The People's Guide to J.R.R. Tolkien

TheOneRing.net
FORGED BY AND FOR FANS OF — JRR TOLKIEN

"... it is vital that a spirit of open inquiry should persist, and that is what *The People's Guide* provides. If you don't agree with any of it, that's fine. TheOneRing.net stands open for disagreements as for further contributions. May they long continue from what must now be a third or a fourth generation of readers."
— From the Foreword by Tom Shippey, author of *The Road to Middle-earth* and *J.R.R. Tolkien: Author of the Century*

"From a global look at mythologies to Sam as the real hero of *LotR*, from Tolkien's love of nature to book reviews and author's interviews, *The People's Guide to J.R.R. Tolkien*, brought to you by the irrepressible scribes at TheOneRing.net, has plenty to delight devoted movie fans as well as serious book scholars (not necessarily mutually exclusive camps)."
— Anne C. Petty, author of *One Ring to Rule Them All: Tolkien's Mythology* and *Tolkien in the Land of Heroes*

ABOUT THE AUTHORS

Erica Challis was born in New Zealand and grew up there and in Australia. A degree in English from the Victoria University of Wellington was followed by a year spent living in Spain. On her return to New Zealand, she gained the position of second horn in the Auckland Philharmonia, where she has played full-time for the past ten years. An accidental meeting on the internet with Xoanon led her to start reporting on *The Lord of the Rings* film project, and shortly afterwards Erica became one of the founders of the fan website TheOneRing.net, where she writes under the name of *Tehanu*. Erica served as editor-in-chief for this book.

Dave Smith, better known as *Turgon*, first read Tolkien in the 1960s, when the U.S. paperback editions sported some supremely awful covers. He is a librarian and lives in a Chicago suburb with his wife, their three children, and one dog, who does not have a Tolkien nickname.

Cynthia L. McNew, aka *Anwyn*, was first introduced to the broad prospect of Middle-earth by her father, who read *The Hobbit* and *The Lord of the Rings* aloud to her mother, her two younger sisters, and herself in her childhood. She has had an unrelenting fascination with Tolkien's writing ever since and is pleased to explore themes and aspects of his work monthly in the Green Books section of TheOneRing.net. Cindy holds a bachelor's degree in music education from Butler University and a master's in choral music from the University of Illinois at Urbana-Champaign.

Cliff Broadway (*Quickbeam*) is a Los Angeles-based writer/actor who has been on stage literally since age five. His numerous performance credits include everything from Shakespeare to playing Darren Stephens in *Bewitched: The Musical*. His first play, *Elevator*, a claustrophile comedy first produced in 1998, was a critical smash. You can hear his voiceover work on TV commercials and radio, most recently as Samwise Gamgee in Black Label Games' *The Fellowship of the Ring* video game. Cliff has been with TheOneRing.net as a senior writer and editor since 1999, helping to found the Green Books monthly magazine and providing his own twisted spin to the online fan experience. Wearing several hats for TORn, he is a Tolkien academic as well as a roving Hollywood reporter. Among his special interests are Dragon Dice, off-road hiking, comic books, and fat purring black cats. And, yes, it really is his last name.

Michael Urban (*Ostadan*) is a lifetime native of Los Angeles and a graduate of UCLA with a Master's degree in Computer Science, supplemented by classes in Medieval Welsh, Philosophy, and other esoteric matters. He works as a computer systems programmer and has been on the internet since its ARPANET days in the 1970s. Since discovering Tolkien's work in the 1960s, he has been active in organized fandom for over 30 years, including a stint as treasurer of the Mythopoeic Linguistic Fellowship. He began writing for Green Books late in 2000.

The People's Guide

to J.R.R. Tolkien

By Cliff Broadway, Erica Challis, Cynthia L. McNew,
Dave Smith and Michael Urban
of TheOneRing.net

Erica Challis, Editor-in-Chief

Cold Spring Press

COLD SPRING PRESS

P.O. Box 284, Cold Spring Harbor, NY 11724
E-mail: Jopenroad@aol.com

Library of Congress Control No. 2002117521
ISBN 1-892975-90-4

Printed in the United States of America
2nd Printing November 2004

Tehanu would like to dedicate this book to her family, who left good books lying around, and to Thomas, for sheer joy.

Quickbeam dedicates it to RLX.

Anwyn would like to dedicate this book to her parents, Buck and Juanita McNew, who showed her the road to Tolkien's world while teaching her to live in our own.

Ostadan would like to thank Glen Goodknight and the Mythopoeic Society for their pioneering work in building Tolkien fandom and scholarship.

Turgon dedicates his contributions to Brenden, Lindsey and Kirsten Smith.

Quotations in Chapter 7, "The Power of Myth," and Chapter 25, "Yin, Yang: The Inward Quest," are from *Lao Tzu Tao Te Ching: A Book about the Way and the Power of the Way*, a new English version by Ursula K. LeGuin, ©1998 by Ursula K. Le Guin. Reprinted by arrangement with Shambhala Publications, Inc., Boston (www.shambhala.com).

Cover and inside art work©Daniel Govar, 2003 (aka Saulone). Check out his fantastic fantasy art at: www.thereandbackagain.net.

Notice: This book has not been been authorized, prepared, approved, licensed, or endorsed by the Tolkien Estate, New Line Cinema, or any of the publishing companies associated with *The Lord of the Rings* and other literary works written by J.R.R. Tolkien.

Contents

Illustrations

Acknowledgments

We would like to thank Tom Shippey for graciously providing a Foreword and for his tuneful singing. Also Jonathan Stein, our most understanding publisher, for guiding us through the process of making this book. We'd like to thank our fellow TORn staff for supporting us, and lastly we'd like to thank our readers for having read, written to, encouraged and occasionally provoked us!

Preface

So You're STILL Reading Tolkien?

Tehanu

You walk into any bookstore and there they are: Three solid-looking books in matching covers, side by side. They've never been out of print since the first volume was published in 1954. Over time, the covers have changed from a gravely enigmatic Ring and Eye symbol to the colorful fantasies of the recent editions, which make the promise plainer: *There are wonders within.*

But wait. What makes these books so special? Are they some kind of classic? Well, they're probably not sitting on the shelves between Tacitus and Tolstoy. You're more likely to find them perched next to books covered in dragons, alien planets, and scantily clad women wearing copper-riveted lingerie. These are the bookshelves where your imagination can run riot.

There's a torrent of new books every year, equally full of magic swords, wizards, and the rise and fall of ancient dynasties. Most of them claim somewhere on the back cover that they are "a worthy successor to Tolkien" or "the greatest fantasy since *The Lord of the Rings.*" But in fifty years' time *The Lord of the Rings* will most likely still be around, and the majority of its "successors" won't. Why is that?

The authors of this book have spent years on this question through our participation in TheOneRing.net, or TORn as it is known to its fans. Started in 1999 to report on the *Lord of the Rings* film project, TORn soon grew into an immense online warehouse of news, commentary and speculation on all things relating to Middle-earth.

Even a volunteer-run website like ours quickly became an insatiable maw demanding more news — even when there was nothing to report. So we created Tehanu's Notes and the Green Books pages to fill in the slow news days with articles about anything we could think of that would interest both ourselves and other Tolkien fans.

That initiative engaged us in a world-spanning dialogue with Tolkien readers from all ages and all walks of life whose questions and insights guided our own search to uncover the meaning of Tolkien's work.

In three years of writing for TheOneRing.net, we have come closer to unraveling the mystery of the books' enduring appeal. We've looked at Tolkien's life, studied his reading, guessed what inspired him, learned what we could about his thinking, and seen how his work has influenced the course of fantasy. We've come to know his fans, too, and the incredible variety of ways that they understand and celebrate his work. It's been a journey too good not to share. So here we offer Tolkien fans the best columns from TheOneRing.net, along with some completely new articles. We hope you enjoy the result of our happy obsession.

Anwyn
Ostadan
Quickbeam
Tehanu
Turgon

Foreword

Tom Shippey
Author of *The Road to Middle-earth* and
J.R.R. Tolkien: Author of the Century

"This is a fearful and wondrous time" for long-time readers and enthusiasts of *The Lord of the Rings*, as *The People's Guide to J.R.R. Tolkien* states at the beginning of Part 5. Wondrous, because of the wave of new readers and new enthusiasts. Fearful, because of the number of take-over bids and attempts to jump on the bandwagon, by which I mean, cutting out the metaphors, people and publications not really very interested in Tolkien but seizing on his renewed popularity as a way of promoting their own particular agendas.

These are now endemic, and well-listed by Turgon. But one thing one can say about *The People's Guide* straight away is that it is not like that. The contributors are all interested in Tolkien as Tolkien, and not as a guide to something else. It might be said therefore that they approach what Tolkien himself, with his collaborator E.V. Gordon, once identified as the proper goal of scholarship, which is to provide a text with "an appreciation as far as possible of the sort which the author may be supposed to have desired" (a goal long since abandoned by his enemies the critics).

But there is a further prominent factor in *The People's Guide* which Tolkien might or might not have wished, but certainly could not have predicted, and that is what we now call "feedback" (a word Tolkien would not even have known). The internet, the experience of continually answering questions and receiving comments, all of it technologically impossible even to as devoted a letter writer as Tolkien, give the organizers of TheOneRing.net a perspective which is uniquely broad, and uniquely full of surprises, some of which would have pleased Tolkien very much, but which he could not have expected.

I am sure, for one thing, that Tolkien would have regarded his time as well spent if his fiction had saved one person from suicide, let alone many, as repeated e-mails declare (chapter 44). More generally if less dramatically, his work is repeatedly acknowledged as life-changing, operating not on the rarefied level of literary culture, but on the domestic level of recovering from grief or sickness or depression.

However, one might say that just as everyone's problems are individual, so are everyone's responses and everyone's roads to recovery. And Tolkien has the potential to offer many such roads, a diversity again well indicated in *The People's Guide*. For another result of its multiple authorship and openness to feedback is the fact that the contributors don't agree, and don't have to agree, with each other. Quickbeam insists that his appreciation of Tolkien is founded on "leaving the real world behind" (chapter 2) whereas Tehanu says (chapter 9) that Tolkien fans "find his words applicable to real-life situations." I am sure that both statements are true, but does the one rule out or disprove the other?

Speaking from my own experience, I would say that you might well feel with Quickbeam that you were retiring into the Never-Never Land of Middle-earth, only to realize — and this might be many years later — that something had stayed in your mind and made a serious difference to your own decisions, and your own way of thinking, without any conscious awareness of it. That is the way great books work. To quote Gandalf, "even the Wise cannot see all ends," or to quote Tehanu's admired Ursula Le Guin, "there are many roads that lead to the city."

I would in fact suggest, modern cliche that it is, that a major if unsung factor in Tolkien's success has been precisely his bone-deep commitment to diversity. This was never the institutionalized and compulsory "multiculturalism" of the modern university (another term Tolkien would never have encountered). Rather it was a deep feeling for leaving people alone, letting them organize their own affairs, and accepting that there are many preferences. Gimli likes caves, Legolas likes trees, hobbits like a well-ordered countryside, and who is to say that any of them is wrong? More seriously, one notes that Aragorn, even when he has come into his kingship, binds himself by his own law, which is that Men shall not enter the Shire.

And, as W.H. Auden astutely pointed out long ago, a critical difference between the good and evil sides in *The Lord of the Rings* is that Gandalf and Galadriel and Elrond can imagine themselves becoming evil, which is why they all reject the Ring, but that Sauron cannot imagine anyone behaving differently from himself, which is why he fails to guard the Sammath Naur. TheOneRing.net is open to just this kind of diversity, at a level much deeper than the token gestures now increasingly demanded of authors, and dealt with in the sections of *The People's Guide* which focus on gender, race, sexual orientation, and much else including language, games, sources, movies and even merchandising.

Other-worldly imagination, real-worldly sagacity — these and many other diversities co-exist in Tolkien and are indicated here. As those with dominating agendas come in to snatch a bit here and a bit there for their own causes and their own preoccupations, it is vital that a spirit of open inquiry should persist, and that is what *The People's Guide* provides. If you don't agree with any of it, that's fine. TheOneRing.net stands open for disagreements as for further contributions. May they long continue from what must now be a third or a fourth generation of readers.

In Defense
of Fantasy

1. In Defense of Fantasy

Tehanu

I should have written a few pert little paragraphs to sum up the first section of this book, but instead this page monstered into an article in its own right; the articles that follow will bounce off it in different ways. In these first essays we're going to talk about our community — that is, people who love Tolkien's work. We want to know what it is that draws us all to the world of Middle-earth. We wonder why we respond to the idea of magic, and we're also curious about those who do *not*. In various ways, we talk about why fantasy attracts us and why we feel it has value.

There are people who feel that fantasy is the mongrel dog of modern literature. To them it's a backward-looking aberration that shouldn't be included in serious discussions about writing. Fantasy doesn't do what modern writing is supposed to do, and it's lousy at winning things like the Booker Prize or the Pulitzer — though oddly enough if it's renamed "Magical Realism," it can manage to nab an award sometimes.

Modern literature favors clear-sighted realism, irony, psychological acuteness and a playful stretching of the boundaries of normal language. Nowadays a good book is expected to catch the nuance of meaning and the way people really speak. Great books make imaginary people vividly alive.

This is true of the old classics too; they revive the past and say "This is humanity, then and now." You can walk in and out of books like *Anna Karenina* or *Moby Dick* and the experience is intense enough to leave you with the tang of tar and salt and starch and perfume in your mouth. However, the further back in time we go, the more demands are made on us in order to understand the speech of that time. The commonplace assumptions of the writers become more alien to us.

People expect this difficulty with Austen and Dickens and Shakespeare; they don't expect it of a writer living in the twentieth century, unless it's James Joyce, but … Hey, people keep breaking the rules!

One problem critics have with Tolkien is this: Tolkien wrote his books in the early part of the twentieth century in a way that ignored the direction that modern literature was taking. He wrote as though Freud had never lived and T.S. Eliot had never written. He didn't care about Hemingway and had no interest in being a forerunner to the beat poets. This is a thing that leaves critics screeching "Wrong turn, go back!" Culture is a dance that we're meant to dance in step, and people can find it disturbing when an artist says "No, instead of moving forward along with everyone else, I'm going to pick up where the *Beowulf* poet left off, around 800 AD." Look, Professor Tolkien, if you can't play with your toys properly the same as everyone else, just get out of the sandpit, OK?

What does it take to make a book "serious literature?" *Beowulf,* despite the presence of a dragon, is serious literature and a long-term denizen of university English curriculae. Whereas *The Lord of the Rings'* half-century of poll-topping popularity hasn't made it a classic — though perhaps that is just a matter of time. Dickens was wildly popular, almost pulp fiction in his day, and now he is both a classic and an author whom other writers name as an influence on them. Still, in most libraries and bookstores Tolkien's work is filed next to the "other fantasy" which is deemed more fantastic than future landfill like *The No-Effort Weightloss Book* or *You Can Sort Your Life out Forever!!!*. Tolkien contains magic, so it's filed next to other books that contain magic in the fast-growing, hard-to-ignore "ghetto shelves." Magic, well, you get that in fairy-tales, so it's basically for children. Why haven't YOU outgrown it? Well, let's see …

Maybe bookshops are right to place fantasy books apart — *The Lord of the Rings* may be a classic, but when we read it, our attitude to what we read is different. Reading fantasy, we're like children let loose on the playground of the imagination. You're welcome there. In fact, fantasy tends to place less value on strong characterization or memorable language, because the slight insubstantiality of the writing is the very thing that allows room for you as a reader to inhabit a space within the world of the book.

When we were very young, we saw fields that seemed to stretch towards distances that shimmered away out of sight, and our most urgent feelings demanded that we run to the edge of our vision. As we grow, it's our minds that want to do the same, and I think this is the enduring appeal of fantasy, horror and science-fiction. They're books that promise a limitless field of play for the imagination. But that playfulness is no trivial thing, because that playground is huge, bordered by stars and space empires and civilizations lost in time past and time to come, full of gods, angels and heroes. To consider these things is also profoundly part of what it is to be human.

The very first art that we know of — the fat, very female "Venus" figurines and the dancing horned shamans found in early cave paintings — is about wonder and magic. I'm not sure the human race has totally outgrown its first stories, its Dreamtime myths.

Fantasy looks at reality from a space that is a few steps removed, and it is at that safer distance that we can tackle the big questions. The simplest stories provide images that we recognize easily; learned early, they're a useful guide. If a person realizes that their life story is that of the Ugly Duckling, they're reassured that their late blooming will be worth the wait. It is comforting to remember Tom Thumb and realize that a longed-for child may never become the Big Man on Wall Street, but he *will* grow — through his own adventures. An expensive therapist could tell you the same thing, only in more words.

Even these simple children's fairy-stories contain a basis in mythic ideas of journeying out, overcoming adversity and recovering the keys to life. But what of the fantasies written for adults? Maybe they're not entirely different — Tolkien still called his stories "fairy-tales" and argued that the monsters they contained are real in the sense that fairy-tale ogres represent real dangers.

If fantasy is to be of any use besides mere entertainment, where do we apply its knowledge of mythical beasts in real life? Who is Smaug then, just for instance?

Well, what is most like that dragon, jealously tending the pile of gold which he knows and lusts after down to the least coin and smallest ring? Are we likely to find something like him in real life, some symbol of pride and greed so bloated with possessiveness that it will scorch the whole earth to remove the slightest threat?

Well, I read in a recent paper that McDonald's is suing a woman in Chile for $1.25 million because she would not withdraw a complaint she made alleging that her son got food poisoning from one of their hamburgers. The allegation led a municipal health authority to fine

McDonald's a crushing $650 after finding "above-normal levels of bacteria" at the restaurant where the sick boy ate. Stung to the quick by this, McDonald's tried to get the finding reversed and the fine returned (while still pursuing the lawsuit against the woman).

If this were an isolated incident you could put it down to a random spasm of corporate greed, but according to Eric Schlosser's book *Fast Food Nation*, "During the 1980s alone, McDonald's threatened to sue at least fifty British publications and organizations, including Channel 2, the Sunday *Times*, the *Guardian*, the *Sun*, student publications, a vegetarian society and a Scottish youth theatre group." These groups were all seen to be critical of the megacorporation, and no matter how small they were, they threatened McDonald's symbolic pile of gold. The culmination of that was surely the famous "McLibel" case where two anti-McDonald's protesters fought McDonald's libel allegations in court. The case dragged on for over a decade and took on mythic David-and-Goliath dimensions.

Reading about Smaug in *The Hobbit* all those years ago gave me a pretty good moral compass to figure out what is going on here. There are any number of individual and corporate Smaugs out there, just as there are many Goldberries and Galadriels with the opposite gift for preserving and enhancing life around them. In good fantasy, what is applicable within them applies to real life too, and it was Tolkien's intention that this should be so.

The Jesuit priest James Schall puts it this way: "Fairy tales, as Tolkien said, 'enrich' creation. The unsuspecting reader who thinks he is only reading 'fantasy' in reading Tolkien will suddenly find himself pondering the state of his own soul because he recognizes his own soul in each fairy-tale."

Not all fantasy has this power, but it was Tolkien's life work to know and understand the great myths of the past and their many reincarnations as Quest epics, fairy-tales, romances and fragments of half-translated poetry. He recast them with all their power into a new form told with a strangely timeless voice. They are tinged with the knowledge of modern things, yet they draw from the wisdom and folly of vanished cultures.

Tolkien was influenced by Owen Barfield, another member of his informal literary club, the Inklings. The Inklings were generally fascinated with the origins of language and creativity, and Barfield's ideas made a big impact on them.

Barfield wrote in 1928 that mythology was something that co-existed with language from its very beginnings because to the first speakers, words were never just literal or abstract, but multi-layered, metaphorical and poetic.

In Barfield's 1926 book *History in English Words,* he says,

> It has only just begun to dawn on us that in our own language alone, not to speak of its many companions, the past history of humanity is spread out in an imperishable map, just as the history of the mineral earth lies embedded in the layers of its outer crust. But there is this difference between the record of the rocks and the secrets which are hidden in language: whereas the former can only give us a knowledge of outward, dead things — such as forgotten seas and the bodily shapes of prehistoric animals and primitive men — language has preserved for us the inner, living history of man's soul. It reveals the evolution of consciousness.

As far as I know Tolkien never communicated with the great comparative mythologist Joseph Campbell, who also thought long and hard about the importance of myth to human culture. It would have been a fruitful exchange. After spending all his long life studying the myths that persist in similar forms through all the civilizations of the world, Campbell regarded myths and "fairy-stories" as the center of our understanding of who we are and what we do.

Campbell believed that the symbols of mythology are a natural indwelling part of us that we do not consciously order or create. Across the barriers of culture we recognize them, like calling to like. "The wonder is that the characteristic efficacy to touch and inspire deep creative centers dwells in the smallest nursery fairy tale — as the flavor of the ocean is contained in a droplet or the whole mystery of life within the egg of a flea."

Campbell finds the same symbols repeated from the mouths of shamans and witch-doctors; he finds them in cultivated poetry and folk fairy-tales. He says, "...it will be always the one, shape-shifting yet marvelously constant story that we find, together with a challengingly persistent suggestion of more remaining to be experienced than will ever be known or told." That sounds like a good description of Middle-earth: a place of endlessly receding borders, the never-ending story.

Growing up in Australia, I'd watch the TV series *Monkey* along with all the other neighbor kids. It was a dubbed version of the famous

Chinese epic *The Journey to the West* and so almost incomprehensible to us, but we were totally hooked. One good turn deserves another; now parts of the Asian world are watching the (sometimes) incomprehensibly dubbed *Fellowship of the Ring* and rushing out to buy the books, so we can assume that they're getting hooked on our favorite myth-epic too.

To my mind, every time must find its own way to understand itself through stories. Much as Tolkien is criticized for his archaic language and his old-fashioned reticence, his sheer popularity argues that *The Lord of the Rings* speaks to the modern reader about the things that still live in our hearts.

Sources:

Joseph Campbell, *The Hero with a Thousand Faces*. Princeton/Bollingen Paperback, 1949.

Owen Barfield: *History in English Words*. Lindisfarne Books, 2002.

Eric Schlosser, *Fast Food Nation*. Houghton Mifflin, 2001.

James V. Schall, SJ. "On the Reality of Fantasy," in *Tolkien: A Celebration*. Ed. Joseph Pearce. A Fount book, published by Harper Collins, 1999.

2. In Defense of Escapism

Quickbeam

I live in Los Angeles, and there are often days when I am afraid to turn on the TV. I ask myself, "Dare I turn this thing on? Do I really want to hear it?" With all the grim coverage of abandoned babies found in dumpsters, innocents shot down in gang-related drive-bys, and various other soundbites of bombings, murder, and rampant corporate greed, who can blame me? Every weekday at 6 o'clock I get a ringside seat to view humanity at its worst. I need not say anything here about the terrorist attacks of September 11. The talking heads have covered that subject so thoroughly that we're at the point of exhaustion. Sometimes I just can't stomach it.

My complaint is how news organizations "sell" the story, for the sake of ratings, by pumping it up to outrageous levels: fetishizing the criminals, glorifying the gore, turning up the barbarous tone of these events until you can't hear yourself think. Despite journalists' attempts to make these happenings more immediate and sensational, I often feel numb and remote, wondering at the enormity of it all. Keeping abreast of current events is one thing, but drowning in media poison is quite another.

The opening scenes of Gary Ross's underrated *Pleasantville* masterfully portray my sentiment. Remember when Tobey Maguire's character wants to spend his weekend watching a marathon of his favorite 1950s show, where life was cleaner, simpler, and certain virtues (or failings) of the human beast were a little more, well, black and white? Some call it nostalgic; I call it therapeutic.

The motivation to "get away from it all" sounds trite, but it's quite real, I assure you, and there are myriad ways to do so. Some are saner than others. My friend Chris goes bowling every Thursday night in Studio City. My brother often goes sportsfishing and brings home the occasional 40-pound mahi-mahi. The other, more unfortunate methods of escapism (like drug use) I won't discuss here ... let's leave that to National Public Radio. As for myself, I choose to dive into the pages of a literary classic.

For me, the appeal of a good book (or play, movie, etc.) is the joy of leaving the "real world" behind to visit another. I have read and reread the works of J.R.R. Tolkien since I was just a sprout. The first book I ever consumed cover-to-cover (and I don't mean those *Hop on Pop* books I shredded as a baby) was *The Hobbit*. I walked through that magical doorway to Middle-earth and was astounded at how familiar, real and beautiful it seemed. I was, in a word, enraptured. I soaked it up like a thirsty sponge and tore through *The Lord of the Rings* and later *The Silmarillion* in quick succession ... by that time I was 12 years old. In another year I read them all again. Sound familiar?

Going back to reread these works is just as rewarding. Ask any fan and they'll tell you straight up: "It's like visiting an old friend." Indeed, I indulge myself with another reading of Tolkien's creation every few years because it's a more welcome place to be than here. Those hobbits and elves are people I want to spend time with — I want to sit by their fires and listen to their songs. As the alarming speed of today's telecommunications brings the world's brutality right into my living room, the comforts of the Shire are more inviting than ever. Haven't you ever wanted to throw a brick at your TV (or computer), run outside your front door to find Bilbo sitting there in the garden, smiling while he offers you a beautiful poppy-seed cake and a seat at his table?

I have, many times.

Tolkien's writing is by turns powerful and highly romantic, true, but there is something in the work that beckons me back, something that continually appeals no matter how many times I read it. Actually, it's a particular set of things ABSENT that I find so wonderful: a world with no obscenities, guns, or sex. I'm quite serious. It makes all the difference to the modern reader's experience.

Consider the gradual coarsening of our American society over the past decade. Once was a time you couldn't say the word "pregnant" on television. Now we have South Park, music videos with endless streams of profanity bleeped out, and a V-chip to help lazy parents block unwanted programs (a technology that never really succeeded, telling you how TRULY lazy these parents are). Hey, I'm certainly no angel; I've been known to cuss like a sailor when my ire is aroused, but sometimes, you must admit ... sometimes it's a relief to be in the company of more genteel conversationalists.

Obviously, the languages Tolkien created for the peoples of Arda were a profound labor of love to him, evident with every page you turn. Can you imagine the devastating effect of adding strident foul language to his characters? Not even the Uruk-hai in their worst moments were given expletives to reveal their anger. That would have been a debasement to the whole construct, destroying the unique tone of his narrative as more of "our reality" crept onto the pages. It was wisely avoided, unlike Jack Chalker's *River of the Dancing Gods* series, where profanities are tossed about on every page. No, Tolkien's efforts were more certain, and his dedication to a pure idiom is a gift to the genre.

And don't get me started on guns! This is a HUGE hot-button for people, and I respectfully don't want to start any controversy about gun control, the Second Amendment, or any such things. It's not about that. I just feel that (a) it's a problem, (b) it has become too complex to be comfortably resolved in my lifetime, and when that overwhelming, hopeless feeling comes over me, my escapist urge kicks into overdrive. Faced with my own personal fears and the politically stagnant landscape, I crave a world with no guns at all. It's unrealistic, I know, but that's my natural, organic response.

Again, I find solace in a fictional account of other dangers, though they be fantastical and drawn only from imagination. I am so grateful for the "medieval" setting of Middle-earth, where modern weaponry never rears its ugly head.

Of course nothing, absolutely nothing, makes our lives more complicated than sexual relationships. You don't need me to elaborate on the painfully obvious. It's a story old as time; just ask Romeo & Juliet — heck, go further back and ask Adam & Eve. This has been the subject of countless Woody Allen films, so I won't put too fine a point on it. I know that there's obviously sex in Middle-earth (Samwise had how many children?), but it's never outright mentioned, thank God. It is good, truly good, to leave *some* things to the imagination.

And yes, I recognize the many romantic conflicts Tolkien drew out in the course of his stories, especially between Elves and mortal Men. I can't overlook those. I'm talking about leaving behind the mundane problems of sex and dating whenever you pick up that book. When you're not thinking about lovemaking, you're able to tackle many more important things. In Middle-earth the more time-honored, dare I say old-fashioned, issues of loyalty, courage, steadfastness, and integrity are at the fore. Tolkien's idiom of storytelling never once strays into the carnal. And you have to agree that heroic battles and adventure are more invigorating than sulking about the house, wondering if she's going to return your call after the first date. Once that book is opened you leave it all behind!

To associate with another place and time, to involve oneself in another "reality," is a basic human need in my eyes. Certainly not as obvious a human need as food or shelter, it is there nonetheless. The world-weary mind finds respite in Tolkien's pages and joy in the victory of his heroes, especially the unexpected ones. Today's world can overwhelm even the best of us. I need to escape to Middle-earth every once in a while. I simply have to. And I won't apologize for how much that makes me sound like a geek.

Much too hasty,
Quickbeam

3. Myth Building

Tehanu

Fantasy, fairy-tale, myth — where does one start and the other leave off? Tolkien wrote a lot about the first two and rather less about the third, but he did once state that he wanted to write a mythology that he could dedicate simply "to England" since he was not satisfied with the grab-bag of Celtic folktales and Arthurian legends that served his country in place of the kind of epic past he felt it deserved. England had nothing to compare with the *Æneid* or the *Odyssey* or the Finnish epic *The Kalevala*.

Now the third example has a peculiar relationship to *The Lord of the Rings*, because the folklorist Lönnrot who collected the folktales that comprise the *Kalevala* has since been accused of making it up — or at any rate, of shaping his collection of small and localized tales into a coherent mythology that defined a nation. Armed with a fresh sense of national identity, the Finns got to work on kicking out their Russian overlords. Well, Tolkien didn't know that the *Kalevala* might be a recent partial invention, or if he suspected he didn't let on. He busied himself making up the mythology he thought England should have had all along.

And this is where it gets interesting. The myriad fantasy writers who've been inspired by Tolkien or who simply copied him are proof that there are plenty of people around who can spin a good yarn and invent beautifully enchanting imaginary worlds to set them in. But it's my abiding interest to discover what made Tolkien's world pre-eminent among them. Mythological, in other words, rather than simply fantastic. It seems to me that Tolkien succeeded in writing something that people embraced as though they *had* discovered their own long-lost mythology.

Tolkien said in his essay "On Fairy Stories" that successful fantasy talks about ordinary things — wood and water, fire and bread — but that "these simplicities are made more luminous by their setting." In one sense that luminous setting is, yes, the dragon-haunted landscape of the fairy-tale, but in the other sense, the brilliance of these ordinary things is their setting within the darkness of the author's mind. There is no one more able to affirm life than someone who has suffered great grief and fear. The terrors of the night hold a weight of darkness for somebody who has been bereaved, and when such a mind fastens on to an object and says, "This gives me joy," then we also see it differently through their eyes. Food and fellowship are luminous things to one who has starved or been alone.

I'm talking about the way a writer gives "weight" to their work. Without that weight a story is just a story — entertaining, but lacking the power to stick in our minds. I'm not sure it's a conscious process. The writer must have a burning need to tell their story, and the story must have something in it that touches the archetypes of myth.

It's easy enough to make a page-turning story of adventures and battles and intrigues. That is what most fantasy is. There is something else at work when somebody dips down into their own inner darkness, their unnameable fears, and pulls out the stories that carry the weight of some truth that we half-know and half-fear.

There is a moment in Peter Jackson's film of *The Fellowship of the Ring* when the Ring drops to the floor, and instead of the light chinking sound of a small object dropping, there is also the muffled clang of a titanic weight. You feel the movement reverberating in time and space.

That is what a fairy-tale or fantasy does when it tips the scale over into myth.

I couldn't study Tolkien without learning about mythology. Now we're not talking fairy-tales and fantasy, or not quite. Myths are the dreams that a people dream in common. The most ancient and earliest myths are those of the Hero's Quest, which exist in remarkably similar forms throughout the world and throughout history.

One of the greatest authorities on the topic is the mythologist Joseph Campbell. His 1949 book *The Hero with a Thousand Faces* looked at Quest myths from many different cultures. To sum up briefly, in all the myriad forms of hero's quests, the same elements recur. The call to adventure comes to the hero, who is small or young or innocent and untried. Perhaps the call is the result of a blunder of some kind, something which has caused an intrusion of the unnatural into the world. The call may be refused, with dire consequences. Usually some kind of supernatural aid or magical object then intervenes — a magic lantern, for instance, or the appearance of an old woman who has some advice.

Bringing that with him, the Hero crosses some kind of threshold that takes him out of his world and into adventure, where he is plunged into "the belly of the whale" or the place of darkness, trials and humiliations. The trials may be spiritual or physical: Frodo in Mordor, or Jesus tempted by Satan, or Theseus in the Labyrinth. After many adventures, the Hero grasps some kind of knowledge or power. Finally he comes home holding some incalculable gift — Buddha with the Enlightenment, Moses with the Ten Commandments, Beowulf with the severed head of Grendel ensuring the safety of the Danes, the countless fairy-tale princes who win the hand of the King's daughter after a thousand adventures.

The first two examples are clearly earth-shattering for the people of the East and West, while the last example speaks of children's fairy-tales. But as Tolkien suspected, the things named so simply in a fairy-tale stand for something else. In the hidden language of fairy-tales, the triumphant royal marriage that closes such tales symbolizes a society put back into balance and made whole.

Older myths tell of the Sacred Marriage, which ensures that life will continue and the social order will abide. Shiva and Parvati in the East, the Great Goddess and the Green Man in the North, Persephone and Hades in Ancient Greece - these archetypes get watered way, way down to the fairy-tale marriage of the King and Queen, and "...they all lived happily ever after." In the original myths, life itself could not continue without that happy ending.

It's not wildly revelatory to say that *The Lord of the Rings* is a Hero's Quest. Most fantasy is. For instance, in the case of *Star Wars*, George Lucas consulted with Joseph Campbell and consciously modeled his story on Campbell's outline of the archetypal Hero's Quest. That is one reason why the middle trilogy of films that begin with *Star Wars* are so successful as stories.

The *Star Wars* films finish with a triumph each time, and that's what you'd expect for the typical Hero's Quest. *The Lord of the Rings* seems to promise the same and then it slyly reshuffles the cards at the end. There's Aragorn's coronation, yay, and his marriage to Arwen, yay, and the hobbits strike their final blow for freedom in the Scouring of the Shire, yippee!

But what's happened to our hero? He literally cannot continue to live in the land he's saved. His quest to destroy the Ring gives Middle-earth peace and freedom, but he buys it with his very life. There is no happy return to the Shire for him — he no longer belongs, the other hobbits are ignorant of his deeds, and his Morgul-knife wound pains him not just physically but spiritually. In his sailing to the West at last we may believe that he will find eternal happiness, but the tone of those last chapters is deeply sad. The writer Diana Wynne Jones comments that Tolkien would have been familiar with the Anglo-Saxon and Norse custom of ship burials, and Frodo's voyage west echoes the sadness of those very final journeys.

It's easy to be fooled by Tolkien's emotional reticence. The biographies talk about how his father died when he was three, and his mother when he was twelve, after lingering illness. Tolkien himself doesn't go on and on about what effect this had on him; the closest he gets is in a late letter to one of his own children, where he talks about how his mother suffered what seemed to him to be the martyrdom of a saint before she died. He talks more about her pain than his.

It only got worse for him. He fought in the trenches in the First World War and lost his closest friends. A whole generation of young men came home from that war and could not talk about what they had seen. There was a feeling that it was "bad form" to talk about the horrors of war, and returning soldiers were made aware that the people "back home" did not want to know the price of victory. Maybe the last chapters of *The Lord of the Rings* are Tolkien's protest, written long years later. Frodo returns to a Shire largely indifferent to his part in saving it, and I think the sadness of his last years in the Shire are as close as Tolkien gets to admitting his own grief.

For the returned servicemen of the First World War there was no Valinor to go to for healing. There was only a silence that was a kind of emotional prison. Tolkien's famous rejoinder to the critics of fantasy is interesting if you read it in that light. In his essay "On Fairy Stories" he retorted that if fantasy was escapist, shouldn't we be asking what we are escaping from, or to? Isn't it the duty of a prisoner of war to escape, for instance? Should we not try to escape an authoritarian regime? Shouldn't we escape the locks on truth? "Why should a man be scorned if, finding himself in prison, he tries to get out and go home? Or if, when he cannot do so, he thinks and talks about other topics than jailers and prison-walls? The world outside has not become less real because the prisoner cannot see it."

Tolkien's talking on more than one level here. Ultimately for him, because of his religious faith he believed that outside the immediate griefs and desolations of the world there was an unquenchable joy. It was his business to see beyond the sadness and ugliness of the world and to bring back news of what he called "the Eucatastrophe" — the sudden turn of events in a story, the grace that for him proved the existence of God the joyous creator, as he would see it.

I've made a portrait of a man with a terrible, sad, dark childhood. Think how easy it would have been for him to lock himself away behind walls of his own making, filling the hours with compulsive scribbling and word-hoarding. Yet we know from his letters and the letters of others that he was a witty, wise and humane person who was very engaged with other people.

As a child Tolkien was learning other languages by the time he was six and inventing his own by the time he was nine. He had a talent, and given the sadness in his life, he could have easily grown into another hopeless introvert using his intellectual games to escape from feeling too much. His chosen field of philology and dead Northern European languages could provide an endless distraction around linguistic detective work and the construction of elegant, logical systems of language. After studying the ways that languages grew naturally he started constructing his own — a time-consuming hobby that he once called his "secret vice." He chided himself for the fascinated hours he spent making up what he called "nonsense fairy languages."

This is a man who could have protected himself from the darker emotions by losing himself in abstractions, and there is plenty to suggest that a part of his nature could easily fall into obsessive-compulsive behavior. It's a common enough way to avoid painful thoughts. But Tolkien didn't exactly do this, or rather, something that could have been a life-limiting compulsive disorder actually became a powerful tool for creating the languages that breathe so much life into Middle-earth. He made it part of his gift rather than his burden.

Am I saying Tolkien was mad? It depends on whether you believe that some kinds of madness are also gifts.

I liken it to something I've noticed about great orchestral conductors. Some of them really do conform to their stereotype: they're megalomaniacs. For them, other people exist mainly in order to do their will. A person using that domineering will for its own sake on their intimates or on a whole society can be a catastrophe. *But* — if they happen to be musical — then it can be a gift. They stand in front of an orchestra and the players submit to their will instinctively, with the discipline of a flock of birds turning in unison, because that focused will stands in front of them like a divine mandate. *Then* the music takes wing. It's not related to having a talent for music, because a much better musician without the megalomania can stand in front of the same orchestra and get mere acquiescence from the players. You can hear that. It just goes to show that there is such a thing as useful madness. If madness is a prison, creativity is one of the keys to unbar the door.

Love is one of the others.

Tolkien loved his family very deeply. Part of the bond between them was cemented by the many, many evenings spent together, with the four children entranced by the stories Tolkien made up for them. Their love and enjoyment repaid the care and time he lavished on stories like *The Hobbit* — indeed, his love for them meant that he finished many of the things he wrote for their pleasure, whereas his academic writing tended to languish unfinished for years at a time.

Trees are another thing that Tolkien loved unabashedly, and it pleases me to imagine his field of study as a kind of intellectual tree, because if you map the development of language, as time goes on you see it branching like a living thing into dialects and eventually into separate languages. The wintry blasts of the Norse invasions shape one branch here, the Norman Conquest cuts another there, then the tree of language sprouts up again with the novelties of the passing times. It was Tolkien's life work to map that net of interlinked branches, and he could have lost himself in it. He would have left a greater body of scholarly work than the rather thin list of commentaries on Old and Middle English that is the result of his long tenure at Oxford. Instead he gave the greater part of his life to the tending of another tree — the Tree of Story, as he called it. It was a natural progression for him.

Had he settled down to a quiet academic career after his marriage, perhaps that is all that would have happened — an Oxford don would have delayed his scholarly work with a slightly obsessive hobby, making imaginary languages and tying them to an elaborate, ever-branching false history in an invented world. Harmless, like train collecting. One day we might have read only *The Silmarillion* as a curiosity. The truest-feeling thing in it is the tale of Beren and Luthien, with the long prohibition that kept them apart, and the love that overcame that. In Tolkien's life, those things really happened — not in the way it's told in *The Silmarillion*, but emotionally that is exactly what he suffered. He met Edith when he was sixteen. She was an orphan, like him. His guardian, the Jesuit priest who brought him up, found out about the romance and forbade him to see or speak to her until he was twenty-one and had got his degree. He must have felt fated to be with her, and he kept loyal to her through all that time until he could see her again — whereupon he immediately proposed to her. It was like a fairy-tale of the sort where long faith-keeping is rewarded. After a long and sometimes difficult marriage he still felt that the fairy-tale version of his marriage was the true one beneath the surface appearance.

After her death he wrote to one of his children saying that if they could have seen her not as their tired domesticated mother but as he saw her when she was young, dancing among the hemlock-umbels in a forest glade, they would understand why she was his Luthien, his Tinuviel, always and forever.

Her grave is marked by that on the headstone: "Luthien." His is marked "Beren."

But the real monument to Tolkien is *The Lord of the Rings* itself. It's become, as Tolkien wished, a mythology. A story whose meanings are dredged out of our collective hopes and sorrows and given voice by a person who understood both.

Here we are, half a century after Tolkien's great story came to light, and the tale is still growing. It's grown past the animated movies made in the 1970s, past the translations into more than two dozen languages. It's out-waited the fall of the Iron Curtain and the Bamboo Curtain and the politics of last century and been received into countries where it is the breath of freedom. It's been painted and made into ballets and plays and now a live-action movie trilogy. There it is: Tolkien's Great Escape. He threw the door open, and look at all the hundreds of millions of readers who've walked into that first innocent-looking gateway to Middle-earth, "In a hole in the ground there lived a hobbit." And all that leads on from there ...

That's what a mythology does — it keeps getting reinvented for each new generation. People take it and build upon it.

We can do that with Middle-earth because it's so huge. It's the result of years of labor from a mind that kept returning to this same compulsion, day in and day out. I was struck by the way that his merest idle scribbles on passing scraps of paper were so often tied into his imaginary world — words, images, symbols from an unreal place. You'd have to be mad to do that, year after year, and in a sense Tolkien was mad — creating endless word lists and linguistic rules to nonexistent languages. He could have sunk himself into that and left no more than an oddity, a handful of imaginary languages and some outlines for the history of an unreal place.

But instead he reached into the very guts of his pain and sorrow and harnessed them to his madness for minutiae. It gave him the power to create Middle-earth, as solid and luminous as it is, and within that he was free. He wrote his freedom down and gave it to us. The choice is always ours, whether to slavishly follow him around the Middle-earth he gave us, or to understand from him that sometimes the keys to anywhere are for our own hands to make.

Sources:
J.R.R. Tolkien, *Tree and Leaf,* Houghton Mifflin, 1989.
J.R.R. Tolkien, *The Annotated Hobbit,* Houghton Mifflin 2002.
J.R.R. Tolkien/edited by Christopher Tolkien, *The Monsters and the Critics and Other Essays,* Houghton Mifflin, 1984.

4. "Yes, Elanor, There Really Is a Gandalf"

Quickbeam

We take pleasure in prominently answering the communication below, expressing at the same time our great gratification that its faithful author is numbered among the friends of TheOneRing.net:

> "Dear Quickbeam — I am eight years old. Some of my little friends say there is no Gandalf. Papa says, 'If you see it on TheOneRing.net, it's so." Please tell me the truth, is there a Gandalf?'
> — Elanor Gamgee
> Bag End, Hobbiton, across The Water

Elanor, your little friends are wrong. They have been affected by the skepticism of a skeptical age. They do not believe except what they see. They think that nothing can be which is not comprehensible by their little minds. All mortal minds, Elanor, whether they be Men's, Dwarves' or Hobbits,' are little. In this great universe of ours, one Hobbit is a mere insect, an ant, in his intellect, as compared with the boundless world about him, as measured by the intelligence capable of grasping the whole of truth and knowledge.

Yes, Elanor, there is a Gandalf. He exists as certainly as love and generosity and devotion exist, and you know that they abound and give to your life its highest beauty and joy. Alas! How dreary the world would be if there were no Gandalf! It would be as dreary as if there were no Elanors. There would be no child-like faith then, no poetry, no romance to make tolerable this existence. We should have no enjoyment, except in sense and sight. The eternal light with which childhood fills the world would be extinguished.

Not believe in Gandalf! You might as well not believe in Elves! You might get your Papa to bring in the Bounders to watch all the chimneys on Yuleday Eve from here to Michel Delving to catch Gandalf, but even if you did not see Gandalf coming down, what would that prove? Nobody sees Gandalf, but that is no sign that there is no Gandalf. The most real things in the world are those that neither children nor stout Men can see. Did you ever see an Oliphaunt dancing on the lawn? Of course not, but that's no proof that they are not real. Nobody can conceive or imagine all the wonders there are unseen and unseeable in the world.

You tear apart the baby's rattle and see what makes the noise inside, but there is a veil covering the unseen world that not the strongest Hobbit, nor even the united strength of King Elessar and all the strongest Dúnedain who ever lived, could tear apart. Only faith, fancy, poetry, love, and romance can push aside that curtain and view the supernal beauty and glory beyond. Is it all real? Ah, Elanor, in all this world there is nothing else real and abiding.

No Gandalf! Thank Ilúvatar he lives, and he lives forever. A thousand years from now, Elanor, nay, ten times ten thousand years from now, he will continue to make glad the heart of childhood.

Much too hasty,
Quickbeam

With apologies to Frank P. Church

5. Are We Not Geeks?

Tehanu

Tolkien and his keen readers are often criticized for being stuck in eternal adolescence and labeled as geeks. I'd like to take a closer look at these labels and find out if "geek" and "adolescent" deserve to be such pejorative words.

Consider how many useful and pragmatic people read therapy and self-help books because they want to fulfill their potential as balanced, self-aware individuals. Many of these books talk about the notion of nurturing one's "inner child." The inner child is that part of us that feels enthusiasm and joy most strongly and that responds most truthfully to the world. Well and good; evidently the "inner child" is regarded as right and precious. But what can we say about the inner *adolescent*? Why aren't we nurturing the inner adolescent?

I think you can hardly say the phrase "teenager" without immediately thinking of somebody rebellious and confused, or remembering one's own years of irritable awkwardness. We haven't got a lot good to say about teenagers, and yet we should. The author Philip Pullman wrote something very interesting in response to a question about why he preferred to write for and about teenagers.

At that age, he said, children are becoming aware of the world in a new way, and they have time to ask the big questions: What is the meaning of life, why are we here, what is our purpose? Later on we get busy, we get cynical, and we are in danger of forgetting we ever cared.

I'd agree with that. I'd go further and say that for many teenagers, those years are a time of great stress partly because it is an age of idealism and yet they are just beginning to learn about the world's tired habits — its petty hypocrisies, callous persecutions, deadly evasions of responsibility, casual negligence towards justice, and the ignoble worms of greed that gnaw away at the heart of every great enterprise... Teenagers rage against the wrongness of the world because they see it more freshly and it wounds them more keenly. As one becomes older, wiser, and tireder, it seems less hassle to take the easy course, to act circumspectly, to be politic more often than honest. I think teenagers rage against growing into that state, and the best of them still believe that they will change the world by virtue of naming and confronting its evils.

I'd like to throw in one of the ultimate Romantic poems I've ever come across. It's by an Argentinean poet, and to me it sums up that idealism of adolescence that rejects the deceitful world with one grand gesture:

FOR AFTERWARDS

I would like to die when the day is ending
on the open sea and looking at the sky;
where the agony of death may seem but sleep
and the soul may seem a bird which mounts in flight.

And in the final instants I would hear,
already with the sky and sea alone,
no other sobbing prayers or sobbing voices
than those of waves in their majestic fall.

To die when life is sadly hauling back
its golden nets from out the tide's deep green
and be like yonder sun that dies down slowly:
some very shining thing that's lost from sight.

To die, and young, before unfaithful time
destroys the delicate and gentle crown;
whilst life still tells us: I am yours
although we know so well it will betray us.

— Manuel Gutierrez (1859-1895)
(translation: Gordon Challis)

Yes, a modern person might find this sentimental and grandiose. It is utterly fantastical in its all-or-nothing approach to life. It offers no gritty pragmatic solutions to the problem of living in a less-than-perfect world. It may be adolescent in its grand gesture of utterly rejecting the world in all its complex awfulness. But would the world be a richer place if everything as great, beautiful and futile as this poem, were banished from our consciousness? I could not bear the loss.

For this is the inner teenager to whom Tolkien and many other fantasy books appeal. They are books that are about honor and justice and the recognition of absolute good and evil; they are books about daring and courage and ultimate sacrifices and grand gestures against hopeless odds.

Nobody has lost that inner teenager who has flung aside their life and decided to change a political system or overturn a scientific belief or who has shrugged off convention in order to embark on a great love affair across continents and oceans. Sadly, it is the inner teenager we appeal to when we send young men off to die in wars; it is my belief that all those who have risked their lives to stand up against oppression and injustice called on their inner teenager too. Because when teenagers look at the status quo they see wrongs, and they name them truthfully, whether society wants to hear or not.

The whole question of geekdom has interested me for a while too. First, what is a geek? During the year immediately preceding the *The Lord of the Rings* movies, we saw many articles like Julian Dibbell's "Lord of the Geeks" in *The Village Voice*. His article summed up a school of writing that wants to deride geeks as a minority of outsiders while simultaneously fearing that they're some vast inchoate conspiracy who control the technology underpinning our modern world. They're losers, according to this view, but by some unfair twist of fate and genetics, they get to spend their lives doing cool things with art, science, technology, popular culture and the media (and I might add that some of them get shockingly rich doing it, too, and have to gad about the world for their pains).

My own definition of geeks is this: people who care about a subject or system so much that they're willing to learn how to master it, whether anyone else cares about it or not. The link between geeks and teenagers exists because before that age, if a child is fascinated by something, we just think they're absorbed in play. It's only when they hit their teen years that we notice geeks because there's some expectation that they should be out partying and socializing. Instead they sometimes — or often — put aside their interest in other people because they'd rather be problem-solving on their computer, or memorizing the entire history of the Plantagenets, or thinking up stories about an imaginary world, or practicing scales for three hours on the violin. Sometimes they're fixed on a goal known only to themselves: sometimes they've found a close-knit gang with similar interests, but in any case they'll follow their own instincts or interests, no matter what anybody else thinks.

The larger group of non-geeks is always going to be nervous of somebody who resists the easiest form of social control, which is shame. In their eyes, you should be able to laugh at somebody and tease them for being different, and that should be sufficient to make them toe the line and make a bit more of an effort to appear similar to everyone else. Geeks resist that, because, well, it'd mean giving up the things that matter more than conformity.

There have always been geeks. Mozart? What a nerd! He had to be a geek. Who illuminated medieval manuscripts? Who preserved literacy during the difficult, violent centuries of the Dark Ages? Geek monks who remembered what civilization was! Who were Pythagoras and Socrates and Archimedes? Total geeks every one of them, with their heads in the clouds.

And so I ask, if anything worth doing is to be done: Are we not geeks?

6. Tolkien & Magic:
The Power of Sub-Creation

Anwyn

...The boy nodded his understanding. "Can I ask you something?" The Jedi Master nodded. "What are midi-chlorians?" Wind whipped at Qui-Gon's long hair, blowing strands of it across his strong face. "Midi-chlorians are microscopic life forms that reside within the cells of all living things and communicate with the Force."...

..."Use the Force, Luke."...

...Raistlin lifted his thin, frail hand and allowed the spell component he had taken from his pouch to fall slowly from between his fingers onto the deck of the boat. Sand, Tanis realized. "Ast tasarak sinuralan krynawi," Raistlin murmured, and then moved his right hand slowly in an arc parallel to the shore....

..."The One Power," Moiraine was saying, "comes from the True Source, the driving force of Creation, the force the Creator made to turn the Wheel of Time."...

Bibbidi, bobbidi, boo.

There seem to be almost as many ways of representing magic as there are fantasy writers. Role-players know the whole system with mages, spell components, spellbooks, the language of magic, etc. Robert Jordan fans can tell you the ins and outs of the One Power, complete with a discourse on the varying characteristics of saidar and saidin and the innumerable levels of strength among Aes Sedai. And Star Wars geeks (a word I use with love, considering that I myself am a dyed-in-the-wool geek!) were stunned when George Lucas started explaining the universe-balancing Force with microscopic middlemen instead of with the innate power of Luke Skywalker and Darth Vader.

What ties them in common is that they each have a *system*, a framework with rules and laws almost more complicated than those of physics. Mages lose their spells after one casting and must rest and recommit the words to memory before casting again. Aes Sedai spend years in training because abuse of the One Power can too easily lead to death, and evidently you've got to be well-stocked on single-celled symbionts (is that even a word? My spellchecker sure doesn't like it) to even make a dent in the Force. Fantasy writers delight in coming up with their own, hopefully brand-new, systems to give *their* books that added twist, that spark that no other sword-swinging Elf-hopping kender-singing dragon-flying books have.

But what about Tolkien? Where is the system? What are the rules that govern the making of Rings of Power, that delineate the powers and limits of Istari, of Maiar, of Valar? He never talks about a framework of physical laws; we see only the results of the power's use. Where does the power come from?

Sam Gamgee, early on in *The Lord of the Rings,* speaks of "Elf-magic." He is almost disappointed when the Company reaches Lothlórien, a place Sam imagines must be absolutely saturated with Elf-magic, only to find that it is quiet and peaceful, with nothing flashy going on. Sam's discussion with Frodo on the subject in Lórien contains just about the only overt use of the word *magic* in all of *Lord of the Rings.* Sam's feeling, as it usually is for most of us, is that if you can't see anyone making it happen, then it must not be the real stuff. But I think Tolkien had another image in mind. He seems to have taken his love of nature and the natural order of things to such an extent that he would rather not impose an unnatural system of rules governing a supernatural power — what we term magic. Instead, it seems clear that Tolkien regarded extraordinary power as part of the natural birthright of *individual beings,* and as such, therefore, the use of that power was simply part of the settled order of events. *Not magic,* but just the use by each individual of the power vested in him or her — to the best and highest of his or her own abilities, be they the greatest of the great or the smallest of the small. And in fact, he regarded the traditional definitions of the word "magic" as tantamount to the evil Machine that tears up the normal fabric of nature.

We at Green Books are constantly getting questions from readers so accustomed to other systems that they almost *demand* a system in Tolkien. "What were the exact powers of the One Ring?" "Does the magic in Lothlórien come from the Elves or vice-versa?" "What can Elrond do with his Elven ring?" "How does Gandalf do magic?" We do the best we can to elucidate, but the plain truth of the matter is that Tolkien just doesn't make rules. He expects us to accept at face value that Celebrimbor and his cohorts "forged" the Three Rings, that Fëanor "wrought" the Silmarils and contained within them the light of the Two Trees, that Elrond, Gandalf, and Galadriel "use" their rings in some vague way for the protection and enhancement of their lands (in the cases of Elrond and Galadriel) and for the furtherance of their tasks (in the case of Gandalf).

Even "What are the powers of Beorn? Why is he the only being in Middle-earth who can shape-change?" Well … because he just was. That was his individual power. Tolkien didn't set out to create magicians who could manipulate a supernatural force. He created individuals who knew how to use their *natural* powers — and he delineated the difference between those who use their power for the sake of creation and those who use it merely for the sake of control.

Tolkien believed that human beings are endowed with creativity in order to share in God's power of creation. He called this "sub-creation" and felt that he was making the most of his abilities in this line through his writing. It follows that the characters in his books would do the same. So everyone is endowed with his or her own abilities, and since he's not limited to real human beings but is free to imagine beings with greater powers of creation, the result is power that to us is supernatural, but to him is merely the result of that being's art. I am speaking, of course, of the wise and wonderful Elves. The forging of the Elven rings is the best example, but their spellbound swords and beautiful works of cooperation with Dwarves also come to mind. The exact quotation that details the nature of the Elves' power and, indeed, the difference between this power and "magic," can be found in *The Letters of J. R. R. Tolkien*. Letter #131 states:

> Their "magic" is Art, delivered from many of its human limitations; more effortless, more quick, more complete (product and vision in unflawed correspondence). And its object is Art not Power, sub-creation not domination and tyrannous re-forming of Creation.

There you have it. Art for Art's sake, and my favorite part — "product and vision in unflawed correspondence." In other words, if they could think it (vision), then they could do it (product). No tiresome mechanics, no industrialized machines — just pure, unadulterated Art: sub-creation. Ultimately, what we would call magic is not, in Middle-earth, any such thing. It is simply the natural powers of created beings proceeding from them in yet another spiral of creation. And we know this power is inherent because Tolkien stated as much. The same Letter tells us that Tolkien uses the word "magic" in reference to external, mechanical forces, thus setting the term in opposition to his design of "inherent inner powers or talents," the Art of the Elves.

So Tolkien divides power into two headings: the natural kind, proceeding from the desire of the being to sub-create, and "magic:" a deliberate use of devices or machines with a corrupted motive. And in the use of the former, he stands alone in his system of creation. No other fantasy writer that I know has gone so far as he has with the Elves, beings with power that emanates as naturally as a flowing spring. True, there are other authors whose magic-users have innate talent, abilities, or senses not available to "ordinary" folks — but these special abilities are usually in existence in order to take advantage of an outside power: the Force, the One Power, or the generic, vague mysticism of "magic." Tolkien's Elves have no need of even the appearance of such supernatural forces, because the force of sub-creation is in them already, without any augmentation.

A pet musing of mine is to wonder how this "sub-creation" applies to beings besides Elves, Valar, and Maiar. Don't bombard me with letters about Gandalf's magic words, either, because he was a Maia and a badass, to boot, and could do whatever he wanted, with words or without 'em, in any language he pleased. I'm talking about mortals now. Aragorn son of Arathorn. Faramir of Ithilien. Samwise Gamgee. I believe very deeply that this power of sub-creation extended very thoroughly to mortals of "uncorrupted motive," even if the results weren't always what we would call "magical."

"The hands of the king are the hands of a healer." So spake Ioreth, wise woman of Gondor, and we know it to be true. Aragorn showed his healing powers many times, but never to greater effect than when he healed Faramir, Éowyn, and Merry of the Black Breath during the last days of the war.

Our darling Faramir, a man of *lore*, yet scarcely less doughty in arms than his brother and with a stern but merciful attitude towards those under his command and in his power, had a gift for governance. We see it "The Seige of Gondor" when the watchers on the walls of Minas Tirith make out at a distance a group of soldiers returning from Osgiliath, fearfully harried by the Orcs and Southrons, and yet holding together in an orderly retreat. The watchers guess from that that Faramir must be there, for they know he can hold man and beast to his will.

When Sam sets out to heal the wounds of the Shire, he wonders how best to use the gift of Galadriel, and Frodo counsels him to "use all the wits and knowledge you have of your own ... and then use the gift to help your work and better it."

That last line sums up my entire feelings on the subject of mortals and sub-creation. Aragorn used *athelas* to help him in his healing, but undoubtedly part of the virtue of it sprang from his own hands. Faramir was versed in the lore and history of men, but he used his knowledge wisely and to good effect, being a good captain of his men and, in time, a steward and prince of his people. And our sweet Sam had a positive gift for growing things, no matter how much he was helped at that juncture by the gift of the Lady Galadriel.

Here's the stickler: just because the results aren't conventionally "magical" doesn't mean that a talent isn't a gift of sub-creation. Any being, immortal or no, Elven or Human or Holbytla, who uses his or her inclinations and abilities to the fullest, and never forgetting that uncorrupted motive, is exercising his "inherent inner powers or talents" — a very personal form of magic that cannot be discounted. So many times in this dreary world we fall short of what we would like to accomplish with our abilities, through sloth or other impediments. Tolkien showed us not only otherworldly Elves whose gifts run to what we would consider outside the settled order of nature, but also very mortal characters who simply used their ordinary powers to the best and fullest extent. And the result, when compared with the many shortcomings and failings of human beings in *this* world, is very magical indeed.

Sources:
Humphrey Carpenter, ed., *The Letters of J.R.R. Tolkien*. Houghton Mifflin, 1995.

7. The Power of Myth

Tehanu

"Tehanu's Notes" began as a series of articles on TheOneRing.net intended to kill some time while we waited for the first of Peter Jackson's films to arrive. They turned into a project that saw me spend more than a year delving into the roots of the power that *The Lord of the Rings* has over our imaginations. I looked at the literatures and mythologies that fascinated Tolkien and found the old myths from which his great tale grew. They were mythologies of life and death, light and dark, fall and redemption, and they've been around a long time. I discovered how Tolkien's Catholic beliefs underlie *The Lord of the Rings* and how his urgent regard for the tension between good and evil gives his writing a power that readers sense without necessarily recognizing the source.

But my questions kept getting bigger, as though I'd only found bigger nets with which to cast further. Why do we need fantasy? What feeds our imagination? What myths inspire all people? Is *The Lord of the Rings* big enough to speak to people outside its purely Western Judaeo-Christian heritage?

What myths exist in a Taoist world that is seen as a balancing of opposites, a harmony in diversity? Who is the hero and who the demon in a world where all created things are aspects of one indivisible divinity, as it is according to Hindu thought? Does *The Lord of the Rings* have anything to say about this?

Three keys fell into my hands entirely through the agency of Tolkien fans who responded to what I wrote on TheOneRing.net. Their letters opened doors to new vistas and led me off on paths that might not interest every Tolkien fan. If so, then I hope my correspondents don't feel ill repaid.

The first key was the *Tao Te Ching*, which set me off on a quest to understand more about the religions and myths of the East. We've long been familiar with slack New Age thinking, to the point where one can feel a certain amount of cynicism for its symptoms — a mania for crystals and incense and small stuffed dolphins — but there is a kind of scholarship underlying some New Age thinking that is absolutely fascinating. It's fueled by ideas from people who have read the Vedas or other scriptures in Sanskrit or translated the *Tao* from its ancient language. It's combined with the thoughts of people who've made anthropology an act of humanist imagination — here I'm thinking of the fantasy writer Ursula Le Guin and her parents, who were anthropologists in Californa familiar with the cultures of the First People there.

There also exists a long tradition of "ecological" writers in California, starting with John Muir and continuing with the poetry of Robinson Jeffers. From there, the wilderness writing of Kim Stanley Robinson and Le Guin's fantasy and science fiction project into the future. All these writers and thinkers are linked somehow, and they seem to be reaching towards some fusion of ideas for how to live that is (to use an overworked phrase) global and inclusive. They all seem to be asking "What does it mean to be human?" and "How should we live in the world?" But Tolkien asks that question too, even with his elves and dwarves and hobbits.

A second key was Bruno Bettelheim's book on fairy-tales, *The Uses of Enchantment*. Bettelheim was a Freudian analyst and an Auschwitz survivor whose work with children centered on the recognition that for them, fairy-tales are the means by which they best understand and recognize the world and their place in it. According to him, they're the highest form of art to a child. The characters and events of a fairy-tale are all parts of the child's life and being. The dark forest and the wolf are part of the child's untamed self, the evil stepmother a plausible explanation for the real-life parent when she's not being the all-loving "good mother," and the triumphant endings with the kingdom won and the princess married are symbols of the moments in life when all is resolved and the child is restored to the centre of its world.

Perhaps Tolkien meant a different thing by "fairy-tales" than Bettelheim did, yet both of them would recognize the power of those symbols and the way the Wolf and the Dark Forest stay in the sediment of our unconscious, as does the desire for justice and happy endings. Fairy-tales are on the whole hopeful, for generally effort is rewarded and evil punished. They are also a prescription for behaving in a certain way. In their original form they don't moralize so much as warn; neither do Tolkien's stories preach. One has only to read his letters to realise how deeply concerned he was with moral issues, and yet one can read *The Lord of the Rings* for years, as I did, without perceiving the Christianity of it. Contrast that with C. S. Lewis, where good and evil are obvious antagonists, the one to be rewarded, the other to be punished. Yet Tolkien, without ever having said "one should behave in such-and-such a way," made more of an impact on me.

The third key that linked everything together was a book by Joseph Campbell called *Myths to Live By*. Anything I can say about it is superfluous; he simply says what I wish I'd said, and better. Joseph Campbell is a comparative mythologist who is at home in many languages and cultures. His glossier and better-known book *The Power of Myth* draws on the art of a dozen cultures to illustrate his ideas, or rather to illuminate the way in which the ideas of one culture find expression in another. It's a kind of big-budget "Tehanu's Notes" written by a great scholar who had a lifetime to devote to it.

In *Myths to Live By* he says something that I haven't heard said elsewhere: that humans are a story-telling and myth-making species as much as a tool-using one; some of the earliest human burial sites show by the ceremonial disposition of the limbs that the first cultures already had rites (and therefore presumably beliefs) concerning death. They must have told stories about what happens after you die; we can assume they had stories to explain what their place was in the greater scheme of things.

We are a unique species in two ways that impel us to make myths: we foreknow our own deaths, and we are, in most cultures, "twice-born." The knowledge of death makes us look for consolation, and so there are myths that tie us into the larger things that continue past us — the life of our tribe, the protection of our gods, the life of the land we inhabit, and the ever-renewing nature of life itself.

The fact that we are each born as strangers to our own culture, unable even to speak the language of our parents, makes us the species that spends years "becoming" before achieving full membership in our society. It takes years to learn to speak our own language and more years to learn to know the rules of our culture and to master the knowledge and tools that our lives require for our survival. Until all this is learnt we are dependent on our tribe and our family, and all through this period there have to be stories and more stories — explaining why some things are acceptable and others not, how things came to be the way they are, and why it is better that it should be so. For a society has to agree on what is good and evil, right and wrong, otherwise every action will lead to endless debates.

In most societies there is then the initiation into adulthood — validation of an individual's readiness to face life as a full member of society. That is the second birth, out of dependence into full participation in society. It's something that the modern world has done away with, and teenagers spend a lot of energy trying to find something that will finally prove to themselves and everyone else that they've grown up. Giving somebody the car keys and the right to vote for total strangers hardly signals that yes, all society acknowledges that this individual is a fully fledged member of society. It's weird in fact that the recognition of adulthood (in terms of giving somebody the vote) is just telling them to go and empower somebody else (a politician) at the very age when the young people need to empower themselves.

Plenty of things in our culture play on the need to find empowerment that young people have. I'm thinking, among other things, of interactive games as an example: they are an arena within which a person is gifted with the power of life and death (or at least some very impressive weapons) and goes through a series of challenges and tests of skill which give the satisfaction of mastery as they're overcome. Within the game, one has the illusion of having great consequence upon the world. However, the games rarely demand that the player develop much skill in making moral choices, and unfortunately in the real world the player is left as unprepared as ever.

How very compelling are our hobbits then, because they are childlike little people starting out without car keys or the vote or a high skill level in Quake. They can drink and smoke and eat as much as they like — a child's vision of freedom — but their little lives count for nothing in the larger affairs of Middle-earth. We've all been there, once. But when the hobbits come to the Council of Elrond, they are told by him that "Neither strength nor wisdom will carry us far…" He goes on to say that the small and weak may have as much chance of achieving the quest as the great and strong. In one of Elrond's visionary moments, he foresees that this particular quest is not laid before the wizards and warriors present, but lies before the humblest members of the Council: the hobbits.

The hobbits' year of journeying makes them independent, self-reliant and powerful, with the kind of power that accepts that an individual's acts have consequences. Thus the journey of the four hobbits is an initiation rite. The hobbits' story is an initiation story, and our culture is short on tales that carry the same intensity of hope for young people.

Is it an impossible stretch to find agreement between Taoism and Tolkien? Difficult, certainly but not impossible. Whether it gives us more insight than reading *The Tao of Pooh* or *Everything I Needed to Know About Life I Learned from a Hobbit*, I'm not sure. Maybe it's trite to say that all major beliefs share some common ground. The exercise was one that I enjoyed, at any rate; perhaps you will too.

"Even the very wise cannot see all ends," says Gandalf, and throughout *The Lord of the Rings* Tolkien gives great value to the hobbits' qualities of innocent virtue. Their Shire would be a little like the Lao Tzu's perfect State in the *Tao Te Ching*:

> ... *So a wise leader might say:*
> *I practice inaction, and the people look after themselves.*
> *I love to be quiet, and the people themselves find justice.*
> *I don't do business, and the people prosper on their own.*
> *I don't have wants, and the people themselves are uncut*
> *wood.*

(Le Guin's gloss on the phrase "uncut wood" is "uncarved, unshaped, unpolished, native natural stuff is better than anything that can be made out of it ... Its potentiality is infinite.")

Tolkien's hobbits, like a Taoist sage, find a personal power made of self-knowledge and acceptance of what is both possible and necessary. None of them wield great dominion over others. Merry and Pippin coordinate the Scouring of the Shire for as long as necessary, and Sam allows his humble wisdom to be recognized in becoming Mayor. He's held the Ring and had visions of himself mantled in temporal power, and he rejects those visions. So the *Tao Te Ching* says:

> *If my mind's modest*
> *I walk the great way.*
> *Arrogance*
> *Is all I fear.*

Or put another way:

To have without possessing,
do without claiming,
lead without controlling:
this is mysterious power.

Here's another verse that intrigues me because I can read and read Tolkien and still not be sure what it would be *like* to meet an elf. We know that elves are somehow alien to us, but most of the art renderings of this come out looking like slightly soft-porn lingerie ads, as though the elves' power were purely sexual (and mostly just affected men, I might add). *This* kind of strangeness I would recognize, though:

Once upon a time
people who knew the Way
were subtle, spiritual, mysterious and penetrating,
unfathomable.

Since they're inexplicable
I can only say what they seemed like:
Cautious, oh yes, as if wading through a winter river.
Alert, as if afraid of the neighbours.
Polite and quiet, like houseguests.
Elusive, like melting ice.
Blank, like uncut wood.
Empty, like valleys.
Mysterious, oh yes, they were like troubled water.

Who can by stillness, little by little
Make what is troubled grow clear?
Who can by movement, little by little
Make what is still grow quick?

To follow the Way
Is not to need fulfillment.
Unfulfilled, one may live on
Needing no renewal.

There's something so weird and "other" about that description …
As though describing somebody who was so evolved that they were beyond humanity, much as Sam found the elves above his likes and

dislikes and impossible to fathom beyond their love of music and dancing.

Another central value in *The Lord of the Rings* is the exercise of compassion, the restraint of judgment, as Sam understands in his last confrontation with Gollum. There on the slopes of Mt. Doom he has Gollum at last in his power, Frodo is out of sight, and Gollum grovels before him in the dust, a creature of abject misery. But he feels something in his heart that holds him back from the killing blow that Gollum seems to have earned. He cannot strike a thing so utterly ruined.

Most major religions with sufficient legs to travel any distance in time or space share those qualities — hardly a blinding insight, but there it is. Compassion is one of the foundation stones of Buddhism, and Hinduism teaches that your self and all of creation are in truth one linked Being (and therefore all things deserve mercy).

And in Tolkien's work, among the most famous quotes are these words from Gandalf: "It was Pity that stayed his hand. Pity, and Mercy: Not to strike without need."

I'm not trying to say that Tolkien ever read the Tao or had any interest in Eastern religions. I've seen no evidence of it. But it's fascinating to make comparisons. At the very least they give an insight into why both Tolkien and Eastern religion made an imprint on the hippie culture of the 1960s and 1970s, when certainly some people were trying to reinvent society. It was a time of innocence and of small hands trying to link into a force that would change the world. Whether you think the Flower Power movement succeeded or failed, it's not surprising that Frodo should have become most beloved of that culture.

Sources:
Joseph Campbell, *Myths to Live By*. Arkana, 1993.
Lao Tzu/ Ursula Le Guin, *Tao Te Ching: A Book About the Way and the Power of the Way*. Shambhala Publications, 1998.
Bruno Bettelheim, *The Uses of Enchantment* . Vintage Books, 1989.

8. How to Express Your Tolkien Ignorance: A Guide for the Media

Turgon

My dear Wormwood,

You ask for a little guidance in dealing with the onrushing tide of media coverage of Tolkien.

The first and easiest way in which to show disrespect is by getting the author's name wrong. Did you see Slubgob's good work the other day in getting the *New York Times* to spell it "Tolkein"? The *New York Times*, no less, succumbing again to such arrogance! We had a good laugh down here. And if the medium isn't print, we also suggest that you plant one of the variously used mispronunciations: tol-kine, or tolk-in. Few will have seen (thanks to our mostly successful efforts to suppress it) that highly useful little book on how to pronounce the most frequently mispronounced names in the arts, *Klee as in Clay*, by Wilfred J. McConkey. It clearly and correctly gives the name as toll-keen.

Beyond these simple starting points, our strategies, by necessity, must be somewhat more subtle and crafty. First and foremost, we must marginalize Tolkien's work. Say it is for children; that's the oldest and easiest way to denigrate a literary work. It worked so well for *Gulliver's Travels* that few now know that it is a scathing and wonderful attack on the idiocies of the human race.

But if Tolkien's work can't be marginalized as for children, the next view to take is to promote it as a cult work. Never mind that *The Lord of the Rings* alone has sold over 100 million copies. Over 100 million copies! And we can successfully pigeonhole it as a cult novel! It feels so good to perpetuate this ruse! (Yet if it doesn't work, try the reverse, elitist approach: anything that is that popular can't be any good. We certainly don't want readers trying the work and making decisions for themselves.)

Next, I suggest attacking the author himself. Make sure he is referred to as a tweedy eccentric, an academic who specialized in boring dead languages and literatures, an absent-minded professor who ran around the dusty libraries of Oxford muttering things to himself about *gollums* and *balrogs*. Show him as a person lost in his own time, a dreamy romantic who looked backwards in time towards a vanished past. He must be presented as a personality that no intelligent person could be interested in.

If you can't find appropriate means to attack the work itself or the author, next comes the readership. Call them geeks of the first order, social outcasts, introspective misfits who stay at home, wasting their lives away by reading books. And the worst of these misfits will spend their time so engrossed in Tolkien's world that they will study the wholly imaginary Elvish languages, or dress up as characters from the books, or worst of all, participate in role-playing games! (The Satanistic aspect of gaming hasn't got much play of late — we should renew this angle.) Never mind that these are wholly legitimate pursuits for anyone who is interested in them. We must present all of this in as laughable a manner as possible.

And by all means, make sure that Tolkien is called controversial. That gives us the chance to work the polar opposites against each other. Forget that the world is neither black and white, but gray, and that nothing is so absolute. Let Tolkien's work be labeled Christian (so non-Christians won't read it), or let it be called an allegory of World War II (which it isn't) — that sounds deadly boring enough to appeal only to high school English teachers. Erroneously root Tolkien's work in the 1960s (much of it was actually written in the 1930s and 1940s), so that we can irrevocably associate it with the hippies and the drug culture (think pipeweed here!). And place it firmly in the despised genre of fantasy. Call it escapism! (Tolkien himself made a perceptive comment that many critics seem to confuse the flight of the deserter with the escape of a prisoner. But we can't let that get out either.) And don't forget to call it a trilogy (or better yet, the Trilogy), because of course it is no such thing — rather, it is a single novel sometimes published in three volumes.

The above ideas are, of course, mere suggestions. Feel free to improvise in new and devious ways. With three movies coming out over a three-year period, we shall have many opportunities to exercise our imaginations. Hah! In fact, everyone down here is looking forward to innumerable examples of ignorance and animosity towards Tolkien. And we are in a unique position to promote these views and keep the usual misrepresentations of Tolkien in the public eye. It is a duty I shall gladly perform, and hope that you too will relish the opportunities afforded.

Your affectionate uncle,

Screwtape

Good & Evil

9. "They're Bad....*BAD!!*"
— *George H.W. Bush*

Tehanu

For me, the events of September 11, 2001 started with a phone call from my boyfriend at around 3 a.m. New Zealand time. For a few moments as I struggled with deep sleep I wondered why he was telling me the plot of some crazy thriller about terrorists and airplanes, and part of me kept right on disbelieving him until I'd turned the radio on. While I was sleeping, the world had changed more than I could take in, and the sense of unreality would return many times over the following days.

I have lived most of my life in cities I love that are built on major fault lines. People ask, "How can you rest easy at night, knowing The Big One could wipe everyone out?" It turns out we were all sleeping on a pretty thin crust. When I turned on the radio words like "Evil," "Justice," and "Punishment," were already beginning to fill the air-waves in a way I have not heard in my lifetime. Sure, politicians throw those words around all the time and with all the relish of somebody slapping down the ace in a game, but we know it's mere posturing. This was different.

After I'd hung up the phone there was nothing to do except go online, because all the world seemed asleep around me and the news was not something I wanted to hug to myself for the rest of the night. There were no lights on anywhere in the sleeping suburb and nobody I wanted to wake yet with the grim news.

Online I would find my friends from other time zones, and indeed there was a surprisingly big crowd in TheOneRing.net's chat room. Barliman's was galvanized, with people typing like wildfire in a dozen impassioned and overlapping conversations. It was surreal and also extremely affecting, for some people in the chat room had seen the towers fall and knew people who were missing. Others were trying to comfort them. The mood was electric with rage, grief, bravado and despair.

Technology is strange, and there are moments when it defines the age we live in. Many of us in Barliman's that night must have been like me, sitting in a room somewhere in the world, completely alone and yet knotted into a web of words and gestures that bonded us across the whole planet. The internet made it possible for people to communicate instantly what they were hearing or seeing in real life or on their local news and to say how they felt about it. There were people who live in war zones trying to comfort these newest victims with the reassurance they could give from their own experience: that everything passes, even the unthinkable. There were expressions of solidarity from all around the planet, and at the same time people who were blind to that, swearing that the whole world hated them. There were arguments as people analyzed the events with the different perspectives of a hundred places in the world. There was, terrifyingly, the cry for revenge, the demand to "Nuke 'em all!" whether we knew who "they" were or not.

If I'd been a near-victim I'd have joined in that demand to hit out at somebody, anybody, and make them suffer too, whether it was fair or not. Anyone other than a saint has moments of wanting to rip the sword out of blind Justice's hands and cut down the scales that measure right from wrong, not caring if we destroy everything, so long as the scales end up equal.

It's too much to expect that I'd *feel* any differently, but I hope I would *know* that the desire was wrong. And why would I know that it was wrong? Standing as I was, further back from the pain, all I could repeat over and over again to people on the brink were Gandalf's words:

> Many that live deserve death. And some that die deserve life. Can you give it to them? Then do not be so eager to deal out death in judgement.

That phrase expressed what I felt, and others took it up both online and in real life, because in those first days we dreaded a worldwide spasm of senseless killing. That conversation between Frodo and Gandalf has always felt like one of the pivotal moments in *The Lord of the Rings*. Now since the film came out, those words have taken on an even greater resonance. I think it is no accident that those words did not end up on the cutting room floor. The film came at a time when people in general were considering things like evil and justice more intensely than they have done in a long time. You can find a meaning in that if you like.

Gandalf does not counsel inaction or passivity. He is involved in a fight that he will see through to the end, and all those fighting on his side are pledged to that too. You hear it in the sad, fierce songs of the Rohirrim, that sing of their courage and determination to fight on past hope and heartbreak as they ride out. Check them out, at the end of "The Muster of Rohan," or Théoden's tremendous call to action at the end of "The Ride of the Rohirrim" and Eomer's war song on the Pelennor field when he sees when he sees the black sails coming up the Anduin.

We were feeling something that Tolkien always felt — that history is full of pain and that events of the far past bear down on the present with an unbearable weight, so that our mere innocence and our best intentions cannot always protect us from its offspring. No wonder then that at such a time, we find some guidance in books like *The Lord of the Rings*.

It isn't nonsense to say that we look to a book for guidance as well as entertainment. In fact we seem to crave entertainment that pits a clearly defined good against a recognizable evil, and our most popular stories show evil being punished and good being rewarded. When you think about it, this isn't just the basis of most fantasy, it's also the basis of other popular genres such as detective stories and police procedurals. How much prime-time television is taken up with the pursuit and punishment of crime? How much television is devoted to shows where we are invited to judge human behavior? How much comedy is based on the exaggeration of a character trait or social trend? While we're laughing at the screen, aren't we also thinking, "I'd better be sure my behavior isn't equally laughable"? While we're enjoying the criminal's comeuppance, isn't some part of us aware that we'd better not be caught doing the same thing?

Although the real world and real people are rarely that simple and easily judged, we do use stories to confirm that our notion of what is good and right and acceptable is shared by other people. We like to know what the standards of our society are, whether we choose to conform to them or not. Somebody who knowingly defies those standards might be a hero or an anti-hero, depending on the situation, but somebody who simply has no idea what society expects is likely to be a blundering tragedy.

There are no easy solutions to the evils that led to the attacks on the World Trade Center and the Pentagon. To us, or to me at any rate, the use of blind force in dealing with it seems comparable to using the Ring to defeat Sauron. Force satisfies us. For a good cause, on the right side, surely it would be justified to … I mean, *we'd* know how to limit the killing …. at this point Gandalf must cry, *"Do not tempt me! "*

We do not wish to become like the Dark Lord ourselves....

In #66 of the *Letters,* Tolkien himself wrote to his son who was serving in the air force during WWII (remember, two generations of Tolkiens served willingly as soldiers). "We are attempting to conquer Sauron with the Ring." I remember those words and keep watch for signs that we are becoming similar to that which we hope to defeat.

A few months later I was one of many people interviewed for a Radio New Zealand documentary on Tolkien fandom and Peter Jackson's film. The interviewer, Camilla Maling, began what she thought would be a very straightforward project documenting Tolkien fan culture, but once she began interviewing the Tolkien fans within and outside the film production, she realized that all her assumptions were wrong. Tolkien fans were not the people she thought we were. By learning what lay at the root of our fascination with the *The Lord of the Rings* she came to create a very different program from what she had expected. Very few interviewers have bothered to notice or find out why we didn't fit their preconceptions, but she was a shining exception.

During the interview our conversation strayed to the events of September 11, and I tried to explain how some of us online were trying to calm the chaotic reactions of rage and hate by reminding people of Gandalf's words. She stopped, surprised, and said that many other Tolkien fans that she had interviewed had also talked about the book in relation to recent events. It seemed that many of us had turned to it for counsel and relief in the days that followed the attack. She found that extraordinary, and yet it made something clear to her about what it is we love so much about Tolkien. She saw that we find his words applicable to real-life situations. Even in times of crisis, or maybe above all in times of crisis, he is one of those writers whom we rely on to regain our sense of values.

Tolkien is remembered by those who knew him as a very kind and humane man who had strong opinions about things like good and evil and how they function in the world. His beliefs about free will, justice, courage and strength are both ancient and modern, and readers still find them emotionally rewarding. Our next essays talk about the way Tolkien's work reveals a moral compass that is, under its deceptively old-fashioned veneer, subtle and profound enough to confront the problems of a changing world.

10. Good & Evil

Anwyn

Good and Evil. The absolute nature of these terms makes them words that modern people have been conditioned against speaking. They involve making judgments that go against the politically correct definition of tolerance. The battle between them, however, consumes the plot of every good fantasy tale ever written, whether it be in print or on the silver screen. The harder modern society tries condemn the concept of objective moral standards, the more its individual members acclaim stories of how the Good fights the Evil, and make no mistake about it: we are speaking of Good with a capital "G" and Evil with a very capital "E."

There is no room for moral interpretation in Tolkien. He had probably never heard anybody say, "Well, I can't force my morality on others." There is no questioning who among his characters is right and who is wrong. Why do people flock to the works of Tolkien, to the films of George Lucas, to action movies involving police officers against drug dealers, to comic book adaptations depicting Our Hero fighting The Villain, in droves? Precisely because when you see a Black Rider standing in your path, you don't stop to debate the merits of his belief system against your own. You draw your sword.

People, no matter how much they publicly deny it, want and indeed need a conscience, a standard against which to measure their own behavior and that of others. What would we think of parents who didn't bother to instruct their children that stealing, lying, cheating in school, and hitting their playmates are wrong? It is the very agelessness of the battle that makes fantasy — especially the incomparable works of Tolkien — so popular. His depiction of Good and Evil leaves no room for doubt; here is how he describes the Lord of the Nazgûl: *"A great black shape against the fires beyond he loomed up, grown to a vast menace of despair."*

Everyone flees before him except Gandalf the White who waits for him, mounted on Shadowfax (the silver horse still free and unbridled), both of them unmoving before the threat.

Darkness, fire, menace, terror and despair are set against freedom, steadfastness, light, certainty and strength. You just can't get much clearer than that.

I think that as much as Tolkien would have stared in disbelief at hearing someone discuss "relative morality," he would have scoffed even more at the culture of victimhood that our society perpetuates. The idea that evildoers cannot be held responsible for their actions is one that should have died a natural death before it ever came to light, and Tolkien had no time or patience for it. He acknowledged that ill usage and sad circumstances could help drive a soul to wrong behavior, but he still believed in the ultimate responsibility of each individual for his or her actions. He makes this most clear through the character of Gollum; we are told that Gollum was shunned by his relations and driven from his home, but although Tolkien allowed Gollum numerous instances of possible redemption, Gollum failed time and again to rise to the challenge. Tolkien displays pity for Gollum's plight but keeps us sternly focused on the fact that it was his choice to continue in his evil ways.

Moreover, he goes back further and shows us Gollum's ultimate motivating force: it was his desire to know secrets and thus have power over his family and peers that first drove him to take and use the Ring. *His own desire.* Gollum wanted to blame his piteous, twisted state on others, conveniently forgetting that it was his action in murdering Déagol and claiming the Ring for his own that led to his ultimate destruction. From the dawn of time, evildoers have tried to blame others for their fall, and Tolkien recognized that this lack of responsibility for actions constitutes a large part of the downward spiral into evil.

Why can't Denethor, Saruman, Sauron, and the rest of our cast of villains see what their lack of responsibility is doing not only to those around them, but to themselves? Like Gollum, they are mired in the root of evil, their focus solely on their own wants. This is why they can never have a comrade, never a team member, but must always be alone while those who work for the good strive together with allies. Those who work for the good can never triumph alone; those who work evil never wish to triumph any other way.

Taking responsibility to strive for the good as part of a team is difficult, no doubt about it. Sometimes the pursuit of good conflicts with the pursuers' own wishes to be safe, to be happy, or to retain their property, but just as Frodo left his home, comfort and safety because he was the only one who could bear the Ring, so Aragorn left behind his heart's desire to guide and assist Frodo. The members of the Company each did the same, each knowing that he could contribute to the good, even if he could not see how. Most of all in faithful Sam do we see this trusting determination.

Tolkien tells us of the doubts and fears of the Company, but he also tells us how they pressed on, convinced that it was their responsibility to do what they could. Each makes a sacrifice for what he perceives as good, not to mention for the good of his allies and fellow creatures, and in the end their rewards far exceed the things they gave up or left behind.

So how is it that Tolkien can get away with painting things this black and white? Don't evildoers sometimes think better of themselves and mend their ways? Don't good people fall? Sure they do. "And what about the Ring?" you protest. "These people were all under some evil influence!" Well, granted, but the fact remains, our villains see something to be gained for themselves, and even though they know it's wrong, they fall to temptation. That doesn't absolve them of the responsibility for their actions. And so might the good fall, as well. Look at Boromir, who fell to sudden temptation. Look at Saruman, whom Tolkien tells us was once Gandalf's superior in the Council. Look even at our Frodo, who stood at the Cracks of Doom and declared that he would throw away in an eyeblink what had cost him and others so much to be able to achieve. Temptation comes to even the best of us, but we only prevail through resistance and recognition that if we fall, it will be our doing, our choice, and not something that has been forced upon us for which we are not responsible.

The reason that Tolkien can tell us so well about the nature of Good and Evil is because he knows that people — individual, fearful, determined, weak, strong, allied, lonely people — are themselves the only variables in what is wrong and what is right. And in the end, it is the people who will answer individually for the consequences of their actions. There will not always be Eagles to pull us out of the fire.

11. Justice, Mercy & Redemption

Anwyn

"So how is it that Tolkien can get away with painting things this black and white? Don't evildoers sometimes think better of themselves and mend their ways? Don't good people fall? Sure they do."

It's true. Tolkien doesn't favor us with any clear-cut examples, at least not in *The Lord of the Rings*, of people who were severe, lifelong evildoers and came to see the errors in their thinking (see *Return of the Jedi* for the best example of this, in Darth Vader), but he does provide us with several prime examples of justice, mercy, and redemption of those who fell to momentary or longer-lasting temptation.

We can define justice as the proper consequences of wrong actions, mercy as a decision on the part of somebody in power to create a way for a wrongdoer to avoid those consequences, and redemption as … well, redemption — the wrongdoer avoids dire consequences by accepting penalties and working to once again earn trust. For example: justice is a failing grade for somebody who cheats on a test. Fairness is making sure that everybody else who cheats will also fail (i.e. fairness equals the same punishment for the same crime), but the justice, the failing grade, is the direct consequence of the action, the cheating.

What about mercy? To continue our line of thought, the cheating student has never done it before, swears up and down he will never do it again, begs for mercy, sits for a second, much harder, "for him only" exam, and keeps the grade he gets on that one instead of the F he would have made for cheating. And redemption? That's if the student studies his keester off and makes an A on the much harder second exam. On a final note, there is (or should be) no mercy for the student who is caught cheating more than once. Justice, for him, is the failing grade, without hope of clemency.

How does this example apply to Prof. Tolkien? It's simple. Boromir lost the first round. He fell to sudden temptation to gain the Ring for his own and tried to take it from Frodo by force. He recovered himself, was appalled at his behavior, begged for mercy, and was given another trial. He was killed, yes. But he was killed in defense of the Good, not in pursuit of the Evil, as we will see later in the cases of Saruman and Denethor. He passed the exam with flying colors. His spirit was redeemed. Tolkien tells us this in no uncertain terms as Boromir lies dying. Boromir is distraught by his sudden horrific fall into temptation, but Aragorn assures him that he has conquered and gained the victory. Boromir paid for his redemption with his life — it was sacrificed in proving that he was better than a gnawing temptation to take the Ring and use it to gain power.

Boromir is our perfect example of all three elements: justice, mercy *and* redemption. Sadly, not everybody can or will be redeemed. Have you ever heard the expression, "You can't help someone who doesn't want to be helped?" My mother used to say that long before "You have to *want* to get better," came into vogue with psychologists/psychiatrists. Saruman and Denethor are two very good examples of people who fell to temptation, fell into evil for however long or short a time, and who refused to recognize that they were at fault, refused to take responsibility or consequences for their evil actions.

Now before I go on with this, I should mention a very nice, intelligent discussion I had with a reader who objected to Denethor being on my "villains" list. His argument was that Denethor was overborne by the power of the palantír and through it by Sauron, and so he was not in his right mind at the end when he ordered his son's death and had himself burned alive. I will go so far as to say that it seems likely Denethor was indeed out of his mind at that stage, but long before that, he had every opportunity to cease the use of the palantír. Tolkien gives us evidence of the fact that he was addicted to using it. But unlike our modern customs that use addiction as the excuse for clemency, Tolkien uses the incident with Pippin and the palantír to make note of the fact that addictions can be cured and thus no longer blamed for wrong behavior. As is still advised in our world today, Gandalf tells Pippin to seek help in overcoming the problem — something Denethor was clearly unwilling to do.

Had Denethor ever been able to unbend his pride long enough to trust somebody of "lower" status than himself, even one of his sons, he might have been turned aside from his path of self-destruction. But ultimately, his overbearing pride was the evil that led to his downfall. Pride whispered that he could control the palantír, pride told him that it would give him yet greater power, and pride shouted at the end of his life that he was still the Steward, still in control, under nobody else's command. Pride even claimed that the Steward's authority was greater than it actually was, that "even were [Aragorn's] claim proved to [Denethor]," yet he would still not bow to "such a one." One of my favorite, but also one of the most heartbreaking, passages in all of Tolkien is Denethor's defiance before his death, and it exhibits this pride and ultimate despair. Gandalf asks him what he wishes, and Denethor answers to the effect that he'd prefer life to go on as he had always known it. But if that cannot be then he would rather have nothing, no half-measures to his life, love and honor, and finally he demands that his will should hold sway to dictate his own end.

His will . . . and ultimately, yes, his own end. Justice was granted in return for his refusal to attempt redemption: a horrible death, a spirit unredeemed, and a death in despair, without seeing the rise of the country that he claimed to love.

Saruman is another almost heartbreaking case: he who was once so knowledgeable and formerly so wise, indeed a Maia spirit, the equal of Gandalf whom we love and revere. What happened? A very similar story to Denethor's, yet with a few notable differences. Saruman's desire for power was for himself alone and not for the people under his rule; his pride was in his own accomplishments, not in a great nation over which he was given Stewardship; and his conceit in thinking he was so much greater than his peers was formed on even less base than Denethor's. Saruman was just a little more down and dirty with his evildoings. He covered them under a much thinner veneer. He made no secret, when he revealed his mind to Gandalf, of the fact that he wanted the Ruling Ring and was prepared to use force on whomever necessary to get it. But just as with Denethor, just as with Boromir, prideful desire for power was the primary evil at work.

Those who will not receive mercy when it is offered are truly in dire straits. Mercy and redemption both were offered Saruman, but it would have meant casting aside his arrogance, ditching his hard-won "power," and abandoning his machines and his tower, the symbols of that power. He simply could not admit that he had been wrong and that he was now caught without any other way out. In his last confrontation from within the walls of Orthanc, Saruman makes it clear to Gandalf that he cannot bend his pride — Tolkien tells us how the pride and hate show in his voice as he succumbs to them.

It's all in those two little words, "pride" and "hate." It seems that Saruman might have welcomed mercy if it were offered, but he could not endure the harder test that would have redeemed him — to turn and use his still formidable powers for the Good. Though Saruman's spirit wavered once more, at the very end, and seemed again to desire mercy, it is clear that this was only *after* the body had been killed. In other words, when you have nothing left to lose, not even your life, sure, why not give up your evil ambitions and try to get back on the good side of the folks in charge? Unfortunately for Saruman's spirit, there is no redemption for those who will not rise to the challenge of mercy — the challenge to prove oneself higher and better than temptation. Tolkien tells us that the West Wind came and blew Saruman's spirit away.

So justice comes to us all, be it a reward or be it consequences — because justice works both ways. Rewards do come, ultimately, to those who follow the straight path, or would you deny the peaceful conclusion to the story of Frodo? The decision is up to us on these things: will we give in to temptation or not? And if we do, will we be able to cast down our evildoings, live up to the challenge of mercy, and be redeemed in the end?

After the original writing of this piece, a reader wrote who objected vehemently to my position on the grounds that true redemption cannot be earned. Because he was following the Christian doctrine that the grace of God is the only path to redemption and that nothing we human beings can do will save us, this reader had a point. However, I will offer the following counterpoints. Between man and God, as a Christian I do believe that it is God's will alone that redeems human souls. But that is not necessarily the kind of redemption I am defining above, and I believe there can be more than one kind. Between imperfect human beings, such as the student and the teacher in the earlier example, redemption can be earned through a combination of grace on the part of the judge (teacher, or in Boromir's case, Aragorn) and hard work on the part of the wrongdoer (cheating student, or Boromir).

And even in a case of redemption of a soul, between that soul and a higher power, there is still one very important task that lies to the wrongdoer: to accept the redemption. Boromir did so. Saruman and Denethor did not, because it would have meant giving up what they considered a better deal: their power and their pride.

Ultimately, grace of God or human judges notwithstanding, the choice will always lie with the wrongdoer: cling to sinking self and accept justice for evil actions, or jump into the boat of mercy and row your way to redemption?

12. Getting the "Eye" Out of Life

Tehanu

When I was writing "Tehanu's Notes" regularly I would often get e-mails from people who had further insights into the things I was discussing. Thomas Goss was one who had wise things to say on the subject of evil:

"It's interesting that the talk has turned to bad guys: I was deliciously spooked by Black Riders, thrilled with disgust at the orcs and trolls, and astounded by the Balrog. These were monsters, naturally and unnaturally evil. They had a feel and a smell to them intoxicating to a young person, and I can still remember the powerful effect that meeting them for the first time had on my imagination: somehow, [the appearance of] these most mythical of creatures bring the sharpest sting of reality to the canon. The orcs have lives and gripes and politics of their own, and the trolls are more natural in their appetites (in *The Hobbit*) than evil in their natures. And of course for sheer, gripping creepiness, nothing quite comes close to the Black Riders. I'm sure that after our first taste of them, you and I never looked at a shadow in quite the same way again.

"But the worst bad guy of them all, Sauron, we never quite meet face to face. Oh, sure, we hear Pippin relate a very disjointed encounter of a long-distance conference, and Saruman, Denethor and Aragorn all struggle with him using various palantiri. Yet it is all second- and third-hand; we never come close to a visceral contact with color and sound. Only in *The Silmarillion* is he described, and that is in the guises (hound, werewolf, etc.) that he took in service of Morgoth. And of course there is the rather dry description of him as having a "fair guise" as a "master of gifts" to the ring-smithing Noldor in the Second Age. But once again, as in descriptions of him in battle before the Barad-dur, we

71

are withheld from any substantive shape to our imagination other than shadow and terror and treachery.

"Lord knows I tried, especially as a boy, to put a face on this evil. I imagined a horribly twisted black wizard, like a shriveled, ogrish man. It didn't ring true. Then a sort of vague, super-Black Rider with a dreadful demon visage: this also fell short. Then I reached for another image with my mind's eye, a vast, angry spirit of hate and malice, in the shape of a man, but huge like a giant, with no tangible body, just a cloak of empty darkness from which no light or hope ever escaped. Nope. That wasn't quite it, either. It was too Balrog-y, somehow.

"It was much later when I realized that the face of Sauron was in his works. He had spread himself so thoroughly across the landscape that there was little left of any central body or being, except for perhaps an organizing will. That was it, all that Sauron was in the end, just pure force of will with perhaps the remnants of a soul clinging to it, sending out its commands through the vast chain of its body. The Nazgul were somehow the nerves, Mordor the bones, Orcs and Men the muscle.

"This is real evil, the ability to create rule by force, perhaps a more terrifying reality, especially to a child of a world at war, than any isolated goblin or wraith. And the results are pure devastation upon the face of the earth: haunted, putrid marshes, poisoned streams, mutated greenery, blasted heath. That was why I never felt right about imagining Sauron as a creature: Tolkien didn't want me to. But he made sure that I knew exactly what Sauron was by the time I finished the book."

I defy anyone to come up with a better analysis than that.

In a wonderful essay, "On Tolkien's Narrative" by fantasy author Diana Wynne Jones, she talks about the way Tolkien makes us fear Sauron's enormous reach. At first it is unnerving to think that he could reach as far as the Shire, but his emissaries there are recognizably outsiders. Once the Hobbits reach Bree it is harder for them to know who can be trusted; it seems that Sauron's spies are everywhere. Then even Nature turns against the Fellowship: the very birds of the air are a watchful threat, not to mention the Wargs.

Like a stone dropped in a pond, the ripples of Sauron's influence spread wider and wider, and so does our realization of this. The Balrog may not be under Sauron's command, but the deep roots of the earth are stirred up by the waking of evil in the land. And most chillingly of all, the terrible song of the Barrow-wight prophesies a Black Resurrection, as if Sauron hoped to rule not only the living but the dead as well, so that all creatures can be in his power not only in the present age, nor only in life, but for all time. The Barrow-wight's spell commands his captives to sleep until the end of time, until the death of the sun and moon, only then to rise again, to what unimaginable existence, at the command of the Dark Lord.

What an absolutely terrifying thought.

When I was a child, I knew the people who could hurt me, and our battles were personal and limited. Books like *The Lord of the Rings* introduced me to the idea of a kind of hatred that I had never encountered in real life, the kind that can destroy you impersonally, in pursuit of its own goals, without ever knowing your name. That was frightening.

So much the worse for Frodo, then, who in his innocence had hardly heard anything of Sauron, yet *Sauron knew his name.*

I sit writing at the computer, and if I switch over to e-mail the chances are that a message will come in promising me the ultimate in spy software and adding the threat that I am being watched myself, so my best defense is to "join 'em, if I can't beat 'em." I could choose to believe this, in which case my life would be dominated by the belief in some Sauron-like entity that knows all about me and can strike at any time. I choose not to believe it — no matter how efficient surveillance is, no matter how efficient the virtual predators on the web may be, I'm in the same relationship to them as a field mouse is to a hawk. Hawks have eyes perfectly adapted for seeing the merest rustle of a rodent, and hawks are masters of the sudden deadly strike. But there are so very many field mice per hawk that all their vigilance and efficiency still leaves a vast and thriving mouse population still living. The odds are high in my favor. Also, it's of no particular economic benefit to anyone to watch me, as no amount of control or surveillance is likely to shake any cash out of me.

What if things were to change, though? I've just seen George Lucas's first feature film, developed out of a National Student Film Festival short. It's called *THX 1138*, and it talks about a future that is totally monitored and depersonalized. I have to think that Lucas has spent his entire career in regression, because his first film is a dark, intelligent, disturbing fairy-tale of the most grown-up kind. The dialogue is laconic, assured and naturalistic, and thus far more believable than his later works. It's a very prescient film.

Right now companies are perfecting software that will enable them to monitor how many keystrokes a worker is making on a keyboard — i.e. how much work they're doing, just as they are developing automated ways of monitoring call center workers. They're aiming to perfect it so you can work from home ... and still be monitored. It's too early to tell how widespread this kind of monitoring is or will become in the future, but given the increasing number of hours that people are spending at work, that's an awful lot of time to have some kind of electronic vigilance over one's life, and the line between home and work is getting blurry. The scary thing about *THX 1138* is that there is no enemy per se, no evil overlord that you can point to or fight with. It's just the system. Once again, why is Sauron so scary? Because he's everywhere and nowhere, and while he may not have noticed you *yet*, there are no guarantees for the future.

Lucas's film is a riff on George Orwell's book *1984*, come to think of it. Again, that faceless, dehumanizing system that watches over everyone, obliterating freedom.

And now this is what's so interesting — the roots of this concern about state surveillance started in the early part of the 20th century. Look at some of the influential writers of that time that Tolkien is criticized for ignoring — such as George Orwell. He was one of the English writers and intellectuals who fought in the Spanish Civil War in 1936. C.S. Lewis introduced Tolkien and the other Inklings to another writer who went and fought on the other side (there were lots of sides to fight on): the poet Roy Campbell. I can join the dots and see that there is a dialogue going on between writers and intellectuals about peace and freedom and the things that began to threaten it in new ways during that century. Tolkien, who was characterized as a stay-at-home, ivory tower academic, wasn't as ignorant of these issues as his critics claim. Orwell wrote about Big Brother; Tolkien had Sauron.

The Spanish Civil War was so important *ideologically* that people from all over Europe and Russia joined up to fight on one side or other — George Orwell on the Communist/Anarchist side, Tolkien's and Lewis's acquaintance Roy Campbell on the Fascist/monarchist/military side, just to name a few prominent writers. It was a complete mess, with so many sides that kept changing alliances and so much ideology being defended, not to mention all the ancient feuds and scores that found an opportunity to get settled. The foreign participants went home with a new cynicism about civil and international politics.

Ten years ago I stood by Picasso's *Guérnica* in Madrid and listened to a teen tourist confidently telling her schoolmates that it referred to "that Franco-Prussian thing." I honestly don't know much about the Franco-Prussian thing, but I know it's nothing to do with Guérnica. Different war, different century. *Guérnica* commemorates a new evil. Generalissimo Franco called on his buddy Hitler to send some planes on over to the small Basque town of Guérnica to bomb anti-Fascist civilians during the civil war. This was something that traumatized the world. Up until then right through human history the main thrust of warfare was directed at soldiers.

To reach deep into enemy territory (or in Franco's case, into his own country, since this was a civil war) and strike sleeping civilians was a monstrosity that shocked the world at the time. Like the V2 rockets that were soon to attack England, it created a new world in which nobody is safe — not even little villages as far from the front as the Shire is from Mordor.

Almost sixty years later, Picasso's painting of Guérnica was as famous as ever, and in Spain it was politically sensitive enough that it was hung under permanent guard in a reinforced room for which you were searched before being allowed to enter. (But the young tourists had completely forgotten the event to which it referred. In sixty years from now will kids think *TTT* refers to a fantasy book or a bombing atrocity? If it's the former then the pen is indeed mightier than the sword. And that, as Gandalf would say, may be an encouraging thought.)

I can hardly forget "the Franco thing," since my own family lived through it. There are old newsreels of the doomed Anarchists marching in the streets of Barcelona with their banners shouting *No Pasarán!* "You/They shall not pass!" That is so very close to what Gandalf shouts first when he faces down the Balrog on the Bridge of Khazad-dum. It sent a chill down my spine. If only good and evil were so clearly defined as in that moment. Gandalf had all the certainty that everyone in the Spanish Civil War lacked, that we lack when we wonder about some nebulous threat to our way of life.

Luckily for us, no centralized will has emerged, no singular Sauron-like personality whose only desire is to control us. It may be impossible for any one person to have that power. Yet many of the effects Sauron had on the land and people seem to be happening by an accidental combination of greed and selfishness spread around a large number of individuals. Who hasn't seen Thomas Goss's "haunted, putrid marshes, poisoned streams, mutated greenery, blasted heath," in some place "where late the sweet birds sang?"

Few of us are likely to form armies marching against pollution or intrusive software or dictatorial workplaces. At least Sauron has a name and a location.

Sources:

Diana Wynne Jones, "On Tolkien's Narrative," from *This Far Land*. Robert Giddings, ed. Barnes & Noble, 1990.

13. Paradise Lost

Tehanu

Okay, evil scary things. Why is Sauron scary? What is the nature of his evil that keeps us so riveted to the page? Did Tolkien base his evil overlord on something else we might recognize? That's an easy one — just look at the baddest of the bad in previous literature. That would be Satan, hands down, no question, I thought. Plenty to learn there, so I dove into Milton's *Paradise Lost*.

> *... I thence invoke thy aid to my adventrous Song,*
> *That with no middle flight intends to soar*
> *Above th' Aonian Mount, while it persues*
> *Things unattempted yet in Prose or Rime ...*

So far so good, while Satan's in the picture. The poem soars all right, with some of the best language ever written. Unbelievable numbers of memorable quotes stud the first few books of the poem, like chunky bits of chocolate in a really good monster chocolate chip cookie. I was continually thinking "That's from Milton? And that? That too?"

Looking at the kind of language Milton uses and Tolkien uses when describing things of a noble nature, I can't imagine that Tolkien was not influenced by *Paradise Lost*. He was a professor of English literature whose knowledge extended well outside his chosen field of Old English and its relatives, and he certainly knew the poem and commented on it. Oddly enough he didn't like Milton very much (for not being a Catholic, evidently!), but on the other hand he didn't much like any English literature more recent than Chaucer. But Milton's language and his vision of Satan's Fall seems to have struck a chord, regardless.

Sure, both writers were reading the same events in the Bible, and it's fair to say that Tolkien imagined a creation myth for Middle-earth that is clearly based on scriptural accounts of Satan's fall. But *Paradise Lost* addresses a problem that concerned Tolkien, veteran of a terrible war that he was: why evil is allowed to exist. Milton took up the theological argument that evil existed because of Man's disobedience, but the existence of evil made possible the contrary gift of free will and choice, since without temptation there would be no virtue in being good. His presentation of the story of the Fall is so brilliant and compelling that it could well have inspired Tolkien to attempt something along the same lines. The first chapters of *The Silmarillion* are part of the result.

Milton had a problem with Satan that Tolkien must have recognized, and I wonder if one reason we see very little of Sauron in *The Lord of the Rings* is that we see so much of Satan in *Paradise Lost*.

Satan leaps off the page, as though he got away from Milton as soon as Milton wrote him down. For starters, *Paradise Lost* opens by telling things from Satan's point of view. Much as Milton himself enjoys describing the torments of Hell that Satan merits after his rebellion and fall from Heaven, Satan immediately gets up, rallies his troops with some of the most inspiring speeches in the language, and sets about making the best of his situation.

> *Satan exalted sat, by merit rais'd*
> *to that bad eminence; …*

and then he proceeds to get all the best lines:

> *What though the field be lost?*
> *All is not lost… th' unconquerable Will,*
> *and study of revenge, immortal hate,*
> *and courage not to submit or yield:*
> *and what is else not to be overcome?*

How many people realize that when they quote that, they're quoting *Satan's* lines?

The trouble is, things are so interesting when Satan is around. He builds his own Dark Tower in Hell (though made of gold and precious stones); he marshals his troops, they hatch plans, Satan flies around persuading the gatekeeper of Hell to let him out, then he flies off daring the perils of the "wilde Abyss" outside, goes to explore Eden and make trouble for mankind… Who cannot be drawn into the action of such language as this:

> Into this wild Abyss the warie Fiend
> stood on the brink of Hell and looked a while,
> pondering his Voyage; for no narrow frith
> he had to cross …

> … At last his Sail-broad Vanns
> he spreads for flight, and in the surging smoke
> uplifted spurns the ground, thence many a League
> as in a cloudy Chair ascending rides
> audacious …

> … Satan stayd not to reply,
> but glad now that his Sea should find a shore,
> with fresh alacritie and force renewd
> springs upward like a Pyramid of fire
> into the wilde expanse, and through the shock
> of fighting Elements, on all sides round
> environd wins his way; harder beset
> and more endangerd, than when Argo passd
> through Bosporus betwixt the justling Rocks …

And then it goes on and on with some more classical allusions that would have delighted the educated readers of Milton's day while flattering their cleverness. (Today some of those allusions are pretty meaningless.)

It's odd how Milton uses so much classical history to illustrate his story, given that his imagination and power of describing things in his own words stretch the limits of fantasy. He didn't need to compare anything to the Argo; his own words would suffice. As though compensating for his blindness, Milton wrote some of the most incredibly visual poetry.

Milton doesn't draw back from describing how Satan looks, his expressions, the way he feels, his long debates with his own divided nature… with the result that this reader for one ends up disliking him less than Milton would have liked. Satan's a trier; you've got to give him that.

Here's an interesting experiment: call to mind all the inspirational corporate catchphrases you can think of, the ones that usually appear on posters with photos of people running across a mesa in Colorado at sunset in front of a rainbow … I mean, take an anti-nausea pill first, and then think things like, "Losing is not an option," or "In order to succeed you must be prepared to fail," or "If you're not living on the edge, you're taking up too much room," and so on. Okay, if you were Milton and had to assign those lines to characters in "Paradise Lost," who would get most of them? Mmmmmm, not Jesus. Not Adam and Eve. God? Nope. Satan.

Methinks that Milton would not like our present century.

Most other characters in the epic walk and talk or sit and talk; Satan flies around all over the place, lying, flattering, making trouble, skiting, losing his temper, getting knocked back and picking himself up again… as soon as he's out of the picture things turn into something of a theological talkfest. Which is what happens later on, when Milton gives us a condensed history of the world according to the Bible.

It's noticeable how few famous quotes there are from the later parts of *Paradise Lost* and fewer still from *Paradise Regained*. I can't help thinking that I'm not the first person to feel their attention wandering once the excitement of the first few chapters is over, with all those amazing descriptions of the fiends in Hell.

Boredom aside, there is a parallel with *The Lord of the Rings* in that you could argue that the true point of both stories exists within the stillness at the center of the action, the eye of the hurricane. With Tolkien, it's in the "negative virtues" described by author Diana Wynne Jones, who says that what wins the war of the Ring are the quiet virtues of endurance, love, and obedience to conscience. Amid all the loud battles, the sieges and victories, we almost lose the two tiny figures of Frodo and Sam plodding, slowly and so alone, to Mount Doom.

In *Paradise Lost* we get the crucial scene amongst the rather static choirs of harping angels, where God discusses Man's freedom of choice.

> *… I made him just and right,*
> *sufficient to have stood, though free to fall…*

and later,

> ... *I formd them free, and free they must remain,*
> *till they enthrall themselves: I else must change*
> *thir nature, and revoke the high Decree*
> *unchangeable, Eternal, which ordaind*
> *thir freedom; they themselves ordaind thir fall ...*

This is the central tenet of *Paradise Lost,* and more than one commentator has discussed how it is central to all the action in *The Lord of the Rings.* Everyone is tempted by the Ring; each responds according to their nature. Though Sauron can compel his minions to serve him, those who fight him must choose to do so from their own free will. Frodo and Sam choose freely to take the Ring to the fire, acting as though prompted by Milton's God:

> *And I will place within them as a guide,*
> *my Umpire, Conscience, whom if they will hear,*
> *light after light well us'd they shall attain,*
> *and to the end persisting, safe arrive.*

That could so easily be the hobbits' story, and it's a way of seeing how Tolkien was keeping his own beliefs at one remove, drawing from Milton rather than the Bible: exercising both a reticence about his own beliefs and the delicacy of allowing each reader the freedom to believe as they choose.

It's impossible not to see the story of the Valar and the fallen Elves of Valinor and the fall of first Melkor and then Sauron who were once fair as an echo of the Biblical Fall of Lucifer. But like Milton, Tolkien uses his story to discuss the things around the fringes of the Bible that theologians and philosophers wrestle with — questions of free will and the seductiveness of evil. The existence of *Paradise Lost* generates powerful resonances in *The Silmarillion's* opening chapters.

Tolkien is very sure that he doesn't want us to have any empathy with Sauron. He's been accused of making his evil characters too one-dimensional, and it's true that we have very little to go on when we try and imagine anything about Sauron besides his utter will to dominate and destroy. Gandalf mentions that even Sauron was not evil once, but became so over time. *The Silmarillion* talks about how Sauron became a lieutenant of Morgoth and enjoyed the scope for cruelty that position allowed him. As for the reasons why he chose that path, we never really know, so we can't really empathize.

There is a tiny clue in the fact that in the beginning Sauron was a Maia of Aulë, the master craftsman among the Valar who delighted in works of skill. To Tolkien's thinking, the wisest and subtlest minds could easily become too enamored of their own cleverness, especially when drawn to the study of machines and science. That was Aulë's domain. Science without ethics horrified Tolkien, and he saw that science and mechanization without morals led to some terrible outcomes. The ability to make powerful and clever machines was something that he saw as a constant temptation for humanity. We invent and experiment without considering the consequences, just to prove that a thing is possible. It's a kind of hubris.

Not surprising then that Sauron became evil through that kind of pride before any other. He had free will, and maybe his first choice was to seek mastery of some powerful art and to prove his abilities as an inventor and craftsman. Innocent enough beginnings, but from there it seems that he fell in love with power for its own sake, and in Tolkien's world that is always the beginning of a fall towards evil.

Sources:
Diana Wynne Jones, "On Tolkien's Narrative," from *This Far Land*. Robert Giddings, ed. Barnes & Noble, 1990.

John Milton, *Paradise Lost and Paradise Regained*. Signet Classic 2001.

14. Ignorance & Knowledge

Tehanu

Recently a few authors in the fields of science fiction and fantasy have defended their field by saying that it is precisely in these genres that you get to write primarily about ideas — more than in modern literary novels, where the prime directive is the exploration of characters and relationships. The science fiction writer Sherri S. Tepper is saying this on the radio in an interview as I write these words, but I first heard it from the fantasy author Philip Pullman.

Writing about ideas ... They're not just talking about learning the facts. Today's children do a load of homework that leaves them carpet-bombed with facts compared to previous generations. But it's not the same as learning what matters or learning to care about anything. That takes imagination and curiosity. Would it be too much to plead for a little time for them to laze around with an idle book now and then?

I don't know how much we're shaped by what we read. Surely our own selves and our family and surroundings form most of our personalities, but occasionally the right book comes along like a key fitting in a lock. That book you love and return to often unlocks your dreams, but while that door's open and you're wandering from Prydain to Avalon, some knowledge comes in to you unbidden.

It's a limited kind of learning — I could read cyberpunk for a year and I bet I wouldn't become remotely cool or any better with technology. I grew up reading the Narnia books and failed either to become a Christian nor, as a lesser goal, to learn to hate the Calormen. Still, the hours we spend sitting deaf to the world and unpestered by our peers do change us. With certain books the door opens two ways — with our entering into the world of the book, and the heart of the book entering into us.

Fantasy tends to be lazier than science fiction in that regard. Most of the time we're there in that book in order not to think about stuff. But every now and then in the middle of all the fun and danger some startling idea whacks you right between the eyes.

Three fantasy authors stand out for me in terms of what they teach. Of course I'm going to mention Tolkien but I also want to talk about other writers too, since people often ask, "So what else is good besides Tolkien?" I think they're really asking, "Who else writes books that can change you?"

Tolkien was a teacher all his life, and not just because it's comfy chair work with no heavy lifting. He genuinely wanted the sum total of knowledge to increase in the world. You might think that his main aim was to get more people to love old dead languages, but he himself didn't consider that to be the most important knowledge a person could gain. The kind of knowledge he regarded as more important than any other is the knowledge of God. There is a famous letter he wrote to his publisher Stanley Unwin's grandaughter, who asked him, "What is the purpose of life?" He answered at great length, concluding, "… the chief purpose of life … is to increase according to our capacity our knowledge of God by all the means we have, and to be moved by it to praise and thanks."

In twelve years spent writing *The Lord of the Rings* he had more immediate concerns than preaching his beliefs, namely unravelling his endless mental yarn ball of history, language and myth and stringing it into a very long but coherent plot. Still, his beliefs were the backdrop to his thought processes as he wrote, so despite the fact that God is never mentioned other than in the most tortuously oblique way, you could say that *The Lord of the Rings* is in fact a 600,000-word koan. The name unsaid is in there like the sound of one hand clapping. Now, I have not become a Christian through reading *The Lord of the Rings* either, but I can't deny that it has affected my attitudes and my way of being in the world. I wish I could say they'd made me a better person, but all I know for sure is that they've made me pretty certain what a better person is. Tolkien teaches things about honor and goodness and hope, which all of us discuss at different points in this book.

So what other writers offer thought-provoking fantasy? There are several whose beliefs and concerns are different or even opposed to Tolkien's. If fantasy has a serious purpose in giving people tools to deal with real life, you'll be pleased to know that the toolkit is large and diverse. Encouraging, because I have yet to find the one universal and infinitely adjustable tool for dealing with all of life.

One series of books struck me very deeply when I first read them and their meaning grew deeper as I grew older and came to appreciate the strong poetry of their language and ideas. They are, as people can tell from my screen name, Ursula Le Guin's *Earthsea* books. I will write more on her later, but say here that her books made me think about things like justice, harmony and balance. Her books are humanist, Tao-centered, informed by cultures outside of Europe.

Meanwhile in the more recent past, another trilogy of books has come out that was worth the patient wait for its completion. This was Philip Pullman's trilogy, *His Dark Materials*. With the publication of *The Amber Spyglass* to complete it, I was certain at last: This was what I'd been waiting for since the year I discovered *The Lord of the Rings* and *A Wizard of Earthsea*. I thought it'd never happen again in my lifetime: A fantasy trilogy to be read over and again. It contains a powerfully enticing fantasy world and a gripping, suspenseful story. Like Tolkien and like Le Guin, the writer was not afraid to weave in questions about the really big things in life.

Pullman was one of the first writers I heard saying that books written for adolescents hit them at an age when they're most ready to think about big mysteries like "Why are we here?" and "What is the purpose of consciousness?" This is the thing with teen fantasy: They may look like kids' books, and the main characters *are* children — or in the hobbits' case, small innocents — but don't be fooled. The best of them are books for people who are ready to desert the easy answers of a child's world. Like *The Lord of the Rings*, the main characters face terrible dangers and make hard choices guided by a mysterious conscience, a desire to do the right thing. In Tolkien's case, if you read his letters, those promptings are part of God's plan for the world. In Pullman's case, there is some mysterious force for good, there are prophecies and judgments from an unknown power, but God as Tolkien would recognize him has been seriously derailed in Pullman's universe. You get no hints about who might be pulling the strings after all.

Pullman's writing celebrates the physical body and the material world:

> If readers take nothing else away from these 1300 pages ... I would like them to take away the sense I was trying to convey of the infinite

preciousness of the physical. The sense of this material universe, full of grass and trees and flesh and skin and sunlight and rain and so on. It is our home. It is where we live.

Shortly after the third book of the trilogy came out, it was unofficially Philip Pullman week in New Zealand. Wham, suddenly everyone was reading *His Dark Materials* and talking about it, and an interview with Philip Pullman featured on the marvellous Kim Hill show on Radio NZ. I can't tell you how strange this interview was. There was Pullman with his mild, educated Oxford voice and his inflexible will, brain as sharp as a tack, sidestepping with a certain practised elegance any questions about whether he was an atheist. Because this seems to be the sticking point with a lot of readers.

Kim Hill brought up another book that bears comparison. Hill's a voracious and insightful reader who doesn't usually like fantasy or science fiction, but she loved Mary Doria Russell's *The Sparrow,* as she did the Pullman trilogy. Pullman and Hill chewed over the idea that it seems to be "genre" fiction that allows itself room to cover the big questions. Science fiction can stretch out and discuss things like origins, the purpose of life, free will and good and evil on the largest possible scale (in my opinion, fantasy *could* but is usually too mentally lazy to try — let's cheer on the exceptions!). Literary fiction, Pullman reckoned, is often obsessed with smallness and detail and cleverness — the angst of twenty-somethings. But children's fiction has the wonderful advantage of being written for people at their most curious age. He said in another interview with the *New Zealand Listener's* Gordon Campbell, "In the early teens, the cosmic issues — the ones that soon get buried in the daily grind of making a living — have a brief chance to flower, as our minds make first contact with the great world beyond."

It was a tremendous relief to hear a writer say these things. Suddenly it felt like there was good reason for loving less literary fiction. I got an image of writers entering into genre fiction with the same unselfconscious joy of a dog let off the lead on a *looong* beach. If it's a working dog bred for running, it'll eat up the distances to the limits of vision. In such a place, writers go off like a hunting dog, following the trails laid down by a really good story ...

That's the other thing literary fiction's had bred out of it — the passion for telling a rip-roaring, can't-put-it-down yarn. That's never been a problem in science fiction and fantasy, or children's fiction. It was good to hear Pullman say this, because I'd just read some of Stephen King's essays on writing in *Secret Windows*. He says:

> My own belief about fiction, long and deeply held, is that story *must* be paramount over all other considerations in fiction, that story *defines* fiction and that all other considerations — theme, mood, tone, symbol, style, even characterization — are expendable. There are critics who take the strongest possible exception to this view, and it is my belief that they would feel vastly more comfortable if *Moby Dick* were a doctoral thesis on cetology rather than an account of what happened on the *Pequod's* final voyage. A doctoral thesis is what a million student papers have reduced this tale to, but the story still remains — "This is what happened to Ishmael."

Returning to Pullman's trilogy: Why that strange title, *His Dark Materials*? It's a quote from Milton's *Paradise Lost*. It takes about halfway through the trilogy before you begin so see why that's relevant. The full quote's on the flyleaf. I remember starting these books wondering if this was another one of these authors who puts up a few favorite quotes in order to show that they're really into literature and up to writing a bit of it themselves. Oh no, no no no. This time it's not a cheap pedigree; it really is a clue to the depths in this book. Pullman's said he hoped it made more people read Milton, and from what I gather, it's worked. Isn't it strange that *two* stories could be based on the events of *Paradise Lost* — the *Ainulindalë* in *The Silmarillion* is another, in my opinion — and use it to reach such different conclusions? Now at last here's a smashing defence for the view that Satan *is* the most interesting character Milton wrote.

Pullman's view of the Biblical story of the Fall in Eden is like a photo negative of Tolkien's or Milton's view, and he continues in the opposite direction from there on. He recasts it as a fall from ignorance into knowledge. It's the same event that propelled Melkor out of the chorus in Tolkien's *Ainulindalë,* yet what a difference! Not the sin of pride, but the gift of curiosity. It's experience and knowledge that make us fully human, according to Pullman, and when I heard him interviewed he argued passionately for giving children the means to escape ignorance: a decent education. I sensed that he saw ignorance itself as an evil, almost malignant force.

I recalled this recently when I had occasion to be at a wealthy private school where the pupils were helping to raise funds by selling artworks designed by them and executed by professionals. Taking pride of place was the national flag sewn out of different fabrics, with patriotic phrases by the children sewn on little patches scattered over the flag's design. Most of them were rather cheering reminders of the way children see life. They said things like "I love our country. It has lots of horses," and "I love our country because it's so pretty." Then there were others that mentioned things like having food and shelter and families. True, I thought, not every country can count on providing those things for its children, and it's good to remember that.

Then there was the one that went, "I love our country because we have freedom. Other countries like Asia and Europe and Australia and Africa have slaves. They don't have choices. We have choices." I spit the binky at that. I've lived in some of those places, and the idea of a school — a supposedly good school — promoting such ignorance about the world was poisonous to me. I can't believe that a real teacher wouldn't seize on the opportunity to teach children to know better than that. Apparently this school didn't mind letting ignorance run amok, fattening up prejudices so one day they'd bloom into an adult hatred of all that's unknown. The point is not which nation's flag these kids were elaborating on. Mine, yours, ours — you don't know, and it doesn't matter. The point is, this was a school, and it was promoting ignorance. It was as though the teachers were taking a flag, symbol of who we are, and using it to bind our eyes so we shouldn't see anybody else. I remembered Pullman's voice, arguing for education, as I saw this.

A major theme in Pullman's trilogy is the difference between childhood and adulthood and the journey from innocence into knowledge. Having knowledge means sometimes you are forced to make a choice, being no longer able to live blindly, instinctively, as a child does. Both Pullman and Tolkien seem fascinated by that moment, when a decision is taken and a choice made freely. Why indeed does Frodo choose to take the Ring? Why does Pullman's heroine Lyra choose to fight? They both seem to act out of conscience. The difference is that in Tolkien's mind, conscience is born out of faith; for Pullman, it is born out of knowledge, the knowledge of consequences.

Ever play that game of imagining a dinner party where you could invite anyone you liked, living or dead? If you're a reader, you'd probably invite your favorite authors. Now, here's the snag: I can't imagine any way that Pullman and Tolkien could inhabit the same room without breaking into some uproar. What fascinates me is that they're so similar: Pullman is a teacher based in Oxford, not unlike Tolkien (in fact they also studied at the same school, Exeter College), he's a mildly spoken writer with a gift for lyric prose, a world creator and fantasist likewise concerned with the state of the human soul and the beauty of the world, be it created or evolved. However, Pullman was born more than half a century later. How the world had changed! As a result, those two wouldn't mildly dislike each other, they'd probably detest each other. Everything Tolkien held to be an irrefutable truth, Pullman would probably qualify with a "Well, on the other hand ..." This is the spirit of our times.

There'd be grievous bodily sarcasm breaking out and possibly even raised voices. Well, raised voices for sure, because I've already heard Pullman raise his voice once when asked what he thought of C. S. Lewis (he thought he was wicked and abominable), and he doesn't think much of Tolkien, besides crediting his ability to write a ripping good yarn. What *The Lord of the Rings* says about human nature is not very interesting, in his opinion. To him, Frodo's reasons aren't good enough.

Meanwhile, Pullman's trilogy has been called "... the most vicious attack on organized religion this reviewer has ever seen ..." and it's been accused of Satanism. In the interview I heard, Pullman retorted mildly that anyone who read his books and found they'd been converted to Satanism was welcome to write to the publisher and ask for their money back. His gracious manner and dry wit seemed cast in the same mold as Tolkien himself, I thought.

Well, isn't it always embarrassing to have similar friends who can't stand the sight of each other? My imaginary dinner party would crash and burn. Yet if in a parallel universe Tolkien had been born 60 years later could they have been twins? Would they meet over a decanter of Tokay and still fight anyway?

Pullman's described himself as a "Church of England Atheist." In the Gordon Campbell interview, he expanded:

> ... the rhythms of the Book of Common Prayer are still deeply in the cells of my brain. I don't want to be rid of them, or be without them. I do believe and try to uphold the injunctions towards charity, but I don't take any notice of the commands to believe ... But the actual textures, sounds, smells of an old country church on a cold winter's morning ...

The light coming through the stained-glass windows on a summer's evening. The sound of the organ. These are all part of my childhood. My grandfather was a country clergyman, and the example he set me of charity and kindness is still profoundly important to me.

There, that's living ambiguity. No line marked in the sand to say, "This is not that. I belong here and reject all that is there. Here is where I stand on this matter; all who do not stand with me stand against me." We live less in a world of absolutes than Tolkien did, and perhaps that's why Pullman's fantasy speaks to us now.

Such different kinds of fantasy leave me feeling enriched and enlarged. I'm glad I've read enough to be happy with both these points of view and threatened by neither of them. The gift of enjoying opposites and being comfortable with ambiguity comes from the fact that I trust that those authors still living are always learning and that their next stories will reveal something new — and possibly contradictory.

It's one of the joys of Middle-earth too — just think of all the unanswered questions, the things that Tolkien never explained further. Tolkien himself never stopped exploring his world and discovering new things about it, and on some topics one feels that he never made his final judgment call at the end of the book or the end of his life. In that, great authors are like great thinkers in any field. We don't even have to be mediocre thinkers to learn something from that.

Sources:

Humphrey Carpenter, ed., *The Letters of J.R.R. Tolkien*. Houghton Mifflin, 1995.

Stephen King, *Secret Windows*. Book-of-the-Month Club, 2000.

Philip Pullman, "Interview with Gordon Campbell," *New Zealand Listener*, January 27, 2001.

15. Fate, Free Will, & the Demands of Conscience

Anwyn

I have an acquaintance whose main objection to Christianity is that while it claims to offer freedom to its believers, it demands total obedience to the commands of God and therefore believers have no real free will. Believers in fate also claim that there is no free will, that our destiny is predetermined and nothing we do can alter it. "But Anwyn, what does this have to do with Tolkien?" Here's the big question: did Frodo have any real choice about whether he would take on the responsibility of bearing the Ring? Or was he A) simply predestined to do so and nothing could release him from the obligation or B) forced into obedience by the knowledge that to refuse would have made him no longer a servant of the Good (equivalent, in my above example about Christianity, to refusing behavior that you know is God's command)?

Predestination has always seemed to me to be a hopelessly circular argument, as is the view of Christianity presented above. As I understand it, if I have two or more choices before me, fatalists will say that whichever one I make, I was incapable of choosing other than what I was fated to. Are you kidding me? I have several choices, the free use of my faculties and reason, and yet there's some unseen force that predicts (though we don't know its predictions until in hindsight) which one I will make? I can't get behind that kind of looped logic.

Yet there are certain passages in Tolkien which seem to smack heavily of a belief in this kind of predestination. In "The Shadow of the Past," Gandalf says cryptically to Frodo that the Ring left Gollum and that some other will was at work to make that happen — some will beyond that of its owner Sauron. He goes on to state right out that Bilbo was meant to find the Ring and thus Frodo was meant to have it!

Now how much would you pay?

So, our Tolkien, Mr. Understated Christianity, Mr. Freedom From Dominion (i.e. Morgoth, Sauron, Saruman, et al), is talking up Fate? Hmmm.

I submit at this point we need to make a clear distinction between two types of fate for the basis of discussion: fate as it affects circumstances beyond our control and fate as it affects our personal choices.

Who could have intended for Bilbo to find the Ring and leave it to Frodo? Who could have *engineered* it to happen thus? Here we step into very deep waters. Backing up in the story, we see that it was Gandalf who dragged Bilbo into the adventure, Gandalf who led Bilbo and the Dwarves through the goblin-infested mountains, and Gandalf who led them through the tunnels. But Gandalf had no way of knowing about Gollum or the Ring. Bzzt! Your answer must be in the form of a question. What, then? The Valar? These are the same Valar who sit on their own island in the Uttermost West, basically forbidden to directly interfere with the events unfolding in Middle-earth, aren't they? Give that money back to Ben Stein! What, then? Ilúvatar? Ilúvatar is not even seen within the confines of *Lord of the Rings* and is only mentioned around the edges of *The Silmarillion*. So . . . is that your final answer?

Who could Gandalf have thought was doing the intending? About this, I can only say that *circumstances came together*. Cosmic forces of the universe? Will of Ilúvatar? Fate? Whatever name you want to give them, these were circumstances far beyond the control of Bilbo, Frodo, or even Gandalf — i.e., their personal choices did not affect this event except the fact of being in "the right place at the right time." Bilbo stumbled along, tripped, found the Ring, that was that. To me, it's what happens *after* the finding that makes the story interesting. Was he fated to find it? Sure, I'll go for that — *with* the understanding that once circumstance, coincidence, fate, or Ilúvatar had played its part, free will kicked in with a vengeance.

All of us have had responsibilities thrust upon us that we never asked for or wanted — circumstantial fate, let's say for the sake of argument. But once the circumstances are before us, we are presented with choices regarding our actions. Bilbo has this Ring. He slowly figures out what he can do with it. Years down the road he is called upon to give it up. *His choice*. Was the choice made easier as a caring friend, in the person of Gandalf, who knew exactly what was best for him to do, stood by unwavering and asked him to do it? Yes, almost certainly. But still, Gandalf says in "The Shadow of the Past" that Bilbo was the only person he knew of who'd had the willpower to move beyond good intentions and actually give it up. Bilbo's choice. So now we come to the crux of the matter: Frodo's choice to take the Ring to the Fire.

In "The Council of Elrond," Frodo offers to take the Ring to Mt. Doom, and he does so feeling as though another will is speaking through his voice. Elrond somehow seems unsurprised and states that if he understands matters clearly, he suspects that if Frodo cannot accomplish the task, nobody can. He makes it clear that he, Elrond, has no right to force so terrible a burden as that on anyone, but continues, "... if you take it freely, I will say that your choice is right."

Ouch! Does anybody besides me hear the ringing of a cosmic gong when you read these words? How do we unravel this tangle? The task is appointed for Frodo, another will is using his voice to volunteer, yet none of the Wise should expect to foresee it, and if Frodo takes it *freely*, it's the right *choice*?

But perhaps it's not so hopeless after all. Elrond tosses in some qualifiers that can't be lightly dismissed. "If I understand aright all that I have heard ..." To me this says that circumstances surrounding and leading up to the Council were what told Elrond that Frodo was right in volunteering to take the Ring. He was its keeper, he was a factor unaccounted for in the counsels of both the Wise and of Sauron, and he had already borne it through darkness and danger. "If you do not find a way, no one will." To me this says that had the Ring landed in the hands of another good person, he or she could just as easily have been the Bearer, but it didn't. It came to Frodo, through circumstances beyond his control, and therefore he should take on the responsibility. Why? Because it was *the right thing to do*.

Here's where our second definition comes into play: fate as it affects or is defined by our own choices and actions. Could it possibly be that the entire concept of fate is simply humankind's catch-all word for the choices a person or a group of people will make based on their own personalities, their upbringings, and the consciences they carry within their souls? In other words, that a person is fated to do such-and-such only because the kind of person he or she is would allow no other action?

I submit the possibility that what might seem to be Frodo's fate was simply the outcome of his responsible, conscience-driven nature. In hindsight things can seem as if they were predestined, but what was it they used to say about the Bagginses? That you could tell what any Baggins would say on any question without the bother of asking them? Very well, then. If Frodo's friends had been asked to say what he would do under such circumstances, they likely would have known that he would have undertaken the task for the greater good, just because they understand the kind of person that he is.

Thus my friend's objection to Christianity is simultaneously given credence and blown out of the water. A Christian *does* have free will governing his or her actions, but also a Christian's conscience, which is shaped by the tenets of his or her religion. Thus the choices made are theoretically linked to those values. Within that framework, free will still plays a large part, not to speak of the fact that the person presumably bought into Christianity freely. For Frodo it was the same. He was raised as a good, responsible, upstanding citizen of the Shire, knowing the difference between right and wrong. His conscience was shaped to certain values, and those values led him to freely accept the responsibility on behalf of the Free Peoples.

So Frodo had a choice. He took the trial of the Ring freely, or under obligation to his own conscience, which amounts to the same thing, thus appearing, from certain points of view, fated to do so. His friends aided him as much as they could on the journey, and when he struck out on his own, they allowed him to go, knowing that they did so for a greater good. With only his faithful Sam he journeyed into the dark lands to rid himself of his even darker burden.

What kept him upon the Road?

Have you ever been in a life-or-death situation? More specifically, have you ever been in a life-or-death situation that required not quick-thinking, decisive action, but rather a slow grind, an endless monotony of wearying tasks that instead of becoming easier, seem only to grow heavier and harder with each step down the Road? A series of days melding into a mind- and soul-numbing existence, where each day is the same as the day before it, and if anything, slightly worse? The readiest example that comes to mind is the care of an aging loved one — the caregiver must manage his or her own life as well as being very constant at the bedside of the ailing one, wondering what the outcome of their suffering will be. This kind of endless cycle can take a huge emotional toll on any person, in some cases leading to near-despair.

What kept Frodo upon the Road? What keeps us going in times of despair?

The answer to both queries is a simple question that hearkens back, once again, to individual conscience and the type of person one is: what will happen to me or to my loved ones if I *do not* continue this task?

Frodo knew that to give up his journey was to doom himself and the whole world of his existence to a horrifying domination at the hands of an evil spirit. He had set himself upon the Road, and what kept him there was this knowledge that to give up meant death, not only for him, but for people and places he loved. So we discover that Our Hero is not totally selfless. There is an element of self-preservation here as well as knowing the right thing to do. If he takes on the responsibility, the way will be uncertain and the outcome iffy, but if he does not, the outcome is certain and will end in enslavement or death for himself and everything and everybody he cares about. Predestination? Hardly. Clear choice between two alternatives, one scary, the other downright horrifying? Definitely. His conscience guided him to the only choice he could have made — thus giving it the appearance, from a certain point of view, of fate.

He had not the nervousness and subsequent relief of a person who has only one day's unsettling or even terrifying business to conduct; he had only the cold comfort of knowing that when his burden was past, then one way or another he would rest, whether it was in his hobbit-hole or in an unmarked ash heap at the foot of the Mountain of Fire.

Frodo did not know the outcome of his journey as he was making it. I would imagine that the first time most of us read *Lord of the Rings,* we were shocked and dismayed at the end of Frodo's Road. He puts on the Ring and claims it for his own, declaring that he will not finish the task he sacrificed so much to do!

We want to weep. All that work wasted. All the weary trudging days, the sheer force of conscience and will that dragged him to the feet of Mount Doom and the patient efforts of Sam that dragged him up it. But here we see the return of our first definition of fate, the forces outside Sam's or Frodo's control that do not allow the faithful work of an honest heart to go to waste.

Right back at the beginning of the tale when they were still in the Shire, Gandalf had his premonition that Gollum might one day serve some purpose and indeed, without him Frodo could not have destroyed the Ring once he had brought it to the Fire. Ilúvatar did not allow the evil power of the Ring or its maker to undo the months of toil by Our Hero and his Faithful Servant. Fate? The last-ditch saving effort coming from outside in the nick of time? Deus ex machina? Justice in reward for faithful service? Or, gasp, the predictable actions of Gollum, based on the kind of individual we know him to be and the years of torture the Ring has laid upon him?

Here is where the two kinds of "fate" I've defined run smack into each other. Frodo's conscience led him to be toiling up Mount Doom on that day. Gollum's insatiable lust for the Ring and his twisted soul led him to be in the same place with objectives of his own. Each was outside the other's control (circumstantial fate, from their points of view), but each one's personal fate, or the actions he was driven to by his nature, played a role in the other's eventual destiny

So we see that what we call fate might really just be another way of saying something was bound to happen because of the nature of the people making the choices with their free will. People and hobbits have free will in abundance, there's no denying, but there is a certain predictability in given situations, based simply on the individual natures of people and hobbits. In hindsight, it's just as easy to label these likelihoods as fate; it gives a bit of cosmic tang to our existence. But I prefer to believe that though circumstances may form around us that are beyond our control, what we do once caught up in them is entirely up to us. Always, of course, as with Bilbo and Frodo, with a little help from our friends.

16. Emotion & Commitment

Anwyn

We have discussed how obedience to a higher good can be the ultimate exercise in free will, and we have discussed how obedience to one's own conscience in the face of exhaustion or terror can keep one's actions firmly fixed on the task at hand. But what about what you feel like doing? Does that not have a place anywhere? Isn't it part of free will to be able to do what you *feel* like doing?

According to my first statements, free will is most highly exercised when one applies it for the greater good *despite* what one feels like doing. This principle results in extremely difficult, but important and good, deeds being accomplished, for depend upon it, if the doing of the deed depended upon how the doer, especially if that doer is a human being, *felt* about it, the likelihood is that it would not get done.

How often have you started a project that you were really excited about and then, as the excitement waned, put it aside or simply let it run out of gas? If you're like me, plenty of times. If you're more grown-up than I, perhaps you have a better track record of finishing what you start, but do you always feel as enthusiastic about it in the middle as you did at the beginning? I'd lay good money that you don't. On the other hand, I'm sure that feeling of excitement comes back when you approach the finish line and then are able to look back on what you've accomplished. But that feeling doesn't return unless you've paid the price of holding your will to the commitment of finishing the project even without the emotion that attended the beginning.

This is not a new principle we're discussing. It's been known since man first began to study his own nature. And believe you me, temptations abound to let these emotions have their full sway. Believe me further when I say that if we constantly gave into them and did just what we felt like doing all the time, not even half so many things would be accomplished. C. S. Lewis, in his wickedly accurate sketches of human nature, *The Screwtape Letters,* has his senior tempter writing to the junior one:

> . . . this disappointment [occurs] on the threshold of every human endeavor. It occurs when the boy who has been enchanted in the nursery by *Stories From the Odyssey* buckles down to really learning Greek. It occurs when lovers have got married and begin the real task of learning to live together. In every department of life it marks the transition from dreaming aspiration to laborious doing.

Lewis follows this with a wonderful piece of advice for us disguised as a warning to the junior tempter. "If once they get through this initial dryness successfully, they become much less dependent on emotion and therefore much harder to tempt."

It's all in that little phrase, "less dependent on emotion." We each, if we are honest and observing, know our own emotions to be as changeable as weather in the Midwest. ("You don't like the weather in Illinois? Wait five minutes!") Most assuredly if we base the majority of our actions on such weathercocks as human emotions, we will find ourselves not only doing and saying things that are at most only borderline acceptable among our friends, but also accomplishing far less of lasting importance and good in our own worlds. It's forcing the will over that selfish line of thought, "But I don't feel like doing [insert arduous task or onerous duty here] just now," and into the mode of either A) "This needs to be done," or B) "I wanted to do this before, and I'll be happy when I've finished," or C) "Something or somebody else will be the better for this when I've done it," that will allow us more stable, more productive, and ultimately, happier, lives.

I can hear you now. "But Anwyn, we've all known this since we graduated college and had to start living in 'the real world.' Just because you're only now catching up is no reason for us to suffer through your ramblings. How in the world does this relate to *Lord of the Rings* or even Tolkien, you silly girl?"

Tolkien knew the traps and pitfalls of human nature just as surely as his friend Lewis did. Though he chose to articulate his views about them in different ways, he knew them and was made melancholy at many periods in his life by them. When you read Humphrey Carpenter's excellent biography of the Professor, notice how easily distracted he says Tolkien was, how many works were stacked around his office all unfinished, how behind he always was because he would stop to play Solitaire (or "Patience"). If he'd had my computer with its instant-access stack of electronic Solitaire cards, he'd *never* have gotten anything done! This problem of being distracted, by allowing emotional or attention-span issues to supersede the duty before him, was a large factor in Tolkien's professional life. I share many of his frustrations in that regard, and I know that neither of us is alone in feeling them.

But did he feel called to a higher standard? To put his will before the emotional ups and downs of human existence? Of course he did. This is proven by the fact that he was often upset with himself and often melancholy for his seeming inability to finish as much work as he would like, but the more obvious proof lies in his works that we revere so much.

His characters, though they have several aspects of our troubled human nature, *take it for granted* that acts of will are more important than fleeting emotions. Aragorn felt his moments of despondency, but all the time his actions unerringly drove towards the goal he had set. Faithful Sam (We use that word so often of Sam, don't we? Think briefly about one word by which you would like to be remembered. *Faithful* is certainly up near the top of my list) knew there was something out there bigger than himself that he had to accomplish, even if the cost were his life. And poor Boromir, the constantly struggling, was wrestling with just this exact problem. His emotions directed him to try to take the Ring under any circumstances he could. His will was simply not disciplined enough to withstand the pounding to which his emotional state subjected it, unlike that of his steadfast brother Faramir.

Our Hero, if he had any doubts about their Quest or their ability to bring it off, mostly kept them to himself. But that doesn't mean he didn't consider what he'd *rather* be doing with his life, were it up to him. If you've ever been pulled to a different geographical location from your lover by a job or some other duty, you'll sympathize with Aragorn immediately. His heart, the center of his feelings, dwelt in Rivendell with the fair daughter of Elrond, but his will, the foundation of his actions, drove him onward to his duties in faraway lands, some of which were prescribed to him by his lineage, some of which he took upon himself. Nobody forced him to escort, guide and guard the Ring-bearer for as long as he could. Yes, it's true, the success of the Ring's journey would definitely affect the question of whether or not he would even have a kingdom to rule when he returned to power, but it is certain that he could have taken up the kingship and held off Mordor, perhaps for long years further. He also could have speculated to himself that the Ring would help him a great deal in taking over the power that rightfully should have been his by birth, but his conscience would not allow consideration of such an action, and his will responded.

Aragorn knows only too well the dangers inherent in doing what you please and not what your duty is. Éowyn, when first we meet her, has not yet learned how this fire can burn. She is petulant and claims that since her duty to Théoden ended with his riding away, she is bound by duty no longer, despite the fact that her royal uncle has bidden her to lead the people in his absence. Aragorn rejects this. His belief is evident that if, having abandoned the road that duty marks out for one through sheer emotional whims, one gains neither happiness *nor* a reputation as an upright person. He makes it plain that he has felt the pangs of human feelings conflicting with duty himself when he speaks of his heart dwelling in Rivendell. But he refused the road that his heartfelt longings dictated to him, and he came to a much greater reward in the end by so doing.

Sam's burden seems simpler, but it is ultimately just as profound. Each of the Company has a role to play, and only through the triumph of their wills over their emotions, whether they be fear, ambition to power, or sheer laziness can those roles be fulfilled. Sam speaks of feeling "torn in two," and in many places he makes choices that are seemingly obvious to us, but which, in the fullness of Sam's loving heart, are agonizing to him. When poor Bill the pony is chased away by the Watcher and the Wargs, Sam states outright that he had to make a hard choice, right there. We may think that nonsense, having to choose between his Mr. Frodo and a horse, but to Sam, the poor pony was also deserving of his love and loyalty, and to allow it to wander in the Warg-filled wilderness with no help or protection was heartbreaking to him. But the higher duty held sway and he went on with the Company.

Again, when Galadriel's tricksy mirror shows him the atrocities that might or might not be happening in the Shire and the abandonment of his beloved Gaffer, he is asked to choose, and this time it is much harder. The choice between his aging father and his duty to

Frodo and the Quest is a wrenching one, and in a fit of horrified frenzy, he cries that he must return to the Shire regardless of the consequences.

Chastised and calmed by Galadriel, reminded that very possibly the things he has seen *have not* and perhaps even *will not* come to pass, unless he should return home to prevent them, he is despairing and confused. Ultimately, Sam is successful at keeping his will focused on his duty because he entrenches himself firmly in that mode from the outset. While still in the Shire, Frodo questions him, not wanting to take him if he will be too torn. He knows that Sam wants adventure outside the Shire, but Frodo knows that their journey will not be a lark. Sam rises to the challenge, for he has knowledge inside him that guides him, a sense that his future lies outside the Shire, that there is something he must accomplish through taking that road to the unknown. To me, that says it all.

So do all of Our Heroes just simply take it for granted that their willpower was enough to get them through, despite the yearnings displayed by their emotions? No. One, in particular, makes a spectacular fall into the temptation of his emotions. Blinded by lust for victory, convinced that only the power of the Ring would help him return to his native land with the ability to change the balance of power to Gondor's favor, Boromir gives in to a temptation that preyed upon him until his strength to resist it was worn away. In the house of Elrond he questions the decision to destroy the Ring, wondering why the Wise do not simply rise up and use it to depose the Dark Lord, but he is silenced by their reasoning. In Lothlórien, Galadriel, in what could be interpreted as an almost malicious use of her power, tests his heart again. What she offers him, he does not say, but it is not too difficult to make a supposition.

Finally, in trying to reason with Frodo, trying to persuade somebody else to think as he does so that he will not have to feel so alone in wanting to give in to temptation, Boromir flings aside the arguments of the Wise. His long speech to Frodo is an impassioned frenzy based solely on emotion. Was there ever a better example of an attempt to rationalize thoughts and actions and feelings which the speaker knows to be wrong? Yes, the cause of Gondor is just. Yes, they need strength to defend it. Every good lie is the stronger for a grain of truth. But from there his arguments lead down a deadly path. He is so able to convince himself that Gandalf and Elrond are merely afraid, that they don't want him to have the power, that he attempts to wrest the Ring from our

Frodo by force. We have already seen the consequences of his actions. His emotions, and the inability of his will to resist them, proved his ultimate undoing.

I would be sorry indeed if any of my readers supposed that I was trying to preach at them out of a higher state. I wrestle with what I know I *should* do vs. what I *feel* like doing every day of my life. The funny thing is, though, when I've done what I felt like doing and neglected what I should have done, I'm almost never the happier for it. When I've had my fun, gone out to eat, or played around on my computer, my house is still cluttered, every dish I own still dirty, my two parakeets still living in a mucked-up cage, and my paperwork still undone. Far from making me happy, the knowledge that not only have I wasted time when I could have been accomplishing something, but also that I still have the tasks ahead of me to do makes me despondent and disgusted with myself. Nothing remains but to ask for help and to try again. It's all a part of growing up.

The immature person is ruled by emotion, unstable and change-able in his or her affections and actions. When we've learned to see the road a little clearer and to know and govern our own responses to it, then we will have a better shot at making our actions subject not to our emotions, but to our wills, which are in turn bound strictly to our consciences. Then let Screwtape have his say! We will fend him off with the *best* the human spirit has to offer.

17. All About Sam

Quickbeam

Most people think Frodo is the true hero of *The Lord of the Rings*. To put it another way: It is accepted by nearly all readers that the novel is about Frodo. It's his quest, his burden, he's the focus. The little blurbs in magazines that are designed for the non-initiate read like this: "The story of a hobbit, Frodo Baggins, who is sent to destroy an evil Ring of power..." Sound like a good pitch? Not quite.

The main character is really Samwise Gamgee, though you may not know it. I'm telling you now, it's all about Sam.

You can safely argue that Frodo Baggins should be the centerpoint of the tale. In *The Hobbit*, Bilbo had the limelight for an entire book, and no one came close to grandstanding him (except maybe Smaug). Seems like Tolkien intended to chronicle the history of the Baggins family, first through Bilbo's adventures, then with Frodo inheriting more adventures than he bargained for.

The story takes Frodo's point of view often enough. Throughout the trilogy we share his experiences though personal sensations, his internal thoughts, and even his dreams. Tolkien lets us inside his suffering. And through that suffering we understand the dynamic of true sacrifice. He's the Ring-bearer, after all.

But a character-driven story like *LotR* is not strictly about sacrifice (or heroism, or the impermanence of beauty, or all those themes that are intrinsic). I must admit the novel is woven of many threads, but the groundwork of the tale, the telling of it, spins on a single proviso: Who is transformed the most between the opening and the closing page, taking the reader through his transformation?

Aragorn is the most heroic character. But it's not his story.

Gandalf is the greatest manipulator of events. But it's not his story.

Sauron is the ever-present antagonist. But it's not his story.

Let me give you the clearest example from another fantasy, familiar to all but the most sheltered — *Star Wars*. You think the original *Star Wars* films are about some farm boy named Luke Skywalker? You think he's the main character? BUZZZ! I'm sorry ... thanks for playing! If you had said Darth Vader, however, you'd be walking home with the grand prize.

The guy in the black helmet is pulling all the strings. Vader begins the first scene of the first trilogy by walking through that laser-blasted door looking for Leia. He is the first character the audience has a relationship with. More importantly, his choices put the plot in motion for all three films. Every facet of the story we experience is an after-effect of what Darth Vader is doing. When *Return of the Jedi* comes to its conclusion, it is only after Vader's most difficult redemption and after we see his glowing form with his predecessors that we know the story is over. He's redeemed. Roll credits. The End.

When you write a 1,200-page novel, you have the luxury of branching off into other subplots and you can take time to work with various characters. But you still need one common thread that thematically brings your story full circle. The transformation of Sam is Tolkien's central storytelling device, though not the most obvious one. There are many clues that reveal Sam, not Frodo, as the main element.

Sam takes an extreme route: from simple gardener to a participant in legend. He starts things off in *The Fellowship of the Ring* as the first new character we learn about, through a description offered by his father, the Gaffer. The old hobbit frets that his son is too caught up in Bilbo's stories, ignoring his true calling of weeding and gardening. Sam is described at the outset as a daydreamer and it seems the unhobbit-like passion for extraordinary tales is already developed in him.

Our dear old Sam is the contact point that we immediately relate to. Just like him, we are daydreaming of fairies, elves, and elephants. That is why Tolkien introduces Sam at once. All the magnificent events of the War of the Ring, the journey, battles, treachery and triumph, are diluted down to this profound effect: Sam is transformed beyond what he recognizes in himself. In the end he becomes the subject of all his dreams. Even he acknowledges that his feats might someday be the subject of future stories and songs.

Sam's conversation with Frodo in the pass of Cirith Ungol, before they meet Shelob, reveals how the rustic gardener has reached a turning point. He speculates that he himself has landed in the middle of some great tale that moves beyond his sphere of understanding. Frodo seems unable, or unwilling, to guess at what current tale they are embroiled in; but for Sam it is an epiphany that the currents of the world are indeed flowing around his actions.

And when Sam realizes that the grand stories of the First Age, of Beren and the Silmarils, are connected to the present unfolding events, he wonders about the final outcome. Will his efforts be in vain, forgotten in the dust of Time, or composed into an Elven-song or even a bedtime story for wee hobbit lads and lasses? As he wonders aloud about his role in history, the reader is keenly aware that this a very different Sam than the one caught eavesdropping below that faraway window. The story moves on after this strangely self-referential musing, and the Professor quietly moves Sam into his greatest moments of peril and deliverance.

As final proof, I offer a closer look at the novel's conclusion. The epic story does not end with the destruction of the Ring, not even with Frodo's departure from the Grey Havens. The final moment we cling to as the story closes its doors is of Sam coming back to his family, sitting at his table and declaring that his role in the formation of a myth is done. Three simple words, "Well, I'm back," are his final admission that there is no more story for him to contribute to.

Sam's perspective is that he can finally return to domestic life without any further adventures. An end has come to chronicling his tale. He is now back with his family, back to his private life and the intrusive eyes of future generations can leave him in peace.

Much too hasty,
Quickbeam

18. *The Silmarillion,* Creation, & Sins of the Artist

Tehanu

Long ago at the beginning of things, when we started a website about a film that was so top-secret that there didn't look like there'd be anything to report on most of the time, I thought I'd fill in the gaps by examining the big picture surrounding the books themselves. I wanted to look at the nature of inspiration and creativity by way of finding out what sets *The Lord of the Rings* apart. Having read *The Silmarillion, Paradise Lost* and then Joseph Pearce's book *Tolkien, Man and Myth* in close succession, I realized that this topic would stray into subjects like ethics and religion. This is always loaded ground, since try as I might I am bound to lay down my own prejudices and beliefs, whether I mean to or not.

I read *The Lord of the Rings* for years without noticing the Christian element in it; after reading *Tolkien, Man and Myth,* I couldn't deny it any more than I could claim the sun rises in the West. It's fitting that Tolkien, who valued free will so highly in the workings of all his creations, would not browbeat the reader with his own beliefs but leave them implicit in all he did, for the reader to choose to see or not.

Anyone wanting to follow this further should read Pearce's book; I'll just mention a few things in it that caught my attention.

The first is a letter from Tolkien arguing against the armchair psychoanalysts who think they can decipher the "meaning" of a book by relating it to the external facts of the author's life, and especially from the follies and misfortunes of that author.

Tolkien went on to list some facts that he considered had a greater bearing on his life as a writer, and in this list he placed what we would naturally expect to be the paramount fact of his life, his occupation as a philologist at Oxford. It is no surprise to report that Tolkien did regard his "taste in languages" as a big influence on *The Lord of the Rings*. But the facts that had the greatest bearing on his writing? According to Tolkien himself, these are the real crux of the matter:

> ... I was born in 1892 and lived for my early years in 'the Shire' in a pre-mechanical age. Or more important, I am a Christian (which can be deduced from my stories), and in fact a Roman Catholic.

I've argued that Tolkien created a convincing world because he was a master of language and myth, for we filter our knowledge of the world through words. Those who can make a world speak to us in a dozen different languages and accents of race, class and character will convince us most. If the writer can create a satisfying, consistent background of myth and history, we are further convinced by the apparent weight and solidity the world gains from that.

I revise my opinion and think that in addition, Tolkien's work gains power from the tension he felt all his life between Good and Evil. Okay, most fantasy novels have some evil to oppose the good, but how many authors consider it as a force in their everyday life? Conversely, how many fantasy authors can you picture wearing a "Sh*t Happens" T-shirt? Even allowing for the changing mores of our time, you could *never* picture Tolkien doing the equivalent of wearing a "Sh*t Happens" T-shirt, because for him, nothing ever "just happened." All his life he was passionately concerned with understanding why and how good and evil operate in the world.

It shows up clearly in the letters Tolkien wrote to his friends and family. In them, he laments the follies of mankind, past and present, and yet sorrowfully accepts them as part of of a world that is inevitably evil. For his Catholic faith holds that Man is fallen and the mortal world doomed to suffer corruption and evil until Redemption, yet to despair and condone evil is in itself a sin. I can see how that belief would generate a kind of tension between joy and despair, and so much of Tolkien's work explores that strange balance.

Right through *The Lord of the Rings* we know that much magic and beauty must pass. All victories are dearly bought and cannot last forever. It's even clearer in *The Silmarillion*.

Now, *The Silmarillion* opens with the creation of the world, which begins in harmony, with the angelic choirs of Valar singing the music of creation according to the plan laid down by the Creator, Eru, sometimes called Ilúvatar. But pretty soon Melkor, one of the Valar, tries to deviate from the music laid down by Eru and add his own individual melodies, causing strife as he insists on his own music. Eventually, as the discord grows, Eru puts a stop to the music and shows the Valar that even Melkor's discords, seemingly unplanned and in contention with Eru's themes, add beauty and power to the whole.

So Tolkien envisions the universe as a kind of music in which even the ugliness, the discords, will resolve at the end into a perfect whole. This reminds me of the way our Western musical harmony relies on tension and discord and resolutions to give it power and beauty. Other philosophers have likened good and evil to the light and shadow in a painting, which can have no meaning without them both. We are overwhelmed by the beauty and ugliness of the world, at times, because we are too close to the picture to see the whole as God sees it; or in Tolkien's terms, we haven't heard the music of the Ainur through to the final resolution.

For a long time Melkor chooses to keep himself apart from his Creator and the other Valar, rather than being cast out of Heaven by God, like his parallel Lucifer in the Bible. Still, Tolkien's text reads rather like the Biblical Fall from Heaven, or like Lucifer's fall in *Paradise Lost*:

> ... He began with the desire of the Light, but when he could not possess it for himself alone, he descended through fire and wrath into a great burning, down in Darkness.

Man enters the tale of *The Silmarillion* long awaited but unannounced, and they have already some strife behind them — there are gaps in the story where the Garden of Eden story could take place, as there are hints that in the future, biblical and known history might begin. *The Silmarillion* continues in parallel, telling the story not of Man's fall and redemption, but, in a sense, that of the Elves. Their redemption comes with Eärendil's returning of the Silmaril. The way that comes about forms the strongest story arc in the book.

What interests me most is Tolkien's notion of the very first sin, the sin that Melkor committed against Iluvatar, the One. Yes, it is like Lucifer's sin, that of pride and of disobedience and rebellion. But in Melkor's case it was also uniquely an artist's sin. He wanted to sing his own original creations, not those imagined for him by the Creator. It's important to realize that in terms of the story, what the Valar sing forms a kind of blueprint for how the universe will take shape and how history will unfold within it, so this is a grave matter.

Discord with his Creator became a deeper sin when Melkor began to desire power over Elves and Men, to have them as servants and perhaps worshipers.

Wanting to boss people around is standard Evil Overlord practice; it is the "corrupted creator" aspect of Melkor that interests me more. Tolkien makes a straight comparison between the two powerful creative Valar, Melkor and Aulë, who both took great pleasure in making new things. This is the comparison Tolkien makes between Melkor and Aulë:

> ... Aulë remained faithful to Eru and submitted all that he did to his will; and he did not envy the works of others, but sought and gave counsel. Whereas Melkor spent his spirit in envy and hate, until at last he could make nothing save in mockery of the thought of others, and all their works he destroyed if he could.

Is Tolkien arguing against creative individuality? That would be a very odd stance for a creative writer to take. Except that he himself never felt that he was inventing his stories — he felt that he was *finding* them. To him, they already existed, and it was his job or his gift to become a channel for them and write them down. As he wrote in a letter to a potential publisher, "... always I had the sense of recording what was already 'there', somewhere: not of 'inventing.'" (*Letters*, #131)

So the story of Melkor's defiant ad-libbing criticizes a certain kind of artistic freedom. Tolkien seems to propose that creativity should submit to certain limits imposed by the will of God or Eru. For another being to assert that they themselves are the wellspring and sole captain of their talent is a sin akin to pride, and in Tolkien's view it runs the risk of turning to evil.

And yet, Tolkien's philosophy is not so simple. The creation myth in *The Silmarillion* seems to imply that discord — Melkor's musical rebellion — makes the final music more beautiful and in some way completes it. Eru, who could surely erase Melkor's music and stop his mouth, does not do so. That discord is the very sound of Free Will — Eru's risky, oft-abused and most precious gift to his creation. So

Tolkien seems to see creativity as perilous balancing act between individuality and the will of God.

I will speak of what I do know: that the moment of inspiration is a mysterious experience for any artist who is paying attention to it; from some source that is incredibly personal and yet unknowably "other," comes a powerful mastery and ease within the medium they work in. Not always, not every time they make something, but there is no mistaking the sensation when it comes: It feels as though the art is coming through one's hands and mind, and the self stands back to observe. From where? Every artist has a different answer.

I was reading something about the arts as they are practised in the East; the book talked about the way the artist who wanted to make a statue of, say, Vishnu, would meditate until they had removed their ego from the process of creation, and in that state they could expect the ideal image of Vishnu to come into their hand and mind. The idea was not to invent a new and individual image of Vishnu, but to achieve the closest approximation of some ideal Vishnu that already exists perfectly somewhere, perhaps within the foundations of the universe.

At the moment when one feels that mysterious knowledge start to guide one's working hand and mind all the things a person might normally desire — power, wealth, status — seem irrelevant.

What Tolkien sees as a God-given gift for creation was corrupted by Melkor in the moment that he ceased to enjoy it for its own sake and turned rather to the love of power. It is no accident that tyranny and the arts stand so often in opposition; they face in opposite directions and are partially blind to each other.

Secondly, Tolkien sees human creativity as part of the way we are created in the image of a creative God. He would regard it as arrogant to take all credit for one's talents on oneself. Some artists are proud of their talent. Some never forget the mysterious nature of inspiration, which does not come at their bidding. I don't pretend to have any answers — from my knowledge, the feeling of inspiration is both part and apart from myself.

The Lord of the Rings is a sub-created world, according to Tolkien. A shadow of the real world. The film of the book is a kind of tertiary world, TheOneRing's website about the film of the book is a quaternary world, people who post on bulletin boards about TheOneRing.net set up a further echo … all of these feed back up the chain to lend greater reality to Middle-earth. The big question is, does The Lord of the Rings lend reality to the real world? Does it make us see the real world differently? Or another question that we'll cover in the next part of this book: What happens if you start asking yourself "What would Gandalf do?"

Sources:

Joseph Pearce, *Tolkien, Man and Myth*. Ignatius Press, 1999.

Humphrey Carpenter, Ed. *The Letters of JRR Tolkien*. Houghton Mifflin, 1981.

J.R.R. Tolkien, Ed. Christopher Tolkien, *The Silmarillion*, Houghton Mifflin, 1977.

Cultural Norms

19. Cultural Norms

Tehanu

"Cultural norms" sounds like a pretty boring topic until we start looking at some of the questions that really rile up Tolkien's fans and detractors — like whether Tolkien was an Aryan supremacist, or if he was misogynistic, or whether the *The Lord of the Rings* is actually a coded text about Sam and Frodo's gay relationship! Or is the book really a manifesto for "treehuggers" and hippies?

Different people have praised and damned Tolkien for all of those things. That's a product of the way in which our culture has changed since Tolkien wrote his books. How could our point of view *not* change? Time has moved on since J.R.R. and his brother Hilary were young boys in Edwardian smocks and long curls, out mushrooming in the English countryside near Sarehole. Hold that image in your mind a moment and compare it to the small boys you know, who match their tech-savvy wits against electronic ninjas. In the late 1890s, the Tolkien boys used to amuse themselves by teasing the miller of Sarehole or trespassing on farmers' fields — resulting in a non-virtual thrashing if they were caught. These days, hitting other people's kids is either politically incorrect or it's part of a "tough love" policy. Back then it was a damn good hiding and about what you deserved for picking mushrooms that weren't yours.

Tolkien's mother was an independent thinker by the standards of the day. She converted to Catholicism, and she resisted her family's attempts to control her until her last breath. She was a widow when they cut off their financial support. She couldn't work while her children needed her, so in effect the family was trying to starve her into recanting. She wouldn't. At the end of the nineteenth century, families could do that to their adult children. Tolkien's guardian could insist that J.R.R. cease all communication with his girlfriend until he was 21, and for the most part he complied with that. It makes you realize that the kinds of freedom and choice we take for granted, or even the kinds that we're still bickering about, are things that Tolkien's generation hardly dared dream.

What would he think about the diversity of today's world? How would he see us? Tolkien looked at the world through different lenses — through his own humanity and tolerance, yet also through his strong and strict old-fashioned principles. He had the comparison between his own time and the older cultures to which he was spiritually attuned through his knowledge of their language and writings. Yet he was fiercely local in his loyalties, loving and valuing most of all his own tiny corner of England above any other place.

The love of place is an appealing thing that draws us into a book even when the place is very foreign to us. I have fallen in love with Tony Hillerman's Navajo desert country through his detective novels, the Greek island of Cephalonia through Louis de Berniere's *Captain Corelli's Mandolin*, Harper Lee's Alabama through *To Kill a Mockingbird*, and on and on. Love of place doesn't repel us — when it doesn't exclude us.

What could repel us as readers is a kind of authorial ignorance or presumption. What if Tolkien was assuming his readers would all be white, European members of a male-dominated culture such as his own? Wouldn't that make a whole lot of people feel excluded? There are critics who feel that Tolkien didn't understand women and denigrated non-European races. Yet the books continue to grow in popularity all over the world, so some part of his tale hits the mark with us despite our differences — and those differences are huge. The Tolkien fans who make up TORN's staff come from all kinds of ethnic groups, nationalities, ages, political biases and sexual orientations, as do our correspondents.

All of the essayists on TheOneRing.net have looked at the various charges leveled against Tolkien by readers who judge him by modern standards of political correctness. We've tried to figure out if he's misunderstood or just plain wrong about some things. We haven't entirely agreed about everything! One thing's sure, Tolkien isn't alive any more to ask, so the best we can do is read him carefully and offer our conclusions. As a dessert topic, Turgon looks at a famous parody of *The Lord of the Rings* as possible heresy.

20. Men are from Gondor, Women are from Lothlórien

Anwyn

If you're a member of the bandwagon that purports to believe that the word *equal* is defined identically to the word *same*, then read no farther at peril of your politically correct sensibilities. The following comments are based on the idea that men and women, no matter how much social equality they may have achieved, act and react in different ways to the people and circumstances around them. This concept is at the core of one of the stickier topics surrounding Tolkien: his handling and alleged neglect/abuse of female characters in *Lord of the Rings*.

"Why are there so few women in *LotR*?? Why do only MEN get to go on the Quest and be in the Fellowship?? Why do only MEN get to do all the heroic things?? Tolkien must be a misogynist..." Good grief! Even ignoring for the moment the radical idea that no one human being is required, in his public or artistic endeavors, to be accountable for anybody *else's* ideas of what may be right and proper (i.e. Tolkien had every right in the world to write his story the way he saw fit — if you don't like it, don't read it), the text of *Lord of the Rings* does not for a moment bear out the idea that Tolkien had any kind of derogatory opinion about women. Three things are clear: that he was far from a misogynist, that the female characters in his masterpiece *collectively* represent everything that is great about being a woman, and that less representation does not equal less importance.

Why does Tolkien get such a bad rap? That, at least, is obvious. Counting the Nine Walkers, the Nine Riders, Sauron Himself, Denethor, Théoden, Saruman, Wormtongue, Beregond, Tom Bombadil, Gollum, Farmer Cotton, Bergil, Faramir, Boromir, Éomer, Imrahil, Elrond, Celeborn, Glorfindel, Galdor, Haldir, Háma, Halbarad, Ingold, Hirgon,

Mablung, Éothain, Glóin, Bilbo, Farmer Maggot, Barliman Butturbur, Bill Ferny, Treebeard . . . well, girls can't count that high, but you get my point, and that's without even opening a book to check. I'm sure I've forgotten at least one. In the opposite corner, there's Arwen, Galadriel, Éowyn, Rosie Cotton, Ioreth, Goldberry, the infamous Lobelia Sackville-Baggins, Mrs. Maggot and Mrs. Cotton, and that's it, unless you want to count Shelob. Personally, I don't. If you're a *real* nitpicker you can throw in Finduilas and Lothiriel of Dol Amroth, but a one-line mention doesn't particularly qualify as a substantial character. We are terribly under-represented! Or at least that is a popular argument. The point is it's easy to see why Tolkien could come across as having a dislike of women. Why does he go so heavy on the testosterone?

Tolkien's personal life is often called into service defending the view that he was a misogynist. His was a predominantly male environment, capped by his regular "guys-to-hang-out-with" group, the Inklings, meeting in a bar and gabbing about their jobs, no women allowed. To me, this has nothing to do with the question of whether Tolkien liked or respected women. It says more about the times he was living in and the job he performed. It can't be doubted that Tolkien was used to this system, having grown up in all-male schools, but none of this means he disliked women on principle. It simply means his circumstances did not lend themselves to a view of women as companions.

To me, the facet of his life (and of any married man's life!) that tells how he truly viewed women can be found in his marriage. Tolkien met his wife when they were both in their teens. Once they fell in love, he remained true to her for many years while the stubborn (and to me, incomprehensible) attitude of his guardian prevented them from marrying. When he finally was allowed to see her, she had seemingly moved on and was engaged to another. His fidelity went to work for him and won her back. Talk about your true romantic! She supported him emotionally and nurtured his abilities and creativity. She moved with him from university to university, bore and helped raise his children, kept his world together. He described her as "my Lúthien." Could there be any higher praise?

Here's the point, supported by this brief glimpse into his marriage: *Tolkien looked upon women as the inspiration for the heroic deeds of men.* Since personal creation comes from personal experience and circumstances, it's only natural that Tolkien would paint women into his mythos as he saw them (or really, *her,* his wife, Edith) in his own world: to be treasured as a gift (albeit sometimes one dearly earned, as in his own case and Aragorn's), to be drawn on for support in times of trial, to be looked up to as a cherished ideal, to be sources of guidance in times of confusion.

Let's look at his female creations. Arwen, beloved of The Man Who Would Be King. What did she do? Sat around in the valley, embroidered a flag, sent an emerald tie-tack. What a gal. But we know Our Hero kept her as the sustaining flame in his heart, perhaps more even than the thought of the throne and the downfall of the Shadow. Her love for Estel was borne through the night with the galloping Rangers to bring hope to Aragorn and his followers. We know she was willing to give up the entire way of life that she knew in order to be with him. (Don't complain to me about how she gave up everything and he gave up nothing, either . . . he *couldn't* become immortal to be with her. She had the choice, and she made it.) Now, maybe you don't want that kind of relationship, but that's the way it fell out for Our Hero and his Lady Fair. On him was the doom of his ancestry; the saving of the West was his duty, and he looked to Arwen, his love, for the inspiration to get the job done.

Galadriel. Does anybody else get a slight feeling of the creeps when we talk about this lady? To me, she is one of the single most powerful characters in the book. It is never overtly stated, but I always get the impression that she is much more of a bad dude than Celeborn could ever have hoped to be. Perhaps it's the phrasing when Tolkien states that she "dwelt" with Celeborn, not that she was married to him — obviously she was making a choice to continue her life with him and could probably revoke it at any time, as it seems she did when she departed over-Sea without him.

Also, when the Company first arrives in Caras Galadon and is having its audience with the Lord and Lady, Galadriel always speaks after Celeborn and always seems to have something to say that upstages him. She always comes off as just a small jump ahead of him in figuring things out. Celeborn theorizes that though he sees only eight in the Company and nine were to set out, there may have been changes; Galadriel knows that there was no change, and she knows who is missing. Celeborn speculates that Gandalf chose poorly when he led the Company into Moria; Galadriel contradicts him. But her inner core of steel is truly revealed when Frodo offers to *give* her the One Ring.

Though she wants it, wants the power for good that temptation is whispering the Ring can give her, she resists, though not without an ominous struggle.

She is wise, powerful, great, sometimes terrible, stern and fair. Yet even in her regal bearing she still takes on some of the same role we saw in Arwen: she is an inspiration, especially to Legolas, her kindred, and Gimli, to whom she becomes almost a mystical mother. He is downcast when it appears she has sent him no message later in the book, and it is not until he receives her words that he takes new heart for the adventure.

Rose Cotton and Mrs. Cotton, Mrs. Maggot, Goldberry, and Ioreth the healing-woman of Gondor. I can hear the feminists putting on their scoffing expressions right this instant. But just because these ladies play the "traditional" female roles of healing, nurturing, and home-making is not a reason to either write them off *or* to start beating on Tolkien. They play their own parts, nothing more, and the other women in the book are not lessened or changed by the fact that these stout-hearted women were back of the front lines, not whackin' off Nazgûl heads but healing those who came back the worse for wear, filling up stomachs after a hungry night's work of driving off "ruffians," handing out mushrooms, and being the devoted "girl next door" when Sam returns from "chasing Black Men up mountains." What else would the front lines be fighting for if not so that they could return to these comforting souls in peace?

Éowyn of the Rohirrim, the standout exception to the "I'm inspiration" rule — or is she? I seem to recall in the end of the book a certain Gondor prince having his heart fall out on the battlements because he was so inspired by her courage. Doesn't everybody's heart, male or female, skip a beat when we talk about this girl? Slender and fair as a lily, sterner than steel, is one of her descriptions. She also had a duty to perform, and it wasn't to stay behind until the men came back looking for their supper. That and roles like it are important, and the women mentioned above filled them admirably. But Éowyn has another calling. She takes her turn on the front lines, and she utters some of the most stirring speeches in the length and breadth of the whole book. She demands to know why she, a descendent of the royal house and one among many valiant warriors, is denied the opportunity to prove her skills along with her brother. She claims no fear and no patience for those who would brand her a serving-woman or a dry-nurse, and she rides to war in disguise and defiance.

The contrast between Éowyn and somebody like Rosie Cotton is crystal clear to me in this one point: it's all in what you choose. Rosie is *content* to make a home, to be a nurturing and supporting influence, and Éowyn is not. Tolkien paints women with different desires, different paths of life, different callings and duties! And THIS is our cold medieval misogynist? That's just barking up the wrong tree. It is Aragorn, Éomer, and Théoden who try to push Éowyn into a mold that is not her own, and she does every individualist in the world proud when she breaks it. My all-time favorite passage, kind of like when Luke throws down his lightsaber and declares "I-am-a-Jedi-like-my-father-before-me," is the confrontation with the Witch-king, when Dernhelm is revealed. He tells her that "no living man" may hinder him. And she laughs in his face!

> "But no living man am I! You look upon a woman. Éowyn I am, Éomund's daughter. You stand between me and my lord and kin. Begone ... For living or dark undead, I will smite you, if you touch him."

Every time I read this I want to stand up and cheer and holler! It is a triumph for a woman, but to me, the triumph is not in the fact that she is doing what a man would normally do; it is in the fact that she has followed her path despite the attempts to push her into another one, and I have just as much respect for Rosie, Arwen, Galadriel, and Ioreth, for following *their* paths, whatever those roles may be, repugnant to some feminists as they may be.

The bottom line is that it's all in what you choose. Men and women are different from one another, but so are individual women. (And men, but that's another column.) My best friend, a sworn-in atTORney and avowed feminist who, when telling her husband to wash the dishes, reminds him, "I cooked tonight, so you clean up" (I think she would wash dishes and make him cook, were it not for the fact that she likes to eat actual food), will still, when we're confronted with shoveling snow or killing bugs, hold me back and say, "This is what we have guys for." That's because she doesn't *like* to shovel snow or kill bugs. Me, I give her my cross-eyed look and go right on shoveling the snow or killing the bug. (Or spider. I dispatched a nasty one for her, off the ceiling, once when her husband wasn't home.)

It's all in what you choose, and Tolkien knew this. His women are as varied in their paths of destiny as they are in their looks and height, and he obviously knows enough about the nature of woman to include the dark side as well: Lobelia Sackville-Baggins chose to behave like a particularly nasty species of shrew, but Tolkien, even so, managed to ultimately put her gall to a positive use. The fact that there are so few female characters is simply a result of how Tolkien himself views women: *as special*. Each had a different, chosen path, with its own responsibilities and rewards, and in the end, Tolkien didn't *need* a passel of women because a surplus would have lessened the individuality of each one.

Can you even remember which Elf Haldir is without looking it up? Or whether Ingold worked for Denethor or for Théoden? How about Hirgon? But nobody I know has ever mixed up Galadriel with Arwen or Éowyn. (Well, nobody who really cares.) Perhaps the men should be hollering about how Tolkien stereotyped them into the roles of wall-building and gate guarding. All I can say for sure is that Tolkien cherished "his Lúthien" and put that perspective into his portrayal of females in *Lord of the Rings*.

Maybe you wouldn't like to be any of the women in the book, ladies, and men, maybe you wouldn't like your girlfriends or wives to take on some of those roles, but in the end, it's a matter of personal perspective, not gender perspective, and really, aren't there enough perspectives to go around? Let's let Tolkien have his cherished vision of womanhood without being beaten up for it. I, for one, would be proud if a man came to view me as a Lúthien. Or as a Galadriel, an Arwen, a Rosie, an Éowyn . . . I could go on . . . and on . . .

21. The Shadow of Racism

Quickbeam

Of the many criticisms brought against Tolkien, this is perhaps the most unwelcome: the charge of racism. I have been warned by friends not to write on this subject. A little too unpleasant, too touchy for some. Whatever. I say if you don't examine things carefully to learn the truth within, then your life will remain rooted in ignorance.

It bears looking at, if for no other reason than to get a clear perspective. Perhaps a rigorous discussion can help dispel the pervasive ignorance that lingers to this day.

Tolkien's use of descriptions like "swarthy" or "slant-eyed" suggests to many that he was a racist. Further, that his entire mythology is a Eurocentric world of white, blond, fair-skinned heroes pitted against a "dark" Enemy, using Black Riders and dark-skinned armies of Southrons. This contention, pitched sourly over the years as a testament to Tolkien's racist worldview, is grievous. Many believe he portrayed races different from his Caucasian heroes as inferior, corruptible, and worth nothing more than deep mistrust.

A more stinging indictment against Tolkien you will not find, but at the core it is very weak and only holds up under the most superficial consideration of his published works. Look deeper and you'll find a more complicated and ultimately redeeming solution. His life and work show that he was not racist, nor was he propagating a hostile attitude towards other races.

First of all, we have to remember his intentions as a writer. In a reductive sense, Tolkien meant to bring forth a powerful myth, because he believed mythology held a most wonderful quality. That is, Man achieves his most basic expression of spiritual truth through his myths. As Humphrey Carpenter put it succinctly in his *Biography*: "Indeed only by myth-making, only by becoming a 'sub-creator' and inventing stories, can Man aspire to the state of perfection that he knew before the Fall."

Tolkien's lifelong linguistic work was not a parlor game or a simple hobby. It was a pilgrimage to him. Few of us see his novels as a spiritual roadmap to a higher philosophy — but myth is never obvious. There is more on this than I have room to expound upon, especially in Tolkien's comprehensive essay, "On Fairy Stories," published in 1947. Within that essay an entire paradigm is unlocked before your eyes, and much of the Professor's vision is made clear.

For my argument, suffice it to say that Tolkien took on the role of "sub-creator" and he took it very seriously. Keeping in mind his deeply personal goals, he went about this mythmaking in two crucial steps. First he gave his invented languages a place to flourish. Thus came about Arda, the angelic powers of the Valar, and what would eventually become *The Silmarillion*.

Second, he chose to ground his mythological world in the "real" by using elements familiar in our modern world. He had to choose a setting that was organically appealing. His heart told him to create what was most important to him: a "new mythology" for England. Tolkien's deep love for the language, the people, the land, and all things English inspired his work. He perceived there was a vacuum in the history of England, that there were no myths the land could call her own. His conviction was fueled by the fact that after studying the rich language of Mother England all his life, still he could not find epic poems or myths she could organically call her own (not of the quality he had seen in other lands).

He explains in his famously long letter to Milton Waldman that he wanted to create a series of related legends that he could make a gift to his country, England. (*Letters*, #131) Even though Tolkien admits this very broad concept was neither his primary focus nor an overnight whim, still throughout his career these many stories formed to match this vision. His tales were grounded in England and Northern Europe, set in a time far gone yet still reachable through epic tales and still distinctly our world. And here is where the cultures clash.

Tolkien's choice of milieu inherently puts Caucasians in all the key roles. It's as simple as that. The characters are white, placed in a distinctly Northern European environment, while everything around them is steeped in Germanic, Norse, and English cultures. By default, the entire affair would focus on white people (some say to the exclusion of other cultures). This does not mean Tolkien was a racist. This was merely his personal taste in legends. If instead he had had a strong taste for Asian or African mythology, he surely would have created stories in that vein. And it's not too far a stretch to think he would have been criticized for going in that direction as well.

If you can imagine Tolkien's scholarly and creative efforts going towards a mythology for the Moorish culture, or any other that he perceived was lacking, then you can also hear the requisite hecklers that would tear him down for it. Oversensitive knee-jerks would spring up all over. Instead of calling him a racist (for allegedly extolling whites as superior) they would call him a bastardizing pirate (for assuming to write about their particular heritage). The pundits would complain loud and long about the white-bread Englishman shoplifting from the rich tapestry of their past. No one can really blame Tolkien for being sympathetic to the long-dead and forgotten culture sprung from the *Kalevala* and the Icelandic Eddas (and of course the void left by the Arthurian cycle) — but someone would no doubt find a way! Cheap opinion comes easy and the PC haze we live in makes it a no-win scenario for any writer building on a historical foundation.

But I digress.

When humans first appear in Tolkien's myths, we must recognize ourselves in them. They are predominantly Caucasian, yes, but do a bit of "geographical overlay" and you'll see other ethnicities of our world start to appear. Go out from Northern Europe far enough to the south and east and not surprisingly you'll find African, Armenian, Turkish and Arab peoples. Thus there are dark-skinned Southrons who live in the hot climate of the Harad. Author and Tolkien historian Michael Martinez adroitly put it this way: "Yes, [the Haradrim] come from the south. And people who live in warm regions tend to be dark-skinned. Funny, that. Should Tolkien have portrayed all the southern peoples of Middle-earth as albinos or something?"

The Easterlings and Haradrim are devices that help place Middle-earth "in the familiar." They are not meant to be horrid stereotypes or to induce xenophobia.

Fair enough. But with his work being decidedly Euro-centric, how do Tolkien's other "races" stack up? Many are fantastical: Ents, Orcs, Elves, and Dwarves, but none are meant to be analogous to the human races of our world. And none of them are represented as disparaging stereotypes. The Elves are depicted as a high race (fair-skinned, beautiful, immortal) but they are not a "supreme white race" — an attitude espoused by several Nazi skinhead groups. There is nothing more pathetic than these "Aryan nationals" with their tiny voices, struggling to justify their views by misappropriating and twisting the works of great writers and thinkers.

The truth is the Children of Ilúvatar, the Elves with their beauty and nobility, are really a lost state of mankind: Adam and Eve before the expulsion from Eden. From the Carpenter *Biography* we learn that Elves:

> ....are Man before the Fall which deprived him of his powers of achievement. Tolkien believed devoutly that there had once been an Eden on earth, and that man's original sin and subsequent dethrone-ment were responsible for the ills of the world; but his Elves, though capable of sin and error, have not "fallen" in the theological sense, and so are able to achieve much beyond the powers of men.

This use of a high race is a far cry from the hate-fueled correlation that other racist groups would have you believe. They are dismissed from the equation and hold no claim to Tolkien's accomplishments.

To set the record straight, the Professor wrote strongly in rejection of Nazi principles, going so far as to refuse the demands of a German publisher in 1938 who wanted proof that he was not Jewish. He risked the opportunity for the first German edition of *The Hobbit* because he objected so adamantly. Writing to his publisher Stanley Unwin (who had the final decision whether to proceed with the German request), Tolkien expressed disgust at having to negotiate with another pub-lisher who was swayed by Nazi race-doctrine, that he was happy to have Jewish friends, and he would rather "let a German translation go hang" before he would be used as a pawn by such insidious policy.

Does that sound like a man who is racist?

But to fans of *LotR*, the most sensitive issue is how Sauron, the hated Enemy, had such sway over the Easterlings, Wainriders, and Haradrim. Why were all these ethnic people under the control of the Dark Lord? Why are the white people portrayed as noble and heroic while the blacks are a misguided lot underneath Sauron? Well, it's not that one-sided. Nothing ever is.

In truth, Men had been corrupted by Sauron's guile for thousands of years, white- and dark-skinned alike. Every individual is an open target for Evil. Just look at what happened to the Númenoreans. Even the Elves of Eregion listened to Sauron (while he was in pleasant form) and forged the Rings of Power. There are tremendous examples of Sauron bringing moral weakness and destruction to many races. Tolkien never suggests that the black Southrons exclusively were prone to evil.

However, he does present a theological plight. The very first Men who allied with the High Elves were exposed to Valinor (the Angelic powers) and its qualities of beauty, nobility, and blessedness. Sauron later took advantage of the wild Men who never traveled west in the First Age and never knew the Elves, playing on their fear and mistrust. Tolkien contends that these Men of the East were corruptible because they never knew the state of "unfallen grace" as embodied in the Elves. Sauron turned their ignorance into a hatred of the West. So you see it was a spiritual schism, not a racial one, that engendered the alliance between these Men and the Dark Lord.

There is a cogent passage that tells us how Tolkien really feels about the human condition, seen through the eyes of Samwise. In *The Two Towers*, during Faramir's attack on a troop of Haradrim, one of them actually crashes through the brush, landing dead at Sam's feet. Sam has not seen a dead man before, and he wonders who he was and what were his origins, and what led him to that fate. Was he evil, or had he been marched to war by lies or threats? Sam imagines that he might have preferred, like Sam himself, to stay peacefully at home.

There is penetrating wisdom here. We examine our own feelings about the Enemy, and what he really is. The forces of fear, coercion, and hatred? Or the man who has fallen prey to these forces?

Tolkien succeeds at what he set out to do — his myths reveal greater truths within. Being a devout Catholic, he felt that Mankind has been separated from its original state of grace. This is a compelling theory even if you do not practice the Christian faith. He wants us to consider that we are all mortal and corruptible, prone to the ways of error, and yet capable of profound acts of beauty and preservation, when we are so inspired.

In its grand weaving, Tolkien's massive epics yield undeniable lessons of human frailty. Sadly, these lessons often fall on deaf ears. His power is diluted by our modern climate, didactically insisting on political correctness (whatever that means .... the phrase "PCs" is overused to the point of losing all intrinsic value). It seems we are too busy looking for slights against our sensibilities, however self-righteous, and we tune out the essence of Tolkien's wondrous accomplishment.

Much too hasty,
Quickbeam

Sources:
Humphrey Carpenter, *J.R.R. Tolkien: A Biography,* Geo. Allen & Unwin, 1977 (revised edition published by Houghton Mifflin, 2000).
Humphrey Carpenter, ed., *The Letters of J.R.R. Tolkien.* Houghton Mifflin, 1995.

22 .... And in the Closet Bind Them

Quickbeam

What's all this I keep reading about Frodo and Sam being gay?

Lately, on various websites (not ours) and message boards, some ostensibly dedicated to "movie gossip," I've seen hostile people going to remarkable lengths to prove that Frodo and Sam were secretly a gay couple, skipping about Middle-earth like lovebirds in Tolkien's "thinly disguised endorsement of homosexuality." Some of these pundits are on a homophobic mission, holding forth in the Talk Back chat room with derogatory claims, trivializing the relationship between Frodo and Sam, using quotes from *The Lord of the Rings* and fervent references to that infamous kiss in the 1980 Rankin/Bass TV film, *The Return of the King*.

Well, shut my mouth and wash my knickers! Roddy McDowall kissing Orson Bean! Now that's unquestionable proof if I've ever seen it. I'm sold. By the way, where do I get my toaster oven for being converted?

The time has come to do some serious debunking, or at least give due consideration to the burning debate before the flames get any higher (Ha-ha). Do we find here some keen insight into Tolkien's life and views on this touchy subject? Is he trying to let us in on a little secret?

In *The Hobbit* we have a little song the Elves sing as Thorin and Company make their way into Rivendell. It is a funny verse about the domestic pleasures of Rivendell, and certainly the Elven singers are making fun of the cold hungry travelers when they sing:

The faggots are reeking,
The bannocks are baking!

To the unenlightened, this little verse almost always gives an image of gay men with disagreeable body odor standing around a kitchen, baking buns. If you had a good copy of the *Oxford English Dictionary* with you, then you'd know better than to entertain such offensive poppycock.

At one point in *The Fellowship of the Ring*, Frodo has awakened from his convalescence in his peaceful room in Rivendell. He has been healed after many painful and dangerous days, and as he prepares to leave his room Sam bursts in, taking Frodo by the hand. Seeing that this once dead hand is at last alive again, Sam strokes it in wonder and blurts out his amazement that it's warm. Then he blushes and quickly takes his distance again.

This episode of hand-holding stands out to many people — the type of people who squirm visibly when two of the same gender show such physical affection. I can hear them now: "It's obvious why Sam is blushing. Because he's embarrassed he was doing gay things to Frodo's hand while he was asleep, that's why!" When I encounter sophistry like this, what more can I do than roll my eyes back into my skull?

But consider for a moment the class system of England in the early 1900s (and as it still exists today) and you'll see another valid reason why Sam is so awkward during this tactile moment. Sam is a gardener. He's a servant, not on the same social rung as Frodo and the other Bagginses. It is made abundantly clear that the socioeconomic structure of the Shire bears itself as a mirror image of Tolkien's rural England. Servants aren't supposed to go touching their masters; it's just not acceptable. Sam was just elated that Frodo survived and his recovery was complete. The fact that he visited Frodo often and held his hand is endearing, showing true depth of concern. However, at the same time he was inappropriately crossing class lines.

The irrational arguer continues: "But wait, there's more proof that these two were really in the closet! In *The Return of the King*, Chapter 3, Mount Doom, we see that Sam is constantly kissing Frodo's hand! And also that one episode where Frodo and Sam lie close, trying to comfort and hold each other, and they sleep together through the night like newlyweds.

"GASP — two people of the same gender touching each other with tenderness! Now that's just too much. Can't be anything else ... Yup. They're gay."

Oh, to laugh. It's not hard to find an audience for this kind of nonsense, unfortunately. I personally don't believe that Frodo and Sam were gay, nor that they were exploring a homosexual relationship. However, I will say that some homoerotic elements are there, quite clearly there, and for a purpose.

I assert, as plainly and sincerely as I may, that J.R.R. Tolkien was a genius. He knew what he was doing every step of the way. He was crafting an epic and he knew exactly how to do it. In its design, *The Lord of the Rings* includes the greatest ambient factors of literary epics as Tolkien knew and had studied his whole life. One could safely argue that he deliberately put homoerotic elements in his narrative. It harkens back to the great epics of the Greeks and Romans. In that mode of epic it was a given that the heroes would share a dynamic of homoerotic expression, it was part of the culture, part of the formula, if you will, and it became the blueprint of heraldic poetry and Homeric writing.

Those stories are about the passion of men, the devotion between men in times of struggle. Though not always in a sexual equation, the passion is still the same. We recognize it as fraternal love and the bond of loyalty and closeness. So if Tolkien put this passion in there, exploring this theme between his characters, then so be it. You can trust that it is part of his work for a reason, and just maybe it pushed as many buttons back in 1954 as it does today.

But tenderness between men is not stigmatized elsewhere the way it is now in modern America. I encourage you to visit Rome, Paris or just about anywhere in Europe and you'll see the climate is very different. I mean the climate of tolerance, of course. People are very accustomed to seeing two women walking down the street, arm-in-arm, or two men greeting each other in a public place with an embrace and a kiss. And yes, they're straight! Completely straight, able to express affection with each other just for its own sake.

You certainly can't find that here, in a country where generations of us have been raised feeling very uncomfortable expressing ourselves with our own bodies and the prevailing sense of machismo has taken its toll. Americans are so emotionally constipated that they can't accept one simple idea: that people can touch each other, with nothing but innocence and caring, a simple dose of humanity that implies nothing else. By and large the American psyche, such as it is, just can't sit still with two men or two women touching each other. *"Don't go there! Too uncomfortable!"* Our minds are filtered through so much cultural detritus that anytime we encounter same-sex affection, without granting it any merit, we are distressed and offended beyond means. I think that's a shame.

Can you imagine yourself crossing the endless volcanic desert, going untold days with no food and only a sip of water? Would you and your traveling companion not be beaten with misery and despair, to the extreme end of your own endurance, just as Frodo and Sam were? Would you not then crave the smallest sign of care, support, and love from the only other human being near you who is carrying you on his back, while you toil with your own madness? You cannot deny it. The simplest touch, the kiss of your loving brother, would do more miracles to keep you alive and sane than anything else would. Yes, a miracle of hope is what we're talking about here, and it breathes power into Tolkien's work like nothing else.

At best, we come out of this with a new appreciation of the Professor as the architect of an epic. Perceptive readers everywhere notice the "gay subtext" between Frodo and Sam. Understanding its purpose in the grand design will only augment our enjoyment of the whole. And for those actual gay readers of *LotR* the subtext is a very personal thing. To them it is empowering to see these characters who are stronger for their physical closeness.

At worst, this "debate" is furthered by true homophobes who use this thematic element to trumpet their own hate — their own self-loathing. They are the ones who deride Tolkien the loudest, sensing something is going on between Frodo and Sam that they can't deal with. Their own discomfort is all you will hear in their absurd claims (which is their own problem — not Tolkien's). I can't abide this ill-conceived minority who seek to drag *LotR* down to the dregs of their own homophobia. To them I say: grow up and leave Tolkien out of it! His work is well out of range of your most inane judgments.

Look, if you want something really gay, I have just the book for you — *Billy Budd.*

Much too hasty,
Quickbeam

23. Tolkien & Nature

Anwyn

Much has been made of Tolkien's pro-nature, anti-industrial outlook on life. Observing, experiencing, and chronicling the beauties of the natural world seem to have taken up a large portion of his time and effort, as seen in his descriptive correspondence as well as in his fiction.

Like all other writers since the beginning of time, Tolkien wrote what he knew. Whether it was his deeply spiritual soul, his intimate capacity for love — both between man and woman and between comrade and friend — or his vast intellectual knowledge, it all came out in his writing, some elements more subtly than others. Some themes are obvious, like the faceoff between good and evil and the representation of the heroic spirit. Other things are less explicit, such as the religious implications of *The Lord of the Rings*, even though we know enough to know that Tolkien himself was deeply religious. What is certain is that all of his material was filtered through the glass of his own experience and beliefs. Reading Tolkien's works gives us an interesting mix of obvious truths about the man and conclusions that are more open to interpretation — such as his devout, almost worshipful attitude towards nature and his hatred of all things industrial.

The professor's decidedly "green" point of view is an established fact and raises interesting speculation as to why he held it and its effect on his convictions about other aspects of human societal life. The tried-and-true explanation for the "why" is that he associated the beauties of nature with his happy childhood home at Sarehole, before the death of his mother — a perfectly reasonable supposition. What one lives with in childhood becomes imprinted on one for life, and the images from his country home (the little mill and its Miller, the spreading trees and quiet country lanes) are so infused into his writing that we have no trouble recognizing pastoral England in the Shire.

As for a hatred of industrialism, well, who among us with even a little country in our souls can pass over a car-jammed interstate freeway, hemmed in on both sides by the dregs of industrial life — abandoned factories, ditto vehicles, mean alleys and dirty streets, giving way to working factories that look and smell almost as bad — without wishing at least a bit that we could have our modern comforts with less noise, less dirt, less nastiness — in short, less industry? Again, not hard to fathom.

So the "why" of his views is fairly established and not difficult to understand. But what intrigues me more is the "how" — how did all this affect his views of society? I believe the effects were shown in a couple of different, very important ways. His love of nature permeates every chapter of *Lord of the Rings*. I could give example after example where almost every new event is prefaced and concluded with a paragraph or two about what the day is like, what the weather is doing, and how everything looks. This love of nature led him down two distinct paths.

First, he was led to a settled and decided distaste and even hatred for all kinds of machinery and for the minds of the men who invented such things as internal combustion engines and airplanes. You can read his opinion of them in *Letters*, #64, where he complains how summer's beauty is ruined by the noise and commotion of passing engines. He wishes that they had never been invented or at least been put to some other use, and accuses engineers of being the most malicious manifestation of human intelligence.

What a sweeping condemnation! Certainly it is a strongly worded diatribe, almost appalling in its scorn of the engineering mind — especially given Tolkien's own creative propensities. His cutting comment implies none too subtly that creativity is the sole province of the artist and that inventive talent is completely wasted on clever mechanisms.

Consider, however, the changes that must have been taking place from the time of Tolkien's childhood to the time of that writing (circa WWII). Cars, once scarce and newly invented, had become commonplace, filling the streets with their rumble and emissions. Airplanes, unknown in his boyhood, filled the skies on their missions against Germany. Factories, certainly fewer and farther between when he lived at Sarehole, were polluting the air, more than ever as part of the machinery of war. All very different and disagreeable to our quiet Professor. Still, I can't excuse Mr. Tolkien from the charge of near-unreasonabe hatred of the man-made and the minds that make it. He went so far as to claim that if a monster would get rid of the uglier trappings of modern life, then the monster could have the works of art, too, and he, Tolkien, would go back to the trees.

It seems Tolkien was convinced that he would be willing to give up some of his modern comforts in exchange for the destruction of the intolerable conditions that produced those comforts. But more than that, he had a higher, more spiritual reason for looking upon the man-made with dubious skepticism. Not only the comparatively smaller crimes of factories and airplanes came under his attack. When news broke of the first atomic bombs, he described them in terms of a lunatic folly that could destroy the world and drew an analogy between the scientists and the Biblical people whose pride led them to build the Tower of Babel, a direct challenge to God (*Letters, #102*).

The ultimate Tolkien reason for despising the man-made: because it affronts God. Babel was the short-lived expression of Biblical man's hubris: a tower purposely designed to reach to the heavens, deliberately to get up in God's face and show him what man could accomplish. God put a swift end to the attempted outrage through a means that definitely must have tickled Tolkien's humor as well as his intellect — He confused the languages of the tower builders, making it impossible for them to communicate and thus forcing them to leave the tower unfinished and go their separate ways. Tolkien obviously looked upon many of the results of human ingenuity as too big for humans themselves to comprehend or handle. I shudder to think how he would have reacted to genetic manipulation and many of the other "advances" humans have made since his time.

"But Anwyn, what about sub-creation? It's going a bit far for Tolkien to glory in the use of his own talents and then want to deny other talented minds the privilege of expressing themselves." Yes, I know. But I would say that nuclear devices are hardly in the category with art and literature (to which Tolkien's "sub-creation" principle was mainly applied), and again, I simply cannot excuse him from the charge of prejudice against the more scientific/engineering minds on the planet, at least so far as they are directed towards industry and "modern" applications. He hated cars and planes and factories because they represented the opposite of what he most loved in this world, and thus he also detested the minds that invented them, whether they were applied to "infernal combustion" or nuclear fission.

Second, the less obvious conclusion: *Tolkien felt that the industrialization of society created and fostered a "lower class" of people.*

An example is Sandyman's mill. Lotho Sackville-Baggins, under the influence of Saruman, automated the mill and brought in rough men to run it.

Old Sandyman ran the mill, kept its mechanism in working order, ground the hobbits' corn and wheat and whatnot, and helped keep their agrarian society running smoothly. In other words, he did his own part in the "sub-creation" scheme. Ted Sandyman, whose father had been the miller and the boss, simply worked cleaning the machines for the men.

Elsewhere I have postulated the theory that Faramir's governing skills, Sam's gardening ditto, and Aragorn's healing hands are all part of the same "sub-creation" that gives us Andúril, the Doors of Moria, and the Rings of Power. So it was with Sandyman and with *every* responsible citizen of the Shire. Each contributed in his own way to the *way things ought to be.* Rush Limbaugh had nothing on Tolkien. In his mind, it was all laid out and each had his or her part, to be played to the best of his or her ability, whether it be milling, cooking, shirriffing, or governing. But old Lotho Pimple was a "progressive," a word that in the lexicons of Tolkien and Lewis equates to "industrial." "Pimple's idea was to grind more and faster, or so he said." So he brought in the *machines* and accomplished two things: he tore the fabric of hobbit society, and he nurtured a class of people like Ted Sandyman, who would rather "clean wheels for the Men" (he might just as well have said "clean wheels for the machines") than to run the Mill and think for himself and be a "sub-creator."

Taking this theme onward, I think of factory workers — armies of human beings making not-so-great wages to spend their days making sure the machines run properly. But Tolkien didn't stop there. He obviously considers the machines' more educated inventors and designers to be doing nothing more than cleaning wheels for the Men. We might say "for The Man."

Tolkien's position was a drastic one. A more moderate point of view would be that there's not a thing in the world wrong with either honest work, even if it be in a factory (I've spent a couple summers cleaning wheels for the Men myself), or with using your brain to dream up new ways of using our resources. But Tolkien's position was that to allow the machines to take over was to devalue the human mind and to abdicate a responsibility both to nature and to the real business of humanity — sub-creation and using it to form a happier, better conducted society based less on power and more on contribution to the Good. He feared greatly the seemingly unstoppable tide of modernism, and of the machines, he wondered ominously, "What's their next move?"

Sources:
Humphrey Carpenter, ed., *The Letters of J.R.R. Tolkien.* Houghton Mifflin, 1995.

24. Quests, Myths & Heroines

Tehanu

"There are only five plots, and every story is a variation on those five."

This is the kind of statement that writer's workshops and how-to-write books love to throw around, rather in the manner of somebody going around putting up "Abandon Hope All Ye Who Enter Here" placards all over what initially seemed to be a little bit of paradise. Maybe children approaching music feel the same way when they're first told, "There are only 12 notes in the Western scale." These restrictions haven't limited our creativity so far, but it's all a bit daunting for the beginner to consider first up.

Being a slow learner, I've forgotten what the Five Plots are. Boy Meets Girl, The Hero's Quest, The Bargain with Death, I can't think of the others. Some dangerous radicals claim there might be Nine Plots. Or Ten. As in all things, there are schisms.

Part of me thinks that there is a way of reading stories that makes them a journey over a map of human emotions; that, and the quality of the writing, are the things on which the plot hangs like a harness on a horse. Equally, one can read a story as though the plot were the driving force and the emotions a by-product. I've talked to people who experience life itself in these diametrically opposed ways, and what's more they live amicably together, sharing the same houses though not inhabiting the same worlds. For one, a day is a series of feelings faintly marked by events; for the other, the same day is a series of events causing emotional reactions.

The fact that we can communicate so well despite these radically different visions is a mark of how adaptable we are as a species. If it weren't for the quality of empathy, why should we be interested in other people's archetypal stories? Why should I care for the outcome of the Young Hero's Quest? None of his struggles and victories are relevant to my life. I used to love Luke Skywalker in *Star Wars*; now I have to bite back the urge to shout at Luke, "Grow up! Stop and think a minute, would you?" When I'm older I'll misremember that it was fun to be so naïve, and then I'll enjoy Luke again.

I've been wondering how we relate to these archetypal stories and whether archetypes can or should change over time. The Quest myth is a good one to look at — relevant to Tolkien, because *The Lord of the Rings* is a quest epic, or a romance. (Tolkien preferred the word "Romance" to "Novel" to describe his book; the word we now use for a story about love used to describe the kind of story that is like a road movie — the characters travel around meeting new adventures one after the other. This older usage is the one that Tolkien, typically, preferred.) *The Lord of the Rings* contains many different quests, but for the central characters, it has the common Quest theme of the hero being tempered by adversity. The hobbits are almost childlike in their simplicity at the beginning of the tale, and by the end of it they have power, wisdom and prestige.

I'm reading another book in a similar vein, Richard Adams's *Watership Down*. You're thinking, "Oh, those widdle fluffy bunny wabbits?" Really, no. What with the quotes at the chapter headings from the Greek tragedies, Malory's *Le Morte d'Arthur*, the *Pilgrim's Progress*, and the musings of Napoleon, Shakespeare and Clausewitz on war, it's clearly not a tale about widdle bunny wunnies. Like Tolkien, the details of the way the countryside looks and smells, the changing of the seasons, are rendered as delicately as a drypoint etching. What Adams has done is a marvel — without once losing the integrity of their animal nature, he's recreated a history of a roving warband with risks and hopes and ventures that reads like a counterpart to *Beowulf* or the Icelandic sagas. The rabbits too have their Thane with his inner circle of seasoned warriors, called the Owsla instead of Eorlingas ... like the Norsemen they inhabit a world where law and custom lay a light hand on the workings of their society, and where the individual relies far more on his strength than on law for his defense, but the wily trickster may succeed too.

But like so many of the books I loved as a child, there aren't many girls leading the ventures. This isn't intended as a criticism of Adams, who wrote some heroic female characters in *Maia*, nor indeed is it a criticism of Tolkien. A book can't possibly contain all things, and

Tolkien's comment that he had a problem with *The Lord of the Rings* being too short shows that he knew there was more he could include — but he was too wise a writer to allow the book to lose focus by trying to contain more than would fit.

One of the things saving fantasy is that people are not static in their lives, and as we grow older we still contain our childhood and adolescence for reference. Otherwise we'd lose empathy for the coming-of-age theme that is such a big part of fantasy and of quest myths. When we're in our teens we start to choose who we are going to be, and part of that choice rests in who we identify with. Then the Hero's Quest/ Coming-of-Age stories exert a powerful fascination for us, because whatever our culture allows or condemns, at that age we're beginning to feel that same need to venture out and test ourselves. But the choice is not made for all time, and we read these stories again and again because they're one of the pathways to rewriting ourselves and remaking our choices.

One day, years later, your former favorite character (maybe it was the permanently angry, hard-done-by underdog who makes good) suddenly loses appeal, and you find yourself casting round for other characters, other Quest myths. Who will interest you more this time? The hard-shelled, fearless warrior from the princely house? The quiet sage-to-be who always guesses rightly? The klutz with the heart of gold? Whatever, they're yardsticks as well as signposts to how we grow and change.

I used to read Biggles and The Hardy Boys when I was small. Excitement! Adventure! Danger! Deserts! Tropical islands! Simple characters and easy plots! (Lots of cigarettes too, at least one a page, but despite that I never took up smoking.) Then I moved on to Henry Treece's wonderful Viking tales and so on.

Then something happened to my books. At some point while I was growing up I noticed that none of the people doing the exciting stuff in my books were girls. This jarred so extremely with the outdoor lives of my friends and me, who did little all summer except play at hunting, fighting, chasing and exploring, that I abandoned that genre of book forever and gratefully discovered books by E. Nesbit, Diana Wynne Jones and Madeleine L'Engle, where girls were as likely to have adventures as boys.

It's not from losing interest or empathy with other ways of being (which is, as I say, one of the greater things of the human spirit), but more from reaching an age where I was casting around for someone to "be like" and I didn't at some unconscious level want to feel like a counterfeit boy, a failed boy. Nor did I want to read about women who waited for the men to do something great and maybe gave them a little bit of help along the way. Our society has changed since Tolkien wrote his tale hoping to create a "Mythology for England," and I'm not sure the myth still fits us as we are today.

That is one of the problems a lot of people have with the character of Arwen in *The Lord of the Rings*. She's the major sweetheart and Aragorn's prize for winning the crown of Gondor. He's her prize for … what? Waiting it out? Sewing him a banner? Giving up her immortality? What is her story, anyway? Is it one you identify with? Sitting and sewing, waiting and hoping are things just about any woman can manage with differing amounts of grace, so they're hardly a mark of female heroism. Giving up immortality is the biggie. The nearest human equivalent might be giving up one's children, since we don't have an immortal life to trade but we do have children (and more frequently than Tolkien's Elves did). They're our immortality, in a way. So Arwen's choice is a big story in itself. You could build a whole novel around it.

Tolkien knew there was an important story about Arwen, but he also knew that it was risky to import another kind of story into the genre he had chosen for *The Lord of the Rings*. He added more details about Arwen in the appendices, where they would tell us more about her without disturbing the flow of the main narrative. He knew how to write a quest epic inside out and backwards and he could see that there wasn't any space in it that would allow Arwen's story to be included, because her story isn't active. Her story would be about the psychological turmoil of choosing mortality, of trusting that love would last and would be recompense for her shortened life span, of hoping that she could leave her own people and be happy among an alien race. Notice how rare it is to eavesdrop on the thoughts of characters in *The Lord of the Rings*? It would be a disjunct in the book to have chapters full of Arwen's internal debate in the midst of all the action aimed at destroying Sauron. Sort of like having a chapter or two written by Virginia Woolf. Other characters in the book are evolving and making choices, but they do it while travelling and striving in the physical world too. Tolkien didn't feel that his female romantic lead should be active. That "ideal woman" archetype must remain passive.

Whose ideal is that, though? I get the feeling that men will be attracted to women who are remotely beautiful and mysterious for some time to come, but a growing number of women don't want to be anything on that list besides "beautiful." They want to add in things like brave, competent, smart and decisive.

What does it take to change the archetypal myth stories, I wonder? On every major continent after the arrival of humans, the vast majority of large mammals (or giant marsupials, in Australia, and giant flightless birds in New Zealand) has died out shortly afterwards, according to the fossil record that remains. (Gee, I wonder why that could be?) What people did then with their tribal storehouse of stories of "you, me and Ugh shoulder to shoulder against the mammoths," I don't know. The mammoths died out, society changed, and after a few generations, the story of the lone hunter versus the ultimate mammoth died out too. Or maybe it mutated into the story of the Quest for the ever-receding, never seen, horizon-glimpsed Fabulous Beast.

Grabbing my attention before it can skedaddle out the open window and get caught up in a lawnmower, I'll drag it back to *The Lord of the Rings* for a moment. And Quests. And the obvious point that the only woman who has an active quest is Eowyn, and it's very much a bloke's quest: to go out and find death in battle as a way of keeping her integrity and freedom. That's somewhat negative, but things turn out surprisingly well for her. Great. She's the Shieldmaiden archetype, and they've been around since the Vikings. And as the story of Beren and Luthien in *The Silmarillion* shows, Tolkien didn't have anything against women taking an active role and being risktakers. Wow, that Luthien! She defies her father, tracks down Beren, and seeks out and confronts both Sauron and Morgoth. Going back to *The Lord of the Rings*: Nor is Galadriel a powerless watcher of events, for all that she stays in one place.

But it's Arwen who's the real sweetheart to so many readers, and she is the archetypal passive woman who waits. People like that, they're comfortable with it; it's a very old archetype. Woman as The Prize, the Goal, the Hero's Reward. Odysseus' Penelope. A character that we speculate about endlessly because the book reveals so little about her. That makes her even more mysterious and feminine. The unknowable Other.

Unless you happen to be a woman yourself, in which case other women are no great mystery and we've got no thanks for some other woman "trying it on" with us, as it were. Don't come over all Mysterious Other with me, honey. Been there, done that. Come on, Arwen, what are you thinking? We don't know, because Tolkien doesn't give us ten minutes alone with her.

People who first discovered *The Lord of the Rings* through Peter Jackson's films might find it strange to know that the role of Arwen in the movies generated a most heated debate among fans. Mysterious as Arwen is, she is a much-loved character. People were not happy to see the film rewrite her to enter the fray as a warrior princess. Early indications before and during filming showed that she was required to do a lot of physical action — riding, archery, swordplay. This was toned down in the finished movie from what was originally intended, though it's hard to tell whether that was because of the strong antipathy the fans had to Arwen's action role (and boy, did this fill up a lot of message boards online for months on end), or whether it was the result of actor Liv Tyler's discomfort with combat and riding scenes, which several people on the set commented on. It was interesting that the person cast to play Arwen turned out to have an innately Arwen-esque horror of the rough and tumble that the original screenplay called for, though to her credit she gave it her best shot. But during the editing process it was as though the Passive Heroine archetype had its own gravity that kept dragging Arwen back closer to what Tolkien had originally intended.

What remained in the movie was a real mix — we saw Arwen hold a sword to Strider's throat, only teasing him yet the implication was that she could sneak up on a Ranger and kill him if she wanted to. She had the skills. She told Aragorn that she was the faster rider of the two. She played a heroic part in Frodo's rescue from the pursuing Ringwraiths. But the image that sticks in my mind was of her standing alone at the Ford defying the Nine. She looked fragile, beleaguered, beautiful. With Frodo being so much smaller than her, she looked like another archetype of heroic virtue — one that has been allowed to women for a long time. She looked like a mother defending her child.

And then she did another thing that was intensely feminine. After the spells of raw power that called down the force of the river onto the Black Riders, she did something that I think can be read as a giving of her life for Frodo's. She asks that what grace is given her may pass to him, to spare him and save him. I wonder whether in a sense she is trading away her immortality right there. One of her "graces" is surely immortality. It's not clear to me that she loses it at the point that she puts on Aragorn's wedding ring, or (as happened with Luthien) at the point where she pledges her love to a mortal, or whether she could lose it by bestowing her lifeforce on Frodo. Either way she is doing what a mother would do to save a child — offering to lay down her own life, since if the offer is accepted she will eventually die.

That is both feminine and heroic. It reminds me of a very different movie, and that is James Cameron's *Aliens*. The scene that sticks in my mind from that movie is Sigourney Weaver facing the alien in the final showdown of that movie. She's encased in a powerful cargo-handling waldo. She's sweaty and bruised and battered. The alien is its usual lethal self and mightily pissed off at the destruction of its brood. But Sigourney's character is taking the place of a mother to an orphaned child in her care since it eluded the monster, and the audience cheers for her determination to save the child. She is the mother tigress archetype. At this point in the film Sigourney Weaver, striking as she is, does not look like some unearthly beauty, but this is a story with a modern sensibility, and some of the expectations for female archetypes have been loosened up. I suspect the women in the audience cheered all the harder for that. We want to see ourselves on the screen, in books, as we are or might hope to be. Bit by bit, it's happening.

What fascinates me is whether the change in our society is permanent enough to generate new myths, or whether it's merely a swing of the pendulum that will be reversed before we have a language of archetypes to cover it. Will Xena the Warrior Princess be a permanent fixture in our culture? Maybe one day there'll be a few more stories added to the Five Plots we started with.

25. Yin, Yang:
The Inward Quest

Tehanu

I'm reading Tolkien's letters, and there's a whole world of ideas there I could talk about — the way his delays must have exasperated his publisher, the way his conscientious committee-sitting and household chores seemed to mire him in pointless makework, and worst of all, that he could lavish so many hundreds of thousands of words on letter writing instead of tackling the dozens of tantalizing projects mentioned in them ... but he may have been a person who developed his ideas via the act of writing them down, in which case the letters helped. And we get to read about his unique creative process as it appeared to him.

He was such a nerd, a nerd's nerd really, and more power to him. I think the 21st century is going to be the Golden Age of nerds anyway. You notice it's all those kids who thought maths camps were the funnest thing who have since grown up to go flying round the world doing interesting work and cycling round France tasting wine in their spare time.

It's interesting that Tolkien had fans the moment *The Lord of the Rings* was published, and they were obsessed about the same details as us. Wondering about who Queen Beruthiel was and why she had so many cats ...

I get called a "Tolkien fan," and it annoys me. "Fan" seems to imply a passive admiration of Tolkien's art, and furthermore I doubt Tolkien himself was a fan of anything much, so it's no way to honor him. His letters give such a sense of the active and participatory way that he admired a vast range of things — philology, dead languages, botany — and the things he learnt grew and changed under the force of his involvement. Not enough to just learn languages, he had to play around with writing his own alliterative poetry (using forms that were only just being rediscovered after centuries of neglect) or create new mythologies. Surely that's meeting knowledge more than halfway, engaging with knowledge until translations and inventions sprouted from it, lived rather than learnt. Tolkien is one of those writers who seems to point towards a way of "living" knowledge, rather than simply collecting it.

Where I live, the winter has a balance point where things decide that, what the heck, it might as well be spring, though it's never gotten quite cold enough to kill anything off before that. If you have roses you have to seize that moment of imminent renewal and prune them. Working my way round the thorny sticks, their buds already fat with potential, I had one of those moments that might not have a name, so I'll call it a moment of comprehension or even apprehension. By that I mean a kind of knowing that is felt unthinking. A knowing-with, not a knowing-of, and it concerned two things I'd been reading.

Tolkien's letters expand a lot on the Elves and their experience of immortality. One letter states that *The Lord of the Rings* contemplated Death and Immortality at its heart. For him the central theme had to do with the mysterious love that mortal beings have for the world they were doomed to leave and the pain of the immortals doomed to stay and witness the whole working of evil in the world they also love (*Letters*, #186).

Another thing the letters mention is the way in which he delighted in words, in their sound and construction. Tolkien spent his whole life from early childhood savoring words for the sheer aesthetic pleasure of a language — not just an appreciation of its beauty, which he could enjoy as well, but something deeper too, like the satisfying of a hunger (*Letters*, #163). In the same letter he describes how discovering a Finnish Grammar, for instance, gave him a thrill as though he'd discovered a cellar full of wines of the most amazing and unexpected flavor.

Now, looking at the rosebuds I suddenly *comprehended* that feeling. The Spanish for "to sprout" is "brotar," and it tastes and feels and sounds more exactly like what I had under my hands than its English equivalent. The word has exactly the kind of ebullient energy that described the potency spring-coiled in each bud. It would be a delight to have more languages and find more words that felt so close to their meaning.

The second comprehension or apprehension related to the Elves and their immortality.

I've made this garden from nothing, and in a few short years it has grown to repay my little efforts with splendid abundance. I made it, and I know it so well that for me next summer's flowers are laid over the winter's dead twigs like a precognition — everything is in embryo, powerful in containment, and utterly untiring.

What would it be like for the Elves, who lavished such love on their garden of Middle-earth, as they once regarded it? Who received this potlatching bounty of flowers as their homage, year on year uncounted? Who saw trees live and die, a mere flicker in their lifespan, the same way I watch one flower grow and fade? Imagine how they would be bound to the land they tended!

I "apprehended" how this endless renewal might also become exhausting to a conscious being that changes little in Time. The contrast of Spring's ferocious energy, year on year, with the sameness of the Elvish experience, must grow wearying and a little frightening.

Tolkien talks about it in *Letter* #181, where he describes the Elves as suffering from a kind of regret for the past and an inability to move forward and embrace change; they are stuck in the world like somebody stuck in a long book that they are tired of, wishing only to settle in one place in the story, their favorite chapter.

When we participate in Tolkien's world, we start to wonder about the huge tales that he left implied at the corners of his stories, where threads lead off into some larger tapestry that we're invited to speculate about. The question of immortality is one.

I was writing about Arwen's story and how interesting it would be if we could have her point of view. But as Tolkien himself said, it was not possible to include her story without destroying the narrative structure of his story, which is a quest romance.

Arwen did have a quest, but hers is a different one, an inward quest, what I'll call a Yin quest. Not an active, fiery Yang quest like you see in Arthurian romances or say, the entire collected works of Goodkind, Gemmell, et. al., where more of the action is busy, external, and leaves a track through the world.

Yin: soft, dark, passive, weak, female, inward .... the Mother, the Valley .... I'm quoting from Ursula Le Guin's translation of *Tao Te Ching* here. If Tolkien had written Arwen's whole story, she wouldn't have *done* any more than she does in *The Lord of the Rings,* but we might have known whether she pricked her finger sewing the banner for Aragorn, and looked at the blood, and considered for the first time that it would one day be finite; a symbol of physical pains that might not heal once she chose mortality.

I imagine Arwen's Quest for the courage to gamble a few decades of mortal love against immortality (and all she might there meet!) would move us through many such symbolic moments. Symbols are the language of poets, and Tolkien knew both his own personal symbols and the icons of a whole literature of Europe. The Yang action in *The Lord of the Rings* is marvelously balanced by the characters' inward search. Frodo and Sam after all have only their own tiny spirits to call on for the endurance to challenge Mordor, and their victory is in the end one of acceptance, endurance and surrender—Yin qualities. That wonderful balance could be seen in Taoist terms, though it might have horrified Tolkien to put it in that way.

One of my favorite writers, and for many of the same reasons, is Ursula Le Guin. If *The Lord of the Rings* is a window into a huge vista, a crowded painting like the ceiling of the Sistine Chapel, then Le Guin's books are like Chinese inkwash drawings, also hinting at vast expanses beyond the borders of the immediate story, but peopled with just a few characters drawn in firm strokes. They travel — most notably Sparrowhawk in his small boat flying on the magewind between the islands of Earthsea — but their quests are tilted more inwards, in the search for self-mastery and for the understanding of balance in the world.

Le Guin is a poet, and I'm always amazed by how much significant action happens in just a few pages, but for that reason her books can seem deceptively *short*. It's magic to be able to write so beautifully, cutting to the essence of each matter with diamond-clear prose, with no words wasted. (Now you can imagine why I find Stephen R. Donaldson's prose so hard to swallow.) As a poet, the action is carried on a series of potent symbols or images. That's a Yin approach to storytelling, I think. Not that people don't go places and fight things, but for instance Sparrowhawk's journey from Roke to Selidor is no longer than his journey between two moments of self-knowledge. Near the beginning:

> ... [he] understood the singing of the bird, and the language of the water falling in the basin of the fountain, and the shape of the clouds,

and the beginning and end of the wind that stirred the leaves: it seemed to him that he himself was a word spoken by the sunlight.

A few chapters later:

Once in that court he had felt himself to be a word spoken by the sunlight. Now the darkness also had spoken: a word that could not be unsaid.

The inward action of the soul is described in these succinct symbolic moments, once again light and dark, like the moments in *LotR* where a last gleam of light reaches under the Mordor pall to touch Frodo at the crossroads of the Morannon; he spies the fallen stone head of the king re-crowned with flowers and says, "They cannot conquer forever." Sam feels the same, spotting a lone star above Ephel Duath. It is so far above and beyond the reach of Sauron and the evils of his day, Sam feels its beauty piercingly, as a beacon of hope even in the forsaken place where they are. The Light against the Dark: almost the small change of symbolism in fantasy literature. It doesn't take a genius to use it, but it's beautiful and moving to see it used well.

I'm always chilled by Le Guin's different vision of Death as the dark slopes into the dry dustlands under a sky of unfamiliar unchanging stars that never set. I'm always moved by Sparrowhawk's return to Life: "… until with a roar of noise and a glory of daylight, and the bitter cold of winter, and the bitter taste of salt, the world was restored to him and he floundered in the sudden, true and living sea." Even in the moment of victory Le Guin does not turn away from the pain of life; there is no "lived happily ever after" for her any more than for Tolkien. The water and the winter are still bitter on Sparrowhawk's return to life.

Like Tolkien, Death and Immortality are consuming interests for Le Guin, and they underlie the Earthsea books as fully as they do Tolkien's work. But when *The Lord of the Rings* came out, she was already enough of an established writer to keep her own individuality in the face of Tolkien's almost overwhelming influence. The third Earthsea book, *The Farthest Shore*, is concerned with the death of magic (and/or the loss of Meaning) when the world is unbalanced by a necromantic grasping after eternal life. For both Tolkien and Le Guin, that's the ultimate greed that reaches outside of what the world can allow. The character Sparrowhawk argues against personal immortality:

"Sparrowhawk reached out and took his hand in a hard grasp, so that both by eye and flesh they touched.

'Lebannen,' he said … 'this is. And thou art. There is no safety. There is no end. The word must be heard in silence. There must be darkness to see the stars. The dance is always danced above the hollow place, above the terrible abyss.'"

Both authors share a sense of the toughness of life and the value of the struggle to do right. Le Guin looks for that reconciliation of light and dark within what Tolkien would call "the circles of the world." The balance must be achieved here, accepting the limits of life and asking no more; not blaming the light for casting a shadow.

> … *For being and nonbeing*
> *arise together;*
> *hard and easy*
> *complete each other;*
> *long and short*
> *shape each other;*
> *note and voice*
> *make music together;*
> *before and after*
> *follow each other.*
> *That's why the wise soul*
> *does without doing,*
> *Teaches without talking…*

— Lao Tzu, *Tao Te Ching*

For Tolkien the balance is achieved in ways beyond our knowing, weighed out by Eru, who sits outside the circles of the world and reveals the fullness of his creation to none. But we are assured that Good and Evil are balanced in His hand.

Some days these appear to me as opposing viewpoints. Other days, I can't see any difference. Tolkien and Le Guin complement each other like the black/white Tao symbol. I'd be poorer for the lack of either of them.

Sources:
Humphrey Carpenter, ed., *The Letters of J.R.R. Tolkien*. Houghton Mifflin, 1995.

From Ursula K. Le Guin's Earthsea series, *A Wizard of Earthsea* and *The Farthest Shore*. Atheneum, reprint edition 1991.

Ursula K. Le Guin, Translator, *Lao Tzu's Tao Te Ching: A Book About the Way and the Power of the Way*. Shambhala Publications, 1998.

26. Literary Sacrilege

Turgon

My desk dictionary defines "sacrilege" as "the misuse, theft, desecration, or profanation of anything regarded as sacred." For many of us, *The Lord of the Rings* is a sacred thing. And here I want to discuss sacrilege specifically in its aspects of desecration and profanation. I am going to discuss a heresy that has been with us for over thirty years in the form of the book *Bored of the Rings*, a parody of *The Lord of the Rings*, by Henry N. Beard and Douglas C. Kenney.

This book first came out in September 1969, and a little background is in order here. *The Lord of the Rings* had come out in paperback in three volumes from Ballantine Books in 1965 and were on the American bestseller lists in 1966-67. The three volumes were latched onto by the so-called hippie generation, spurring various sorts of subway graffiti like "Frodo lives!" and "J.R.R. Tolkien is hobbit-forming." Everyone seemed to be reading Tolkien, and those weirdly panoramic covers by Barbara Remington on the three volumes of the Ballantine edition of *The Lord of the Rings*, with spiky mountains amid red skies and strange lizardy beasts, truly recall that long-ago time of the late 1960s.

The original cover of *Bored of the Rings* is actually a parody of these specific Ballantine covers, even to the point of poking fun at the famous statement on the back of the book by J.R.R. Tolkien (in counter to the pirated Ace Books edition of *The Lord of the Rings*), that "this paperback edition, and no other, has been published with my consent and co-operation. Those who approve of courtesy (at least) to living authors will purchase it, and no other." The version by Beard and Kenney on the parody reads: "This paperback edition, and no other, has been published solely for the purpose of making a few fast bucks. Those who approve of courtesy to a certain author will not touch this gobbler with a ten-foot battle-lance."

So who were Beard and Kenney to attempt to line their own bank accounts with a riff on Tolkien? Wunderkinder at Harvard University, in the first place, but they were also the bastard sons of that irreverent college humor magazine, the *Harvard Lampoon*, where they co-wrote parodies of magazines like *Time* and *Life*. *Bored of the Rings* is reported to have been so successful from the start that it inspired Beard and Kenney (with a third partner) to found the *National Lampoon* in 1970. The three founders had a five-year buyout clause with their financer, and in 1975, Beard took his share of the money and departed. In the years since he has been a very successful writer of books of humor and wordplay, including *Poetry for Cats*, *French for Cats* (and its sequel *Advanced French for Exceptional Cats*), *Latin for All Occasions*, *Zen for Cats*, etc., along with various dictionaries on sailing, gardening, fishing, cooking and golfing.

Kenney, on the other hand, stayed on with *National Lampoon*, and co-wrote the screenplay of *National Lampoon's Animal House* (1978). He even has a bit part in the movie (typically, he played the weirdo Stork). From there he went on to co-write the movie *Caddyshack* (1980), which stars Chevy Chase, Rodney Dangerfield and Bill Murray. Kenney had frequently suffered bouts of depression, and for years he had abused drugs like cocaine. In August 1980, on a visit to Hawaii, he died after falling from a cliff. Suicide has been suggested, but the claim is unproven.

Tolkien purists are quick to scoff at *Bored of the Rings*, and I can't imagine that the Professor himself felt very kindly towards the book, but I confess that I find it hilarious. It's very clever and well thought out, from names (Bilbo Baggins = Dildo Bugger; Frodo = Frito; Tom Bombadil = Tim Benzedrine; Gimli son of Gloin = Gimlet son of Groin, etc.), to specifics of the world, as well as to certain poems and scenes. I immediately think fondly of the wizard Goodgulf (i.e. Gandalf) and his solution to the closed door at the entrance to Moria: "Suddenly the Wizard sprang to his feet. 'The knob,' he cried, and leading the pack sheep over to the base of the gate, stood on its back on tiptoe and turned the great knob with both hands. It turned easily, and with a loud squeaking the door swung open a crack."

Bored of the Rings is a slim book, and while it begins as a close parody of Tolkien's work, the authors knew humor well enough to know that it would by sheer nature become less interesting if it got too long. The part covering the events of *The Fellowship of the Ring* takes up two-thirds of the finished book, leaving only one third in which to cover both *The Two Towers* and *The Return of the King*. Basically, the book tells the story of Frito and some boggies from the Sty who are on a quest to throw the Great Ring into the Zazu Pits of Fordor.

I think it must be admitted that a few sections of *The Lord of the Rings* seem almost to invite parody, and Beard and Kenney have done devastatingly funny things with Tim Benzedrine and Hashberry as druggie versions of Tom Bombadil and Goldberry. And they have also, like Peter Jackson in his film, simplified the plot considerably. Arwen is gone, and the love interest for Stomper (Strider) is a German warrior-woman, Eorache (Eowyn), "daughter of Eorlobe, Captain of der Rubbermark und Thane of Chowder." *Bored of the Rings* has undeniable filmic qualities — hint, hint! — and it would be fascinating someday to see a film version of the parody.

Humor is a personal thing (and some of the humor in *Bored of the Rings* is dated), and many folk can't abide having things they love made fun of. As for me, I'm all for more iconoclasts like Salman Rushdie, whose *Satanic Verses* caused such a stir a decade ago, and James Morrow, author of the truly wicked *Bible Stories for Adults*. I enjoy pulling *Bored of the Rings* off of the shelf every few years for a re-read. Yes, it's irreverent and sophomoric; yes, it's obscene; yes, it's in very bad taste. And no, it doesn't have any of the joy I get from reading Tolkien, but it has a different sort of pleasure. And I don't think I'm alone in thinking this. *Bored of the Rings* has been in print for over three decades, which is a remarkable feat for a parody. It is currently available as a trade paperback with a glammed-up cover. If you're in the mood for a very twisted look at Tolkien, give it a try.

Let me close here with a sample from the opening section to the book, which is a kind of teaser-prologue. This ought to be enough for anyone to figure out if *Bored of the Rings* is a book for them (or decidedly not for them):

> "Do you like what you doth see . . . ?" said the voluptuous elf-maiden as she provocatively parted the folds of her robe to reveal the rounded, shadowy glories within. Frito's throat was dry, though his head reeled with desire and ale.
>
> She slipped off the flimsy garment and strode toward the fascinated

boggie unashamed of her nakedness. She ran a perfect hand along his hairy toes, and he helplessly watched them curl with the fierce insistent wanting of her.

"Let me make thee more comfortable," she whispered hoarsely, fiddling with the clasps of his jerkin, loosening his sword belt with a laugh . . . .

"But I'm so small and hairy, and . . . you're so beautiful," Frito whimpered, slipping clumsily out of his crossed garters.

The elf-maiden said nothing, but only sighed deep in her throat and held him more firmly to her faunlike body. "There is one thing you must do for me first," she whispered into one tufted ear.

"Anything," sobbed Frito, growing frantic with his need. "Anything!"

She closed her eyes and then opened them to the ceiling. "The Ring," she said. "I must have your Ring."

Frito's whole body tensed. "Oh no," he cried, "not that! Anything but . . . that"

"I must have it," she said both tenderly and fiercely. "I must have the Ring!"

Frito's eyes blurred with tears and confusion. "I can't," he said. "I mustn't!"

But he knew resolve was no longer strong in him. Slowly, the elf-maiden's hand inched toward the chain in his vest pocket, closer and closer it came to the Ring Frito had guarded so faithfully ...

Sources:

Henry N. Beard and Douglas C. Kenney, *Bored of the Rings*. New American Library, 1969.

Deep Wells

27. Deep Wells

Tehanu

Writers always get asked: "Where do you get your inspiration?" Wondering what the answer might be in Tolkien's case, it's worth considering Julia Cameron's book on the creative process, *The Artist's Way*. Cameron says that in order to draw on any deep wells of inspiration, you've got to fill those wells up with something else first, whether it's your own experiences or the appreciation of nature or art. Surely in Tolkien's own literary experience there must be a clue to what triggered his imagination? As part of our never-ending quest to find what went into making *The Lord of the Rings*, we had a look at the things that Tolkien himself read.

Not surprisingly, we found that he didn't particularly read a lot of fantasy and science fiction besides the works of his fellow Inklings — like C. S. Lewis's Narnia tales (which Tolkien disliked) and his space travel trilogy (which he did like). I say "not surprisingly" because it's my belief that in order to write something original or profound, a writer had better read *anything* other than existing books like the one they're trying to write. The best fantasy is still written by people who have a passion for many other things besides — history, science, mythology, politics, languages, you name it. The imagination gets fat on reality. The alternative — fantasy written by people who only read fantasy — suffers from a kind of anorexia of the imagination.

In Tolkien's case, he fattened his imagination on a mixture of sharply observed reality and mythology. He took note of Andrew Lang's *Fairy Books* and George Macdonald's fairy-tales, which he read as a child, but the bulk of his interest lay in things that were serious works from ancient cultures. Not, as you'd expect, wild, fantastical distant cultures. It seems that Time itself serves to make his own homeland strange enough.

Tolkien studied almost solely those cultures whose history and mythology had affected his home turf in some way. His heart was bound to a small area of England in the West Midlands, and he was fascinated by the Britons, Celts, Saxons, Vikings and Gaels who'd left a mark there, as well as having a passing interest in the ancient Greek and Roman cultures whose laws and literature cast a feeble light even to those far Western outposts.

C. S. Lewis's comment that "he had been inside language" points to something very special about Tolkien — he understood the past not just as an historian or an archaeologist might understand it, but as a poet of that time. Or to put it another way, he understood the heart and soul of the people whose languages he studied because their words, the words of their bards, expressed as strongly as possible what they considered to be the crux of their human nature and desires. As Lewis said in his obituary for Tolkien, he had "a unique insight at once into the langage of poetry and into the poetry of language."

Sometimes the old texts he studied contained words whose meaning was lost. While pursuing his philological work he would pick away at the discrepancies in translations and imagine how a certain word had come to take the form it had. In the process, stories came to him, as explained in detail in Tom Shippey's outstanding book *J.R.R. Tolkien: Author of the Century*. Shippey makes fascinating reading for anyone interested in how philology, "the love of words," could provide such a rich vein of story materials.

From the moment Tolkien first read of Sigurd and the dragon Fafnir, his heart was turned to the tales and the languages of northern Europe; and if we want to understand how he came to write as he did, it makes sense to look at the Anglo-Saxon world of *Beowulf*, the Norse sagas and the poems of the Eddas, the *Kalevala*, which he loved for the beauty of the Finnish language it was written in, and the Middle English poets.

Further than that I can't follow him. He simply knew too many languages. For instance, his biographer Humphrey Carpenter looked at Tolkien's work on the Oxford English Dictionary and found entries such as "wasp," which he cross-referenced to Old Saxon, Middle Dutch, Modern Dutch, Old High German, Middle Low German, Middle High German, Modern German, Old Teutonic, primitive pre-Teutonic, Lithuanian, Old Slavonic, Russian, and Latin. Presumably Tolkien didn't just know the words of those languages; he could also read the things that were considered worth writing down in all those languages and times. Although time has destroyed much of what must have once existed, the labor and expense of making a manuscript on parchment meant that things did not get written down at all unless they were important.

But without consciously trying, those early writers were also including the commonplace things of their world that strike us now with a strange loveliness. The Vikings and the Anglo-Saxons wrote lovingly of the sea and their ships and their horses; they wrote of the passing of time and the wreck of human hopes by time, fire and sword — all things that are echoed in Tolkien's stories. The *Kalevala* is full of the celebration of nature — something that fascinated Tolkien too, for he was highly aware of the magic of the real world. He knew a great deal of botany, astronomy, geology and history, and yet he linked that to the ancient world's sense of involvement with the natural world of earth, sky and creatures under heaven.

Most of all he loved the speaking creatures, humankind, and all their various forms of language. That empathy and sharp curiosity gave him a deep well of ideas to draw on when he came to write *The Lord of the Rings*.

28. There and Back Again, with Gorbo the Snerg

Turgon

In his 1977 biography of Tolkien, Humphrey Carpenter cited an almost unknown children's book as an influence on *The Hobbit*. The book is *The Marvellous Land of Snergs*, by E.A. Wyke-Smith, and it originally appeared in 1927, some scant few years before Tolkien began writing *The Hobbit*. Carpenter even quotes a letter from Tolkien, who described the book as something of an inspiration for *The Hobbit*, even if only subconsciously. These were enticing references to me, but finding a copy of the book to read proved for a long time impossible.

In *The Annotated Hobbit* (1988), edited by Douglas A. Anderson, there are a few more tantalizing bits about the Snergs book, including the following from the editor's introduction:

> This story concerns the adventures of a Snerg named Gorbo. Snergs are "a race of people only slightly taller than the average table but broad in the shoulders and of great strength."
>
> The Land of the Snergs is described as "a place set apart." There a small colony has been established where children who are uncared for by their parents are taken. The story centers on two children, Joe and Sylvia, who, along with Gorbo, proceed on a rambling adventure into unknown lands; they encounter a reformed ogre who no longer eats children but has become a vegetarian, and a sinister witch named Mother Meldrum . . . .
>
> Its playfulness and humor are strongly suggestive of *The Hobbit*. For example:
>
> "[The Snergs] are great on feasts, which they have in the open air at long tables joined end on and following the turns of the street. This

is necessary because nearly everybody is invited — that is to say, commanded to come, because the King gives the feasts, though each person has to bring his share of food and drink and put it in the general stock. Of late years the procedure has changed owing to the number of invitations that had to be sent; the commands are now understood and only invitations to stay away are sent to the people who are not wanted on the particular occasion. They are sometimes hard up for a reason for a feast, and then the Master of the Household, whose job it is, has to hunt for a reason, such as its being somebody's birthday. Once they had a feast because it was nobody's birthday that day." (*The Marvellous Land of Snergs*, p. 10.)

The Marvellous Land of Snergs has many admirable qualities. It remains a delightful book even today, and ill deserves its sixty-odd years of obscurity. (*The Annotated Hobbit*, pp. 4-5.)

Invitations to stay away? I love the idea! (I can fondly dream of its applicability to many family barbecues ....)

Really, these Snergs do sound an awful lot like the Hobbits that we know and love.

A few years ago *The Marvellous Land of Snergs* was finally reprinted, thus solving the problem of its scarcity. The new edition was published in a very handsome trade paperback by Old Earth Books and has an introduction by the editor of *The Annotated Hobbit*. It includes all of the illustrations by George Morrow from the original edition, which add a visual charm to the book. And on the front cover, there is a new comment by Tolkien on the book recording his and his children's love of E.A. Wyke-Smith's *Marvellous Land of Snergs*. It reads: "I should like to record my own love and my children's love of E.A. Wyke-Smith's *Marvellous Land of Snergs*, at any rate of the snerg-element in that tale, and of Gorbo, the gem of dunderheads, jewel of a companion in an escapade."

If I had needed any other persuasion, that quote in itself would have sold the book to me. And the book itself is a charm! The language is rolling and the humor delightful, and from personal experience I can say that it is a great book to read aloud to children. The Tolkien connections — and there are a few more than just the hobbits — are all well and good, but the book stands on its own merits. It has the true flavor of a fairy-tale, mixing knights and kings with witches and ogres, and there is a truly charming map of the whole adventure by the author's daughter, which reminds me a bit of Ernest Shepard's panoramic maps accompanying *Winnie the Pooh* and *The Wind in the Willows*.

The further points of similarity with *The Hobbit* come in when Gorbo, Sylvia and Joe get lost in the Twisted Trees, which will remind Tolkien readers of Bilbo and his party getting lost in Mirkwood. Another of George Morrow's illustrations looks especially Tolkienesque — it could easily stand for Gandalf riding on a pony, but it's actually the villain of the story, Mother Meldrum, in disguise.

The Marvellous Land of Snergs has plenty of attractions for fans of *The Hobbit*, and there are many reasons to recommend it beyond the Tolkien connection. In fact, my favorite part of the book has no Tolkien connection at all, but it is rife with real fairy-tale richness. It's the part where Gorbo goes hunting in the forest at night for true mandrakes — the true ones are distinguished from the spurious ones because they squeak when you pull them out of the ground in the moonlight! There is even an appropriately atmospheric illustration by George Morrow to go with this episode.

Several months after posting the above review of *The Marvellous Land of Snergs*, I was delighted to receive a friendly e-mail about my comments from the author's grandson, Charles Wyke-Smith. Mr. Wyke-Smith graciously agreed to answer some questions, and I'm pleased to share some of his replies below.

Q. Tell us about your grandfather's book and your own connections with it.

A. My grandfather's book, *The Marvellous Land of Snergs*, was published by Ernest Benn in September of 1927 and was the eighth and last one he wrote before his death in 1935.

It tells the story of two small children, Joe and Sylvia, who have been rescued from their different but equally awful lives by a Miss Watkyns, who runs The Society for the Removal of Superfluous Children, which is located in a "world apart." She transports the children there, where they join numerous other children saved from bad circumstances. The two children are always up to mischief together and end up meeting Gorbo the Snerg and getting into a series of adventures with him.

The Snergs are a race of dwarf-like people who love to feast and enjoy life, and many aspects of the Snergs can be seen in Tolkien's *The*

Hobbit published in 1937. Tolkien himself wrote of his children's love of the story, and apparently they even made up Snerg stories of their own.

Tolkien, in a letter to W. H. Auden in 1955, mentioned that his children enjoyed The Hobbit, then adds in a footnote that the Snergs book was an unconscious source for Hobbits (see *The Letters of J.R.R. Tolkien*, edited by Humphrey Carpenter, p. 215).

My grandfather's books were on the bookcases at home, and I particularly loved two of them — *The Last of the Baron*, about three young boys from London sent to kill an evil baron in the north of England in medieval times, and *Some Pirates and Marmaduke*, a wonderful and rather unusual pirate story. I kept starting *The Marvellous Land of Snergs,* but I was in my late teens before I pushed past the rather strange beginning and discovered what an imaginative and original story it was.

Q. What did you and your family think of Tolkien's works before it became publicized that Tolkien had much admired your grandfather's book, and that his Hobbits are, in terms of literature, closely related to your grandfather's Snergs?

A. I loved *Lord of the Rings* as a teenager and read it several times. I've always known through my aunt that there was a connection between my grandfather and Tolkien and that Tolkien's children had liked the Snergs story, but really it was only when I read the book again after it had been re-published that I really saw how many parallels there were.

Q. What do you and your family think of Tolkien now?

A. The Tolkien connection has served to get my grandfather's book out of years of obscurity, and that is very gratifying. That said, my Aunt Nina has always felt that Tolkien simply saw how much his children loved the Snergs book and so took all of the parts he liked about the story and used them as the basis for *The Hobbit*.

And certainly, you don't have to look far to see numerous connections between the Hobbits and the Snergs — in their physical descriptions, their love of communal feasting, the numerous similar locations through which the heroes of the two stories travel, such as dangerous forests and underground caverns, and even the heroes' names — Gorbo and Bilbo — indicate to me that Tolkien must at least have been influenced by Snergs.

I think perhaps that when Tolkien read *Snergs*, which we know he did, the sense of place and the characters stuck with him, and when he was inspired to write *The Hobbit*, these influences came through in his story.

Also, very similar use of the author's voice in *The Hobbit*, meaning where the writer addresses the reader directly, and in the ironic style of the humor, are to me less obvious but stronger indications of the influence the Snergs story had on him, as if Snergs provided a basis for a stylistic framework in which he could tell the story of *The Hobbit*.

Of course, Tolkien took the "world apart" concept much further in creating Middle-earth and combined it with many other ideas. Also, the success of *The Hobbit* inspired him to write *Lord of the Rings*, one of the greatest fictional novels of the twentieth century, to which he gave a sweeping sense of scale and linguistic and historical dimensions that *Snergs* simply does not have.

So although I have a more open-minded point of view than some family members, it's not unreasonable for anyone who has read both books to think that Tolkien used Snergs as more than an "unconscious source" for *The Hobbit*. At the same time, if Tolkien did indeed draw ideas from *Snergs* for *The Hobbit*, by the time he got to *Lord of the Rings*, he had certainly elevated them to a far more sophisticated level.

Comparing the two, Tolkien's book is certainly more accessible. My Edwardian grandfather's strong and often parental-sounding "author's voice" throughout the Snergs story, and the somewhat rambling opening make it slow going at first, unlike *The Hobbit,* which introduces its main characters very quickly and gets right into the story. So I can see why *The Hobbit* was such an instant success and *Snergs* slipped into years of obscurity.

Q. You have recently written a screenplay of *The Marvellous Land of Snergs*. Tell us a bit about the problems and pleasures in translating a book from one medium to another.

A. Firstly, regardless of my family connection to it, I find *The Marvellous Land of Snergs* to be very entertaining and humorous — the characters are so well drawn and the outcomes of their actions so well matched to their personalities that you just have to laugh out loud in many places.

The problem that I considered long and hard before I started the screenplay was that the story is made much less accessible by the long narrative opening and some of the rather old-fashioned writing, references and moralizing.

So I decided that if I just focused on telling the story, letting the characters speak for themselves and starting them on their adventures right from page one that I could perhaps release this wonderful story from the rather outdated style of the book.

The limitations of using only action and dialogue can make screenplay writing very demanding; you can't write "He felt very sad" as you can in a book, because you can't film that — you have to write action or dialogue that shows the character is sad.

But with *Snergs*, that's exactly how the book is written; once it gets under way, there's lots of action and dialogue (which is also why it's such an easy read after that point), and where there wasn't any, it wasn't too tough to create it from the descriptive parts, because the characters were so well defined that I had a good basis on which to decide how a character might speak or act in a given circumstance.

The beginning was the toughest challenge. The first 24 pages of the book that set up the story have virtually no dialogue at all, so I spent almost four weeks (of the four months it took to get to a first draft of the script) planning and trying ideas for what turned out to be the script's first 10 pages.

However, once I started to see the story unfold in the script, it became very exciting and I would spend long days with my grandfather's book and my laptop, slowly inching forward and just retelling the story within the script format as faithfully as I could. Much to my surprise, I kept most of the dialogue as is. I'd expected to have to re-write large chunks, but the dialogue "speaks" very easily and realistically, each character with his or her own speaking style, so my grandfather obviously had a great ear for the way people talk.

There was another unexpected pleasure I got from writing this script. I never met my grandfather and only knew of him from photographs and family anecdotes, but as I worked on the script, I felt his personality so strongly evoked in his words, which of course I read and reread in excruciating detail, that it was like actually getting to meet him in some way. Anyone who has read a book and felt the presence of the writer, which probably includes a lot of Tolkien fans, will know what I mean.

Q. One of the charms of the book is the author's wry style. Do you think that translates well in a script?

A. Yes, I do, although I think you get the strongest sense of that wryness in the extensively used authorial voice, specially at the book's opening and close — stuff like "It occurs to me here that there is some difficulty in providing a really useful moral from this tale ..." etc etc. I made a conscious decision not to go down the obvious and rather clichéd path of having a narrated voiceover take the author's part and to drop that whole aspect of the book and only retain the story.

However, within the story itself, that same ironic humor is there in the character's actions and dialogue, even though perhaps it's not so obvious as in the author's comments to the reader, and so that did translate very well.

In working with the book, I found my grandfather had given real dimensionality to the characters — each is very individual and clearly drawn and has their own strengths and weakness — and I finally realized it's the characters' actions that are truly at the heart of humor in *Snergs*, and that humor not only translates, but can actually be intensified in the screenplay format because a screenplay is a very action-based medium.

Q. How do you see your screenplay of *The Marvellous Land of Snergs* being made into a film — as an animated film, or a live-action one? And what might be the pros and cons of each way?

A. I think I really see it as live action — I even had specific locations in mind, in Devon and in Derbyshire, England, where I grew up, as I was writing.

That said, a live-action version will still require some special effects, but not so much of the whiz-bang variety — particularly, I want to represent the Snergs as George Morrow's imaginative and wonderful illustrations depicts them and as my grandfather describes them: "only slightly taller than the average table but broad in the shoulders and of great strength," and not simply slightly modify real people as Jackson did with the hobbits, so that will probably require computer-generated characters to be combined with live action.

I saw Hallmark's *Dinotopia* on TV this week, which showed just how far that technique has come, with a very believable sequence of a small computer-generated dinosaur playing ping-pong with a real person — if only the simplistic and predictable storyline had been as sophisticated.

Snergs is set in rolling countryside, moorlands and mountains, and I think when your story is set a real-looking world, then go with live action, which seems more real to the audience simply because it *is* real, and use the animation effects to enhance and modify when you reach the limitations of the real world to convey the story's vision. Perhaps Peter Jackson came to that same conclusion when he decided to use primarily real locations rather than computer-generated settings for LotR, although he clearly used massive computing power when he needed it. Ultimately, it doesn't matter to me how the end result is achieved; I just want to see the movie made, and made well.

Finally, I want to say that while the Tolkien connection is very tantalizing and certainly has caused a lot of interest in my grandfather's book recently, I think the subject is somewhat academic. I know I will be forever quizzed about my feelings on the suggestions that Tolkien "ripped Snergs off," was subconsciously influenced by, based Bilbo on Gorbo, and so on, but there is little to be gained from such debate.

I think *The Lord of the Rings* is a true literary masterpiece, and if my grandfather's book in any way set Tolkien on the path to writing it, then I see that as a cause for pride for me and my family rather than any resentment. What is gratifying is to discover that so many people are once again enjoying Grandfather's book, and I would love to see it made into what I believe would be a marvelous movie.

Sources:

E.A. Wyke-Smith, *The Marvellous Land of Snergs*. Reprint edition, Old Earth Books, 1995.

Douglas A. Anderson, ed., *The Annotated Hobbit*. Houghton Mifflin, 1988.

Humphrey Carpenter, ed., *The Letters of J.R.R. Tolkien*. Houghton Mifflin, 1995.

29. Beowulf, Icelandic Sagas, & the Genesis of Middle-earth

Tehanu

Scores of people wrote in to defend Iceland's national literature when one of my online articles described it as "dull," and I learned a lot from them. I've learned so much more about *Beowulf* too since the first time I read it, looking for some secret of the genesis of Middle-earth. I was looking for the wrong things, and realized it when I finally tracked down a copy of *Beowulf: The Monsters and the Critics*, which is the written record of a speech that Tolkien gave to the British Academy in 1936. It's crunchy reading, but reveals a great deal about how *Beowulf* influenced the writing of *The Lord of the Rings*.

One of the things it makes very clear is that Tolkien was aware of something that certain critics dislike about his own work:

> But there is also, I suppose, a real question of taste involved: a judgement that the heroic or tragic story on a strictly human plane is by nature superior. Doom is held less literary than ἁμαρτία *["amartia," which I can only translate loosely as "sin" or "failing" -Tehanu]* The proposition seems to have been passed as self-evident. I dissent, even at the risk of being held incorrect or not sober.

What I believe he is saying is this: at the time of his address to the British Academy, the prevailing critical opinion put a high value on the kind of tale where the action is driven by the conflicted hero and most especially by the tragic flaw in the makeup of the hero. In that genre, the hero is not "doomed" to fail because of some outside force, such as

Fate or the fate-weaving Norns of Northern myth. Nor is he confronted with evil in the form of a monster or supernatural antagonist. According to that prevailing critical opinion, stories have more literary merit if they portray the fall of a hero due to their own internal weaknesses. Less value is given to stories where the hero fights against magical evil itself. The kind of story where the hero is pitted against his Fate or doom is un-modern, and Tolkien is knowingly swimming against the tide by embracing it as a worthwhile artform. Tolkien's stories are exactly so — filled with dooms and prophecies that their heroes must carry out.

Tolkien's great essay goes on to argue why *Beowulf* is a great work of literature despite the monsters that uphold the central conflict. In doing so he gives away some important hints about the composition of *The Lord of the Rings*.

Before biting into the crunchy bits of the essay, I want to talk about what first struck me about it. This is the work of a very intelligent, well-read man, and I don't think we get many insights into his brilliance quite as accessible as this one, where he is talking about his chosen field of study to a gathering of some of the finest minds in the same field. It is revelatory to see how Tolkien would flip between languages with apparent spontaneity, and presumably his audience would be expected to follow him as he dropped in a word of Greek here, a bit of Latin there, some German, a bit of Middle English banter and of course a lot of Old English, since this is the language *Beowulf* was written in, some time between the 7th and 10th century AD.

Along with that he marshals a diverse pile of books to illustrate his argument, sometimes seriously, sometimes in jest — this would have been a fun lecture to hear, if you'd been able to keep up with the pace. As well as the expected Old and Middle English texts and their critics, he mentions in passing Shakespeare, Homer, Milton, the *Aeneid*, and even describes his fellow academics in terms drawn amusingly from Lewis Carroll's poem *Jabberwocky*. I found that interesting because it fed my idea that Tolkien was more widely read than most people realize, and if he ignored or discarded modern preferences when he wrote his own books, it was done consciously.

For me, reading *Beowulf* wasn't easy, and ditto for the Icelandic Sagas. My first attempts kept me thinking about the effort it takes to read things like that, which were Tolkien's lifeblood. For me in the 21st century to look at the world of *Njal's Saga* or *Beowulf* took a leap of the imagination far beyond what it takes to read most fantasy literature, of which "sensible" people say, "Oh, it's so unconnected with everyday life."

The world of Njal and Beowulf is the real world, or was, and yet it seems further and stranger than half the fantasy novels I've read, whose main characters could come and live here and now; they'd adapt in no time. McDonald's and a nine-to-five job, thank you very much.

The characters in those sagas would never adapt, they would never compromise their suicidal honor, their crazy passionate ideals, their love of glory and of courage for courage's sake. We would never understand them or they us, and they'd kill everyone for reasons that we couldn't fathom. The only things I've read lately that achieve the same sense of "otherness" in a race of people are Paul Park's *Soldiers of Paradise* (check out his antinomial berserkers as they go singing into battle!) and Mary Doria Russell's *The Sparrow*.

In the sagas and *Beowulf* you have to do the work of getting your mind into that world yourself ... but then, the sagas were read or spoken aloud to a group, and the bard could do with his eyes and hands and voice and silences what it would take Stephen R. Donaldson three "Refulgents," two "Scintillatings," four "Suppuratings" and an "Orotund" to achieve — which is why sentences in *Njal's Saga* can afford to be shorter.

I also imagine that in a saga that is read aloud, the listeners' responses save the writer from having to witter on about fiery hearts like red-hot cauldrons of seething hatred, etc. etc. Imagine a saga being read aloud:

> "And so Thord fell dead," said the bard.
> There was outrage amongst his listeners.
> "No! Not Thord?! He was my favorite character!" cried one.
> "Well, that Thorgeir better watch out, the cowardly scum, he'll get his comeuppance soon, I hope!"
> Everyone in Thorstead denounced Thorgeir bitterly until the bard was able to continue ...

You have to remember that the original audience for the sagas were descended from and related to characters in the stories, so that they had a memoryhoard of family characteristics to identify each character where we see only a wilderness of Thords and Thorgeirs.

All of which is off the track from *The Lord of the Rings,* but does remind us that while Tolkien's vocabulary was larger than most, his style is not highly ornamented. He spends little time on clever language but ensures that the story is told clearly. You always know where you are, what it looks like, what is happening, and who is speaking.

While the Icelandic sagas don't waste words on describing a place that all the listeners knew anyway, they, Tolkien and *Beowulf* share a strong *sense* of place and a preference for being understated rather than overwrought.

Some copies of *Beowulf* are set up so that each left-hand page is in Old English, and it looks like gibberish. And then certain words start to spring out. "Wealle" becomes "wall," "scild" becomes "shield," and suddenly there are a raft of familiar words: the Eorlingas, Theoden (once I'd figured out the odd rune standing for "th") and Thengel ... not as names now, but titles and nouns: Prince, hero, warrior ... (Old English scholars'll get mad, I'm being indiscriminate here!) Eomer turns up as a prince, and so do the *mearas,* the horses of Rohan in elder days.

And then the lovely line, "On him the mail-coat shone, an armour net woven by a smith's ingenuity."

The word for "ingenuity" appears to be "orthancum." Orthanc is the tower of wizards ... or of skill, cunning ... ingenuity. Orthanc. Suddenly *Beowulf* seems very familiar: old heirlooms are "mathoms," the floor is "flet" ... There is a scene where Beowulf and his troop come to the golden hall of Heorot, and lay their arms outside as custom demands, and go in to offer their services to the king to cleanse the land of evil, and the king's advisor Unferth attempts to discredit them ... it was surely in Tolkien's mind when he described the arrival of Aragorn and the others to Theoden's hall.

Except that Tolkien's characters are facing a different kind of evil. No single monster but an alliance of dark forces governed by a single calculating will. They can't offer to kill Sauron with their bare hands like Beowulf does Grendel, in fulfilment of a boast. In a way, the humble hobbits (miles away from Theoden's mead hall at this point) are a rebuke to such Beowulfian boasting, since that is also what they do in the end: defeat evil unarmed.

Beowulf is really beautiful, and Tolkien used his famous British Academy lecture to remind people of that. How those people loved the sea! "The swan's road, the gannet's bath, the whale's way." They spoke of their ships "… floating foamy-necked over the waves like a bird." Some things were common figures of speech back then that strike us with their novelty now. Things like, "Then he answered him, unlocked his word-hoard…"

The great thing about *Beowulf* and the Icelandic sagas is their sense of personal courage against the odds, against the "doom" that is laid upon their central characters. Their values are not our values; we don't believe our lives are spun out by the Fates or that we should die before allowing one skerrick of our pride to be marred. Opposites attract: Tolkien found the sagas' heroes a model that he freely admitted he could not emulate when he himself went to war. Not many could.

The first time I read the sagas, I asked, "How can anyone write a story with hundreds of characters all called Thord and the main characters die about two-thirds of the way through?" Every few chapters, one would get killed in the following manner:

"Thjostolf raised his axe a second time and drove it into Thorvald's head, killing him instantly," and variations thereof. Sometimes you get more detail about collarbones shattering, legs being severed, and blood gushing into lungs. I rather preferred lines like:

"He snatched up a spear and hurled it at Hrut's ship. The man who was in its way fell dead." Deadly understatement. When I came to think about it more, this is very much in the vein of Legolas and Gimli's competition at Helm's Deep, where they keep a casual, lighthearted tally of the orcs they've killed. But we know — and this is Tolkien's skill as an author — that their apparent sangfroid is a game of manners, a kind of chivalric manner, which hides the desperate danger and fear of death that everyone would really be feeling. Death'll always get you in the end, so all you can do is hold on to your pride until the very end. I call it "battle panache," and the Icelandic sagas show again and again how far that was admired in that culture. In *Njal's Saga*, Thorgrim the Easterner climbs up onto the roof of Gunnar's house, which he is besieging. Gunnar strikes him with his halberd through the window. Thorgrim drops his shield, slips, and falls off the roof. He strides over to where the other besiegers are sitting.

"Is Gunnar at home?" one of them asks.

"That's for you to find out," replied Thorgrim. "But I know that his halberd certainly is." And with that he fell dead.

In Tolkien's essay *The Monsters and the Critics,* he talks about the heroic temper of the North, which he saw in both the Sagas and in *Beowulf* (and another revelation to me in that essay was his conviction of English superiority — one of his conservative quirks that would be less warmly received nowadays).

Another great early English poem, *The Battle of Maldon* (dealing with a catastrophic defeat), ends with the lines, "Will shall be the sterner, heart the bolder, spirit the greater as our strength lessens." This is the reigning sentiment of much Anglo-Saxon and Norse literature, and Tolkien comments that these words "... are not, of course, an exhortation to simple courage." Nor do they persuade us to hope that victory is the reward of an indomnitable will. Tolkien believes that those words are meant to school the warrior to continue the struggle even past the death of hope.

He says that one of the outstanding features of Northern literature is the "theory of courage" that those lines embody. Heroic lays show,

> ... the exaltation of undefeated will ... but though with sympathy and patience we might gather, from a line here or a tone there, the background of the imagination which gives to this indomitability, this paradox of defeat inevitable yet unacknowledged, its full significance, it is in *Beowulf* that a poet has devoted a whole poem to the theme, so that we may see man at war with the hostile world, and his inevitable overthrow in Time.

Beowulf, according to Tolkien, does center the story that way; it means to show how man is set against the hostile world, doomed to be defeated with the passage of time. This is very much the sense that Tolkien conveys in his history of Middle-earth, which is, as he would put it, a tale of a long defeat, for evil is never banished from the world; Elrond says he has seen three ages come and go with many defeats and many fruitless victories, and through all the slow decline of the glory and magic that was.

Tolkien believed that the world was and always would be in decline since the Fall in the Garden of Eden, and he recognized both the sense of hopelessness in the old Northern works and the belief that one must stand against the dark, against evil, no matter how hopeless the odds. In Catholic belief, failure to do so is a sin; to the old Norsemen, it makes your name mud forever.

The prevailing opinion about *Beowulf,* prior to Tolkien, was that it was a well-written poem dealing with a trivial story — a hero's defeat of some folkloric monsters, namely Grendel and a very Smaug-like dragon. In passing the poem mentions some famous events in Scandinavian history — feuds, the rise and fall of various kings, some limited genealogies. But these important events are at the fringes of the story, and the monsters at the center. Most people thought that was a mistake and reacted as if Milton had decided to set a children's fairy-tale to great poetry. Tolkien goes on to say that they forgot to wonder whether Milton's treatment of such a simple story might not have affected the trivial theme and lent it some weight. Whatever dragons and monsters may represent, the truth is that people are still writing stories about them; they are not writing stories about the historic feuds of the Scyldings also mentioned in *Beowulf.*

Tolkien recalled that people of the dark ages lived their lives bound within small limits, hardly larger than the light cast by their primitive hall fires; the surrounding dark was wholly hostile, and they had little more than their own courage with which to tackle the "monsters" outside. They knew that the children of the dark defeat the greatest champions and highest lords in the end. For Beowulf it is enough of a tragedy simply to be a man, and mortal, according to Tolkien. And the monsters are both real adversaries and symbols of the forces of chaos that hate life and laughter. Tolkien did not feel this was a trivial theme.

This same melancholy pervades Middle-earth and gives it much of its power to move us. Not that I want to persuade you that *The Lord of the Rings* is a book full of misery; it is not, largely because the tale is told from the hobbits' viewpoint and they are by nature optimists who truly know how to enjoy the present and don't dwell on the past.

The past is brought up again and again in *Beowulf* — mostly by bards singing at Beowulf's victory feasts — and Tolkien realized how the writer used those historical references to give his story a sense of truth, a sense that it was based on the real world. Merely alluding to some of the dramatic events of the past, the old feuds and wars that Beowulf's listeners would already know, gave the story a place to stand among these events that were already old when the poem was written. It made the story part of a pattern made up of still more ancient stories, some of them true. The people in the story remember their own history.

This is the pattern that Tolkien followed in *The Lord of the Rings*. From the very beginning the reader is treated to songs and sayings that are thrown in, beginning in the first chapter with the very local history of hobbit genealogy, customs and folklore, and leading up to the great Elvish lays, sometimes untranslated, which hint at the vast wilderness of history underlying the visible action of *The Lord of the Rings*.

A lot of people have wondered how Tolkien, a devout Christian, could write at such length about a world in which Christianity is not part of the history. *Beowulf* gives a clue to how he approached that, for it was written long after the time in which the story is set. It was written by a literate and therefore almost certainly Christian person, most likely a monk, yet all the characters in it are of the old, pagan order of heroes, and the writer never allows them to have direct knowledge of anything else. His own comments may be interpolated — as in his description of Grendel as part of the Biblical Cain's clan, condemned by the Almighty — but they are separate from the knowledge of the people in the poem, who sometimes prayed for help at pagan shrines, for "such was their way" in those times. They praise the Almighty, but Whom they so name is left untold. The poet, whoever he was, understood the way that his forebears thought and respected it.

Tolkien imagined forebears from an even more distant past who populated Middle-earth, part of our history but not yet involved with the workings of Scripture. Tolkien simply acts as the scribe who comes later but who separates his own beliefs from the history he's recording. In *The Monsters and the Critics*, Tolkien talks about his interest in the fusion of the old heroic lays and the way they were understood by writers who came later after contact with the stories of the Scriptures. At this transitional period, the old monsters and dragons were not quite like medieval demons, out for your soul, or symbols of evil that the soul must struggle with — they were physical creatures walking on the earth as well.

The Northern imagination, as Tolkien put it, put the monsters in the center, giving them victory but no honor. In their myths, the gods themselves are doomed, and they enlist mankind in their battle against the monsters of the dark. This is a contrast with the myths of the ancient Greeks, for instance, which make mankind pawns in the pointless whims and feuds of their gods. There is no sense of one side ranged mightily against the dark — a division that gave the Northern mythical imagination such enduring power.

There are two places in the essay where Tolkien mentions with regret that we do not know the pre-Christian English mythology as we do that of Finland or Scandinavia. Link that to his famous remark that he created Middle-earth because he wanted to make a mythology for England, and you suspect that he went on from there to apply the same process that philologists use for tracking down the origin of a word. If you have two similar words for the same thing in two related languages, you can extrapolate what the original root word must have been farther back in time before the two languages diverged, provided you know the way in which languages tend to evolve.

Tolkien was doing a similar thing by looking at the shreds of Old English tales that survived the Norman invasion, and the much more fully preserved mythology of Scandinavia, and extrapolating from them what England's mythology might have been in the more distant past. This was the seed from which Middle-earth grew.

Sources:

J. R .R. Tolkien/edited by Christopher Tolkien, *The Monsters and the Critics and Other Essays,* Houghton Mifflin, 1984.

Trans. Magnus Magnusson & Hermann Pálsson, *Njal's Saga,* Penguin Classics/Penguin Books, 1960.

Trans. Michael Swanton, *Beowulf.* St. Martin's Press, 1997.

30. "Breathed Through Silver"

Anwyn

I have fielded inquiries from many readers over the years who are struggling with the relationship between *The Lord of the Rings* and Christianity. Several readers have wanted to impart Christlike qualities to various characters, notably Frodo, Aragorn, and Gandalf. Others seem to regard the whole of the story as a Christian allegory much in the mold of C. S. Lewis's *The Chronicles of Narnia*, ignoring the views of Tolkien himself upon allegory. While it seems obvious that there are Christian elements throughout Tolkien's myths, to assume along the lines of the above interpretations would be at best wishful thinking and at worst a consummate disregard for the way Tolkien operated, the places in which he found inspiration, and the ways in which he used it.

Tolkien's opinion of allegory such as Lewis employed in the *Chronicles* is well known. Lewis depicted a world of anthropomorphic animals, most notably Aslan, the Great Lion, who is from beginning to end a perfect, if slightly simplified for children, icon of Jesus Christ, including his suffering and sacrificial death at the hands of wicked creatures and his subsequent resurrection.

Tolkien gave a poor review of Lewis's Narnia stories. Whereas the purpose of most of Lewis's later writings was to defend and propagate Christianity, Tolkien's spiritual views were held much more privately and kept between himself and God, his family, and his intimate friends. Moreover, he vilified the mode of expression Lewis chose. He said in the foreword to *The Lord of the Rings* that he disliked allegory of all kinds, much preferring what he called "applicability," which leaves the reader free to draw conclusions or notice analogies. Allegory, he felt, intends to put the reader's thinking more firmly under the author's thumb. He mellowed enough to admit that allegorical language is the natural mode of trying to explain the meaning of a myth or fairy-tale. He added that a story with a great deal of internal "life" has the tendency to breed allegorical interpretations (*Letters,* #131). But he still adhered to the notion that his mind did not work allegorically. Thus we see right away that any attempt to fashion the tale of *The Lord of the Rings* or any other of his works into a wholesale allegory falls flat as regards the stated intention of the author.

Yet it is undeniable that elements of Christian thought and even Biblical story everywhere abound in Tolkien. The creation story outlined in the beginning of *The Silmarillion*, the concept of an "Eden" and exile from it in the story of the Elves and Valinor, the creation and fall of imperfect man in the story of unhappy Númenor, the isolation and paradoxical leadership responsibilities of Aragorn, the sacrificial death and resurrection of Gandalf ... the list is virtually endless. A concrete reason for this emerges from a study of Tolkien's letters and of the dialogue between Tolkien and Lewis that eventually helped lead the latter to Christianity.

I've stated elsewhere that Tolkien wrote what he knew. He was in a very particular place intellectually and spiritually; he was a profoundly religious Catholic who at the same time made the study of non-Christian myth and legend his dearest hobby and even a professional study. Though bonded with Lewis in a love of "northernness" — that is, the stories of the medieval Norsemen — he was also, like Lewis, grounded in the mythology of other peoples and lands. And perhaps partially as a result of his studies, he included the Christian story under the heading of "myth," though he regarded it, unlike other myths, as one he believed to be literally and historically true. It was his pet theory that all myth sprang from the well of "sub-creation," and when Lewis was struggling with the leap from belief in God to definite belief in Christianity, it was Tolkien who tried to help Lewis understand that he did not have to give up a certain form of belief in the power of non-Christian myths in order to become a Christian.

Lewis derived his quandary from what he perceived as a breakdown of logic. He believed in the power of myths as beautiful stories but looked upon them in the end as human-invented lies "and therefore worthless, even though breathed through silver" (Lewis quoted by author Humphrey Carpenter, *The Inklings*, p. 46). Conversely, even if he believed in the historical truth of the death and resurrection of Jesus Christ, he failed to see its relevance or how to believe in it on a deeper level.

It was Tolkien who postulated the idea that non-Christian myths did not have to be dismissed as lies *and* that the Christian myth, despite its ultimate truth, still retained the mystical qualities and the human resonance of a legendary story. Tolkien believed that the story of Christ was the ultimate expression of myth, perpetuated by God, and that all other myths were derived at least in part from this central true myth. He contended that man was a sub-creator of the story under God and thus spun out the timeless saga, or parts of it, in various forms from the beginning of human time.

Thus by conflating what he saw as the central truth of all myth (the sacrificial god) with its essential beauty as story, Tolkien drew Christianity and myth together down a new path, one that embraced the ancient legends of mankind with his deeply held belief in one God. He talked of this in a letter to his son Christopher. In speaking of persons who under outside pressure had given up any form of believing in Judeo-Christian "myths" like Creation or Eden, he says they have in consequence lost sight of the beauty in those myths (*Letters*, #96). Essentially his whole argument was that untrue myths can be spiritual nourishment as stories, while the beauty of a good story should not be forgotten even in the true myth of Christ.

Since Tolkien deliberately set out to write a mythology for England, it would have been impossible for him to produce any such thing without myriad references to the myths he already knew, both Christian and otherwise. He admitted as much, yet insisted that the ways that an author's life feeds into the stories he creates are ill understood. He felt that one can only guess at those complex processes of transformation. He says this in the foreword to *The Lord of the Rings*, in attempting to fend off speculation that the story can be equated to the circumstances and events of World War II. But perhaps it is not entirely hopeless to discuss a few of what are seemingly the most attractive "allegory theories" under the light of Tolkien's beliefs about myth and his Christian experience.

Though we have already shown that to assume a wholesale allegory out of *The Lord of the Rings* is impossible, still there are specific elements that commend themselves very earnestly to allegorical examination. By far the most popular submitted for the consideration of Green Books staff is the idea that either Frodo, Gandalf, or Aragorn is a Christ figure. To me, the very fact that there are Christlike elements seen in *each* of these characters already completely belies any allegorical intentions. A more perfect allegory surely would have chosen only one. Still it is worthwhile to understand which characteristics of each seem to beckon the Christ comparison.

The weakest among these arguments is that on Frodo's behalf. Looking at Frodo's pastoral innocence, his subsequent reluctant assumption of crushing responsibility, and his passage from naïveté to world-weariness, it's hard to see any direct correlation to Christ. Those who have postulated it to me seem to be trying very hard to equate the destruction of the Ring with the death of certain parts of Frodo's personality; thus he becomes in a sense a sacrifice for the good of the world. While it is true that Frodo made sacrifices, the loss of his time and his happiness pale in comparison with the torture and death of Christ, and while Frodo's plight tugs our hearts, it is important to remember that at the last it was not he who deliberately and knowingly made the ultimate sacrifice — of the Ring and with it the parts of himself over which the Ring had gained ascendency. He was unable to do so, and other powers took a hand. In contrast, Christ's will stayed the course and followed the divine plan — a plan he was privy to from the beginning, whereas Frodo had no foreknowledge of his fate. A comparison between the two inevitably breaks down.

A slightly stronger case can be made for Aragorn. The phrase "son of Man" used so often about Christ rings ominously close to home with the heir of Isildur. The descendent of David was the heir to the kingship of Israel, just as Aragorn was in line to claim the kingship of Gondor. Both were born in obscurity and raised with the knowledge of what they were; each had a responsibility to lead men to the good. But where Jesus eschewed an earthly throne to follow God's plan for his human life, the plan for Aragorn's life *was* the kingship. He proceeded towards it cautiously, striving to do even more than his duty along the way, in order to purge any false motives and be sure that he could claim his destiny with a pure heart. But the fact remains that Aragorn was an earthly king, not an otherworldly one.

Speaking of otherworldly, how about Gandalf? The most obvious choice to represent Christ in an allegory theory, he carried out the ultimate Christ imitation: he suffered, was buried and died; after a certain number of days he rose again to bring judgment to the living and the dead. ("Was buried" and "died" are deliberately reversed from the Christian creed; Gandalf was for all intents buried in the pit with the Balrog before his physical form actually perished, as opposed to Christ, who "died and was buried.") His sacrifice was for the good of the Fellowship and therefore for the good of all the Free Peoples of Middle-earth, just as Christ's sacrifice was for all of humankind.

Yet even with this eerie similarity, there comes a point where the comparison will go no further: namely that Gandalf was not God in human form, but a created being subordinate not only to Ilúvatar but also to his intermediaries, the Valar. Some might consider the distinction trivial; after all, Gandalf was an immortal spirit and the closest thing to a manifestation of a god that the Hobbits, certainly, would ever see.

But to me the distinction is crucial. Tolkien is very careful not to step past the bounds of *sub*-creation; he does not cross the line into godmaking. He is very conscious that Gandalf is a created being and as such is subject to the will of Ilúvatar; moreover, it was not through any premeditated plan of sacrifice (as was Christ's death) but through a series of circumstances that Gandalf met his death, and Tolkien implies that Ilúvatar took his time in considering whether Gandalf would be allowed to return. God had foreseen the necessity of his descent into humanity as Jesus Christ and his subsequent sacrifice; Gandalf, for all his worth, was merely another created player in the vast web of circumstance that was the Third Age.

So we see that Tolkien, while deftly drawing together skeins of truth from Christianity with which to weave his tales, also keeps himself within boundaries of his own making. Besides despising purposed allegory, he also seems to have depicted his Christian elements with the utmost reverence and without presuming to step directly into the realm of God's original creation and plan. Tom's country ends *here*; he will not pass the borders.

In addition, Tolkien's use of elements from other myths is also permeated with a certain Christian reverence. He tells us of created beings of spirit subordinate to Ilúvatar and yet more powerful than any Man or Elf and who each have a specified sphere of influence. The Valar are designated to the realms of air, water, the stars, nature, the afterlife … a decided Olympian flavor. But these planetary spirits (and it is interesting, though tangential, that *both* Tolkien and Lewis chose to retain the concept of created subordinate spirits bound up in the fate of the physical world), very much *un*like those of ancient Greece and

Rome, comport themselves in modes of behavior far removed from human ones.

Where Zeus et. al. have sexual dalliances with humans, take a direct hand in earthly events, arrange matters to their own selfish likings, pout and use humans as pawns to perpetrate petty quarrels with one another, the Valar and Maiar are far above such nonsense. The only recorded liaison of spirit and physical being is the marriage (whole marriage, not just passing sexual encounter) between Melian and King Thingol in *The Silmarillion*, and even then it is between the spirit and an Elf, an immortal, not a human being. The Valar, the Maiar, Elves and Men are all created from a clearly visible source; nobody just "appears" in the sea or springs out of anybody else's head. Tolkien had very definite ideas about the natural order of creation, and it is undeniable that these ideas came in large part from the Bible and his faith. But even so he is still a far cry from the charge of allegory.

Ultimately, Tolkien created a story on a vast canvas, drawing influence and inspiration from sources varying from the Norse to Genesis to Matthew and far beyond. Though it is clear that he used his own experiences, both studious and religious, he shied away from merely clothing old stories in new garments. Instead, he regarded the use of his own powers of invention and arrangement as the foundation of his claim to sub-creation. He undoubtedly saw allegory as a tired formula that yielded little in the way of originality, and he sought to build a mythos for England that carried within it both the beauty of pure story and the grains of universal truth. That he succeeded is evidenced by the ongoing love people continue to bear for his work. He is the foremost storyteller of his age: legend resonating with truth, human spiritual experience "breathed through silver."

Sources:
Humphrey Carpenter, *The Inklings*, Allen & Unwin 1978, p. 46.
Humphrey Carpenter, ed., *The Letters of J.R.R. Tolkien*. Houghton Mifflin, 1995.

31. Narrative

Tehanu

Somebody's innocent request for a list of other good fantasy to read turned into something of a mission as I started to rack my brain for books to recommend. I needed to look at my favorites again to decide whether they were good writing or whether they were just fun that happened to appeal to me at the time I read them. Fun isn't in short supply to fantasy readers; good writing is. Soon it was clear to me that there is a lot of good children's and teenager's fantasy around, but it was harder to name many writers for adults that I would call "good" by my own definition — that is, well crafted, intelligent, original and written with an awareness of language for its own sake. That's not everyone's cup of tea, but if it's me who's being asked, that's my criteria.

Enjoyable, yes, plenty of that around. Lots of people are inventing interesting worlds where you can read about all kinds of quests and adventures. I read them and then forget them. They pass the time pleasantly whenever I don't want to be aware of things like buses or income tax or housework. One day the dustmites I have failed to clean up will mutate into some kind of fantasy horror that will inject a little action into my life, but meanwhile there is a never-ending supply of imaginary worlds where this can happen without exercising me unduly.

But with the stuff I read when I was a kid, I *cared* what happened at the end of the book. I've been rereading some of that stuff and admiring how good some of it is. Writing for kids is no simpler than writing for adults, but it is a different craft.

One of the fantasy authors I always enjoyed was Diana Wynne Jones, and it turns out that in her youth she took some of Tolkien's courses at Oxford. She's written an essay on Tolkien's narrative structure in LotR which I found illuminating, and I can't recommend it highly enough. You can find it in a collection called *This Far Land* where it is usually overlooked by Tolkienophiles because the other essays in the book are written by people who thoroughly despise Tolkien. If you're reading this book, you may not have the stomach for that one.

I can only touch briefly on some of the things that she says far better than I can. I think she was one of the first people to guess at the complex structure hidden under the simple surface of LotR, and she was able to relate it to techniques that would have been familiar to Tolkien from the Anglo-Saxon and Middle English texts he worked with.

First of all, she says how hard it was to learn anything from Tolkien at all, given that he appeared to hate lecturing, always mumbled, and turned to face the board if there was any chance that anyone had heard what he'd said. The class shrank to a handful, but she stuck it out and became aware that Tolkien had a valuable hoard of knowledge about the way plots are constructed and also of the next step beyond plot building, which is narrative.

Jones describes narrative something like this: The plot is what happens. The narrative is how you pace those events; how you make things in the plot foreshadow or echo other things that will happen or have happened, so that as you read the book, the events have a kind of unconscious "rightness" due to the way they have been prepared. Rather than have a series of random adventures, it is possible to make things happen in such a way that certain events cast a shadow over the past so we see the things we thought we knew in a different way. Or an action can cast its shadow over the future so that we have a subconscious expectation that the writer can later confirm or confound, according to how he chooses to play the game.

A lot of fantasy writing is a bit like somebody daydreaming. They dream up a world that's pretty nice, interesting things happen in it, they think up a plot, they write it down, and with enough imagination and intelligence it develops its own complexity as the characters and motives start to work against each other. But to make a good story into high art, the writer needs to control the narrative.

One of the things that Tolkien shares with his earlier models — the Icelandic sagas and the Old and Middle English texts that he studied — is the habit of standing right back from the characters and letting their actions and words reveal their personality. That places the reader's point of view at greater distance from the characters than is usual for modern fiction. You rarely read anywhere in Tolkien — or in the ancient and medieval works that he loved — a sentence containing the words "he thought ...." Occasionally you get close to it with a character saying something "to himself" or when "his heart tells him" something, or when his speech is qualified by an emotive term such as "he exclaimed *in amazement.*" But it remains relatively unusual compared to modern writing, which lets us inside people's heads more explicitly.

I'm just rereading the chapter "The Shadow of the Past" now and thinking on how Frodo's shock and Gandalf's forebodings are conveyed largely by their words and actions. It's a highly emotional chapter, and yet it's all conveyed without much emotive language like "Frodo felt sickened and his heart pounded as he thought about the danger he was in." Just as well, really. We learn that Frodo secretly thought Gandalf looked older and that Gandalf was thinking about the beginning of Bilbo's journey nearly eighty years ago, that Frodo thought how beautiful and precious the Ring was when he tried to throw it away — but once you start looking for them you realize how rare such statements are in this book. The only time we're told what Frodo feels is in one paragraph near the beginning where Tolkien describes how the urge to wander abroad begins to grow in Frodo after a number of years during which he was contented enough and not worried about the future. Later on he imagines fear like a dark cloud rising in the East and stretching towards him. We're given a rare glimpse of an image that is inside Frodo's mind, where we can't see it unless Tolkien outright tells us. But the vast majority of what we know about the characters comes through their speech.

This kind of thing is a choice, a conscious decision, as anyone who has ever tried to write fiction soon discovers. How much do you allow the reader to peek into the mind and heart of the characters? Do you allow them an all-knowing intrusive viewpoint so they can read everyone's minds? Or do you stand back and make the reader guess what the characters are thinking and feeling? Do you allow your reader to fly free of the main characters and see things happening all over the map, far out of their sight and hearing? Or do you limit what the reader knows to the things that the main characters can see themselves? Do you allow the reader to see that the character's point of view is false or mistaken? Once you decide to tell the story from a certain point of view, you more or less have to stand by it for most of the novel, and you have to make it work for you so that the readers gain knowledge of the characters and the events that you want them to have.

In Tolkien's case the characters are defined by their words, and it's fascinating to reread the book and mentally zoom in on the words of one particular character for a while. For instance, Boromir — once I started analyzing everything he says from the moment he enters the story, it's blindingly obvious how proud he is. In fact "proud" is the very word Tolkien uses to describe him the first two times he's mentioned at all (kind of like awoogah, awooogah, sirens going off: This man's weakness is Pride in all its archetypal glory) and his first speech is at once boastful about the valor of the Gondorians in holding off Mordor — where he mentions their pride and dignity — and slightly whiny because he thinks nobody else is pulling their weight to help.

By the end of the speech when Boromir says he took the journey to Rivendell instead of his brother because the journey would be full of danger, we would be right in suspecting Boromir of boasting about his own courage and prowess compared to his brother. By the end of the chapter, reading it carefully, we also know that he has the courage to ask the hard questions and to challenge the answers, and that he is impatient to act quickly and directly.

How many people can really tell Merry and Pippin apart? When you look hard at everything they say and do, you'll notice how consistently different they are. Pippin takes things lightly and often blurts things out in a rather gauche way. Merry tends to be more practical and to take charge, as for example in Fangorn, where Merry knows where they are because he had the foresight to study some maps way back in Rivendell. But Tolkien doesn't spell any of that out. He lets the characters reveal themselves by their speech. It's easy to lose the tone of each character's speech, as it's mixed up with so many others, not to mention all the action and the descriptions of landscape and weather. That's why it's so much fun to really pay attention to one character at a time.

This kind of thing is a dance between the writer and the reader — the writer seems reticent and yet you're invited to look harder at what is really going on, and you're rewarded by discovering more.

Diana Wynne Jones analyzed the narrative structure of LotR and ended up feeling that she could she look and go on looking, and still wonder how Tolkien does what he does. It's done so well that the artifice is invisible. Yet she detected an immense cunning and fore-thought to the structure of a tale that appears to unfold very fluidly and easily, like any pageturner of a novel.

She relates it to the way a symphony is constructed, and that seems a good analogy to me. Music often has an underlying structure that makes its episodes feel "right" and logically inevitable and that occurs at a deeper level than the things one is aware of, like the melodies or rhythms or colors of the instruments.

How can you tell when a symphonic piece is nearly finished? Certain expectations have been set up and then resolved. There are a dozen subconscious cues in the structure of the piece to say that we are reaching a conclusion, not because the composer ran out of tunes at that point, but because of the way the piece is "built," though we don't really notice it.

You can probably find a structure in anything if you look hard enough, but to Diana Wynne Jones, *The Lord of the Rings* is built in a series of movements, each of which has a "coda" section. The coda gives a foreshadowing of what comes next and reflects on what has been. She marvels at how this structure is so hidden in the telling of the story, "...which appears to march forward and to unfold with the utmost clarity and regularity." I'm not sure the book segments out as neatly as she implies, but I'll present her analysis of the first "movement."

The opening scene copies the way some of the Arthurian tales started, like *Sir Gawain and the Green Knight*, with a feast at which the hero is present ... and then shortly afterwards the mirth is interrupted, and we hear rumors of strangeness, a quest to be undertaken. Magic enters the safe, homely world of the party; a quest is begun. This is a tradition of storytelling, the medieval Romance, that Tolkien knew backwards and inside out, but here he begins it disguised as a children's fairy story, with a birthday party. Very homely.

But as the quest begins, the book opens out from small to large: Tolkien's hobbits start out innocent and ignorant of the wider world because of their distance from it, as well as their determined compla-cency. Frodo's only aim at first is to get to Rivendell. After that, greater ones than he will decide what is to become of the Ring. But on the way there are light premonitions of the wider world: Meeting the Elves singing of places far distant in space and time; then Tom Bombadil and the mention that he has been there since the beginning of the world;

next the encounter with the barrow-wights. Jones describes them as the dead hand of the past reaching to disturb the present. They're carrying the leftover hatred of the wars of Angmar. This is a foreshadowing of the way the Ring has reached out of distant history, loaded with the weight of an old evil that will flourish in the present. And it's part of the history of the Ring, but not directly, not in this story.

Until Bree they've been mostly in a Hobbit world. At Bree they meet Men, and we become aware that people are on the move from distant parts of the world with which the Hobbits have never been concerned. We've known that the Elves are passing through the Shire on their Elvish errands, but now it seems that there is a wider disquiet. The world opens out from our point of view.

The coda is the journey to Rivendell. We meet the trolls — a touch of the past again, Bilbo's past (remember Bilbo was saved by Gandalf? But where is Gandalf on this journey?) — and then we meet the Black Riders again. But this time they are far more dangerous, and there is the real sense that the hobbits might not survive. The autumn road is harder and more desperate.

The first movement sets up an expectation that the hobbits would be rescued again on Weathertop or on the way to Rivendell, as they were in the Shire by the Elves, or by Tom Bombadil when they were helpless under the Barrow. But instead, after Bree they barely escape the dangers that beset them, even with all the help they can get from Glorfindel and with their strongest efforts. The "first movement" makes us expect that somebody will always be there to rescue them: the coda gives us the dreadful foreboding that the hobbits are in greater danger than we realized and the help we expected may not come.

Jones points to another thing about the way the book is built: the way the perspective widens from a purely hobbit's-eye view of the world, very cozy and lots of meals, to the world of Bree, which has men in it, to the Council of Elrond, where we become more aware of the size of Middle-earth and the length of its history, and we are introduced to more of its races.

The perspective widens again when we see Gondor, the Rohirrim, the vast intake of peoples going to Mordor .... but the view has been prepared in stages. Each step of the way, verses and songs and passing comments give the hobbits and the reader a growing awareness of the age and size of Middle-earth.

Jones describes volume II as "the great choral movement." Yes, that seems a fair comparison. Or you could hunt out a recording of Mahler's 6th Symphony and hear that same structure turned to music: skeined music, each strand different, all conflicting and color and tension, yet finally all drawn to march in the same direction. From a certain point in LOTR's second volume, our perspectives are vast and the people caught up in the wake of Frodo's quest become a multitude.

But all of that has been foreshadowed by the snatches of songs about past deeds and the meetings with Elves intent on their alien concerns. This is a technique that Tolkien would have been familiar with in his own reading of older literature.

Beowulf uses the device of having a harper sing to Beowulf about the glorious deeds of the past, namely the legendary slaying of the dragon Fafnir. The song reflects Beowulf's own deed in slaying the monster Grendel, but it also foreshadows Beowulf's death, for he is killed by a dragon in the end. Tolkien also uses songs, these "insets" of history, to set up the atmosphere of Middle-earth a little more clearly for us, but also he uses them again and again to make us sense the weight of doom-laden history that is pushing the living characters forward with a terrible necessity to act.

Take the scene at Weathertop where Strider sings about Beren and Luthien and the trials and the love between the mortal man and the Elf princess. This prepares the way for the appearance of Arwen and her story and hints at what she means to Strider. Another example might be the moment in Rivendell when Gandalf looks down on the sleeping Frodo and sees him (or foresees him) for a moment slightly transparent, slightly luminous, like a glass filled with clear light. Right at the end of Frodo's journey to Mount Doom, that transfiguration is complete when he appears to Sam as a figure robed in white towering over Gollum, blazing, radiant, holding a wheel of fire — borrowing power from the Ring, perhaps, yet also filled with the power of his own resolve.

There are the dreams, too — Frodo's dreams in the house of Tom Bombadil and both Frodo and Sam's visions in the Mirror of Galadriel. Frodo's dream of the curtain of rain rolling back to reveal a far green country doesn't come true until nearly the last page, and when you read it for the first time you feel the wonder of recognition, though you probably can't quite remember by then why it seems so familiar and "right."

Jones points out what a tour de force it is to tell the tale the way Tolkien did, working it up to a complexity that required him to split the narrative strand into two or three "braids." Tom Shippey, in his outstanding book *J.R.R. Tolkien: Author of the Century,* draws a kind of diagram so you can see the complexity of the narrative braiding during the middle third of the story and the way the stories leapfrog over one another in time.

Yet certain moments tie all the characters together, such as the sunset that Frodo and Sam see at the crossroads in Ithilien. We learn many chapters later that Pippin sees it from Minas Tirith at the same time. Moments like that prod us into remembering that nobody in Minas Tirith knows what's become of Frodo and Sam, or where Aragorn is, and they're mistaken about where Merry is, since he's not supposed to be part of Theoden's warband — and even their arrival seems like a lost hope by then. As Shippey says, Tolkien uses this complicated form of storytelling, known as interlace, to build suspense very successfully. He gives the reader the sense of confusion that the characters themselves experience as they labor in ignorance of what anyone besides themselves is doing. It's a feat that Shippey admires:

"One might feel that a more experienced writer, one who wrote novels or fantasies professionally rather than passionately, would have known not to risk such finesses or trust so much to the ingenuity of his readers: but Tolkien knew no better than to try it."

Most fantasy novels flick between the various characters and their adventures, chapter by chapter. Tolkien stays with Merry and Pippin and the others for *half a volume* and then goes back to Frodo and Sam.

Why in that order? Why the glorious battles, the bustling, active, triumphant adventures of Merry and Pippin and the three pursuers, the battle of Helm's deep, the overthrow of Saruman, *first?* Shouldn't a narrative be structured so the quiet stuff happens first and then the more exciting stuff? Like a symphony that ends with a loud fast finale?

Tolkien takes a risk. He is only *distracting* us with all the chasing and battling. It is not this *action* that is going to save Middle-earth, but the operation of quieter virtues in Frodo and Sam. Steadfastness, loyalty, determination and love, what Jones calls "negative virtues." The negative virtues often consist of non-action — of patience, of endurance, or of choosing not to slay, not to run away. Of course there is also Sam and Frodo's courage and love and concern for each other making up another trio of virtues.

She points out that volume II is built in two parts that work in contrary motion, which is again a musical structure, one that you might find in a fugue. At the beginning, Merry and Pippin are captive and pursued. The first half of the volume deals with their adventures, their growing sense of self-reliance, and their involvement with the greater realm of Rohan. The second half of the volume is the antithesis: Sam and Frodo have only a kind of dogged determination and loyalty to get them through their trek *away* from civilization and into the wilderness. The volume ends with Frodo as a captive and Sam as an ineffective hero who only *nearly* succeeds when he attacks Shelob.

Both sets of hobbits attack a tower: Merry and Pippin at Orthanc, Sam and Frodo at Cirith Ungol. But Sam and Frodo fail, and set against the successes at Orthanc it only deepens our sense of despair and our belief that the hobbits in Mordor face an impossible task. To write half a novel that is about the quiet virtues of steadfastness and love *after* all the heroic action scenes in the first half is a real risk, and Tolkien carries it off. The scene where Sam attacks Shelob, or much earlier the moment at the crossroads when the setting sun gilds the fallen statue of the King — they are some of the most moving episodes in the book.

Jones says that some things are deliberately presented twice, like the Dead Marshes, which are foreshadowed in the Midgewater Marshes, but the later version is twisted into horror by that same entanglement of a futile evil past. It's like we're revisiting familiar ground (a marsh), but Tolkien shows us how much worse it can get. Or the Ents, foreshadowed in the Old Forest outside the Shire. The creatures of the Old Forest will not involve themselves in the War of the Ring, but by the time the hobbits encounter the Ents, the evil in Mordor has become so pressing that the Ents are at last persuaded to fight.

I can see another way that the narrative works in contrary motion: Right near the beginning we are presented with the Shire in autumn and the rumors that the Elves are leaving Middle-earth for good. Hints of this decline of the elder races recur throughout the books, so that the image of autumn at the beginning can be read as an image of the decline of the Third Age and all the noble, wild and magical things in it. (You'll notice in Peter Jackson's film that whenever the story moves to Rivendell or Lothlorien, truckloads of autumn leaves are always falling — a good visual cue to the state of the Elves in Middle-earth.) The story of the war of the Ring opposes the victory over Mordor against the failing vigor of the Elder Races. Victory costs them their tenure in Middle-earth, though the price would have been higher had they lost.

So, to return to the narrative structure: The great and notable people continue the War of the Ring in the beginning of the third volume, but once again it's a red herring; everything depends instead on two very ordinary and unprotected travelers far off in the wasteland of Mordor. It's a stomach-turning moment when the battle of the Pelennor Fields is over and the reader realizes that it has availed nothing, Middle-earth is still not safe, and more lives must be lost in the terrible gambit in front of the Black Gate.

Strangest of all, then, to return to the terrible journey across the wastelands of Mordor and to see the great deed achieved by a triple failure. I'm going to quote Wynne Jones here because there is no clearer way to put it:

> … despite their courage, and their wholly admirable affection for one another, and Frodo's near transfiguration, their action is indeed negative. At the last minute, Frodo refuses to throw the Ring into the Cracks of Doom and puts it on instead.

And the other failures from the past:

> Frodo, not lovingly, spared Gollum's life. Sam, not understanding Gollum's loneliness in the marshes, threatened him and turned his incipient friendship to hatred. So Gollum bites off Frodo's finger and falls with it and the Ring into the Cracks of Doom.

And then just where any other author might have stopped, at the triumphant moment of Sauron's overthrow, Tolkien instead lets us see how these ordinary folk, the hobbits, return home and slide back out of History. The scale is shrunk down, as Jones puts it, back to the Shire. But Frodo … he has become more Elvish, and Tolkien has hinted that the Elves, with their immortality, their never-aging, their bottomless memory, are "… widowed from history." They are forced to withdraw from the world in which the memory of every act must live forever, every grief over a mortal death is endless. Tolkien hints at the burden that immortality would be.

So Frodo joins the Elves in their retreat from history, from the world where things happen. This is not a happy ending, as I once thought. The journey West over the sea has a couple of antecedents in medieval literature — Arthur's voyage to Avalon after his final defeat or St. Brendan's journey to the western Paradise. But there was also the ancient custom of shipburial among the Vikings and Anglo-Saxons, which was solely associated with death, not renewal. Does Cirdan's boat really go to an earthly paradise whose shores are made of gems, like St. Brendan's island, or is it a funeral voyage? Despite what Tolkien tells us about Valinor, it's hard to avoid the resonance of these other journeys to the West.

There is simply no better way to say it than Diana Wynne Jones said it: "So the ending is heart-rendingly equivocal. You can see it as Frodo moving into eternity, or into history — or not. You can see it as a justification — or not — of the negative side."

And this is how the Arthurian romances would often end, with a sense that no victory was final, that every gift had its price, that life went on regardless and left the likes of King Arthur ensorcelled under his hill, and Frodo forever parted from his Shire.

Sources:

Diana Wynne Jones, "The Shape of the Narrative in *The Lord of the Rings*," Robert Giddings, Editor, *J.R.R. Tolkien, This Far Land*, Vision Press, 1983.

Tom Shippey, *J.R.R. Tolkien: Author of the Century*. Houghton Mifflin, 2001.

32. Northern Magic

Tehanu

I read one day, I read two,
on the third day I was still reading
It was not a great book, no
Nor a very small one ...
It was a whacking huge great read that went on forever and ever
It started on Monday and carried on 'til Sunday
And I had issues with the translation.

I thought I might elevate whinging to an artform in the epic style after I read the old Finnish epic poem, the *Kalevala*. It's long, and the repetitions that the singers use to prompt their memories make it even longer. People who've read *The Iliad's* repetitive "rosy-fingered dawns" too often will recognize what I'm talking about. Both of them existed for centuries only because of the bards who memorized and recited them, year after year. That sort of oral poetry often uses a few repeated lines that can give the singer stalling time while they recall the next bit.

All I wanted to do is find out what caused the excitement that Tolkien felt about the great Finnish national epic. It fired him up with a desire for England to have a national epic too, written by him. What else seeped into his own writing from his love of the *Kalevala*?

It would have been nice to be able to read it in Finnish but even without that you can get the Quenya flavor of the names, and Tolkien did credit his knowledge of Finnish for the inspiration behind his Quenya language. I couldn't believe that Väinämöinen the wizard and Ilmarinen the Smith weren't really Tolkien characters already — the names seemed that familiar! But in fact I'd never come across them before. There is one curious thing, though: the creation myth that begins the *Kalevala* names Ilmatar as the creator of the world, and she is the all-mother (or Water Mother), born of the "high airs." In

Tolkien's world, it's Ilúvatar who is the All-father of creation. Interestingly, Tolkien language scholars note that the prefix *Il-* is All, *ilm* is "high airs."

Another familiar thing is the *Kalevala's* setting in an open wild country where anyone can build a farmstead and rule their individual lot in the vast forest. In the *Kalevala* there is no government and no towns; everyone seems to live like Beorn, in a homestead buried in the wilderness. Those empty spaces on all the maps of Middle-earth could be filled with such lonely, self-sufficient homesteaders, and indeed that seems to be the way the first people lived when they arrived in Middle-earth. *The Silmarillion* describes how one of those first clans, the Haladin, lived in scattered, self-governing homesteads without overlords (*The Silmarillion, p. 175*).

Like Tolkien's female characters, the women in the Kalevala don't adventure much, but they are important. Their lives and feelings are described in detail, and their thoughts and opinions are reported. The heroes Joukahainen and Lemminkainen never set out without asking their mothers' advice, which they suffer for ignoring. The women are wise and outspoken. Lemminkainen dies wishing he'd known the words of wisdom his mother had that might have saved him, though all she might have said is "Next time, *follow* my advice." She's pretty active in restoring him to life with her spells afterwards. Meanwhile up north there's always the old woman of Pohjola who seems to protect her mysterious land with magic, like Melian and Galadriel.

Men boast of their weapons, but there are no details of the fighting — in fact even though the heroes carry swords, and so do the sorcerers and magicians (I immediately think of Gandalf with Glamdring), the only contests described in detail are spellmatches.

The *Kalevala* talks a lot about herds and hives and not much about war. It's a contrast from reading the battle-ready Norse sagas, though there are also similarities in the deep love they share for the places they made their home. Even more than in Norse Sagas, though, the Finnish tales celebrate the beauty of nature and describe it with intense affection:

> *Therefore is the birch left standing,*
> *as a perch for thee, O Cuckoo;*
> *whence the cuckoo's cry may echo.*
> *From thy sand-hued throat cry sweetly,*

With thy silver voice call loudly,
With thy tin-like voice cry clearly,
Call at morning, call at evening,
And at noontide call thou likewise,
To rejoice my plains surrounding,
That my woods may grow more cheerful,
That my coast may grow more wealthy,
And my region grow more fruitful.

Or:

...Belt the fir-trees all with silver,
Birch-trees with their golden blossoms,
And their trunks with gold adornments.
Make it as in former seasons
Even when thy days were better,
When the fir-shoots shone in moonlight,
And the pine-boughs in the sunlight,
When the wood was sweet with honey,
Smelt like malt the heathlands' borders,
From the very swamps ran butter.

Tolkien must have felt an empathy with this loving appreciation of the natural world. He certainly felt something similar for the country of his childhood, the rural fields and woods around Sarehole.

For my second reading of the *Kalevala* I used the same translation that Tolkien used, that of W. F. Kirby. It avoided some of the grating colloquialisms of at least one later version (who's a "foolish fellow," then?) but I still thought a lot about how quickly some words date. To call somebody a "fellow" sounds pretty naff right now ... "naff" will be a dead word soon too. Where I live it's not particularly rude to call a "foolish fellow" a "silly old bugger," but in other parts of the world they're not going to forgive you that in a hurry. The generation before me might have used the word "joker" in its place, but that's becoming a dated, rural word now.

Hard to translate those equivalents from Finnish, which doesn't have close relatives in the European languages. Tricky to translate gracefully. I wondered how Tolkien might have done it, because he had a prodigious store of colloquial dialect words. Of course, for centuries the *Kalevala* stories were told by live storytellers who could select the most current slang if they needed it.

The Kirby translation has this unvarying rhythm all the way through, for thousands and thousands of lines:

DA-da DA-da DA-da DA-da
DA-da DA-da DA-da DA-da.

Longfellow was for some unfathomable reason so inspired by this that he wrote *Hiawatha* in the same meter:

"BY the SHORES of GITCH-ee GUM-ee"

The epic oral-poetry-saga thing was once hot news, and with the Kirby translation making the Finnish epic available to the world, people tried their hand at it, thinking that's how it should be. There are a few tantalizing lines at the back of Kirby to show how the original might sound:

Lenteleikse, liiteleikse,
Katseleikse, Käänteleikse.

Bilbo and the hobbits often make up rhymes in a very similar meter that keeps a steady four beats per line (with a preceding upbeat added), for example, *"The Road goes ever on and on."* The dwarf Gimli is responsible for *"The world was young, the mountains green,"* which also uses that four-beat meter.

Something about the use of magic struck me in the *Kalevala*. In the Icelandic sagas there's very little magic, if any. In the *Kalevala*, it's everywhere, and it hinges on the power of the sorcerer to know the right words and understand the origins of things. Here's some magic, for instance: the power of the word to bring things into being. It's also similar to what Ursula Le Guin's mages do in *A Wizard of Earthsea*:

Then the aged Väinämöinen,
He the great primeval sorcerer,
Fashioned then the boat with wisdom,
Built with magic songs the vessel,
From the fragments of an oak-tree,
Fragments of the shattered oak-tree.
With a song the keel he fashioned,
With another, sides he fashioned,

> *And he sang again a third time,*
> *And the rudder he constructed,*
> *Bound the rib-ends firm together,*
> *And the joints he fixed together.*

That all reminds me of the way the Valar could sing things into being: Yavanna singing to make the Two Trees of Valinor. Later Galadriel seems to form the land of Lothlorien when she sings, "I sang of leaves, of leaves of gold, and leaves of gold there grew:" And as I mention elsewhere, Tom Bombadil's domain seems to be maintained by his singing and his making.

After this Väinämöinen needs three more words to finish the boat, so he looks for them from the brains of swallows and under the tongues of reindeer. It seems to me that much of the magic in Tolkien's world is of this understated kind: Wizards are people who have knowledge of words of power and of the origins of things. That is the way magic is practised in the *Kalevala* too. Remember Gandalf trying to find the right word to open the Gate of Moria? Or how part of his holding the Balrog at bay consists of naming its origins ("Flame of Udûn!")?

This is Väinämöinen, trying to find the spell to cure a wound. To do that he must understand the origins of iron and speak of them to the wound, which is a cut from an axe:

> *Then his magic spells he uttered,*
> *And himself began to speak them,*
> *Spells of origin, for healing,*
> *And to close the wound completely.*
> *But he could not think of any*
> *Words of origin of iron,*
> *Which might serve to bind the evil,*
> *And to close the gaping edges*
> *Of the great wound from the iron,*
> *By the blue edge deeply bitten.*

The spells in the poem are believed to have an immensely old history — some are drawn from magic beliefs dating back to Neolithic times, thousands and thousands of years ago. As one *Kalevala* translator said, some parts of the poem are a window into the deepest past, maybe as much as 15,000 years ago when the bear was the most worshiped totemic animal in Europe. The Norse berserker "Bearsarkers," the furious shapechangers and magic warriors, are another remnant of this old, old belief in bear-magic. Other parts of the poem must have come to life later, when metalworking was an arcane knowledge and metals were venerated as powerful in themselves. You can almost imagine Tolkien thinking about how, if the legends of the northern shamans might survive so long, the mythical events from his First Age of Middle-earth might also survive in song and story down to the present.

The life the *Kalevala* describes was hard and it seemed that people had enough to do to get fed, and not much left over to worry about fighting. Who in the western world now would write longingly:

Do not weep, my dearest daughter,
Do not grieve, (and thou so youthful);
Eat a whole year long fresh butter,
That your form may grow more rounded,
Eat thou pork the second season,
That your form may grow more charming,
And the third year eat thou cream-cakes,
That you may become more lovely...

The characters in the *Kalevala* have a lively appreciation of food that is hobbit-like, and their praises of milk, cream, butter and honey would grace Goldberry's table.

Other writers have pointed out the similarities between Tolkien's "Tale of Túrin Turumbar" in *The Silmarillion* and the *Kalevala's* tale of Kullervo, who unwittingly sleeps with his long-lost sister. She throws herself into a cataract and drowns, like Túrin's sister. He slays himself with a sword that speaks. Like Túrin's sword Gurthang, it says it would gladly take the blood of one so wicked, since it has slain so many blameless ones before.

Something I noticed in the *Kalevala* was a kind of prototype for the Ents, or at least an awareness that trees might have wisdom and opinions of their own. In one canto, Väinämöinen wants to build a boat and he sends Sampsa Pellervoinen, a kind of spirit of crops and trees, to find the right wood. Sampsa talks to an aspen and a pine, and they give excuses for why they'd be no use. Finally he asks an oak tree.

And the oak-tree answered wisely,
Answered thus the acorn-bearer:

"Yes indeed my wood is suited
For the keel to make a vessel..."

Either the oak tree is a willing collaborator in its new destiny as a boat (Sampsa cuts it down immediately) or the verse is being ironic: unlike the "wise" oak tree, the other trees manage to persuade Sampsa to leave them alone. Throughout *The Lord of the Rings* we also meet trees that are fairly opinionated about axes! And of course, we meet trees that talk.

Reading the *Kalevala* made me stew over with questions; it was so full of mysterious unexplained characters. Who is Pellervoinen and why is he "earth-born?" Why is Väinämöinen's mother Ilmatar a goddess sometimes, but later can only speak to him from her grave "beneath the billows?" Why are the Hiisi sometimes malevolent spirits, sometimes magical helpers, and sometimes a single entity, lord of the wilderness? It reminded me of a thing that some Tolkien fans find so irritating about studying Middle-earth, and that is Tolkien's inconsistency. Anyone who's studied his invented languages in depth knows that Tolkien kept changing his preferences for certain words and grammatical constructions. Some early works use the older forms; while writing stories, though, a new version of an existing word would suddenly seem more poetic or appropriate to him and so he'd use that instead. Later he might or might not try to develop a link between earlier and later forms of the same word. His own etymologies did not agree amongst themselves nor with all his written work.

The same applies to his stories: the Gandalf of *The Hobbit* is pretty inconsistent with the great wizard of *The Lord of the Rings*. Both Tom Bombadil and the Ents are called Eldest by different inhabitants of Middle-earth. Little things like that perplex scholars of Middle-earth.

Tolkien struggled to get all his stories to agree with each other, but I think a small rebellious part of him was perfectly and delightedly aware that all real mythologies have these discrepancies. Over time, competing versions of the same tale appear. Successive storytellers misremember and embellish the legends they tell until it becomes a sleuthing game to try and find out what the first and possibly the truest version might be. In every author's mind is a mountain of possible truths, and Tolkien was assiduous in mining his from every direction and extracting as many stories as he could. The result is that his

Middle-earth almost achieves the bewildering contradictory richness of real mythology. Nothing could have pleased him more.

Sources:

Kirby, W.F. *Kalevala: The Land of Heroes*. J. M. Dent & Sons, London, 1907.

33. Tom Bombadil &
the Green Man

Tehanu

In the years since my first reading of *The Lord of the Rings*, I found myself more and more tempted to skim quickly through the chapters that featured Tom Bombadil. I lost my childlike acceptance of him as a necessary character in the War of the Ring. Frodo's quest was so much more of an adult concern, and I couldn't see how this humming, capering joker matched the gravity of the rest of the story. Many readers get hung up on the same point — and sadly some readers never get past Tom in their *first* reading to find out what happens in the rest of the story. Wasn't Tolkien taking a risk in asking us to accept Bombadil as part of a serious epic?

Tolkien once spoke of the long-simmering "broth" of folk-tale where elements of truth and fiction are tossed in over the years and boiled together until retellings and the passage of time develop the perfectly seasoned story. His own writing seems to work the same way, throwing in bits and pieces of mythology and folklore and religion and poetry and stewing them in his mind for decades until the finished story becomes something original and different. We can go on forever picking out bits and pieces of the *Rings* and identifying their origin from earlier sources, but for the most part, Tolkien's mind worked on them to shape something new. The trouble with Tom Bombadil is that to many readers he remains a fairly indigestible and odd-flavored lump in the soup.

The screenwriters for the *Fellowship of the Ring* film saw those chapters as a problem. In the time that they had, they couldn't afford to let the story lose the urgency of the chase, which it had built up almost since the beginning. We feel that the Black Riders, and through them Sauron, are pursuing Frodo and his companions. The film can't afford the time to introduce the viewers to another strange character while the hobbits spend two days in a suspenseless state of song-lulled security. Can a book afford any time to linger there above the Old Forest with Tom in this day and age where we're so admiring of books that are "tautly written?"

Elsewhere I've written about the fantasy author Diana Wynne Jones, who studied (insofar as possible) Tolkien's use of narrative. While examining the way Tolkien builds and releases tension and sets up a pattern of foreshadowing events, she comments about Bombadil: "Tolkien was quite right to put him in, but I wish he hadn't." Which leads me to ask, "What would we miss if he wasn't there?" It's not enough to say, "Without Tom, who'd rescue the hobbits from the Barrow-wight, and where would they get the magic blade that Merry used to slay the Witch-King?" Those things could be made to come about (in a "tautly written" way!) using characters we've already connected with, like the Elves. Why write a chapter of this meandering nursery silliness, as it appears? Why does Diana Wynne Jones say, "But Tolkien was right to put him in," when she admits that he irritates her?

It's worth looking at how Bombadil arrived in the story. He was there right from the beginning — even before Frodo! In fact Tolkien started developing the character of Tom Bombadil some time before *The Hobbit* was published, and his poem, *The Adventures of Tom Bombadil*, appeared in the *Oxford Magazine*'s issue for February 1934. Years later when it came time to write a sequel to *The Hobbit*, it seems that Tolkien toyed with the idea of reviving his old friend Tom Bombadil and making him the protagonist of the next book.

There's a fascinating series of letters that Tolkien wrote around the time that *The Hobbit's* success was becoming a certainty and Stanley Unwin, his publisher, was pestering him for "a sequel." In October 1937 Tolkien wrote to Stanley Unwin that he felt he'd said everything there was to say about hobbits. He hinted coyly that there was a great deal to be said about the world hobbits lived in. In December he asked Unwin if he thought Tom Bombadil could be the main character in a *Hobbit* sequel and alluded to Tom as a spirit of the countryside around Berkshire and Oxfordshire as it once was. He expressed some doubt about that as a story idea, but then as matters stood, he thought the first chapter of *The Lord of the Rings* was "poor stuff" and only changed his mind when Stanley's son Rayner gave it an enthusiastic thumbs-up.

Without that he may not have continued. One can only speculate what would have happened if Unwin Senior had encouraged Tolkien to make Bombadil the hero of his *Hobbit* sequel.

There is also a fairly famous remark that Tolkien made about getting the characters as far as Bree. At that point, he said, he didn't know who Strider was, or where Gandalf had gone, or how Frodo was going to get to Mordor. But he did know a great deal about Tom Bombadil. I think that he was still under the impression that he was writing a children's tale where fanciful characters could be expected to pop up and entertain us one after another. Once he'd finished the book he went back and revised the whole thing, and much of the comfy fairy-tale flavor of the beginning would have been raked over pretty thoroughly and tuned to the weightiness of later events. I'm pretty certain that episodes like the terrible Black Resurrection speech of the Barrow-wight and Frodo's prophetic dreaming in Bombadil's house are things Tolkien added in later. But there remains the structure of the first draft of the story: apparently a cozy fairy-tale where the hobbits are going to leave the Shire and get into a number of alarming scrapes from which they'll be rescued by other odd and charming inhabitants of Middle-earth. What Tolkien left in that is charming and childlike is there deliberately, and Tom is there for a reason.

The Shire is a bounded, safe place with no real interest in the distant past or future. Tom's world is also bounded. He will not leave its borders, and so the strange wonders within it are part of the fading world of magic that is leaving Middle-earth or shrinking within smaller and smaller bounds, as the Old Forest has shrunk. But through Tom Bombadil we become aware that the history of Middle-earth is so long that its inhabitants can't know it all. The Dwarves reckon Durin as the eldest living thing, Elrond states that Bombadil is the first being on earth, and the Ents call the Elves Eldest (they themselves are "only" as old as the mountains!) and after all those years they still don't know all there is to know about each other. So we're left, as Tolkien intended, with a world too large to be hemmed in by any one story he tells about it.

Tom introduces us to the length of history in Middle-earth quite casually. He is "Eldest." The dead who have lain for centuries adorned with treasure inside the barrow-mounds are recent memories to him. He remembers the fair lady who wore the brooch he picks out of the barrow. He remembers the days when the Old Forest covered much of the world, and he was there before the first tree and the first raindrop. When the hobbits hear his stories, they learn how their world is much wider and older than they had considered. Tolkien sets up a pattern, for when they leave Bombadil's house they immediately come across one remainder from the old wars Tom talked about — the Barrow-wight. Tom has to save them from the Wight, just as he saved them from Old Man Willow. There is a difference though — when the hobbits met Old Man Willow, they lost their heads completely and panicked. All Sam and Frodo could do was run around aimlessly yelling for help. For this second entrapment, Frodo does little enough to save them, but he does gather his wits, resist the temptation to use the Ring to save himself alone, and steel his nerve to strike at the Barrow-wight. Somehow during his sojourn in the house of Tom Bombadil, while listening to tales of history and old wars, he's learned something about courage. And so he saves the hobbits: he sings the song that will call Bombadil to rescue them.

What's with all this annoying singing? For Tolkien, singing *is* magic. It's at the very heart of creation. He pictures the world and all its history as the unfolding song that the Valar sing, in the creation myth that opens *The Silmarillion*. I could happily live without the rest of that book, but I find great beauty and satisfaction in the vision of Eru and the Valar singing the world into existence and patterning its history through vast choral harmonies.

We're told that the Elves have "magic" and yet we never see them do any magic to conjure up their feasts in the Shire woods, for instance — they just sing. But when Frodo is in Lothlorien, Galadriel tells him of the things that maintain and defend her land against the Enemy and shows him the Ring she bears, which he is able to see. Her comment is that the land is defended by that as much as by the elven bows and elven singing. The arrows you would expect as a defense, but the singing is somewhat unexpected on that list. Evidently music is power in Middle-earth.

In the ancient Anglo-Saxon world that Tolkien knew so well, the word for "bard" — *scop* — is formed as the past tense of *scieppen*, "to shape, form, create" and is related to *scieppend*, "creator, shaper, God." In Ancient Greek there's a similar relationship between the verb "to make" and the word which has come down to us as "poet." In old Scots dialect, "poet" is *makar*, "maker."

If all that would ever come to be in the world had already been sung by the Valar at the Creation, then there would be no free will, for our history would simply unfold what they had already elaborated. Within the created world Tolkien put further singers, the Elves and, yes, Tom Bombadil. Then he leaves it very open for us to guess how much their singing creates novelty and chance in courses of the world. Tom Bombadil turns down the hobbits' invitation to adventure by saying he has his house to mind. And what does he do there? His making and his singing! Is Tom Bombadil such a silly old fart, or is he akin to Väinämöinen, the supreme magician in the *Kalevala*, whose singing creates trees and stars out of nothing?

I think Tom Bombadil is more than a diversion, and I think Diana Wynne Jones's comment, "… he was right to leave him in" accepts this: Tom Bombadil and all the episodes from the Old Forest to the Barrow-downs serve to make Middle-earth wider, deeper and more mysterious. They give it the sense of limitless horizons and deep time. Look at all the old myths and folk-tales that are hinted at here: the soporific spell of Old Man Willow turns the Withywindle into a kind of River Lethe out of Greek mythology, giving forgetfulness, drowsiness, death. The forest itself, vivid and alive, is a relic of pagan mythologies that gave trees powers and a vegetable intelligence.

Beyond all doubt Tolkien loved trees. In the preface to his essay "On Fairy-stories" he comments sadly on the "barbarous" mutilation and removal of a large willow near his house. "I do not think it had any friends, or any mourners, except myself and a pair of owls." I found even more evidence of his feeling for trees in an essay by George Sayer in Joseph Pearce's *Tolkien, a Celebration*. Sayer was invited to join some of the hikes around Malvern that Tolkien took with C. S. Lewis and his brother. The Lewis brothers got irritated by Tolkien's habit of stopping to talk and look at things — flowers, birds and insects but most especially trees. "He would often place his hand on the trunks of the ones that we passed. He felt their wanton or unnecessary felling almost as murder." Sayer recalls how Tolkien said "ORCS!" when he heard a chainsaw in use. Tolkien said he "… had sometimes imagined an uprising of the trees against their human tormentors."

He was also very knowledgeable about the historic associations of various plants, telling Sayer about how picking a plant such as celandine was once linked to a tradition of saying certain combinations of *Aves* and *Paternosters*. He pointed it out as an example of a pagan custom that had later been adopted into Christian folklore. Originally, there had been certain runes to speak before picking such a plant.

Now, for all that people laud the Christian impulses in *The Lord of the Rings,* I'm pretty sure that Tolkien was not only fascinated by earlier religions but quite comfortable with their existence in historical times. He was a devout Catholic who loved trees enough to feel a good deal of empathy with earlier cultures that worshipped them. He might have put it to himself in these terms: "If *I* had lived in a time before the revelation of Christ's message, in a culture ignorant of the God I know, wouldn't I fall naturally into a worship of those manifestations of divine creation that I saw all around me?"

Linked to the worship of trees is the figure of the Green Man. Who is he? Nobody's sure, because despite his long survival into the Christian era, and despite the fact that the Green Man is carved among the saints and icons of countless churches in Europe, he's never named and never explained. He's like something so common to the Gothic minds of the cathedral builders that they never felt a need to say more about him. To them, clearly, if you wanted to build an enduring fantasy in stone that would stimulate worship, then the logical place for the arches to begin and the corbels to end is in the mouths or heads of the Green Man.

You can identify the Green Man whenever you see a head, often bearded, either made up of leaves or sprouting vegetation from his mouth. Used in architecture, the vegetation is often carved to form the starting point of arches, columns and buttresses. The message seems to be this: The Green Man's speech is life itself, the vegetable life on which other living things depend, as the building's structure depends on the columns "uttered" by the Green Man carved at their base. While you are in a stone church you are also in the sacred grove, and the whole drama of life takes place within the setting of life itself, not just within the minds and hearts of human beings. The pagan tree is now the Tree of Life, the Tree of Knowledge of Good and Evil, the Tree of the Cross. The tree, vine, the barley-sheaf — all the things that wreathe the Green Man — flourish, nourish us, die and are reborn.

To the medieval mind, which was Tolkien's area of greatest empathy, that pagan "cycle of life" was recast as the Resurrection, but the earlier meanings remained — the belief in a green force that engenders life. The Green Man used to be a symbol of how humankind is connected with the rest of creation. Tolkien's essay "On Fairy-stories" suggests that fairy-tales about talking beasts reflect a yearning to undo the sundering of human and other life, as though in some Edenic past we could speak to the birds and understand the secret life of plants. Tolkien's own desire for such a possibility is an undercurrent in his work, I think.

To the Gothic cathedral builders the Green Man also symbolized the creative force of the imagination. A surprising number of old books have the Green Man pattern engraved on the title page too, making a further connection between him and the creation of words. Just as the carved leaves and fruit pour endlessly from the mouth of the Green Man, just as Tom Bombadil's "making and singing" sustain his green land, so does the artist and creator pour forth the works of his mind. They, like Tolkien, may well have felt that to create imaginatively was sacred — one of the attributes of God that are gifted to humanity.

The Green Man myth has some manifestations that Tolkien leaves out, such as Cerunnos the Horned Man, also known as Herne the Hunter. Interestingly Cerunnos has a consort, usually the Great Goddess of the earliest myths we know of in Europe. Later on she's the May Queen, crowned in flowers. Tolkien would have no truck with a pagan earth-goddess of fertility, but he does give Tom Bombadil a consort — Goldberry, daughter of the River, crowned in lilies. Maybe she's just a straight lift-out from the ancient Greek myths of river nymphs — or a kind of locus genii, the spirit of that place. (Didn't I say this was a big stewpot of mixed-up folklore?) She has her own power over water, as Tom has his over wood. Tolkien leaves it open to interpretation whether his own mythology of Valar and Maiar would make Tom and Goldberry related to — or echoes of — Oromë and Vana. Orome's the closest thing in Middle-earth to Herne the Hunter.

But again, is it just a simple one-for-one translation, making Vana the quickener of flowers into Goldberry? The Great Goddess is also Ishtar, goddess of love, and perhaps Tolkien's filtered that to turn Tom and Goldberry into the book's most happily married couple. They're the only couple we see and hear moving and speaking and acting together, who are living in love, day in and day out. Not pledged to it, not waiting for it, not mentioned as a future possibility like Sam and Rosie or Aragorn and Arwen, but visibly there in the book.

That will endure, we hope, if Tom is "last as he was first."

Soures:

J.R.R Tolkien, "On Fairy-stories," George Allen & Unwin Ltd., 1964, reprinted in *The Tolkien Reader*. Ballantine Books, 1989.

Introductory Note to "Tree and Leaf" (1964), 1989 Houghton Mifflin hardcover edition.

Joseph Pearce, Editor, *Tolkien, A Celebration*. Harper Collins, 1999.

34. Tolkien & the Realm of Arthur

Tehanu

I keep thinking back to that famous quote from one of Tolkien's letters, where he said he wanted to create a mythology for England. For him, even the Arthurian legends weren't English enough. There had to have been a time, before the Norman conquest, when parts of England had an oral tradition that is unknown to us now, because their very language was lost. Tolkien took the Norman conquest rather personally because of that, it seems, and he went about rescuing such fragments of older English tales as still remained, and of course inventing his own imaginary languages.

Perhaps it started as a game, to fill in the gap left by the death of ancient Anglo-Saxon culture, but it was a game he played according to his own curious rules. The languages he invented aren't anything like Old English — the principal inventions, Sindarin and Quenya, are based on Welsh and Finnish. And then, as he famously said on a few occasions, the mere process of creating new languages seemed to spawn tales, histories, cultures and characters to inhabit them.

I was interested to find out whether Tolkien completely rejected the Arthurian stories or whether they influenced his own imaginary mythology.

It turns out that he did indeed begin a long poem called "The Fall of Arthur," in an alliterative meter like that used in *Beowulf*. He avoided the Christian and Grail legends and concentrated on the end of Arthur's life and the treachery of Mordred. It seems as though he was trying to see how an heroic English story would sound if it had been left in the hands of the native Anglo-Saxon storytellers instead of being told by the troubadours in the French of the Norman invaders. Once again, we get the feeling that Tolkien is writing a kind of "what-if" literature. ("What if the Norman Conquest had never happened? What far older literature might have survived into the present?") In any case, "The Fall of Arthur" was never finished.

I should have realized how big a topic King Arthur was when a handful of people in casual conversation could recollect about 12 versions of King Arthur's story. They weren't even regular fantasy readers. Now, months later, I have seen an awful lot of Arthurian literature and history and picked my way through names and characters that merge and change with each telling.

Such books are often illustrated with fourteenth-century manuscript pictures that show such a determined loathing of the human face and figure that King Arthur and his knights look squinty-eyed and even Guenevere looks laughably prune-faced. The illuminators seemed to take more trouble to get the draped folds on the clothing right. It might be that somehow nobody in medieval Germany, France and Britain even *accidentally* discovered how to draw people well, but I see it as evidence that the monasteries where these tales were copied and illustrated had a strong international grip on the way images were transmitted. And there was a good deal of mortification of the flesh and denial of earthly pleasures in that.

All the while, as manuscripts were copied in monasteries, the religious and mystical aspect of the tale grew. That interested the people who were largely in control of preserving and transmitting the stories; I see the uniformity of those squinting, pursy-mouthed medieval illustrations as a measure of how influential that control was.

One of the interesting things about the Arthurian myths is this antagonism between piety — as in the Grail stories — and the natural impulses of these brawling, jousting knights with hair-trigger tempers, decked out for war in all their finery. It's rather a thin veneer of civilization, you feel sometimes. I don't think Tolkien approved of those characters, on the whole, or at any rate where his characters have honor they act without such extravagance. Aragorn and Boromir are war-weary and tired of the road they travel, and their lives have little of the idle feasting and contests that fill much of the time at Camelot.

I'm starting the tale of Arthur's legend somewhat in the middle, at the point where it was written down. Based on Arthur, the (probable) 5th-century war leader of the Britons, seven centuries of bards and troubadours stitched a tale of enemies routed and monsters vanquished, pieced out of history and maybe pre-existing myths. When Arthur's story came to be written down, the preoccupations of the writers came into play. Geoffrey of Monmouth sought to establish a quasi-divine precedent for the rule of the Norman Conquerors. Troubadours of the French courts softened the tales and added the dimension of courtly love, their audiences being composed of more women, who were whiling away the time until their lords should return from the Crusades. Lancelot appeared then, and the tales of his love for Guenevere. The growing climate of religious fervor turned the focus from the mystery and magic of the old Celtic tales to the reinterpretation of Arthur as a near-Messiah for Britain. So the Grail tales grew in importance to reflect that.

I reread *Sir Gawain and the Green Knight*, knowing that it was one of the Arthurian legends in Middle English that Tolkien had studied extensively.

Reading *Gawain*, I felt like I was reading some kind of Celtic wonder-tale, full of mystery and hidden meanings. Sir Gawain, brave and impetuous and a little arrogant, goes on a quest that, in the end, humbles him and makes him wiser. The ending seems tacked on by medieval monks, making Gawain's new-found wisdom no more than a realization that all women are false since Eve. But at the same time, the growing influence of the code of chivalry bends the story in another direction, showing a dozen ways that a true knight wins honor through his gentleness, courtesy, honor, truth, defense of the weak, humility and self-control. At one point Gawain says to a lady who taunts him to use his strength to take what he wants:

> "Bot threte is unthryvande in thede there I lende,
> And uche gift that is geven not with goude wylle."
>
> [But force is ignoble in (the) country where I live,
> And (as is) each gift that is not given with good will."(freely)]

That's a contrast to earlier tales like *Beowulf*, which seem to inhabit the kind of culture that would consider kicking sand in the faces of 98-pound weaklings an honorable pastime and fine sport for all. When the meadcasks are broached in Hrothgar's hall, you'd want to be very very big or stay very very quiet.

Later still after the Middle English *Sir Gawain,* Malory combined earlier French and English traditions to make, in *Le Morte d'Arthur*, the "Standard" version of Arthur, with its Camelot, Round Table, questing knights, Merlin, Lancelot and Guenevere.

Malory himself had a life of adventure. Not only did he fight in various battles, but he tried to murder the Duke of Buckingham in an ambush, and he broke into Coombe Abbey, where he robbed and insulted the abbot; he was at various times charged with forcing somebody's wife, with highway robbery and cattle rustling. He was imprisoned eight times and escaped twice, once by swimming a moat, once by means of an armed breakout. During his final imprisonment, he wrote *Le Morte d'Arthur*.

That certainly explains why much of the book is such a spun out, one-thing-after-another time killer. Horrifyingly enough, it's meant to be a considerably tighter read than its main sources, the Alliterative *Morte Arthure* and some Norman French romances. We have a lot to be thankful for in the many fine 20th-century retellings available now, which pick the eyes out of the tales but leave aside 80 percent of the jousting, hunting and warring and the historically absurd bits like the war on Rome. The sheer squandering of horses, the pointless tournaments that bred feuds, the contempt for commoners, the meaningless quests for white hounds and magic harts boggle the attention somewhat. It goes on and on inconclusively, rather like reading all the sports pages in last century's newspapers.

Some bits of Malory are wonderful — the world he creates that is so full of chaos, surprise and magic, the tale of Arthur's beginnings, and later on, the tale of the disintegration of the Round Table, with the betrayals and defeats of the main characters. There they come into focus as individuals, loving and suffering as people do.

During the course *of Le Morte d'Arthur*, Arthur himself becomes less of a leader and more of a pawn in the hands of the rival factions at court. By contrast, Malory follows Lancelot's career with greater and greater interest, and our sympathies lie with him more and more. It seems that Lancelot never fails any test of chivalry by his own judgment, though he can be beguiled. Arthur adheres to rules that would see him burn his own wife for adultery; Lancelot trusts his heart and somehow breaks those laws without compromising his honor and truth. By the end of the book, the story seems to me to be really about Lancelot and Guenevere. We're given more of their speech and thought than we ever get of Arthur.

One of the great things about the Round Table is that it provided a wonderful format for reinventing old tales. One could simply invent another knight of the Round Table and polish up a favorite tale to add into the existing romances and quests. In this way the Arthurian legends reflected their time. It's interesting that as time went on, the Grail quest assumed greater importance; the independent women such as Morgan le Fay, Guenevere, and Viviane become more and more evil. Their scheming and betrayals are simply not there in the earliest versions. Even Malory, though he tacitly approves Lancelot and Guenevere's love, paints her as capricious and even a little stupid.

Now, Malory couldn't copyright his work; Tolkien could and did. If it were not for that, some of the thousands of works of fan fiction set in Middle-earth would have burst into print, and within decades Tolkien's creation would be as rich and multi-branched as Arthurian legend. There would be versions and inversions, inconsistent and competing stories, updates and extrapolations, because fans have found in Middle-earth a playground for the imagination unmatched by anything since Camelot. It's an incredible feat for one man to have created a parallel world so compelling as to have drawn the world's imagination to it as strongly as it has; given half a chance, in a few decades fans would have done for Middle-earth what it's taken centuries for Gramarye and Avalon to achieve. As it is, Tolkien altered our expectations of fantasy. Very few modern writers would dare to portray Elves, for instance, as wee little people who live under toadstools.

So what influence did the tales of the Round Table have on Tolkien? Surprisingly little, it seems. He seems to have known intuitively that his own imagination would grow best if he didn't plant it in the shade of the vast ramified grove of Arthurian tradition. I think that says a lot about Tolkien. He could (and did) write "fan fiction" of a sort — translating *Sir Gawain and the Green Knight* into modern English and working on the above-mentioned poem "The Fall of Arthur." But in the end he must have wanted a totally free vision within a new world, a world so new that he'd have to construct about 11 languages to give his people an intellectual home.

There are a few things that Tolkien borrows, but in a shadowy and transformed way — the King who will return, the rightful King whose claim is recognized by the sword he bears (in the one case, reforged, in the other, drawn out of the anvil), the Lady of the Lake who gives the magic scabbard as well as the magic sword. In *The Lord of the Rings*, the

Lady is Galadriel, whose kingdom is reached by crossing water, like that of the Ladies of the Lake. (That's not in Malory's version, but it's in the earlier Celtic tales.) Notice Frodo's sense that he has entered an enchantment as soon as he crosses the Silverlode; it lasts until he leaves by the Anduin. There's also the final journey across water to Avalon, or in Tolkien's case to the Undying Lands of Valinor. Although Avalon is sometimes identified with Glastonbury, in other tellings it is more vaguely described as being "to the West somewhere." You can even hear a linguistic connection in the sound of the names "Valinor" and "Avalon."

It's fascinating to look at the parallels, but more than anything I get a sense of distance between Middle-earth and Camelot. Tolkien had strong religious feelings, and his stories illustrate the way he felt God moves in the world. Was there something about the Arthurian legends that repelled him, that made him uncomfortable in that world? Even given the religious overtones of so many of the tales where Good and Evil are in contest?

I can think of some possibilities. One reason is best described by a quote from T. H. White's wonderful, quirky 20th-century revision of Malory's *Morte d'Arthur*. Many people will have read the first book, *The Sword in the Stone,* with its bumbling Merlin, good-hearted boy Arthur, and its strange scholarly jests and digs at British nobility. The later books become dark and cynical. They're matter-of-fact about the quests and wonders, deeply sad at human folly, terribly moving and beautiful. At the end Arthur muses:

> Looking back at his life, it seemed that he had been struggling all the time to dam a flood, which whenever he had checked it, had broken through at a new place ... It was the flood of Force Majeur ... But he had crushed the feudal dream of war successfully. Then, with his Round Table, he had tried to harness Tyranny in lesser forms, so that its power might be used for useful ends. He had sent out the men of might to rescue the oppressed and to straighten evil ... the ends had been achieved, but the force had remained in his hands unchastened. So he had sought for a new channel, and sent them out on God's business, searching for the Holy Grail. That too had been a failure, because those who had achieved the Quest had become perfect and been lost to the world, while those who had failed in it had soon returned no better.

Tolkien might have found that to be a futile conclusion. Perhaps he wanted to write about a Quest that *did* alter the world in its fulfillment.

Perhaps Tolkien also understood that perfection leaves us cold. Sir Galahad, the purest knight, can't hold our sympathy as much as the more flawed characters. Some of the best recent versions of Camelot, like Mary Stewart's or Marion Zimmer Bradley's, avoid the perfect Galahads and take the stories back to their simpler, earthier roots in a Celto-Roman setting, stripping away a lot of the later accretions of chivalry and medieval religion.

I don't think we should confuse Tolkien's history of Middle-earth with his storytelling gift. His "historic" style is what you get in *The Silmarillion,* with its declamatory epic language. It's moving in a certain way, but it's not meant to engage our emotions the same as when he "tells a story," as he does in *The Hobbit* and *The Lord of the Rings.* There the tone is completely different, and in those stories the point of view is wholly that of the ordinary characters, the yeomen. The hobbits are not lords and athelings they are homely, comfort-loving characters. Civilized, moderate, and commonplace. There is nobody in the world of the Round Table like that, and it seems that Tolkien wanted to write from a point of view that never existed in the old romances and epics of chivalry.

I think Tolkien wanted to tell a story that left us with more hope and which is more universal. It's prophesied that King Arthur will return if his Isle of Gramarye is invaded; that's something of a sterile hope if you don't live in Britain. It's also a passive hope; it doesn't leave much for the common folk to do. They're barely mentioned in Arthurian legend. Tolkien wanted to put ordinary people (well, hobbits) at the center of the quest, so their striving is something that encourages us because we can identify with it.

Sources:
T. H. White, *The Sword in the Stone.* Collins, 1970.
Sir Gawaine and the Greene Knight. Christine Franzen, Department of English [internal publication], Victoria University of Wellington.

35. Ancient & Modern Wars

Tehanu

Around 1926, Tolkien formed a group among his Oxford colleagues called the Kolbítar, which met every few weeks to read and translate portions of the Icelandic Sagas and the Elder Edda. For Tolkien, who could translate fluently and perfectly, this was an opportunity to share his love of a subject that had captivated him since childhood. As much as anything, this early fascination prompted him to attempt his own "Ring Cycle."

So after the *Kalevala* it made sense for me to read more from the Icelanders. The two cultures did after all have some cultural connections as well as a similar background, always snatching life from the jaws of winter. The Norsemen, like the Finns and Laplanders, lived a life on the edge, though perhaps as much because of their violent culture as because of the intrinsic harshness of their climate. Where the Kalevalans praised their foggy islands, their misty marshes and endless small lakes, the Norsemen contended with the sea, which they both loved and hated. I can't imagine that when Tolkien wrote about the Elves' yearning for the sea that he had in mind the tame seaside of Lyme Regis where he took his holidays.

Life was tough, and fine words were about the only luxury most people could afford, much as we might remember the Vikings for their hoards of gold and weapons. Sagas don't mention the long, dark, cold and claustrophobic winters in households that must have cried out for songs and stories to send the imagination elsewhere for a while.

Egil's Saga has a poet as the central character who always has a verse ready for his latest exploits:

> *So I rise up early*
> *to erect my rhyme,*

215

My tongue toils,
A servant at his task;

I pile the praise-stones,
The poem rises,
My labor is not lost
Long may my words live.

These people didn't believe in much of a life after death unless a person died in battle, in which case they went to Valhalla, feasting and fighting in the company of the gods until Ragnarok. My math suggests that since women, children, and any man who died of some mischance were ruled out, *most* of the population could expect no afterlife worth mentioning. You died, that was it. In such a society, words were a valuable thing that might hold and preserve a person in shining memory after death, giving them a kind of existence that endured beyond the grave.

...poet's power
gold-praised, that
Odin from ogres tore
In ancient times,

Purest of possessions,
Poetic craft, power
The dwarf-devised,
Drew first breath...

...I muse how my mother met her end,
First that, then my father's
Fall I sing
In a poem of praise
From my palace of words,
From my temple the word-tree
Tells its growth-tale.

I notice that phrase "word tree." Tolkien lived his whole life erecting a word tree, a tree of tales.

Egil's Saga, like the other Icelandic sagas, gives a sense of people living on a knifeedge, always close to sudden death. I wonder how much of a spur to creativity that kind of thing is? How many subsistence cultures have built the most sophisticated art out of words that vanished forever as soon as their language died out? Who knows what poetry the cavemen may have had to complement their paintings? You can't pretend that people used to be dumber or less alive to the world about them, or less able to read the visible world as a metaphor for the unseen mysteries of life.

Modern living provides plenty of grief and sharp edges for people to rub up against, but we don't expect famine and slaughter as commonplace events. I wonder if our ancestors' greater awareness of mortality gave them an urgent need to create, with word and song, something out of nothing.

"In the beginning was the Word .... " And indeed in most cultures the power of the word has been set against Unbeing and against Time. In *Egil's Saga* it's put like this: Odin is the master of battles and death, but his compensatory gift is poetry.

Like the other sagas, Egil's tells of a life where murder was common, unpredictable and closeup:

> *Now the bitter bearer*
> *of the blazing war-blade*
> *has taken ten*
> *of my trusted followers:*
>
> *But my salmon-like spear*
> *Settled the score*
> *When I cast it through*
> *The curved ribs of Ketil.*

Tolkien fought in the First World War and spent three months on the front line in the battle of the Somme, where the ranks of men walked into machine-gun fire. I wonder if he was drawn to recreate the heroic ideal of the far past because in his life he saw this instead, chillingly described here by Gil Elliot:

> It is reasonable to obey the law, it is good to organize well, it is ingenious to devise guns of high technical capacity, it is sensible to shelter human beings against massive firepower by putting them in protective trenches.

The end result of this complex organization was the manufacture of corpses, 6000 a day for 1500 days. Historian Richard Rhodes calls this an "essentially industrial operation." We take it for granted now, but in 1914, and for Tolkien, it was a fresh and horrid invention. He wrote very little about it directly, but the reeking wasteland of Mordor matches descriptions I've read of the Somme in midsummer, blasted and pocked with craters where poison gas lingered and an oily scummed water collected only to torment the men parched with thirst whenever the watercarriers couldn't make it through the trenches. When it rained, the Front turned to mud where a few green things still struggled to live and a year of corpses lay unburied — not unlike the Dead Marshes, where Tolkien imagines how it would be if the war dead lingered for thousands of years, never transformed into poppies and crosses but always present as a reminder of Sauron's wars.

Tolkien's education in history and literature had prepared him for the kind of ancient battles where a fighting man could see his attacker and where it mattered a great deal whether he had the force of will, the confidence, the belief in his own luck as well as the skill and strength to counter him. The berserkers, for instance, were believed to be men who were proof against iron's bite. Notice the conjunction of two things considered magical to the early Iron Age of the Norsemen and the Finns — iron and bears. The berserkers were supposed to be able to change into bears, and they wore their bearskin shirts ("sarks") as a reminder of that. I think the berserkers were so terrifying in their self-belief that few opponents could strike at them with conviction. It must have seemed like magic.

It made a difference, in that Iron Age culture, whether somebody faced their battles with courage or not, and individuals want to feel that their spirit makes a difference in the world. Courage had a survival value then in a way that it doesn't now. If you've seen the movie *Gallipoli*, or the first few minutes of *Saving Private Ryan*, you'll know what I mean. It's one thing to fight for what one believes in and quite another thing to be mown down for it. Tolkien himself uses a haunting phrase in one of his letters, "The toad under the harrow."

To be sure, bad luck and stray arrows could kill an Iron Age warrior, but his own bravery and attitude improved his odds in a fight. Tolkien saw the culmination of a process where this was no longer the case and would never be again.

I wonder whether *The Lord of the Rings* is about finding some other kind of courage, the kind that Sam and Frodo must use to get themselves to Mordor. The Tolkien scholar Tom Shippey believes that it is, and that while *The Lord of the Rings* celebrates the more ancient kinds of warrior courage that you see in Boromir or Faramir, it also attempts to find some other kind of courage that can withstand the grinding uncertainty and relative helplessness of trench warfare. For instance there's the courage of plodding, simple Sam, with his determination to see it through to the end, with or without hope. And the gentleness and good cheer that he keeps about him through all his trials are a kind of outstanding courage that you do not see in the old Germanic sagas and epics.

Whatever else *The Lord of the Rings* is about, it *is* a response to the World Wars, this new thing in Tolkien's world, and you could hardly expect such a powerful book to spring from a less compelling need to make sense of the world. You can argue all day whether heroic fantasy is or isn't a good and useful response to war in the twentieth century, but it seems that creative imagination is one of the few things we have to set against it.

In Tolkien's world, Death is the Gift of Men denied to the Elves, and that is taken to have a purely Christian meaning: Death offering the hope of Heaven. I bet that Tolkien's breadth was great enough to encompass a second meaning : that Man's cruel and poignant mortality lends urgency to our imagination and lights as many fuses as it burns out.

Sources:
Hermann Pálsson and Paul Edwards, trans. *Egil's Saga*, Penguin, 1976.
Richard Rhodes, *The Making of the Atomic Bomb*, Simon & Schuster, 1987 (for the Gil Elliot quote).

Present
Dreams

36. Present Dreams

Tehanu

This is a fearful and wondrous time for those of us who've been devoted to *The Lord of the Rings* for most of our lives. The advent of the films has brought Tolkien's work into the mainstream in a way he could barely have imagined, and we're not exactly used to the idea either! On TheOneRing.net we've followed the *Rings* film project with a mixture of feelings as it went from highly secret beginnings to a triumphant appearance around the world. We're proud of the wide success of something that we felt deserved the attention; it's a pleasure to chronicle the growing fame of the book we love and the filmmakers whom we came to admire.

On the other hand, there's the sense of loss that comes with sending anything you value out into the wide world. Would the book survive the transition to celluloid? Would our too-unlikely-to-believe film conquer the world or fall on its face? All along the way, the film project seemed crazy, quixotic, charmed. It was an adventure to watch it grow from a rumor to a reality.

Like no other fans, we felt protective of this Middle-earth thing that we'd come to feel was our private world, a special place that we shared only with a select few — a place that only a certain kind of person would love and understand as deeply as we did. Would the film bring in a new kind of *Rings* fan, one who cared nothing for the books themselves? Would the story become simply another action epic, larger than most, but missing the layers of meaning that patient readers had gleaned over the years? Would everything to do with Tolkien become commercialized beyond recognition?

The film has brought about some changes all right, with the arrival of a new breed of Tolkien fan. For them, Frodo and Legolas will always be Elijah Wood and Orlando Bloom, and as such the subject of their

221

fantasies (TORn gets regular fanmail from girls pleading for us to send their declarations of eternal love on to them). We can laugh about the critics' dire predictions that the films would fail because *LotR* was too much of a *Boys' Own* story to appeal to women. Heh!

And yet we get those touching e-mails from people who saw the film, rushed out and got the books, and were jolted out of some hole their life had dumped them in — sickness, depression, illiteracy, creative impasse. They're grateful the books exist and amazed that they never came across them before.

Now that *The Lord of the Rings* has become even more popular, how do people celebrate their love of the story?

Well, as never before, there are more books to read, games to play and things to collect. Quickbeam predicted the wave of Rings merchandise right at the outset, and we offer his take on that here. Turgon talks about the way religious groups try to claim Tolkien as exclusively theirs; Ostadan offers an article on the attractions of learning Elvish, and I observe how strongly Tolkien has established himself in popular culture.

In the next section, "The Films," we look at how Tolkien's work has fared as it is translated into the medium of film.

37. Wake Up and Smell the Dogma

Turgon

Unlike his close friend C.S. Lewis, J.R.R. Tolkien did not make Christianity the central topic of his writings, and he seems to have viewed his religion as a personal matter. I would welcome an informed study of Tolkien and his Catholicism (his friend Lewis was not Catholic but Anglican) that balances it with Tolkien's other interests, including his professional ones. And at least one such consideration already exists in Verlyn Flieger's fine volume *Splintered Light*. However, there is a change going on in the landscape of those who write about Tolkien and his works. The Christian proselytizers have entered the field. For years they were few in number, and their one-dimensional Christian interpretations of Tolkien seemed to be branches that reached out from the C.S. Lewis devotees, most of whom are doctrinally in sympathy with Lewis's works as a Christian apologist.

The expansion into Tolkiendom began to gather momentum in 1998 with Joseph Pearce's *Tolkien: Man and Myth*, a workmanlike consideration of Tolkien and his spiritualism by a Catholic convert. It's not really a bad book, but it suffers from its singular point of view. The movement picked up even more steam around the time of the release of the first of Peter Jackson's films, with the uninteresting, sermon-like book *Finding God in The Lord of the Rings* by Kurt Bruner and Jim Ware.

Then came what is simply the most vacuous and unnecessary book I have seen in years, *Tolkien's Ordinary Virtues: Exploring the Spiritual Themes of The Lord of the Rings*, by Mark Eddy Smith. This latter book has some thirty chapters on topics such as "Friendship," "Temptation," "Suffering," "Trust," "Hope," "Mirth," and "Love." The platitudes in this book, and the poor quality of the writing, should make any educated fifth grader groan in disgust: "History is a two-edged sword and in some instances it is a broken sword;" "Wisdom is not so much about intelligence, or the ability to strategize, or see all possibilities. It is about the heart;" and "Love is the goal and object of every other virtue."

The bandwagon rolls on. A magazine called *Touchstone: A Journal of Mere Christianity* devoted an entire issue to "J.R.R. Tolkien and the Christian Imagination." *The Catholic World Report* focused an issue on "The Enduring Catholic Vision of J.R.R. Tolkien." More books on various aspects of Tolkien and his religion have since come out. These include *Bilbo's Birthday and Frodo's Adventure of Faith* by Robert E. Morse; *J.R.R. Tolkien's Sanctifying Myth: Understanding Middle-earth* by Bradley J. Birzer; and *Frodo's Quest: Living the Myth in The Lord of the Rings* by Robert Ellwood. There is even a Christian study guide to *The Hobbit* by one Michael Poteet that offers this scintillating instruction: "What might we infer about the nature of elf weapons from the goblins' reaction? Read Ephesians 6:10-18. What connection can you see between the elf weapons and the 'full armor of God' we Christians are to wear?" Well, *none*. And more of these books are forthcoming.

What I object to about these types of works is not that they attempt to study Tolkien's spirituality (though I do object to the ones that do it poorly), but that the essential motive behind many of these books is for the fundamentalists to claim Tolkien as one of their own. Tolkien, during his lifetime, certainly never went on the lecture circuit or on the radio promoting Christianity, as his friend C.S. Lewis did. It is one thing that people seek to use Tolkien's works to validate their own faith; it is another to move from there on to salesmanship and to try to sell one's own version of God to the reading public. What seems to be happening now is a further development: some of the fundamentalists who write these books are attempting to use Tolkien to promote their own political viewpoints. This is apparent in the main essay "*The Lord of the Rings* as a Defense of Western Civilization" by John G. West, Jr., in the recent collection he edited called *Celebrating Middle-earth*.

Many of these writers quote Tolkien's letters in support of their viewpoint, forgetting that these were private letters, written to individuals, not public pronouncements, lectures or apologetics. That we have a volume of published letters is indeed a wonderful thing, and the discussion of Christian matters in the published volume has a balance in proportion with the rest of Tolkien's interests. It is also worth pointing out here that the one Tolkien letter that is most frequently quoted in Christian interpretations, written to the manager of a Catholic bookshop in Oxford, was never even sent. The text published in the *Letters* volume came from a draft which Tolkien kept, and on the top of it he noted that it was not sent because it felt like he was taking himself too importantly (*Letters*, p. 196).

Some months ago I was in the science fiction section of a bookstore, checking out what new Tolkien-related books might be there, when I observed an elderly woman with a young teen who was evidently her grandson. She was forcing Tolkien on the youth, who clearly wasn't happy and was squirming in resistance. I wondered what was going on, when I overheard a portion of the conversation. The old woman, her eyes glazing with the fever of a proselytizer, spoke to him with an unctuous coaxing voice: "Tolkien was a Christian!" I squirmed myself and felt sorry for that kid. What an awful way to be introduced to any writer, let alone one so wonderful as Tolkien. Unlike the poor young fellow who wasn't able to walk away, I could and did.

I think using Tolkien's Christianity as bait to lure to the young into religion has at its core the process of sleazy salesmanship. The friendly Tolkien coating on the pill doesn't change the fact that someone's trying to get you to swallow something. I'm certain that Tolkien himself would not approve. To a correspondent who labeled him as "a believer in moral didacticism" he retorted that his intention was the opposite in The Lord of the Rings; the book was not a vehicle with which to preach or teach (*Letters*, p. 414). And as to Tolkien being labeled a Christian writer, here I'm also certain that he would object. In the same letter quoted above he said that it was a small-minded and childish pastime to go about fixing "labels" to writers (*Letters*, p. 414).

Understanding Tolkien's Catholicism is without question a vital part of understanding Tolkien as a writer, but it is only one part of his multifaceted genius. A proper balance must be maintained if one is truly to understand the whole.

38. Glossopoeia for Fun & Profit

Ostadan

One of J.R.R. Tolkien's less famous works is *A Secret Vice*, a lecture first presented in 1931, and reprinted as an essay in *The Monsters & the Critics and Other Essays*. The "vice" to which the essay refers is the peculiar practice of creating languages, not as a code, but as an art form, perhaps to be shared for the use or appreciation of interested parties, as one would share a painting or manuscript. The word glossopoeia is a coinage derived from Greek, meaning "the making of tongues." As Tolkien explains, the creation of languages offers both intellectual and aesthetic satisfaction, but at the time he wrote, there were few such creations known to the public.

As we will see, this situation has changed considerably since that time. In this article, we will consider the genesis and effects of the three best-known glossopoeic works in chronological order: the international language Esperanto; the Elvish cluster of languages; and tlhIngan Hol, better known by its English name, "Klingon."

Esperanto was conceived and developed during the 1870s and 1880s by L.L. Zamenhof (1859-1917). Dismayed as a child by the mistrust that followed when people did not share a common language, he made it his life's work to create a language that could be learned by people in many lands as a common second language. Zamenhof's language was first published in 1887 as La Lingvo Internacia, with Zamenhof assuming the pseudonym of "Dr. Esperanto;" the word esperanto in the new language meant "one who hopes," and indeed Zamenhof hoped that his language would help the cause of international peace and understanding by encouraging communication among ordinary citizens of the world. Before long, the name became associated with the language itself, rather than the author. Esperanto was designed to be easy to learn and understand, at least relative to other European languages. As an example of what Esperanto looks like, here is a couplet, translated by Bertil Wennergren, that may seem familiar:

> *Unu Ringo ilin regas, Unu ilin prenas,*
> *Unu Ringo en mallumon ilin gvidas kaj katenas.*

This example shows a few of Esperanto's interesting features. The vocabulary is largely derived from Latin roots (reg-, "rule"), but has some Germanic or English roots like ring- in the mix as well. The word mal-lumon for "darkness" demonstrates how the vocabulary is extended by using affixes; the word can be literally analyzed as "un-light."

The number of Esperanto speakers grew steadily after its publication. A number of literary translations, as well as original articles, prose, and poetry, appeared during the next twenty years, and the first international congress conducted entirely in Esperanto was held in France in 1905.

Among the people who eventually learned Esperanto to the point of being able to write in it was a young English Boy Scout named John Ronald Reuel Tolkien. In 1909, he wrote a small sixteen-page notebook, the *Book of the Foxrook,* partly in Esperanto, describing a "privata kodo" for scouts. This private code consisted of a rune-like alphabet and a set of ideographs and represents the earliest known alphabet invented by Tolkien. The first page of this notebook was exhibited by the Bodleian Library as part of a Tolkien centenary exhibition in 1992.

Tolkien maintained some interest in Esperanto even while his own linguistic creativity was in full bloom. He refers to the language favorably in *A Secret Vice* and in 1932 wrote an open letter to the British Esperanto Association. In part, he wrote,

> ... technical improvement of the machinery ... tends ... to destroy the "humane" or aesthetic aspect of the invented idiom. This apparently unpractical aspect appears to be largely overlooked by theorists; though I imagine it is not really unpractical and will have ultimately great influence on the prime matter of universal acceptance. ... [one rival language] ... has no gleam of the individuality, coherence, and beauty, which appear in the great natural idioms, and which do appear to a considerable degree (probably as high a degree as is possible in an artificial idiom) in Esperanto ...

227

Here Tolkien, echoing some of his thoughts in *A Secret Vice*, is observing that the creation of a language is more than the simple creation of a tool or code; it is an endeavor that must give not only intellectual satisfaction, but aesthetic pleasure in the arrangement of sounds and meaning. Indeed, Zamenhof evidently spent a fair amount of time "taste-testing" his developing language before deciding on the words and sounds that would finally be part of the language.

Tolkien's feelings for Esperanto apparently cooled in later years based on his belief that language and myth are inseperable. In a letter to one Mr. Thompson in 1956 he asserted that Esperanto and similar languages like Novial and Ido had less vitality even than extinct ancient languages because of a lack of Esperanto "legendarium." (*Letters*, #180).

Nevertheless, it is worth observing that, of the dozens of prospective international language projects that have appeared in the last 150 years (including the three others Tolkien mentioned), only Esperanto has continued to grow substantially after the death of its creator. Estimates of the number of competent speakers range in the hundreds of thousands, and a Google search for "Esperanto" produces more than 500,000 matching web pages. There are even Esperanto translations of *The Lord of the Rings* and *The Hobbit* in print.

Arguably, Tolkien was wrong about Esperanto — but for exactly the right reason. Unlike the other languages he mentions, Esperanto does indeed have its own mythology. It does not consist of magical legends, but is a kind of political mythology of hope, a shared belief among its speakers that the world would be a better and friendlier place if everyone in the world could communicate across borders as easily as Esperantists do, in a language that belongs to no single nation or people. This notion, called the *interna ideo* by Esperantists, is sometimes a source of embarrassment. Nevertheless, this idealism pervades much of Esperanto literature, especially from the first fifty years of its existence. Many, if not most, biographies of Zamenhof tend to mythologize his life, treating the behavior of some of those who tried to gain control of Esperanto's development with the sort of language usually reserved for the likes of a Lucifer or Sauron. So, if Esperanto is not dead, it is precisely because there are legends and myths connected with the language.

In *A Secret Vice*, Tolkien distinguishes languages like Esperanto, devised for the practical purpose of serving as an interlanguage, from the real subject of his article — languages constructed as an Art or

Game. Tolkien, indeed, was addicted to this "game." Over the years, he created perhaps a dozen or more identifiable languages, including Dwarvish, Adûnaic, Black Speech, Valinorean, and several dialects of Elvish. He wrote:

> You must remember that these things were constructed deliberately to be personal, and give private satisfaction — not for scientific experiment, nor yet in expectation of any audience.

The Elvish languages, and Qenya (later Quenya) in particular, were thus a way for Tolkien to express his individual taste in languages. As has been discussed many times elsewhere, Quenya was strongly influenced by Tolkien's attraction to the Finnish language. In early Quenya, for example, the word for "twenty-three," his age at the time, was *leminkainen*, quite similar to Lemminkäinen, one of the major heroes of the Finnish epic, the *Kalevala*. Similarly, Goldogrin, the Gnomish language of the Noldor, was heavily influenced by Tolkien's love of Welsh. There is no question that the Elvish languages represent the most complicated such creation ever seen. Not only did Tolkien devise Quenya and Goldogrin, but also a common proto-language from which those two were (within the mythology) derived, and hints of several other related Elvish dialects.

Closely bound up with the Elvish languages was Tolkien's own emerging mythology, recorded in the *Book of Lost Tales*. In *A Secret Vice*, he wrote:

> ... for perfect construction of an art-language it is found necessary to construct at least in outline a mythology concomitant. Not solely because some pieces of verse will inevitably be part of the (more or less) completed structure, but because the making of language and mythology are related functions ... The converse indeed is true, your language construction will breed a mythology.

So closely bound were the languages and myth that it is impossible to tell where a phrase or word in the language inspired a new part of the story and where the languages were expanded or changed to suit the tale.

Unlike a practical language like Esperanto, in which stability is (as Tolkien himself observed) critically important to its goal of widespread propagation, Tolkien's languages were dynamic and changed as his own tastes changed and, indeed, as his mythology of Arda itself grew and evolved. "There is no finality in linguistic invention and taste," Tolkien wrote in 1932, and his own languages demonstrated that dramatically. But Tolkien's private game took a different turn when his fiction was published. In *The Hobbit,* there are a few hints of the Gnomish language — names like Orcrist, Glamdring, and Elrond, with English meanings given for the two weapons. *The Lord of the Rings*, however, entailed the publication of dozens of such names and examples of complete sentences and even poetry in both Quenya and Sindarin. In fact, the names and relationships of Sindarin and Quenya themselves changed during the writing of the novel, another example of how the mythology and languages influenced one another reciprocally.

The publication of so much Elvish had two profound effects. The first was that substantial parts of Sindarin and Quenya became essentially "frozen." With few exceptions, the names and interpretations that had appeared in print were no longer subject to revision and had to be considered definitive. To Tolkien, this was just a new feature of the game. Previously, if a word was changed or added, the existing languages were retroactively modified, sometimes extensively, to accommodate the change. But after publication, whenever he devised or revised a grammatical construct or vocabulary element, he felt bound to make sure it conformed to the published material, even when this was inconvenient.

The second effect was that the game was no longer private. Fans of the books quickly learned to write (at least in English) using Tolkien's Cirth and Tengwar and began their own linguistic game, that of reconstructing the Elvish languages based on the "linguistic evidence" that appeared in *The Lord of the Rings*. Tolkien, for as long as his time and energy permitted, encouraged and even participated in this activity.

For example, an important source of information about Quenya nouns is the so-called "Plotz Declension," which was explained in a letter that Tolkien wrote to Richard Plotz showing standard Quenya noun declensions. He would answer language-related inquiries and prepared a detailed analysis of two Elvish poems for publication with the *Road Goes Ever On* songbook. As a result, Elvish linguistics became its own sub-fandom within organized Tolkien fandom.

The journal *Parma Eldalamberon* first appeared under the auspices of the Mythopoeic Society in September, 1971, and contained articles on writing English using the Tengwar and on the formation of plurals in Sindarin. The journal is still irregularly published; the most recent issue contained extensive samples of the Sarati of Rumil (a predecessor to the Tengwar) and word lists and fragments of the Noldorin language prior to the writing of *The Hobbit*. Many other journals relating to Tolkienian linguistics have appeared over the years, and with the rapidly expanding use of the internet, we now see electronic mailing lists and dozens of web pages devoted to this esoteric field. One can even find translations into Elvish such as this Sindarin couplet by Ryszard Derdzinski:

> *Er-chorf hain torthad bain, Er-chorf hain hired,*
> *Er-chorf hain toged bain a din fuin hain nuded.*

In all likelihood, there are some thousands of Tolkien fans around the world who, like the herb-master in the Houses of Healing, "know somewhat of the Valinorean."

With the publication of *The Silmarillion, Unfinished Tales,* and each volume of *The History of Middle-earth,* more of Tolkien's linguistic invention has been revealed. Nevertheless, even Quenya, the most well documented of Tolkien's languages, will never be fully known. Nobody can hope to speak Quenya fluently because neither its vocabulary nor grammar is complete — Tolkien never intended for them to be! Nor is there ever likely to be an official Academy of Elvish that can expand and establish some kind of "canonical" Quenya or Sindarin that everyone can agree upon. In a private correspondence, one professor of linguistics expressed his personal dissatisfaction with Elvish as an area of study:

"Elvish satisfies a very different need, I think. In some ways, it strikes me as studying Latin. The language is basically dead. It exists in fragments as a fascinating puzzle, but it's not going anywhere. Klingon, on the other hand ..."

Perhaps the most profound effect of the prominence of the Elvish languages in Tolkien's hugely popular work was that it made glossopoeia respectable. Indeed, it seems that fantasy and science fiction works in the post-Tolkien milieu practically require the appearance of some exotic language spoken by alien or mythic races, or at least some systematic phonological structure in the names of people and places. One can now find several web pages devoted to glossopoeia, or "conlangs" as such constructed languages are sometimes called.

It was in this post-Tolkienian world that Paramount and Gene Roddenberry created the *Star Trek* motion pictures of the 1970s. The first film had a short subtitled dialogue among the Klingons, as well as a snippet of Vulcan dialogue, but these were ad hoc creations, not part of any systematic language. For the 1982 *Star Trek* film *The Wrath of Khan*, the studios were looking for a linguist to construct a few lines of Vulcan dialogue and recruited one Dr. Mark Okrand, a linguist with whom a producer's secretary happened to be acquainted. It represented a few days' work, but the producers called upon Okrand again for the somewhat more extensive Klingon dialogue in the 1984 film *The Search for Spock*. Unexpectedly, and perhaps himself inspired by Tolkien's work, Okrand created an extensive phonology, grammar, and lexicon for the Klingon language and even retrofitted the haphazard speech from the first film into his language as "clipped" Klingon, a battle dialect. The first edition of *The Klingon Dictionary* was published in 1985 and has had several reprintings (including updates based on additional material appearing in later films).

In a sense, Klingon is a linguistic joke. It disobeys certain rules recognized as human language universals by linguists, and its Romanized orthography uses upper and lower case letters in a most idiosyncratic manner. As an example of the language, here once more is the familiar couplet, rendered into Klingon by Ivan Derzhansky:

> *Hoch SeHmeH wa' Qeb 'ej bIH maghmeH wa' Qeb,*
> *Hoch qemmeH 'ej ramDaq bIH baghmeH wa' Qeb.*

With the many harsh aspirants and glottal consonants, the Klingon language would likely have struck Tolkien as an Orkish "brutal jargon," and indeed does have superficial phonological resemblances to Black Speech.

The Klingons, however, are a much more richly depicted culture than Orcs and have captured the imagination of many viewers. Consequently, *The Klingon Dictionary* has sold hundreds of thousands of copies, a figure that usually leads to rather inflated numbers claimed for the number of Klingon "speakers." There are instructional language tapes available, and the Klingon Language Institute even produced a Klingon version of *Hamlet* not long ago, largely as a result of a joke in a *Star Trek* film (although many agree that the play is better in the original Esperanto).

In the case of Klingon, the popularity can be attributed to the mythology that produced it: the mythical future world of *Star Trek*. While only a small number of people can actually speak it fluently — the head of the Klingon Language Institute has said that he does not know of a hundred such people, although the criteria for judging fluency are necessarily nebulous — it is nearly certain that there are a large number of fans who can, with the aid of the dictionary and grammar, construct a grammatical Klingon phrase or sentence, or who have memorized some of the "useful phrases" such as "Surrender or die!" (bIjeghbe'chugh vaj bIHegh) — almost certainly more than the number of people who can do the same with Quenya or Sindarin.

All three of these invented languages have had considerable success in their own rights. Perhaps to understand why, we can compare the "cultures" associated with Esperanto, Elvish, and Klingon. The stereotypical Esperantist is a slightly naïve idealist who sees Esperanto as a way of increasing the brotherhood of mankind through improved communication and tries to correspond with pen-pals in as many countries as he or she can. The stereotyped student of Elvish is inspired by a language in which one routinely says things like, "a star shines on the hour of our meeting," and may write Elvish poetry filled with natural imagery about oceans, forests, trees, rivers, and clouds. The Klingon speaker enjoys the dark irony of a language in which the standard greeting translates as, "What do you want?" and even "I love you" is expressed in a guttural phrase like "qamuSHa." If you really like stereotypes, the Esperantist is a 1940s-style leftist, the Elvish scholar is a 1960s hippie, and the Klingon speaker is a biker in black leather.

While this is obviously too facile a characterization, we can see that each of these languages fulfills some need (albeit not necessarily practical) of its community: aesthetically, politically, literarily, or indeed, mythically. They enjoy unusual success out of the hundreds of glossopoeic inventions that have doubtless occurred in the past because they touch some part of the human linguistic facility in ways that other efforts have not.

There are many sources on the web for information about Esperanto. In North America, a good starting point is The Esperanto League for North America, while those in other countries might look at The

Multi-lingual Esperanto Information Center. Two good websites to find out more about Elvish are Resources for Tolkienian Linguistics and Ardalambion. The leading organization for Klingon is The Klingon Language Institute. There are dozens of other conlangs that you can read about on the web, including the logical language Lojban and the Tsolyani language from the fantasy role-playing world of Tekumel. One useful starting point is Richard Kennaway's Constructed Languages List, which has an astonishing number of links and thumbnail descriptions.

Sources:

Patrick Wynne and Arden Smith, "Tolkien and Esperanto," in issue 17 of the journal *Seven*.

The Klingon Dictionary, Pocket Books (Simon & Schuster Inc.) 1985, 1992.

J.R.R. Tolkien/Edited Christopher Tolkien: *The Monsters and the Critics and Other Essays*. Houghton Mifflin Company, 1984.

39. The Game's the Thing!

Quickbeam

I am a fervent fan of gaming. Be it strategy game, party game, dice, trivia, fantasy role-playing, collectible card — you name it, I have surely played it. One of my favorites has become something of a hobby, the wonderful Dragon Dice game (imagine a cross between Risk and Magic: the Gathering and you've got the best collectible dice game there is). I've played in tournaments across the West coast, even claiming the title of Western Regional Champion.

But there is a special place on my table for board games. Ah, the joy of Scrabble with close friends who allow vulgar words! The glee of popping Mousetrap's plastic contraption into chaotic motion! I even get a kick out of the prehistoric Clue; now there's a new edition with *The Simpsons* characters.

But the most satisfying board games of all are those bearing the name *Lord of the Rings*. And strangely enough, there are only two licensed with that actual name at the time of this writing. Only two.

For the record, I have found a variety of other strategy games and TCG's (trading card games) that have been based on Tolkien's legendarium, some more loosely than others. Every month at our Green Books pages on TheOneRing.net we get several misguided letters from people trying to correlate the names of the nine Nazgûl with the Middle-earth: The Wizards TCG published by Iron Crown in 1995 (check your head, there are many apocryphal names on those cards, made up by the company to fill in details Tolkien did not record).

But here I will explore the two delicious board games that (through the magic of overpaid lawyers and tricky licensing) actually claim the name of our beloved epic.

Harking back to late 1978, we uncover the treasure of Ralph Bakshi's rotoscoped animated film. Surely many people wish to leave it buried, but that's another story. Within months of the film's wide release in the US, the classic game company Milton Bradley had store shelves piled high with The Lord of the Rings Adventure Game. My stepmom and I were wandering through Sears, of all places, and my eyes lit up like a certain wizard's fireworks when I saw it. I squealed and begged to get one, succeeded, and spent the next ten years adoring it like no other game.

The board, cards, and character tokens all bear designs from the Bakshi film. Cell animated characters are reproduced on the cards and game board just as you saw them on the silver screen.

Even though the maximum number of players is four, a player may choose any of the Nine Walkers and insert the token in a colored plastic base. (I always choose yellow, along with my faithful Sam — a habit unbroken after all this time.)

The most striking feature of this game is the oversized board. Actually, it's kind of wacky. The general map of Middle-earth, just like the one found in any edition of LotR, is reproduced on a grid of hexagons. To the distaste of many there is a great deal of abstraction in the layout of this hex-map, but it really is clever. Places along the travel route are given names (Bree, Rivendell, Lórien), and some are designated by color. For example, the Mines of Moria spaces are colored black, indicating underground darkness.

Players each take turns trying to move from Start, adjacent to a homely picture of a hobbit-hole, across the entirety of Middle-earth to reach the last space, labeled Mt. Doom. Thus the game mechanics are standard: whoever gets to the end of the board first is the winner.

There are a variety of obstacles, culled from the adversarial creatures that appear in the book: Nazgûl tokens that can be shifted about to block opponents, stationary Orcs marked on a quarter of the board's spaces, and even Shelob qualifies for her own hex. The mountains are especially difficult to cross, for each player has to roll a "delaying die" that determines how many turns you lose before you get to move out of the terrain.

The real meat and potatoes of this game are in the playing cards. They allow remarkably ruthless and cruel behavior among the players. You can steal little plastic Rings from your opponent, move him helpless into a posse of Orcs, or even bring a Nazgûl back from the dead to haunt his progress. I wonder what power of the Valar could ever conceive of resurrecting a Nazgûl! Yikes ...

Admittedly, the designs are simple, even a little silly at times. Looking at the goofy icon used for the Orcs, I wonder: "Who on Earth was paid to *draw* that?" It looks like a strange toothy walrus wearing a Viking helmet. But given the way United Artists was trying to sell the LotR property with a juvenile appeal back in 1978, it makes sense that the same flavor would sneak its way into this game.

The only way to play it is to know going in that you will be mean, heartless, and opportunistic at every chance. Two-player games end up being dull, really, because the dynamic is all wrong. I strongly advise three- or four-player matches played with gusto. The Bakshi film never actually completed the story, but thankfully this game allows you to fulfill your quest and destroy the Ring. But only at the expense of other players!

Nowadays the '79 LotR Adventure Game is a rare collector's item. Never reproduced in later editions, you will have to scour through eBay auctions and Gaming Conventions to find a decent copy that still has all its pieces. I am very lucky to own one in superb condition and an extra full game for replacement pieces.

In stark contrast we have the just-released Lord of the Rings board game designed by Reiner Knizia and released in America through Fantasy Flight Games. (Well, originally it was Hasbro aka Wizards of the Coast ... no, no that can't be right. The box has the Parker Bros. logo — and also the Tolkien Enterprises logo. This is confusing. Seems the licensing lawyers have been at it again.)

Anyway, take everything I just said about the old Milton Bradley game and reverse it. This extraordinary new game is lush, detailed, considerably more complicated, and rides on a principal that may just shock: You have to *help* your opponents, not *hinder*.

Knizia's design turns the traditional formula of board games on its ear. The spirit of cooperation reigns over the players as they struggle against the game itself. It is the truest representation of "fellowship" a board game can hope for. Even better, it keeps an amazing fidelity to themes and events in the novel, as you will see. At the risk of drooling, I declare from the mountaintop how much I love this new game.

It is difficult to dilute the essence of the mechanics, but I'll try. The main action is split along several game boards: the "Corruption Line" and the four "Scenario Boards." Each player (as many as five) takes the role of a hobbit from the story: Frodo, Sam, Merry, Pippin, or the estimable Fredegar Bolger. Why Fatty? It makes sense, since he too was one of the friendly conspirators and knew about the Ring, so you can extrapolate how he could have been included in the traveling company if the story had taken that course.

The hobbit players take turns being the Ringbearer, making their way through various adventure boards (Scenario Boards). The "Corruption Line" is the constant element, and a rather ominous piece that resembles an Eye atop Barad-dûr is placed at the darkest end of the spectrum. The hobbits begin over at the light end, and appropriately, the Ring corrupts everyone throughout the game. The only winning outcome is if everyone stays in the light and somehow keeps the Sauron piece at a safe distance. If he catches any of the hobbits on the Corruption Line, they're removed from the game.

You have to be a very sharp strategist to get through this. Typical of a Knizia game, there are many choices to make and they become increasingly hard as you go. Generosity is key — you will spend your best cards and life tokens for your fellow player, giving support and advice as events get worse. At the end, several others may willingly die so you can have one last chance to destroy the Ring. It's marvelous.

Instead of simplified iconography, we have John Howe's excellent artwork covering every inch of the play area and cards. It is no surprise that Peter Jackson hired Howe to stay in New Zealand for a year, alongside Alan Lee, producing conceptual work for the films. The rich textures and colors are exemplary. I want to put the Helm's Deep Scenario Board in a nice frame!

Who knows what fun things are yet to come from these clever designers? Knizia has released two expansions to his award-winning game (ah, more Howe artwork!), so I can only guess at what other LotR games may be coming down the pipe. I better throw out that forgotten old Pictionary and make room in my closet.

Much too hasty,
Quickbeam

40. Welcome to Merchandising Hell

Quickbeam

Emblazoned above the gate: "Abandon all disposable income, ye who enter here."

Let us wind back the clock to, say, April of 1999. Certainly you remember the unprecedented hype that surrounded *Episode One: The Phantom Menace*? All the local news channels were interviewing people in line outside of Mann's Chinese Theatre (myself being one of them)... people rushing Toys 'R Us at 3:00 a.m. to secure some pre-release action figures ... then of course the many magazine covers: *Time*, *Newsweek* (and yes, *Popular Mechanics*). Remember the little C-3PO coffee mugs? Maybe you own a set?

No one was immune from the hype when it rose to its highest pitch. None could hide from it. Every merchant was saturated — be he bookseller, 7-Eleven, or Taco Bell. Shopping malls across the country were awash with countless toys, confections, and doo-dads. Even the Pygmy tribes in the secluded Amazon jungle had little Darth Maul T-shirts. Yes, truly! I saw it on the Discovery Channel. I bore witness to a frenzy of marketing campaigns executed throughout Hollywood: banners, billboards, and signs, oh my! It's an Industry Town, after all.

Well, I now admit fretting somewhat about the same thing happening with New Line's film trilogy for *The Lord of the Rings*.

I suspected that when Peter Jackson's first installment was released late in 2001, something would happen that Tolkien fans had never seen before. I warned everyone ominously: "Mark my words, it will come upon you like a huge, unstoppable wave. It is the powerful tide of COMMERCE, and you can swim with it if you like, because struggling against it is quite pointless."

Sure, there was Ralph Bakshi's 1978 adaptation of LotR, but come on! It was so poorly received it didn't make a dent. What limited merchandising there was has now become a specialty market for eBay auctions. I recall there was a handful of silly action figures, a nice calendar, and one exceptional board game from Milton Bradley (still my all-time fave). Maybe a coloring book for the little ones. That's about it.

All signs pointed to the new version of Tolkien's classic being given the *Star Wars* treatment by its studio. Hey, I don't blame them for their approach. Everyone from the lead actors down to the distributors anticipated that PJ's film would be a juggernaut, the kind Hollywood execs glibly refer to as "instant franchise." I tried to prepare my readers for the hype, the glory, and more junk than Santa's big red sleigh. You see, merchandisers are very smart people, and likewise Saul Zaentz, who holds all licenses for products related to Tolkien's work.

My zaniest predictions for film-related products (long before the theatrical release of *Fellowship*) shows a bit of my cynical voice. Confident that anyone above the age of eight would cringe at the new stuff, I certainly did entertain the ridiculous:

•*Gollum Toothpaste* — helps to keep your kids' teeth shiny clean, even if "we only has six."

• *Twirling Ringwraith Lollypops* — the little battery operated kind with a handle shaped like a Nazgûl. Follow one of these with a generous brushing of Gollum Toothpaste.

•*Shadowfax Pony Food* — for all you equestrians who want your pony to grow up big and strong.

•*Samwise's Gardening Kit* — this is inevitable. A spade, nutrient-rich soil, and some *ch-ch-ch-chia* seeds conveniently packaged and sold at drugstores.

•*LotR Multivitamins* — tart and colorful with 100 percent Daily Value of vitamins and minerals. Kids love biting the head off Aragorn.

•*Happy Orthanc Playset* — plastic construction toy for pre-schoolers to build their own Orc stronghold. Sold in conjunction with:

•*Hasty Ents Playset* — for the pre-schooler who wants to see his trees win the day! The ultimate environmental message for your kids.

•*Gandalf in Moria Coin Bank* — plastic figure of Gandalf standing next to a deep "coin well." Every time you drop in a quarter, the voice chip yells out "Fool of a Took!"

•*Butterbur's Fax Service* — when you absolutely need that letter sent RIGHT AWAY.

•*LotR Breakfast Cereal* — crunchy Rings of toasted corn with little marshmallows shaped like Morgul knives.

•*Phial of Galadriel Nightlight* — plug it in and your child's room is immersed in glowing elf-light. Chases all the unpleasant bug-a-boos away.

•*Shelob Roach Traps* — rid your home of ants, roaches, and flies. Better than spinning your own web.

•*Lórien Lembas* — tasty nutrition bars sold at fitness clubs. Dairy-free, low carbs, and high protein for those long jaunts on the Stairmaster.

•*Pippin's Palantír* — works just like a Magic 8-Ball, only it doesn't take over your mind.

•*Wormtongue Shoe Polish* — in honor of the best bootlicker in Middle-earth.

After the first movie came out, I saw how New Line did not avalanche the fans with a *Star Wars*-type mess. Maybe they watched carefully and learned from George Lucas's mistake. His oversaturation of banal product was not selling well (no wonder, *Episode One* was poorly received by its fans). I sense that New Line pulled back somewhat, fearing similar over-hype and backlash, and the resulting licensed merchandise was a mixed bag. I didn't see as many silly T-shirts as I thought might appear. Consider some of the stuff that actually did emerge from the tie-in machinery:

•*Burger King Glass Goblets* — the goblets light up red from the bottom. HA!

•*Houghton Mifflin tie-in books* — Brian Sibley's *Official Movie Guide* for example, with fun behind-the-scenes photos.

•*Decipher's LotR Trading Card Game* — terrific for people like me who enjoy strategy/fantasy games á la Magic: the Gathering.

•*Sideshow/WETA collectibles* — with gorgeous busts, statues, and figures created by the movie's Oscar-winning design team.

•*Toy Biz Action Figures* — in the spirit of all franchises, a figure for every hero, villain, and monster.

•*Playmates Sets* — I was dead right on this: Isengard Caverns has its own plastic construction set!

•*Candy and Cereal* — European kids could eat Kinder Surprise chocolate eggs and even Cinnamon Grahams with Christopher Lee grinning evilly at them on the cereal box.

It was shocking, amusing, and ironic all at once for us literary types who had *never* imagined Frodo's picture on the side of a milkshake cup. Who could have dreamt up a wacky Super Bowl commercial, complete with Celtic flutes and a shadowy wizard, using the Ring Verse while flashing the championship ring given out to winning players?! Tolkien connected with American football? It was enough to pull us outside of our comfortable notions of "the typical fan experience" (others just wanted to pull their hair out).

The ugliest business of all was the announcement that during the summer of 2002 Kia Motors America would launch a huge LotR campaign for their new Sorento off-road vehicles. I spit as I type this now. Poor Tolkien is surely turning over in his grave. Toys are great fun and nobody could argue with a chocolate egg, but using LotR to sell a sport utility vehicle? The Professor hated cars ... he absolutely hated what they did to the English countryside. Everyone knows this. Motor-cars and the building of roads to accommodate them were like the spirit of Mordor to him: destructive, polluting machines that eroded the green landscape he held so dear. If Kia SUVs had existed in Middle-earth, then Saruman would have been behind the wheel — smashing vegetation and underbrush and filling the air with poison fumes. Now this idiotic automaker wanted consumers to associate the beautiful pristine world of Tolkien's imagination with a combustion-engine car that would rip right over it. What were they thinking?

Fans of the original books find themselves in a brave new world of pop culture associations and merchandise. Back in the 1960s no one would have guessed it would be like this now. You either love it or despise it. Both sides have something going on here. Art and Commerce are two dancers locked in a strange waltz. They always go together, moving, sometimes stumbling, across the floor. On a good day they are capable of creating lovely dances that mesmerize and entertain. But often they miss a crucial step and fall flat on their embarrassed faces.

Much too hasty,
Quickbeam

41. True Fans, Truly Obsessed

Quickbeam

When you get right down to it, no one on earth has fans quite like the late John Ronald Reuel Tolkien. Ringaholics, Tolkienites, Tree-hugging hobbit-knockers (or the new trend: pervy hobbit fanciers); whatever label you want will fit just fine. Of course, "fan" is a state of mind as much as it is obvious behavior ... and you can color fanhood any number of ways.

I've been to concerts where fans are utterly enraptured by the performers. Dead Can Dance is a prime example. Rare is the musical artist who casts such a spell of reverence over the audience; they act like they're in church. Have you ever been to a large comic book convention? I have twice met Neil Gaiman, author of *The Sandman*, at such functions. It never fails that he is quickly mobbed by stumbling, sweaty fan-boys everywhere he goes (alas poor Neil). Pop diva Cher has several websites furnished by her adoring fans. Some focus on her music, some her acting career, and one even profiles her cosmetic surgeon. You get the idea.

But Tolkien fans — that's a whole different ball of wax. As a lifelong aficionado of Middle-earth, I speak with authority when I say: something sets us apart. We are a breed so unique that others pale in comparison. In fact, we're kind of nuts. Spell that N-U-T-S. As a group we spend more of our lives poring over Tolkien's writings and artistry than is reasonable and certainly more than we'll admit. We live and breathe his fictional world as a basic factor in our lives, even using the term *secondary reality* to describe it.

It's a genuine measure of our devotion when this man's work has seeped into our everyday world. What compels someone (me for example) to permanently mark their body with a tattoo of fiery Elvish letters? Have you ever memorized any phrases of Quenya that inspire you or named your goldfish Frodo? How many times have you corrected someone in conversation: *"It is not pronounced tahl-kin, it's toll-keen."* Go ahead, admit it.

Now a whole new generation of Tolkien fans will come to the fore, via the movies. The fact that Peter Jackson is even attempting to film the *LotR* Trilogy raises the hackles of a huge population. You may call these people purists. They are worried the films will not be true to the source. Indeed, they despise any adaptation of Tolkien's work, for the stage, radio, or any visual media. "It's all blasphemy," they say. "Nothing can hold a candle to the original. Ultimately these people will fail to manifest the profundity of his work." There are Shakespeare purists, too, who function much the same way. Personally, I greatly anticipated Jackson's films, but I didn't envy him one bit. He has the toughest of all possible audiences to please. It was a near impossible feat.

[Post-movie editorial: I must interject that at the time of this original writing in April 2000, most fans on the net had no idea how wonderful and satisfying PJ's version of *The Fellowship of the Ring* would be, nor could we have guessed it would become so successful worldwide, earning well over $850 million at the box office, garnering 13 Academy Award Nominations (four wins) and galvanizing the online Tolkien community. Everyone had their fingers crossed, but we could never have known, not really, that the film would hit THAT kind of bulls eye! — QB]

In the other corner, the really overbearing beat-you-to-death-if-you-forget-an-accent kind of fans can get out of control. Take the debate of nasturtians vs. nasturtiums. Our very own Sir Ian McKellen —yes, Gandalf himself—has been embroiled in the fixation of zealous Tolkien fans. Not long ago he wrote a wonderful Grey Book entry on his official website (www.mckellen.com) and in his description of the Hobbiton set, he mentioned the little orange flowers planted there.

He used the name Tolkien used, "nasturtians" (Indian Cress), and then started to get e-mail from some smartass who presumed to know better, "Don't mean to be picky, but nasturtiUMS."

And since Sir Ian is a detail-oriented man, he decided to do some fact checking. You really must when you're dealing with these types. He asked for clarification from his webmaster, Keith Stern, who is easily one of the most avid Tolkien buffs on the Pacific Coast and has a keen eye for details. This was the correspondence that followed from Mr. Stern to Sir Ian:

> The spelling "nasturtians" was a quirk of Tolkien's but he was very definite about it — remember he was a philologist. In *LotR* he refers to "nasturtians" and never "nasturtiums," so if the set designers are using *ums* instead of *ans* then they have made a mistake (I don't think they have, as *ums* would have only yellow or white flowers).
>
> Even the editors for Allen & Unwin's printers changed the spelling to "nasturtiums" when setting the first printing and felt Tolkien's wrath as a result.
>
> So, to Tolkien at least, "nasturtian" was used to refer to Indian Cress (Tropaeolum Majus). "Nasturtium" might be used to refer to Watercress (Nasturtium officinale). ...If you want to remain effortlessly true to Tolkien, spell it with an *an*.
>
> You will certainly find gardeners, herbalists, and experts who call Indian Cress "Nasturtium" and that is the most common spelling, but for some reason Tolkien (who was an avid gardener) was touchy about the difference — therefore so am I.
>
> Your e-mailer better have some documentation to back up his/her claim. My main source is Tolkien's letter to Katherine Farrer of 7 August, 1954.

You could not ask for a better source. Within Letter No. 148 Tolkien shares a funny anecdote about how he clashed with a *LotR* proofreader who was changing out words like "nasturtians," blindly assuming the author was mistaken. It seems that the earliest 1954 edition of *The Fellowship of the Ring* contained numerous misprints because changes were made without anyone checking with Tolkien himself. The nerve! So he had to go back, slap the guy around a bit, and ensure that his specific use of elven (instead of elfin), among others, would go unmolested. The Professor ardently recounts his efforts to keep "nasturtians" pure. Having a small chat with a college gardener (whose tone of voice sounds suspiciously like the Old Gaffer), we learn more than we need to know about these plants, and Tolkien shows us he is a master of exactitude.

So now perhaps you have an idea of how the man operated. Without his obstinate efforts to consider every word, every phrase, every color of language, the results would not be nearly so successful. His rigorous attention to detail brings out the best in his stories. It also brings out the most rabid fans.

But why are we so involved?

The answer lies with JRRT himself. He was more than a writer, he was a historian. He did not simply impose a plot on his characters and roll out mechanical dialogue. Deeper than any author of the 20th century he delved into the meticulous creation of a *world*. A world replete with its own genesis, geography, civilization, organic infrastructure and upwards of a dozen original languages (with dialiects and alphabet systems!). Although we have only five books set in Middle-earth, within them Tolkien really gave us many thousands of years of history, sweeping and self-inclusive. This was his great achievement: an elaborate history wrapped within itself a hundred times over. He spent nearly 50 years writing *The Silmarillion*, and at the time of his death he still considered it incomplete.

As much as I enjoy the work of Isaac Asimov, Orson Scott Card, Ursula K. Le Guin, and occasionally Piers Anthony, they never came close to what Tolkien did. Where do you find millions of passionate Terry Brooks fans who are as nuts as we are? You don't.

I know you've heard this phrase a million times but think about it once more: "the scope of Tolkien's creation ..." Think again and then reflect on the focused mind that brought it to fruition. We recognize this man as a creative singularity because we grasp the Herculean effort that went into his books. That's the quality in his authorship that most inspires us. We readers who see beyond the trappings of the "adventure tale" and sense the affectionate labor within are truly receptive to Tolkien's sagacity. That is why we are the fans we are. Other readers give him credit only as a writer of charming children's books, in the manner of *Harry Potter*. Excuse me, those poor souls just don't get it.

Right now, I look out my window and see the bright blue swimming pool below. There I see my friends, glowing with sun-worship and sharing strawberry margaritas. The light plays on the water, and I hear laughter and camaraderie. But I'm not down there with them. Instead, I'm examining my first edition of *The Silmarillion*, double-checking my maps in Fonstad's *Atlas of Middle-earth*, and making sure

PRESENT DREAMS

I put the perfect little accents on every Nazgûl and Palantír. I am driven to be thorough, to show respect for Tolkien's work, no matter the time or effort it costs.

Spoken like a true fan.

Much too hasty,
Quickbeam

42. Uqbar, Orbis Tertius, Middle-earth

Tehanu

Many years ago I read a short story by the Argentinean writer Jorge Luis Borges, and that story influenced the way I've thought about the Tolkien world-building phenomenon.

The story was called "Tlön, Uqbar, Orbis Tertius," and like most of Borges's stories, it breaks most of the conventions of storytelling. It's cast in a form like some sort of essay-cum-letter from a scholarly person who assumes you know his friends and his background and that you share their knowledge of all philosophers, living or dead, in six languages. It's a disturbing little tale, under all the scholarly fussiness.

Over dinner (the author begins), a friend quotes a philosopher from Uqbar. Nobody's ever heard of such a place, but the friend insists it's in the *Anglo-American Encyclopædia*. Further investigation shows that four pages on the mysterious country of Uqbar exist in some copies of the 10th edition of that work, but not in others.

It all would have ended there except for the death of an acquaintance who left behind him *A First Encyclopædia of Tlön. Volume XI: Hlaer to Jangr*. The author (or at any rate, the protagonist) says:

> It was two years since I had discovered, in a volume of a pirated encyclopædia, a brief description of a false country; now, chance was showing me something much more valuable, something to be reckoned with. Now, I had in my hands a substantial fragment of the complete history of an unknown planet, with its architecture and its playing cards, its mythological terrors and the sound of its dialects, its emperors and its oceans, its minerals, its birds, and its fishes, its algebra and its fire,

its theological and metaphysical arguments, all clearly stated, coherent, without any apparent dogmatic intention or parodic undertone.

Can you see where I'm headed with this?

Since no other volumes turn up, but there is an explosion of detective and scholarly effort to try and find the other volumes, somebody eventually suggests "that we all take on the task of reconstructing the missing volumes, many and vast as they were." He figures that one generation of the so-called "Tlönists" will be enough to carry out the task.

Eventually the complete encyclopædia appears in a library in Memphis, and by then it's more or less proven to be the work of a secret society that has labored for centuries on this hoaxing game, the Orbis Tertius.

> The popular magazines have publicized, with pardonable zeal, the zoology and topography of Tlön. I think, however, that its transparent tigers and its towers of blood scarcely deserve the unwavering attention of *all* men. I should like to take some little time to deal with its conception of the universe.

And in that dry, unassuming tone, the story goes on to startle and confound.

Walk into any bookstore and that is exactly what you see: shelves of books about the Tolkien universe, the *Star Wars* universe, the *Babylon 5* universe ... the places we wish were real. The places we would *will* into being if we could.

All well and good. In Borges's story, all seems explicable, if rather odd, until objects begin to appear in the real world, just as mysteriously as the books did. A woman orders a dinner set from Poitiers:

> Amongst them, trembling faintly, just perceptibly, like a sleeping bird, was a magnetic compass. It shivered mysteriously ... the letters on the dial corresponded with one of the alphabets of Tlön. Such was the first intrusion of the fantastic world into the real one.

And later the author comes across a drunkard lying dead with a few coins and a small metal cone the "of the diameter of a die," which weighs almost more than a man can lift. "These small and extremely heavy cones, made of a metal which does not exist in this world, are images of divinity in certain religions in Tlön."

Suddenly everyone wanted to be a Tlönist, to believe in Tlön, to write about it, study its philosophy and so on. Reality gave way under the onslaught of publications from and about Tlön. "Contact with Tlön and the ways of Tlön have disintegrated this world. Captivated by its discipline, humanity forgets and goes on forgetting that it is the discipline of chess players, not of angels ... "

I guess some people watching their friends or family submerge themselves for hours and weeks in imaginary game worlds must recognize this uneasy sense that the tangible world is being disregarded, ignored, fled away from.

In Tlön, things can be forced into existence through the desire for and belief in their being, and it seems to me that the *Silmarillion* was a little like this and the *Unfinished Tales* even more so. It's fanned the flames of a mania for medievalism, for fantasy, for historical re-enactment, for swords and sorcery ... would that have come about without *The Lord of the Rings?* And now, people are insatiable to know more, to invent every detail of Middle-earth, as though somehow to force it into being. And so more is revealed. Not only by Christopher Tolkien, who has access to his father's notes, but also by the legion of fans who write fan fiction based on Tolkien's world, much of it online.

But it was Tolkien who originally desired to bring this world into being and almost had the genius to carry it off.

I say "almost" because unlike the secret society of Orbis Tertius, Tolkien is able to show his world only in the light of his own knowledge (which is vast, admittedly — he was a well-read man). So *The Silmarillion* and the histories are full of languages and legends, myths and poetry, stars and trees. I've argued before now that the invention of convincing languages is one of the most powerful ways of making an alternate world credible. We respond to language subconsciously and intuitively, every one of us. So many fantasy authors, hoping to command the same sense of authenticity in their works, "try it on" by elaborating their own area of expertise. If their obsession is medieval armor, good on them, but it's not an interest shared by about half the human race. (Those people called, y'know, "women.")

Tolkien's works are not full of architecture or geology or math or political intrigue or criminal law or housekeeping or physics or any of the things he didn't know in detail. Borges's Tlön was supposedly created by a committee of experts in many disciplines who handed the task down to successors. In Borges's story it takes hundreds of people to create a world credible enough to obsess the public interest. Measure that against the fascination that Tolkien's world exerts over us, and consider that it was done by one man working with very little precedent.

Living as I do not far from where Peter Jackson's films were being made, I would sometimes get a strange sense that there was a light overlay of another country, almost visible, only waiting for the lighting and camera crews to bring it closer into being. These are places I know well, in some cases, and yet they are being *fantasticated*. The process is entirely imaginary, but the more minds share in the imaginary process, the more force it gains.

It's like when somebody decides to build a stone tower in the middle of an otherwise ordinary suburb, as has happened in the film's capital, Wellington. What books were they reading when they made that decision? And since the first film came out, various people have stated that they will build a hobbit-hole to live in themselves, by hook or by crook, even if they have to rewrite city planning ordinances to do it. Some of them will carry out their dream, I expect. And so the real country of New Zealand will edge a little closer to our dream of Middle-earth.

So far the good people down at Richard Taylor's props and effects workshop, Weta, have behaved like responsible and sober-minded citizens about this, which is a shame in my view. As far as I know they've resisted the temptation to put on Ringwraith costumes and go out one night to freak the living daylights out of some kids taking a shortcut through the Shire woods, which are right in the middle of the nation's capital. Imagine the impact that would have! How much more interesting it would be if a trip to the local shop had the possibility of encountering one of the Nine ...

"I couldn't see it clearly, officer ... but I heard it sort of *sniffing* at me!"

To go add to the rash people who thought they'd seen Sean Connery (the wrong Sean, as it turned out, but in the early days of the movie there was a rumor that he'd play Gandalf), I've been expecting a proliferation of false Ringwraiths, Balrog wannabes, people who claim to be Aragorn, people who really think they *are* Aragorn, people who claim to be actors who are Aragorn (and will want you to buy them a drink on the strength of that), and so on. I'm hoping that New Zealand will never recover from having *The Lord of the Rings* filmed in it.

So far all I've encountered is a realistically grumpy Gandalf taking part in San Francisco's famous Bay to Breakers footrace, but it's early days yet. I took it for a hopeful sign that this particular mania is spreading.

Fun is where you make it, really, and the opportunities have never been so good.

Sources:

Jorge Luis Borges, *Tlön Uqbar Orbis Tertius*. The Porcupine's Quill, 1983.

The Films

43. Set Your Sites on Hollywood

Quickbeam

Venerable film critic Roger Ebert once posited that the internet would change the landscape of showbiz forever. "The movie industry has the same relationship to the Internet today that it had to talkies in the 1920s: Plug in or quit." He emphatically predicted that the old-timers running Hollywood would suffer if they did not get wise to the Net. The studio suits sitting around their boardrooms would have to rethink their development of projects, press relations, and of course their marketing schemes. All because of one simple thing: shared electronic media.

I see it happening. Compared with Hollywood in its '50s heyday, nothing seems the same now. Back then powerhouse studios kept a tight lid on things; only the most controlled leaks got out. The movie-going public knew precious little from what gossip columnists could dig up. A successful studio knew how to feed ticket-buyers exactly what was best for them.

That Golden Age is long gone. The net has demolished the carefully guarded walls of movie making. The driving forces behind Hollywood are demystified now that every person online has access to them. Nowadays you just point, click, and *voilà* ... you are on the backlot. The best movie fan sites give the scoop on films long before they reach production. People post their "dream castings" on message boards before casting directors even get out of bed. Movie geeks are now an empowered clan. Advance buzz, that most elusive of commodities, can build up a movie to a flying success (New Line's *LotR* trilogy) or sink it beneath the waves (Paramount's sadly failing *Star Trek* franchise). The old notion of limited access is extinct — for regardless of who signs a "confidentiality agreement," furtive movie spies go online anyway and post stories anonymously.

That's how TheOneRing.net initially started out. Fans clamored for photos of the New Zealand countryside and ripped through spy reports as fast as we could get them up. As popular interest in *The Fellowship of the Ring* grew, Tolkien fans wanted to air their concerns for how Tolkien's work was being treated as a commercial movie product. Our site charted the progress of the films over two years, and behind-the-scenes reports opened a new lifeline to a distant country in the South Pacific. Now the barrier between movie production and movie audience was completely shattered, for at this point Peter Jackson (and many of his cast and crew) were actually reading TORn to get the scoop! The director and screenwriters visited our site to get wind of what the fans wanted .... and what they feared. Not a production day would go by without the effects team at WETA logging on to see what new developments we reported. I say this with some pride, yes, but no one was more surprised to learn of it than we were.

What we do at TORn is something like alchemy. We take myriad small comments and turn them into a larger voice that even Hollywood listens to. In "We Cry at Beauty," Tehanu speaks of "the growth of a fan community that is in worldwide communication to such an extent that it involves the world media and the filmmakers themselves."

We relate strongly to Tolkien's work in the cinematic medium. Whether it is me waxing nostalgic over the old TV cartoons ("Love/Hate Rankin/Bass") or Anwyn carefully finding a comfort zone with the new *LotR* movies ("A New Direction for Tolkien Purism"), we are all in the same audience. No longer a passive audience, mind you, as we now have the ear of the creative people behind the camera. This section presents a very personal record of my journey to the New Zealand film sets ("Where the Stars are Strange"), alongside all our original movie reviews of Jackson's first two installments, *The Fellowship of the Ring* and *The Two Towers*. So it seems that Mr. Ebert's vision of a paradigm shift in the Hollywood machinery is coming true. Movie studios now have the fans looking over their shoulder every step of the way. Out of necessity, the film biz is paying close attention to the net and its vocal denizens.

The fans have been heard. Their fingerprints are on the lens.

Much too hasty,
Quickbeam

44. We Cry at Beauty

Tehanu

In June 2002, the *San Francisco Chronicle*'s Steven Winn wrote an article musing on why people cry in the presence of beauty. It's "our most fundamental and mysterious response to art" that makes tears flow when we look at things that are not sad but piercingly beautiful — that feeling Tolkien describes in "The Field of Cormallen" chapter of *Return of the King*, where the minstrel sang to the assembly "until their hearts, wounded with sweet words, overflowed ..."

The *Chronicle* did a follow-up to the article inviting readers to write about the things that called up their tears in that way. They got dozens of replies. Among them, the movie *The Lord of the Rings* got two mentions, and in each case it was for the quality of the friendship between the characters. One writer mentioned that their "unwavering commitment" got his tears flowing; another man recalled the "depth of loyalty and friendship ... the saving of one life by another, the utter simplicity of devotion and love acted out."

There were other films mentioned: *Casablanca, It's a Wonderful Life, Death in Venice, Babe, Field of Dreams, Gone with the Wind,* and Charlie Chaplin's *City Lights*. Many of them are unarguable classics, so it's nice to see a *Lord of the Rings* film in that company. Not only that, but it's telling to see so many films mentioned in the same breath as Mahler's *Adagietto* from the Fifth Symphony, Martin Luther King's "I Have a Dream" speech, Tchaikovsky's *Swan Lake*, The Beatles' "Eleanor Rigby," arias from *Der Rosenkavalier*, the voice of Frederica von Stade singing *La Vie en Rose*, Schubert's piano trios, Shakespeare's plays, Keats' poetry, Beethoven, Mozart, Rembrandt, Rodin and Picasso.

Right back when I started "Tehanu's Notes" on TheOneRing.net, I wrote about the possibility that cinema will be the art that defines the 20th and 21st centuries in the same way that Baroque music or

Renaissance painting define the spirit of their times. The cinema is something that is capable of being great art and also very much part of everyday popular culture, and few people have no opinion about it. A lively art is like that — there's an easy ebb and flow of ideas between the people making it, learning to make it and those appreciating it. There is a cinematic mainstream and there are strong currents that build on it or challenge it. Special effects-laden movies using CGI (computer-generated images) may be the defining genre of the turn of the millenium, the works that will be remembered as our Old Masters.

I have felt for a long time that art, music and architecture are losing that sense of being a living popular art by becoming increasingly fragmented. You have to be educated to follow the trends in art and architecture. How much modern architecture do we inhabit with the same easy pleasure and admiration we feel in, for instance, Chartres Cathedral or Venice's Plaza San Marco? While pop music remains in touch with pop culture, "art" or classical music seems adrift, with no agreement on what is central and what is not. Once upon a time even the street vendors could whistle themes from Rossini's latest opera. Nobody is whistling the themes from a contemporary opera around here now, except for the pianist downstairs from me who's just spent four hours slaving over a hot metronome trying to learn something arrhythmic and atonal and who consequently can't get it out of his head.

I'm not saying that modern art and music are bad; it's just that we can't seem to agree very widely on where their center is and where they are headed, exactly. They no longer seem life-changing to very many people.

If cinema is our great art form, then the *The Lord of the Rings* came from something like Rafael's workshop. The technicians at WETA doing the special effects were pleased by the comparison when I first made it before the film came out, and I still believe it to be true. Those old masters of the Renaissance did not paint alone when they had a really big canvas to cover. They had helpers who specialized in many tasks that formed part of the final creation: grinding the pigments, preparing the canvas, or painting details such as drapery folds, hands, and haloes. The many, many unknown artists involved in making a big film are like that — painting, writing code, designing software. Imagine them as Tolkien's dwarves, hidden away in their caves, ruled by a passion to make a thing that is beautiful. The people I met in the film worked as if in the grip of a fever to create.

The *Fellowship of the Rings* movie marks a coming-of-age for fantasy films and for big-budget special effects films. All of that wonder and imagination and creativity were there in the first amazing *Star Wars* film, and since then the techniques have only gotten better. But now they've been made subordinate to the story, and the story has the power to make people cry. It's like we've been admiring the painting technique and marveling over the transition from tempura to oil paint for too long. Instead, let's look at what the picture is about! It might move you to tears.

Moved to tears by *The Lord of the Rings* ... I notice that people are still saying that books "change their life." The *Lord of the Rings* movie changed my own life more than the books did—without it there would have been no urgent reason to start up another website for Tolkien fans. Without that, there wouldn't have been the growth of a fan community that is in worldwide communication to such an extent that it involves the world media and the filmmakers themselves.

All these things came to mind when I went to a "Pot-luck Picnic and Lembas Bake-off" for "Ringer" fans living in the area who'd met on the net. Three years ago, it's doubtful that it would have crossed any of our minds to hold such an event. Nor could we have organized it so conveniently.

The announcement of Peter Jackson's film project just happened to coincide with the time when e-mail and the internet began to grow exponentially among people (like me) who had no previous interest in computers. Without that timing, there wouldn't be the fan community that exists today. There have been online discussion groups for Tolkien fans since the net began — the large crossover between computer jocks and Tolkien fans is not just a stereotype — but TheOneRing.net started at the same time that the net began to be commonplace for everyone, not just technophiles. So now this particular global village of ours includes children and matriarchs and village elders, you could say. When people ask what difference the films have made to Tolkien fans, that is one answer — it's given us the community to which we belong.

At the picnic it came up in conversation how *The Lord of the Rings* had changed people's lives, and it's a thing I've seen discussed in TORn's chat room and message boards often enough. If stories are to be believed, then it is true that *The Lord of the Rings* has dragged people back from the brink of death. More than one person has said or written to me that at some point they were about to give up, they were about to die, and they found the strength to go on because they thought something like "Frodo wouldn't have given up!"

Now, this is not a recent thing. In some cases they were speaking of a turning point long ago in their life. But before, there wasn't really a place where they could speak about it and expect to be understood.

Recently there was a discussion on our website messageboard about obsession. People talked about falling in love with books and movies, and how that was sometimes an infatuation that burned out, and sometimes an enduring love.

They wondered whether they'd look back at their current LotR-mania as a craze, or whether their collection of Tolkieniana would always sit around taking pride of place on the mantelpiece. Others said that discovering Middle-earth for the first time felt like a homecoming, and they would always want to be in contact with others who shared that feeling. In a less dramatic way, people who've always enjoyed the books privately have found that once they were drawn into the never-ending online discussion about Middle-earth, they too had no end to their curiosity and imagination concerning the topic.

The sheer invention that goes on around the Rings is a joy, really. In three years of running TORn, I've come to take for granted the in-jokes, crazes, spoofs, traditions, acronyms and new words that sprout up continually on the website. There is something especially funny about a joke that nobody but another "Ringer" or "TORNado" would get — the very feature that makes in-jokes so irritating to outsiders. I'm still not sick of the Middle-earth song parodies or the witty spoof images that people create every day. I don't even scratch the surface of the whole response to the Rings — every month TORn's Green Books staff read through a gigantic pile of fan fiction sparked off by Tolkien's writing. People paint and draw Middle-earth, they make costumes, they write poetry and songs, and they even figure out how to forge their own One Ring.

If there's one thing the film influenced more than we could have foreseen, it's the growth of interest in Tolkien's languages, especially Quenya and Sindarin. Seeing them written down in books was no preparation for how beautiful they actually sound. It's like a secret that hardly anyone knew besides Tolkien, who invented them with the intention of making something as sensual and aesthetically pleasing to the ear as a great wine is to the palate. Hearing them in the film was a revelation. We know from our e-mail as well as from talking to the owners of Elvish linguistics websites that the result has been a surge of interest in learning them. What really made my day recently was a conversation with a high school kid who was teaching herself Sindarin along with her friends. They thought it was the coolest secret language to have!

In *The Silmarillion* there is a story of how the Valar Aüle secretly created the dwarves. He wanted to create a race of beings that would perceive the beauty of the world that Ilúvatar had created and to whom Aüle could teach his lore and craft. He created the dwarves, but without the power of Ilúvatar they could not take on an independent life of their own. Ilúvatar granted this power. Tolkien may have wondered whether his own sub-created world of Middle-earth could take on a life of its own, or whether it was like Aüle's first attempt at making Dwarves — a pitiful attempt, unable to move save by his direction.

The answer is that his work has taken on more life than he could have imagined in his wildest dreams. There is no end in sight to the creative energy that is still rolling on like a wave spreading in all directions outwards from books to art to film to music and dance. It's absurd when you think of the tiny ripple that started it all — a blank page on an examination paper that Tolkien was marking, and the unbidden sentence that came to him then, "In a hole in the ground there lived a hobbit ..."

Sources:
Steven Winn, Arts and Culture Critic, *San Francisco Chronicle*, June 11, 2002.

45. Love/Hate Rankin/Bass

Quickbeam

Remember the buck-toothed Bilbo who was so pudgy that it was anatomically impossible for him to walk? Remember the very slimy, frog-like Gollum who frightened you so much? Remember Glenn Yarbrough singing with that ridiculous warble? Anyone over the age of 40 might not understand what I'm going on about. But the others of you — those children of the 1970s who were too young to understand Watergate yet were the first audience enraptured by *Star Wars* — you will know exactly where I'm about to go.

This little trip down memory lane is brought to you by a man who really loves those Rankin/Bass animated versions of Tolkien. I grew up on them. But at the same time I can't stomach the oversimplified scripts, the treacly songs, and the rampant silliness that makes you think, "That is so NOT Tolkien." Yes, even as I adore them, I realize how awful they are as well. Is it nostalgia or schizophrenia?

Back when I was just eight, Arthur Rankin Jr. and Jules Bass were famous names in my house. Every Holiday Special they made was cause for celebration, eventually leading to havoc in front of the TV set while my brother and I jockeyed for the prime seat in the living room (our father's reclining chair). We always lost that fight to our father, because he wanted to watch too. We sat on the floor, staring up at the television in awe. Nothing brought me more joy than the "Animagic" stop-motion animation Rankin/Bass used for *Rudolph the Red-nosed Reindeer* and *The Year Without a Santa Claus* (ah, Heat-Miser, greatest camp villain of all time). Nothing, that is, until *The Hobbit* was broadcast by ABC in 1977.

Having no idea what a hobbit was or where the "Middle-of-the-Earth" could be found, I still trembled with excitement when the movie came on. How thrilling to see a story about "Elves, Dwarves, Wizards,

261

Goblins, Dragons .... and Hobbits." With eyes wide and breath held, my little imagination went wild! I instantly fell in love. So deeply did I fall under the spell of this little movie — well, not even my mom could stop me from crying uncontrollably when Thorin died at the end. Hey, whatever, I was eight years old!

When Messrs. Rankin and Bass acquired the rights to *The Hobbit* they assembled some of the best voice talent available while bringing on board a Japanese production company for the animation itself. This creative assembly would work together years later on *The Return of the King* (RotK). So fruitful was the collaboration with key animator Kazuyuki Kobayashi that he would again work with Rankin/Bass for *The Last Unicorn* in 1982, which is why that film bears such a strong artistic resemblance to their earlier Tolkien efforts.

A small history tangent for you: after Ralph Bakshi's 1978 abbreviated version of *The Lord of the Rings*, no sequel would follow. Very rude to leave the story hanging like that! Very unhappy fans arose, too. So Rankin/Bass picked up the rights just for RotK — a sensible move to conclude the story, as Tolkien was enjoying a mighty wave of popularity in the late 1970s (right after his death, sadly enough).

Do you realize the caliber of talent that contributed their voices? The cast list reads like a Who's Who from the Golden Age of Hollywood. Thorin was Hans Conried, the most prolific character actor ever, who freaked out kids worldwide in *The 5,000 Fingers of Dr. T* and was also the voice of Snidely Whiplash on *The Bullwinkle Show*. John Huston provided what I always felt was the ultimate Gandalf (until Ian McKellen came along and incarnated the wizard for real). Yes, the legendary John Huston — director of *The African Queen* and father of Angelica. Even Otto Preminger came down to slum with the locals. The great director of *Laura* and *Exodus* (last seen as Mr. Freeze on *Batman* in 1966) decided to give Thranduil of Mirkwood a thick German accent.

We cannot forget Paul Frees, the distinguished voice of the "Ghost Host" from the Disney parks' Haunted Mansion ride. Paul did several characters here, including big fat Bombur. When Cyril Ritchard, the original Elrond in *The Hobbit*, died unexpectedly of heart failure, Paul was able to perfectly match Cyril's voice in RotK. How funny is that: every time you listen to the "Ghost Host" you are also listening to Elrond Half-elven. I kid you not.

There is much to enjoy here. For a start, the character designs are truly unique and the backgrounds lovely. The soft watercolor style of Bag End and the countryside looks strikingly like Tolkien's original painting of "The Hill: Hobbiton-across-the-Water." A very nice touch on Elrond's design was the blinking halo of stars around his head; he seems almost angelic. The Goblins were murderously wicked .... Every child I know is frightened at them popping up out of the shadows, vicious teeth and huge mouths. But the Great Goblin had the greatest mouth of all. It looked all the world to me like Thorin REALLY was about to get his head bitten off.

Sadly, Bilbo Baggins was drawn as a giant lump of fat with girly hair and stubby arms. How could a roly-poly like that hoist and throw a huge rock at a spider? And I'm afraid Smaug too much resembled a large crimson pussycat. Not nearly enough like a dragon. Looking at his feline eyes and fluffy hair (and with Richard Boone's I'm-so-finicky voice), I was convinced that it was a giant litter box he squatted over, not a dragon hoard.

But the supreme design, the crown jewel of these productions, was Gollum. He was a brilliant creation all around. This Gollum was so much rolled into one: creepy, sniveling, utterly pathetic, and more than a little amphibious. You could not take your eyes off him. The throaty voice of Brother Theodore was a kindled vat of poison. What wickedness! When he cackles and screams, you truly believe it. He was nightmare material for the little ones, and still is. Even though Tolkien suggested Gollum should never be represented as a monster, I must acknowledge character designers Tsuguyuki Kubo and Lester Abrams (who later created more wonderful beasties for *The Last Unicorn*).

The plus side: many set pieces were done just right, remaining very true to Tolkien in mood and style. The Unexpected Party eschews a lengthy performance by the Dwarves, instead having Gandalf narrate the Dwarven song, while soft music evokes faraway and dangerous lands. Huston's voice elicits such beauty out of Tolkien's verse. The conversation with Smaug is delicious. The dragon (the crimson cat) is so good at playing Bilbo for information, yet the clever hobbit is playing him right back.

RotK is very, very, VERY dark for an animated children's film. It must be, by default. Check out Éowyn's confrontation with the Witch-king for a sublime jolt (even if she looks like she stepped out of an episode of *Cowboy Bebop*). Other moments squarely hit the bullseye:

the battering ram Grond spits up blood, a fine moment when Sam leans over to kiss Frodo's forehead, that last shot of the white ship leaving the Grey Havens. These moments work so well because they stick so close to the original book. Credit the screenwriter, Romeo Muller, for knowing his source.

The minus side: well, yes, plenty of things are horribly wrong, I must be honest here. Mistakes and stupid choices abound. This stuff has no business being in a Tolkien adaptation. The names Smaug and Sauron are consistently mispronounced (it should sound like "Smowg" not "Smog"). The runes on Thror's Map are screwy, with the wrong letters showing up in the moonlight! Every time a spider dies we don't really see it: instead we get this cheesy twirling kaleidoscope effect. Notice how the Battle of Five Armies is just a bunch of little dots moving about the valley? It looks like an ant farm gone haywire. For crying out loud, in *RotK* the Nazgûl flying overhead are fully visible, skull-faces and all (while the Witch-king is correctly drawn as invisible)! Denethor is laughably misused as a character. You can't take him seriously while he cackles and croons for five straight minutes. And what about Aragorn? He has nothing of interest to say, no conflict to resolve. He is just so damn boring. Impressive how they took the romantic hero of the movie and neutered him like that.

Of special note is a long, peculiar monologue in *RotK* belonging to Gandalf. Just as the fighting on the Pelennor really gets heated, the whole movie comes to a screeching halt when Gandalf looks up at the sky and muses about the nature of Sauron, of all things. It has to be the strangest thing ever seen in a Tolkien adaptation. Male singers chant as if in they're stuck in a bell tower: *"Doom! The Cracks of Doom!"* while the wizard asks bizarre, rhetorical questions such as: "Who causes the minutes to fall dead, adding up to no passing hour?" Witness two little hobbits floating in a psychedelic swirly cloud, and then we see a weird, floating jellyfish that is supposed to be an "Eye." I cannot explain any of this. It's just too weird.

However, I do love the fun music. True, both films suffer from cheap, static animation techniques, but you forget all about that with Maury Laws's zesty scores. His contribution is critical to the storytelling, and the music cues lift and zoom terrifically when required. If the fight with the spiders doesn't look very exciting, it sure sounds exciting! At other times quiet orchestration frames several scenes of beauty and loss and strangeness. Gollum's main theme is based on one of Tolkien's original riddles (the one about "the dark"), given life by a single, dignified oboe — gliding quietly through the entire Riddle Game scene like a snake in the dark. When Sam holds the Ring close and suffers his hallucination of becoming "Samwise the Strong," the orchestra kicks off like a rocket. Laws gives us a full thrashing of wildly colorful music; without him the scene would never work.

Before I faint from gushing, I suddenly remember those awful Glenn Yarbrough songs. Who was this guy? What's the deal with his vibrato? Whatever his claim to fame, he's just WRONG for Middle-earth. Seventies folk kitsch has no place here (yet it can be argued that such kitsch was influenced by Tolkien). Yarbrough sounds an awful lot like Cat Stevens in *Harold and Maude*, singing relentlessly at every scene transition and ruining them along the way.

You want an upbeat musical number for your movie? A real showstopper? Give it to the Goblins. Who knew Goblins could sing like that? They get two delightful musical numbers in *The Hobbit*, singing with jolly evil as they set fire to the pine trees. Conversely, the Orcs in *RotK* suffer the worst embarrassment. "Where There's a Whip, There's a Way" is quite possibly the most awful, awful song ever in the history of the universe. But it will live forever. A classic, fondly remembered by all.

Now do you see what I mean? My comments are going back and forth to extremes. I have such internal conflict! Love and derision at the same time. I do sound schizophrenic! Oh, how I love/hate Rankin/Bass.

But after all, that wee eight-year-old boy was rewarded for his infatuation. After seeing *The Hobbit* on TV, I got hold of the book. My first "real book" book. You know where it goes from there .... my life changed, my active imagination blossomed, my love of literature flourished, everything in my young mind just leapt forward from that point. So I guess, in a sense, I shouldn't complain about how hokey those cartoons are. Because of Rankin/Bass I was led directly to J.R.R. Tolkien — and the world of language was opened to me.

At the end of the day, I am quite grateful. Just as the younger generations of today will be grateful to Peter Jackson and his films. For they too will be led to the books when their imagination is sparked. I see a pattern here. Ain't it grand?

Much too hasty,
Quickbeam

46. A New Direction for Tolkien Purism: Looking for Authenticity in the Work of Peter Jackson

Anwyn

In the summer of 2000, long before the release of *Lord of the Rings: Fellowship of the Ring*, I had the pleasure of being interviewed by Andrew O'Hehir over at Salon.com. When he asked where I fell in the camp of rabid purism (i.e. those who are filled with righteous anger over Peter Jackson daring to change any little iota of Tolkien's work), I was able to respond that I was keeping an open mind until I saw the movies. I almost surprised myself with how truthful that statement was, because I had been as upset as almost anybody else over the reports of Arwen's expanded role, the excising of Tom Bombadil, etc.

As the time of the movie drew nigh, I became ever more concerned that my summer-2000 "open mind" was going to backfire on me in a big way, and I drew in on my pessimistic purist self. Sure enough, many of my later misgivings were justified in my ultimate opinion of the film, but at the same time, I still believe that a soft purist touch and a somewhat open mind are the best tools with which to approach the far-reaching work of Mr. Peter Jackson. Rabid unbending purism, in the end, will not make it very far, no matter which film we measure it against.

At the time of the original writing, I was convinced that it was fitting to consider carefully, while we still had time, how we wished to enter the theaters the next year, 2001, The Year of the Film Reels. Did we want to walk in with cut and dried preconceptions, or even worse, dead set on hating anything that wasn't verbatim Tolkien, at the expense of our enjoyment of other elements of the films? Further, I thought it important to try to encourage ourselves (and yes, I included myself ... as a reputed purist I needed to consider my mindset most carefully) to think over what it means to adapt a story from print to screen, how a filmmaker's vision is justified in that task, and how authenticity can be found in the work even in light of changes that might be made to the author's original texts.

Mr. O'Hehir's request for a chat came at a time when many other seemingly chance observations had come together in my mind about the nature of authenticity. I was writing a paper for one of my last university classes that summer and reading an excellent article that postulated two definitions of "authenticity:" that which is posed by "textual critics" and that used by "moral philosophers." The two definitions are not complicated and are well worth the read.

Basically summarized, a textual critic takes the position that every effort should be made to find out what the composer (or author, in this case) actually wished and intended to say or accomplish and then abide strictly by that in all things. Musically speaking, for older composers, this is not always so easy. Matters of tempo, acoustics, the kind of ensemble and venue available for performance — all these things change radically over even short periods of musical history, making the realization of a deceased composer's wishes problematic at best. Even with the cut and dried black and white printed words and the glorious austere drawings and paintings of Tolkien before us, attempting a film that adapts restrictively to his vision would be a tricky proposition. There is simply no way to measure his imaginative images against our own; time and again words are pictured differently from person to person. A textual critic would nevertheless say that we need to have Tolkien's final version and then adhere strictly and solely to it in any artistic format that spins off the book, i.e. Jackson's movies.

A moral philosopher, on the other hand, again according to the article, takes the position that an editor should use his powers of judgment and his knowledge of the subject and author to aid him in producing his addition to the saga of the work in question. (The article was referring mainly to editors who create critical editions of composers' works, but we can take license in our application of the concept.) Moreover, the article's writer felt that any editor who descended to the level of being *solely* a textual critic was simply looking for a way to abdicate the responsibilities of his judgment so that he could produce a work that adhered, parrot-like, to the work of the original author/composer, without any need for potentially painful or dangerous decisions on his part.

I take the view that in reading, enjoying, contemplating, absorbing, and cherishing Tolkien's work, it is right to first be a textual critic, reading the final versions as Tolkien sent them to print (changes to the storyline of *The Hobbit* notwithstanding), and *then* to be a moral philosopher, using your own judgment, your own experiences, and the filter of your own reality to incorporate the stories into your existence. The fact of the matter is that it is next to impossible for a normal human being with ordinary interpretive/imaginative faculties to do otherwise; everything we take in is filtered through our own experiences.

So if we accept that as a working method of making Tolkien's book, in a sense, our own, then why should we judge Peter Jackson for wanting the same for himself? "Because, Anwyn," I hear you saying, "He's not just taking the stories into the closet of his mind and carefully storing them there; he's turning them into a completely different animal and spewing them out again onto the movie screens of the universe!!" True, he is. But does that mean he has to negate his own judgment and expertise in favor of simply regurgitating our best-beloved story? Personally, I don't think so.

In translating Tolkien to the screen, each person involved, from Jackson on through the ranks to the costume designers, sword-fighting coaches, production artists, etc., has a personal commitment, a personal responsibility not only to the production but to himself and his vision. If a person vacates this responsibility and goes under strict orders from a rabid textual critic, it invalidates his personality and makes his contribution to the project not individual; that is, anybody could have done his job, like so many Borg drones assigned to a power conduit. It would be possible to make the movies this way. You could get an army of human drones with the appropriate technical filmmaking knowledge and actors to spin out Tolkien's lines letter by letter. And don't think I wouldn't be mouthing *all* the dialogue along with them.

There was a wonderful *Foxtrot*, a comic strip by the hilarious and culturally insightful Bill Amend, published during Jackson's production run that showed his two principal child characters, Jason and

Marcus, as Frodo and Sam in Lórien, deviating from the script and just rattling off the correct dialogue because they had the books memorized! How many of us true fans haven't dreamed of the same opportunity? If it was done that way, though, in the end, *we would have nothing that we didn't really have already*. Think about it — sure, the action would be visual and we would hear the lines audibly, but there would be nothing there that we hard-core geeks didn't have playing in our heads to begin with.

Now some will ask, "What about the people who don't read the books? Don't they need to know *exactly* what really happened, step by step, line by line?" Under those circumstances, given a choice between a verbatim, automaton movie and a creative effort that takes a few liberties on the way to being brilliant, I say, "Make 'em read the books!" (Insert rant here about who *wouldn't* want to have the "true" Tolkien vision internalized along with whatever films come to light. Imagine a person who got his or her Tolkien knowledge strictly from a movie — thinking here of the mangled animations of the 1970s, I shudder at the thought.) With responsibility, a solid creative vision, and a firm grasp of storytelling, the filmmakers' vision can *enhance* our beloved stories without taking anything away from us.

Have you ever considered the difference between a bad film adaptation and a good one? I've eagerly gone to the theaters waiting for a new adaptation of one of my favorite books. Many's the time I've come away unspeakably disappointed, discovering only a few genuine gems along the way. Interestingly, though, I find that the difference does not lie principally in how much the filmmakers changed or did not change the story. Impossible? I don't think so, at least not in my experience. Two of my favorite all-time adaptations are *Shawshank Redemption* and *Anne of Green Gables* (the Kevin Sullivan miniseries). I've read the books and seen the movies both, and what shines through both films is the integrity of their respective stories. Some plot lines were changed or omitted in the interest of time or dramatization, and Kevin Sullivan in particular has a knack for combining several characters into one multipurpose character so that he can trim bewildering, extraneous people who would be too much for a film scope. But I found that this in no way detracted from the vision, the authenticity, of the story he was telling.

One of the worst adaptations I have ever had the misfortune to see was the version of *Little Women* starring Winona Ryder and Susan

Sarandon. How dreary and lacking in anything approaching storytelling! Chopping dialogue in the wrong places, adding it where it made no sense, hitting viewers over the head with concepts that would have been obvious in a sensitively told story ... Help! Let me out of the theater! And yet the characters were identical, much of the dialogue was intact, and most of the events unfolded the same way. But the film still suffered through either not enough creative vision or a lack of a plan as to how to convey the vision. I do not believe that Peter Jackson is lacking in that vision, and reports would seem to indicate he is not lacking in plan either. (An ironic side note: The excellent Sullivan adaptation of *Anne* uses almost verbatim a bittersweet love scene from the book *Little Women* — and uses it, I might add, to much better effect than the film of *Little Women* did!)

Therefore at the time of first writing, I appealed to all of your creative sensibilities and respect for filmmakers: keep an open mind! I'm as much a Tolkien purist as the next. I did not want to see Arwen parading around the countryside wielding a sword, and now having seen *Fellowship*, I still feel that way. That's what we have Éowyn for! (See, despite my prattle about open-mindedness, I would still love to force PJ to change that whole Arwen thing back to "normal!") But have you ever noticed how often purists disagree? They disagree on pronunciation, among scores of other things ... you start to read the book pronouncing things one way, and unless you very quickly read and begin to adhere to Tolkien's pronunciation guide, pretty soon "your way" is fixed in your head. Purists disagree on matters of interpretation, such as Boromir's dream, omens, magic, Entwives, Balrogs, Elven physical characteristics ... a multitude of other details.

I would bring to your attention one of my favorite quotations. I've seen it attributed to Edmund Burke, and it was used in the play *1776*. It states, "A representative of the people owes them not only his industry, but also his judgment, and he betrays them if he sacrifices it to their opinion." Just remember that even if Peter Jackson were inclined to bow to the will of fans, he would not be able to do so, because even the most rabid purists disagree amongst themselves constantly. He would wind up like the old story, attempting to please everybody and ending by pleasing absolutely nobody. Under such a dilemma, it is more than proper that his own creative interpretation should be the final authority.

Authenticity is a matter of using your own carefully informed judgment, based on research and knowledge. Therefore, knowing as we do that Peter Jackson has a vision that he believes is right, an open mind until we see the films and a soft critical touch afterwards are appropriate. (A soft critical touch with respect to his handling of the story, that is. Bad filmmaking would be another question altogether.)

Just because it is not what we would do does not mean the Jackson fims do not have integrity that is true to Tolkien's story. We of course will be busy measuring his ideas of authenticity against our own for decades to come, but provided he has lived up to the dictates of his own heart about Tolkien's work, we will have to grant him a certain measure of authenticity, regardless of his actual "purism."

47. Where the Stars are Strange

Quickbeam

In December 2000, Cliff ("Quickbeam") went to New Zealand at the invitation of Sir Ian McKellen, who played Gandalf in the film. He spent a week observing and eventually participating in the making of Peter Jackson's The Lord of the Rings, which was then less than a month away from completing its extraordinary 15-month shoot. This is Quickbeam's record of a week he will never forget.

The original article was serialized and shared with TheOneRing.net readers over five days.

Part I
* * *

My little cat died right before I left for New Zealand.

On November 27, 2000, Icarus died of kidney failure after many months of pain. He stopped breathing in my arms. I held him as his eyes went glassy and cold. We raced down to the veterinarian, driving through the traffic lights, but there was no hope for him.

This is hard to convey without sounding overly sentimental. Forgive me.

He was an orange tabby with golden eyes. Muscular and talkative, he was a "big old tomcat" who walked around like he owned the place. I named him after the Greek myth of Icarus because he was often uncontrollable and would never listen to discipline. He was my constant companion for 13 years. I always slept with Icarus curled up in the crook of my arm, the sound of his purring a lullaby for the weary.

He was more than just a cat, to me anyway, and I loved him with a full heart. I fell apart when the vet took him away, wrapped in a towel

.... I wept for seemingly hours, unaware of time.

The following morning was not easy. How could I feel good about a long trip, even if I was going to Middle-earth? What, leave my home to visit a strange country? Now? Not knowing any friends there? I couldn't even stand upright without crying and blubbering. Everything felt wrong. Leaving for New Zealand was the last thing I needed. All enthusiasm vanished: I simply did not want to go.

Indeed, I was THIS CLOSE to canceling my tickets.

I wrote an e-mail to Sir Ian McKellen and told him how I felt. His response was very kind, with a warmth I did not expect. He wrote:

> So sorry about your cat: your trip couldn't be more timely. Looking forward to seeing u. I'll take u to Minas Tirith and u can meet Shadowfax.
> xoxo Ian

My perspective changed a bit then. I carefully thought it over and realized how unique this was. This trip was a singularity. It was, trite though it sounds, a once-in-a-lifetime chance. To see the secretive sets. To meet the powerful talent behind (and in front of) the camera. To give the fans a closer view of the magic.

To heal.

Maybe this was exactly what I needed. To take my mind off things and heal. What else was I going to do — sit around Los Angeles and mope, missing out on everything? Insanity. I would work through it, somehow, and I could stand some fresh air.

Then I suddenly recalled that awful Glenn Yarbrough singing in the old Rankin/Bass version of *The Hobbit*. "The greatest adventure is there if you're bold, let go of the moment that life makes you hold."

Ahhh, I'm such a child sometimes.

* * *

I left L.A. behind on Wednesday night, November 29, 2000. It was a cramped, uncomfortable, jittery flight. You try sleeping *in coach* through eighteen hours of bumpy flight — some 37,000 feet aloft — while below the vast expanse of the Pacific churns ....

Deep ocean. Vast sea.

With my CD player in my ears, I tried to doze. As the hours stretched on, even half-dreams of Peter Murphy's spiritual songs held no comfort. I tried the Carpenter biography of J.R.R. Tolkien but failed to get through two whole pages. I closed my eyes. I thought of Icarus and wondered if I would be joining him in heaven soon. Then, it seemed, funny things played out before my vision. I looked out my window, down the huge length of the metal jet wing, and thought I saw something. It was very strange. There was my little orange cat, sitting on the wing, enjoying the wind flowing through his fur.

I know, I know. But there he was, all the same. He stood, walked softly towards me and jumped into the cabin, passing right through the wall. He curled up in my lap and slept. A waking dream ....? Maybe. I felt comforted and calmed, soon falling into my own slumber.

* * *

Morning arrived on the other side of Planet Earth. I missed a day completely, so I opened my date book and crossed a big scratch through November 30. A day that would never exist for me in any universe. I couldn't get my mind around that, even though I've read all of Stephen Hawking's books.

But indeed there was Auckland in the bright sunshine. Some tingle of imagination started to leap-frog in my brain. I anticipated the delights yet to come. Wizards and orcs, hobbits and oliphaunts waited for me! All would turn out well.

Just look at that gorgeous island ... The high air was startlingly clear. Surf pounded the jagged shoreline, leading up to green-swathed cliffs and alongside them endless fingers of beach. Little white dots on the green signified sheep.

O splendid New Zealand! Am I really here?

Have you ever felt that certain "new" feeling that comes over you when you travel? Like when you take a deep breath and think to yourself, "Those are brand new, alien molecules of air, little bits of oxygen that would never have been in my lungs." Everything is novel; and you are sensitive to signs of life all around you. "Look! there goes a species of bird I've never seen. I feel like Magellan!" Hard to explain but incredibly satisfying.

Now connected to Wellington, I enjoyed a second breakfast and by chance found a picture of Sir Ian in the morning *Herald*. In the image, he gestured his hand in welcome. Nice touch.

An hour later I touched down at a place just off the edge of the World, catching my first glimpse of the Stone Street Studios. To the untrained eye it was just a clump of white buildings adjacent to the airport, but to me it was a menagerie of magic.

My spirits rose. Down there one might find things, myriad brilliant *things* — like a giant foam-rubber Shelob, and thousands of shiny helmets, and famous Shakespearean actors foaming at the mouth. I felt electricity in my veins. Fantastic!

Soon a taxi shepherded me to the center of Wellington. I admit to freaking out when the driver went down the wrong side of the road! How bizarre. I had better get used to the myriad differences around here.

Destination: Downtown Backpackers Youth Hostel. My friend Tehanu told me it was decent, and she was right.

I took out my camera and walked around all afternoon, making a fool of myself. Well, basically, I could pass for a Kiwi as long as I didn't speak. I'm sure my accent would give me away, eventually. I wanted very much to see the city, and I had chanced upon the perfect day to do so.

I basked in the air, the gentle sunshine, the soft breeze from Lambton Harbor. Though it was the first of December, it was early summer here and heaven was all around me. My heart was at ease.

Wellington is strikingly similar to San Francisco. There were quaint houses in colorful rows, all up and down the hills. A cluster of skyscrapers, promontories of commerce, snuggled close to the harbor's edge. Boats innumerable: towing, docking, and receding out across the water. And there across the harbor lay the hills of the Lower Hutt. There be the magnificent Helm's Deep set, now converted into Minas Tirith. On my right was Mount Victoria, glorious green, where the four hobbits hid from the sniffing Nazgûl.

"Good Lord, I'm in Middle-earth."

I toured all day (wow, Parliament Building!) and went out clubbing all night (wow, Courtenay Place!). In the morning, however, a certain White Rider was expecting me at Stone Street Studios.

* * *

At dawn my ride appeared out of the mist, and in minutes, we were coursing through the Mt. Vic tunnel, Miramar just ahead. Whatever was about to happen — and I could not have known — would change my life.

There I was at the unassuming Stone Street facility, nestled in a middle-class suburban neighborhood. Rather ordinary-looking, the buildings once housed a paint manufacturing plant, or so I'm told. Outside the gate, a guard sat listening to a small radio. Not at all like movie studios in L.A.; there was no imposing security gate, no barricade, and no attitude. He asked us all to sign in, and easy as that, we were inside.

Part of a giant dead Oliphaunt lay on the asphalt just ahead. It was not the whole prop, just a section of it. The thing was so huge it had to be taken apart into manageable sizes for transport. The truck-sized piece I saw had a hide of dark brown matted fur and, assembled across the top like the masts of a huge ship, wooden poles and platforms. From there, on the back of the beast, the evil Mordor Orcs and Haradrim would ride. If this was only a piece of it, how colossal the entire thing must be! In *The Return of the King* it will appear as an Oliphaunt corpse left on the burnt Pelennor Fields. I heard rumor that this huge beast, fully assembled, would break the world record for the largest stationary film prop ever made.

Now we were lost in a labyrinth of stars' trailers. There were signs on many of the doors:

FRODO
THÉODEN
GANDALF

We went straight towards this last one and stopped at the door. My friend said, "Maybe we should call over at the Production Office. He might be working on-set."

I replied, "Why don't we just say 'friend' and knock real loud?"

The door swung wide. There stood a tall, imposing wizard dressed in shimmering white robes. The fabric was embroidered in magnificent silk patterns. His beard was less than two hands in length, tapered to a point, and he wore no hat. I walked up and said to him, "We're here."

At first Sir Ian said nothing. He had a very sweet, gentle smile on his face and a script in his hand. He put the pages down and opened his arms, giving me a hug. "Oh, I am sorry," he said, as warm and generous as my own family.

There, on the other side of the world, as Gandalf the White comforted me, I let my feelings go and cried in his arms.

Part II
Gandalf Tea Wednesday.
* * *

Sir Ian McKellen, dressed in what looked like 20 pounds of white fabric, was in between takes. Since he was not needed on the set until later, there was enough time for all of us to relax over tea and fresh apples. My sense was that he was comfortable, if a little tired. Apparently the work schedule they had him on was intense. As this was the last four weeks of principal photography, the general intensity was bound to increase.

Yet Middle-earth was all around me, begging to be explored.

In a few moments, Gandalf led us through a grid of trailers and on towards the soundstages. To our right was the Production Office, filled with busy people and mountains of paperwork. The wise wizard moved cautiously about, looking for a door with lights on the outside. Specifically, he wanted to make sure the lights were OFF so we could enter without disturbing the current shoot.

Soon I was inside a private chamber within Meduseld, the Golden Hall, home of King Théoden. Lights and equipment surrounded the smallish set. The room suggested a cozy log cabin with horses carved upon the horizontal beams. It was decorated with lovely tapestries, each with an equine motif. Brad Dourif stood there, though I did not recognize him at first. Here was Gríma Wormtongue, adorned in rich ebony robes: a slender figure with slicked wet hair and an evil look.

We stayed out of the way to watch from the shadows. They were ready to roll film.

A woman dressed in gauzy white flitted from the doorway to hit her mark close to the camera. Who was this lovely creature who knelt by the bedside? This was Miranda Otto as Éowyn! With long tresses and makeup, she looked nothing like her small publicity photo I had seen a year ago. Her movements and manner were amazing to watch. This was Éowyn, in the flesh, her shining eyes filled with sadness.

Captivating ....

The scene seemed to be about Wormtongue's behind-the-throne scheming. He spoke to Éowyn from the doorway, leering at a safe distance. I was so fascinated that I stood rooted to the spot, unaware that Ian was beckoning us to leave the set in search of other wonders.

Down another hall I found myself in the Silent Street.... the Rath Dínen.... and within was a larger tomb where lay the Stewards of Minas Tirith. Fittingly, the space was quiet and grey. Only the work lights glowed softly overhead.

With a glint in his eye, Ian said, "This is the leftover set where we filmed the Pyre of Denethor last week. I came crashing down that ramp on Shadowfax. Quite a dramatic entrance!"

The plywood walls were convincingly painted like ancient marble. Along the perimeter loomed a dozen bas-relief figures. Nearly two meters tall, these specter-like forms were draped with robes covering all the features of the face. Each solemn figure held a down-pointed sword. Very chilling indeed.

Lo and behold! Each tomb had a name and date below its mysterious Grim Reaper sculpture. I walked around the room, reading each one. *They were accurate!* These weren't just made up names like Charlie Brown or Henry Kissinger. I recognized them from Appendix A: "Annals of the Kings and Rulers."

Mardil 2080 — Belecthor I 2655 — Ecthelion I 2698

Brilliant! How totally brilliant to apply this much effort to something that will hardly register on the screen. When you sit in the theater watching *The Return of the King,* you won't even notice them. So why put them there?

Think about it: Somebody at WETA spent a lot of time going through the Appendices and assigning very clever artisans to create gorgeous, creepy sculptures — with accurate nameplates. Thus the actors were surrounded by real "history" that would help center their performances. I would see more of such fidelity during the rest of my visit.

The room took on a new aura. I had a sense of true place. A raised platform stood center where the pyre had burned. It was charred and black. Although the props, fuel, and actors were gone, the horror still weighed oppressively in the air. Denethor's raging madness. The bloodshed. The screaming.

I had to get out.

* * *

Gandalf, amused by my ardent enthusiasm for the tour, took us down to the Golden Hall itself.

Entering the set, I could not see for the bright lights blasting in my eyes. We were on the wrong side of the prop walls and had to maneuver around great stands of reflective material and rows of cables. I nearly tripped on one of these and stumbled on top of Peter Jackson himself.

Nearly.

He sat in a classic director's chair watching a configuration of monitors. I was an explosion of nerves the minute I saw him. No time to compose myself — there was Ian already introducing me. "Peter, you know Quickbeam from TheOneRing?" Peter smiled with recognition, got up from his seat and shook my hand.

OMIGOD OMIGOD OMIGOD I'm shaking hands with Peter Jackson!

He had the finest Kiwi accent I ever heard. "Yes, of course, I've been to your site."

"You have? Really?" I asked disbelieving.

"Sure." He smiled again.

Like I said, I was nervous as hell but had no reason to be. He seemed just like a normal guy. Laid back, casual, loosened up. *He's just a cool guy. Okay, I can do this.*

And here is where the stupid Yank in me came roaring out. The lamer-than-lame joke I used for an opener was: "You know, I wanted to get a better sense of your work style, to see what it's like on one of your sets, so I rented a copy of *Meet the Feebles*, and I expected things would be much worse." Hey, you can't expect a man to be pithy when he's so worked up.

Strangely enough, Peter Jackson actually laughed. "Did you like it?" he grinned.

"Oh, I totally love that movie!" I replied. "My favorite sick-out twisted comedy ever. I'm surprised you got away with it."

He continued with ease. "So what do you think of all this?" He gestured at the impressive Golden Hall. Seeing it now full on, I felt a warm wave of love washing over me. The words *amazing detail* cannot do it justice. The vaulted ceiling was crossed with thick pine beams, each bolstered with a horse's head at the column joints. Wrought-iron torchiers stood alongside columns like tree trunks (intricate Celtic knot designs covering all). And were they beautiful! A giant woven tapestry adorned the far wall, like a museum piece from a Scottish castle. Some of the prop walls swiveled open to reveal huge lights positioned before Théoden's throne. This striking wooden chair, high-backed and richly stained, was now the focus of the camera.

Was I in another world? How could all these things from my imagination be *real??* Look at the white horse on the tapestry! Is that Eorl the Young? I took a moment to breathe and said to Peter, "It's just fantastic. In my own mind's eye I had never thought of anything so detailed and wonderful." I sincerely meant it.

PJ was actually beaming. He was quietly proud and confident. "Yes, it is nice, isn't it?"

"I'll let you go back to work, I know you're busy ... but I want to say it's all wonderful and I'm thrilled to meet you."

The director was then pulled away by harried production assistants and other crew, all vying for his attention. I thought, *I don't envy him a bit.*

Ian was on call now, as they were ready to shoot the healing of Théoden. Miranda Otto and Brad Dourif appeared. Bustle and activity everywhere. I looked for a hiding spot next to the makeup crew, so I could sit and observe.

There was Bernard Hill. He was not wearing the heavy aging makeup today, rather he looked fully robust and sharp-eyed. I went over and we spoke. This guy is a real barrel of monkeys! Boisterous and congenial, he made a sly reference to *Titanic*, saying, "Do you know the movies I've starred in that have ended up being the highest-grossing, most successful films of all time? This one included."

Work began now in earnest on the scene. Cameras were rolling. ACTION!

Gandalf the White spoke in a commanding tone to the King, "Arise, Théoden, and be healed. Too long have you sat in shadows ...." Éowyn ran up to support him, tears of joy flowing. Théoden had the most stunned look on his face. Wow!

Then they shot scenes of Wormtongue being cast down on the floor, squirming with anger. The camera rolled toward him for a close-up. I could see in the monitors a huge dangle of snot dripping from his flaring nostrils. *Wow!*

The prop assistant stood adjacent to me holding a wizard's staff of white ash. It was Gandalf's version of Saruman's staff. Once more, with feeling — WOW!

"Can I hold it?" I asked.

"Oh, I don't think that would be a good idea," he apologized.

"I promise not to run off with it."

Too late. He was called over to the actors to get ready for the next shot. I was crestfallen. *Damn! That was a missed opportunity!*

* * *

Lunchtime already. The main dining hall was a cavernous soundstage with rows of tables unending. I got a crash course in Kiwi "fine dining" and was all the happier for it. Everything on the menu was rich in sauces, creams, and dairy.

While I ate, the room filled with Rohan extras and a gaggle of armored soldiers. My friend the wizard came over with a plate of grilled veggies and breads. Sir Ian, as you may know, follows a vegetarian diet. He is truly one of the Wise. What you might not know is that he has an incurable sweet tooth.

Orlando Bloom came by and sat next to us. Here at last was Legolas. A smoother fellow you could not ask for. I showed him a new softcover copy of *LotR* that had a little gold emblem on the front: "An epic motion picture trilogy — Coming soon from New Line Cinema."

"Can you believe they're marketing it like that already?" Orlando said.

I answered, "That's nothing ... just wait until we get closer to the film's release. The merchandise will be like *Star Wars* ... insane."

And thus the spell of camaraderie came over me. I felt I was at home here, sharing the table with old buddies, although it still seemed surreal that I was even sitting there at all.

A few handsome Maori and Samoan fellows came in, sitting with the young soldiers. Loud laughter came from their table. Gandalf leaned in and said, "You see that big lad over there? He played Sauron in the battle scenes. You'll have to go meet him." I blinked. Sauron? The Dark Lord of Mordor — sitting one table away from me?? In minutes I had myself another fateful introduction.

His name is Sala Baker. Although young he's still a very LARGE Samoan lad who commands an instant hush when he walks into a room. Unlike his character, he was very friendly and kind. Originally a stunt person for key battle scenes, he ended up moving around the production, doing some assistant work, and of course he became friends with everyone. One morning PJ, Fran Walsh, and the ladies from casting were having a big meeting, unable to decide who was going to play Sauron. Then somebody said, "Hey, get Sala! He's perfect for it!" Boom. Unanimous agreement from everyone in the room.

He wanted me to join him and some of the crew later that night for Karaoke. "I'll be there with bells on," I said.

* * *

The weather changed that afternoon when I went looking for Nazgûl on top of Mount Victoria. The day turned blustery as I marched my way uphill. Low clouds raced across the sky at tremendous velocity. The cheerless sun showed itself intermittently and the cold wind gusted sharply.

The slopes of Mt. Vic loom above Wellington: heavily wooded yet laced with many walking trails. It is an island of green bisecting the city. The wind became my companion, blowing me uphill.

The pines were roaring on the height,
The winds were moaning in the night.

A warm spot of sun teased across the tall pines and was gone. I perceived small spirits were watching me. Maybe just one. What was that familiar sound? Meowing? Am I hearing things again....?

I pressed onward. Plunging through the trees I soon found the fateful spot. It was instinctive. Like a frightened Frodo, I knew the danger was near. I just knew it. The sniffing Ringwraith would round the corner any second and I had to get off the path to hide. But I stood alert, watching the movement of every leaf.

Prickling sensations on my neck. I was there — in the Shire, standing in the Green Hill Country, and it was an Eastfarthing sky above me! This is what it felt like to have my imaginings become real. I wanted to stay forever.

Still no Nazgûl appeared.

At the top of Mt. Vic you will find a fantastic view. Sort of like the Seat of Seeing atop Amon Hen. All the lands about open up like a book.

You will also find at the summit a distinctive memorial for Admiral Richard E. Byrd, an American actually, famous for his Antarctic expeditions and for his pioneering flight over the South Pole in a tri-motor airplane in 1929. It seems I was in the good company of a fellow adventurer.

* * *

That night I found myself at the Steam Boat Karaoke Bar. Once upstairs, I thought I was in the wrong place. It was a complete dive. Yuck.

All doubt fled when I saw folks from the Second Unit and from WETA looking through the songbook, trying to choose their next number. And then the Dark Lord came up and shook my hand. "What are you having?" he offered.

I begged off. "No thanks, Sala, I really don't drink much."

"Dude, come on!" he insisted. "Don't wuss out on me, you big Yank. What're you having?" I couldn't say no to him — *and neither could you*. When Sauron wants to buy you a drink, you better not piss him off.

When the Lord of the Nazgûl came into the room, the energy picked up. In real life he was a tall devilish Yul Brynner look-alike named Shane Rangi. That's right, folks, I spent my evening with the most horrific, nefarious beings in all of Middle-earth. Sauron and the Witch-king. Truly, all the WETA people were fresh-faced youths, and drinks poured freely. Miranda Otto arrived on the arm of David Wenham. Faramir and Éowyn together at last! Was this an off-camera romance? I was a little too fuzzy to hold up a conversation with them, so I stayed in my seat.

Before long, these total strangers melted the barriers of indifference and welcomed me as a friend. Not once was I uncomfortable. We drank. We sang horribly off-key. We laughed. I kept saying, "No, I don't want another one, really ..." but my glass was always full.

"What's it like working on *LotR*? Is this lengthy project driving you crazy?" I asked those around me. The answers were unanimous: "Oh, It's brilliant." "We love it." "Wish it would never end." "Best two years of my life." "Incredible." What a difference from a Hollywood set where you hear mostly bitching and complaining. I kid you not, there is always a cloud of "This sucks, can we just get through this and go home?" Diva actresses and their demands. Lofty directors who scream at everyone. Every set. Every time.

But then I realized that *these people are really into it!* They all respected PJ, they loved the work, and they went at it with true passion. I knew then that Mr. Jackson was way ahead of the game.

When I was quite drunk I got up and sang *Do You Really Want to Hurt Me?* which is just about in my range. Solid applause. Sitting back down, a striking redhead with fantastic eyes grabbed me and said, "That was brilliant! Full-on, mate!" This young woman was Sukhita, who wrangled armor and painted miniatures ... she and I would become quite close. But my singing would go on to haunt me.

Lor' bless me, Master Frodo, I'll never drink that much again!

* * *

It was a crisp, lovely Sunday morning, December 3, 2000, though my hangover stalled my enjoyment of it. I was honored to have breakfast with Shane and his striking girlfriend, Carleen. They took me to a small shop to find my first greenstone necklace, sometimes referred to as "New Zealand jade." The Maori call it *Pounamu* and everybody wears one (or a kindred bone carving). The pendant that is made out of greenstone or bone is called *Taonga*, which means "treasure." Now this is an essential bit of Maori culture ... so I picked one carefully. There was one: triangular, flat, it felt good in my hands. The shape signified protection.

But you can never buy one for yourself! It absolutely must be *given* to you. I put my money in Shane's hands; he made the purchase — the man behind the counter was of deep Maori ancestry and he blessed it with a special chant, *Karakia* — then Carleen lovingly placed it around my neck, giving me a kiss.

No turning back now. I was officially a Kiwi by adoption.

* * *

Up the road on Kio Bay there was an afternoon party being held for Sir Ian. Some pretty big people were in attendance: members of Parliament, Peter Jackson himself and some higher-ups from *LotR*, and several luminaries from New Zealand's gay and lesbian community (writers, dancers, politicians). It was a *thank you* for Sir Ian's contributions to the community during his time in NZ, and also a fond *adieu*. And a successful party it was. Good cheer flourished and the kitchen overflowed with food.

PJ came into the garden with Fran Walsh at his side. She had the kindest demeanor, like some kind of angelic being; and I felt rather like Sam meeting Galadriel for the first time. She had a vibrant energy that drew people to her.

"I have to ask, Peter, what is it you'll miss the most when this project is over? What will you do when all is done and you wake up in the morning and say, 'I don't have *LotR* to work on today?'"

He replied, "Oh, the people, certainly. I will miss them the most. We've all gotten so close: it will be very hard to not have them near when all is finished." Fran nodded in agreement. After meeting so many of these wonderful people, I knew he meant it.

There was Alan Lee, standing by himself! We struck up a great talk. He shared how he had created those amazing tapestries inside the Golden Hall (insider's secret — they were only painted to LOOK like tapestries). So much of the architecture, props, and physical elements were created from his designs. I say they should give special Oscars just to Alan Lee and John Howe for their staggering efforts.

It was a party of special magnificence and Sir Ian was in a jovial mood. He was presented with a special award from the Prime Minister and many other gifts. PJ gave him a specially framed portrait of Ian himself, in Gandalf costume, but with his pointy wizard's hat all backwards. It was crooked forward on his head, and the title proclaimed BENT in large letters. Throughout the evening several people generously offered to let me stay with them instead of at the hostel. I'll say it again, the very word *hospitality* is defined by New Zealanders. I found another friend in David Eyre, one of the top brass at Te Papa National Museum. He offered his apartment in Rongotai, which was a short walk down from Studios K and L. Now I would be only a few blocks away from Fangorn Forest!

As the sun lowered in the sky, I stepped outside and saw PJ standing further off, Fran close to his side. Watching them together at the garden wall, something clicked. There was an unspoken quality in their relationship that eluded me before. She was his love, his support, his inspiration — he was Beren, and she was forever his Lúthien.

Part III

* * *

At the front desk Monday morning there was a message waiting for me:

Cliff Please call Sauron URGENT

I raced back upstairs to phone the Dark Lord. After checking out of the hostel and getting all my mundane possessions over to David's place, I was ready for more eye-opening adventure. Soon Sala Baker and I would be on our way to the WETA workshop. Holy Eureka, this was the day I struck gold!

Sauron showed up (driving a sporty little black car, of course) and soon we were driving back to Middle-earth. I was about to gain entrance to the creative powerhouse behind these movies: WETA. A relaxed and informal introduction was called for.

It helped that people were starting to recognize me. A woman from the production office stopped me in my tracks and said, "Oh! You're that guy who sang Culture Club the other night! Bravo!" I wasn't a complete stranger, then.

* * *

In an hour we arrived at the gate of a nondescript two-story building. What was inside this place? What kind of magic, horror, ancient history, and phantasmagoric wonders were hiding within?

We signed many copies of "Confidentiality Agreements" (not that Sala really needed to), and the administrative assistant, Hannah, appeared. She guided us upstairs to an office decorated with some of WETA's great creatures — most of them from Peter Jackson films. From *Heavenly Creatures*, I saw Diello, heir to the throne of Borovnia! In another corner was the wacky baby zombie from *Dead Alive*. Many other critters I simply didn't recognize. There at the reception desk was a gorgeous bust of Arwen. Ah! I swore I wouldn't touch anything. I kept my hands tightly clasped behind my back the whole day.

The very tall and articulate Richard Taylor came out to greet us. Now this was a treat! If you don't know his name yet — you will soon. He is more than company director and F/X supervisor; he is a visual genius ... and also a genius at bringing together the right mix of skills, sweat, and passion from his team. He has collected under his wing a throng of outstanding talent. These people are shockingly good! And they are all huge fans of Tolkien. If you like the way Andúril is crafted, Richard's people forged it. If you like Alan Lee's beautiful details found on the Weathertop ruins, again, Richard's people built them. Most of Middle-earth's organic construction starts here, under his watchful eye.

Richard would oblige my request for knowledge. After making several promises that I would not touch or take pictures of anything (which made me a bit more nervous) I was ushered down a hallway to see sculptors hard at work. A work table was filled with hard clay sculpts of Nazgûl on horseback and several fantastic Ents!

Ents. At last I was among my kind.

But the Nazgûl was most captivating, and I locked eyes with it. The hooded Wraith was searching, and I was amazed that an inanimate, stationary figure could capture so much dramatic tension. Just stunning! His evil cloak was so finely detailed it actually looked like real black cloth. These were the prototypes that would become special polystone sculptures sold through Sideshow Toys.

I met the young and stylish Daniel Falconer (this guy is a real lady killer). His design team worked on Treebeard in many aspects: drawing, models, giant animatronic. He laughed at my nickname, saying, "Oh yeah, I spent quite some time drawing early versions of that character!"

He pulled out a portfolio that was carefully tucked away. Dozens of pages ... dozens of amazing Ents! None of them were cartoonish, nor even remotely similar to the Ralph Bakshi design for an Ent (I'm sure you folks remember THAT Treebeard design, which looked like it just stepped off the front panel of a box of cereal). No, these were seriously botanical Ents! They were utterly realistic as trees, in their own right, with a little anthropomorphization here and there. It is sad that not all of these creations will end up in *The Two Towers*. I also saw Daniel's version of Quickbeam!! Woo-hoo!

Man, have I got big roots down there. I had no idea.

We said farewell to the sculptors and Sala then showed me an armor prototype for Sauron. It was fierce and spiky-looking, a giant warrior coming forth from Barad-dûr to engage Isildur. This 16-inch armored figure seemed to burn with malice. You can imagine how proud Sala was to wear that outfi t ... but the version we looked at was not the "final," of course. All these early designs get modified and re-sculpted a thousand times before they end up in the approved, completed state.

Hannah walked us down to the work rooms and soundstages. Orc heads were piled on huge racks everywhere. Ghastly!

Here's how it works. Orc actors closest to the camera would spend several hours in makeup, with fully movable facial features, special contact lenses and teeth. These were "Hero Orcs." "Hero" means the designers provide great detail on an item because when it's blown up on the silver screen 40 feet high, the audience will see all that detail. All things made especially for close-ups are categorized this way: Hero Armor, Hero Mallorn Leaves, etc. If you're an Orc actor further in the background, you will end up wearing a latex mask instead.

These Orc heads were just as ugly as could be. Barely humanoid, they all looked bloody and bruised. That was what made them so beautiful. There were great racks of Orc prosthetic limbs, too, for the stunt players working in combat scenes. You can't be an Orc with pale human-colored skin showing from underneath your gauntlets, can you? Ergo these arm pieces were created to cover any exposed length of arm or leg. Hannah admitted it got bloody hot in them, too.

In another room sat the chain mail workers. Tiny ringlets of steel lay everywhere, an ocean of little washers spilling from table to floor. Two Gondorian mail shirts were carefully being sewn together. It was insanely complicated. Weaving and linking was their daily task. They would sit at this table for days on end putting it all together, each mail shirt an original ... custom-made. Can you imagine the arthritic cramps in your hands after your day was done?

Soon we were in a storage space filled with a mighty ship. Though it was a scale miniature, it was still as large as a moving van. It was one of the Black Fleet — indeed the foremost ship in which Aragorn sails up to the Harlond, unveiling the great standard of Elendil. What a magnificent piece of work! The ship looked ancient and sleek, fitted with great shining masts and ebony smooth planks. I only wished I could see Aragorn's standard waving in the wind from this baby!

My admiration was cut short, for on the other side lay a thing of deepest terror and evil.

Grond!

There it was, alongside the great ship, seething with ruinous magic.

I moved in closer and saw it was scaled with hundreds of pieces of steel, and on each scale was crafted an evil rune marking. It was just as Tolkien described, with a hideous lupine head. Just think of the effort it took to make this baleful battering ram so malignant, so profane, so perfect!

I believed then that WETA's painters, craftsmen, and designers were living spirits of *pure artistry*. Everything they touched sprang from the raw imagination — only to become tangible. These things were real! You could touch them, smell them, be crushed into a wincing pulp by them.

Then I saw the corpse and jumped out of my skin. It was Boromir, lying on the floor. However, he was only painted from the shoulders up. Very odd. My mind was convinced it was real. Shivers of gooseflesh ... Blinking a few times I realized it was a giant foam-latex body. Only the face would be visible after the costume was put on. It was the prop sent over the falls of Rauros in the funeral boat.

Behold! A great purple Shelob! She was hanging on the wall right above Boromir, looking all the more guilty. It was a bas-relief painted in bright colors, and it represented one of WETA's earliest designs of the creature. If they didn't change a thing (yeah right) and used this exact design, it would be perfect. So many evil eyes staring. Horrible prickly legs and mandibles. Huge swollen belly of darkness.

Help. I can't breathe. She has poisoned me.

Then Hannah brought me back, showing me something more pleasing: Hobbit ears and feet. The latex ears were laid out, being carefully painted with an airbrush-type tool. These are not Vulcan ears; they are warmer, smaller, and have a different pointed tip. Total number made for these films? 1,600 or so.

The waggish Hobbit feet live up to the hype — big and hairy. They doubled for actual shoes, so it was imperative they be tough on the outside to walk through rain, mud, and across mountains. They are some kind of super-industrial latex with real yak hairs implanted.

We walked into an adjacent room brimming with pikes, halberds, scimitars, and axes. The place was wall-to-wall medieval weaponry. The variety was exhaustive! These were totally gorgeous pieces, many of which weren't even made of metal.

I kept gushing to everyone I met. "Wondrous! You guys are absolutely amazing. Wait until the world sees what you've accomplished!" Every word was true.

* * *

On we went into a warehouse adequate in size for a jumbo jet. There, a great Stone Troll leered above me. It was bearing down, ready to smash my fragile skull.

Goliath brute! Massive hulking thing!

It was over 10 meters tall (two stories) or I have no sense of space. This was the prop to end all props. While I cowered underneath it, I almost lost my balance and fell on my butt. How could such an elephantine thing be put together?

I stood under its stony gaze for a long time. Was that a bird's nest behind its ear?

Truly, I had seen many wonders at WETA that day. But the most breathtaking, the most absurdly grand of all, waited on the far wall. There was Minas Tirith, built to exacting detail, filling up the entire warehouse to the rafters. It was a scale model built at a ratio of 75 to 1. As wide as two Greyhound Buses and more complex than Chaos Theory, it cleanly took my breath away.

Adjectives fail me.

All the great circles of the City wound up and up the slopes of Mindolluin. Within each circle were halls, houses, fountains, stables, plazas and infinite columns. Each ramp and walkway was built to the finest realistic detail. It was a "miniature," technically speaking, but the assemblage was so towering you just couldn't use such a word!

May it go down in history as the most celebrated scale model of all time.

* * *

The only downside to this visit (and I must be mad to even name one) was missing the chance to hang out at WETA Digital. There you could find plenty more magic, of a different sort. The Army of the Dead, the Cave Troll from Moria, and of course the best-kept secret in show business: Gollum.

Our tour ended and my feet came back to touch the ground. Back in the front office people were buzzing about some exciting news — a certain redheaded film geek who runs a certain film geek website was coming down next week to pay a visit. Hannah and the others clapped their hands in delight. Of course, this meant one more spotlight shining on WETA. No wonder they were happy. A little acknowledgment can go a long way.

The WETA team was duly proud. I sensed a unifying feeling of satisfaction and pride from every one I met that day. They knew in their hearts this stuff was brilliant ... and it was time the world knew.

* * *

Back at the Stone Street Studios I was met with several warm smiles by the Casting people. All the young women said, "So you're the American who was singing on Saturday? That was great! Yeah, come on in!"

I had heard — somewhere along the way — that they needed extras. Word on the street was that they could use another tall, strapping lad to play a soldier. After a couple of phone calls my Polaroid was taken. I received my instructions and timetable. All was set.

The next day I would be on the full-size set, living the dream of Gondor.

* * *

Sala said good-bye then; evidently he had some Easterlings to enslave, and I was left to my own devices. I checked out the call sheet and learned where they were filming Fangorn Forest. I was on my way to Studio K in a scant 10 minutes.

Gaining entry at the gate, I made a beeline straight for the first bluescreen I could see. There was Treebeard himself, the great Shepherd of the Trees. He was built on a rolling platform with great handles and controls along the bottom. He was an animatronic puppet about 50 times bigger than any Yoda! Bright optic-blue cloth hung around the perimeter.

My first impression of Treebeard? I've already used the word *brilliant* a million times. He looked every bit his age, very tree-like, with a dominant mossy beard pouring down from his large, deep-set eyes. There was a feeling of Old World about him. How shall I say — he looked like a soberly British old tree.

Dominic Monaghan and Billy Boyd were getting strapped into a safety harness, while touch-ups were applied to their feet. Merry and Pippin, the greatest mischief makers in hobbit history, were about to go for an unconventional ride.

Up the back of Treebeard they went, and perched atop they looked like hapless birds. The wind machine was turned on and the remote operators started to manipulate mouth, beard, and bushy eyebrows. Pole-arm operators gently moved the Ent's branchy arms. The whole apparatus was heaved and rocked on its platform with the poor hobbits bobbing up and down on their perch! From the camera's perspective the rocking translated to a reasonable semblance of *Ent-strides*. Sitting near me was voice artist Ken Blackburn. Holding a small microphone, he read pages from the script while Treebeard's mouth moved. After a time I started to feel bad for Dom and Billy. They were getting the worst of it, being tossed around like that all day.

I was very glad to meet Second Unit director Rick Porras, a man of infinite patience. He had to take remote instructions from PJ (who was watching the scene himself on his "wall of monitors" and would phone in every so often), keep track of all the off-screen dialogue, and plan a series of camera movements that would fit the digital effects yet-to-come. I don't know how he kept up with it all.

Daniel Falconer soon came in to admire the new Treebeard. It was his first time seeing it complete and operational. After he and his team worked on it for so long ... Ah, the glow that he had around him! The emotions going across his face were delicious. He drew me in closer and pointed to the beard. "See that? We put a lovely little snail in there."

* * *

In the adjacent soundstage I discovered the actual Fangorn set. It was empty. It was dark. Alone I walked in and found myself taken to another imaginary world.

The trees were "rooted" on various platforms and raised scaffolds. The forest sloped upward to an invisible wall at the back. Extinguished lights stood silent, watching me from behind the trunks. Overhead, deep green branches and blankets of moss dripped down.

The smell of wet dirt became strong. A small babbling stream came down towards me, and as I walked further in the soil gave gently under my feet.

Under the darkling eaves of Fangorn, I stood still. I kept my quiet thoughts to myself.

Part IV
* * *

In the predawn mist of December 5, 2000, I stood outside Wellington's grand Railway Station waiting for a charter bus to carry me off to the White City. There it was, on the farthest right, and a throng of young men in their twenties stood around, bristling in the cold. It was the kind of cold where your breath crystallizes and falls to the ground with a soft, tinkly sound.

Soon the bus pushed off and we left the city limits, headed north up into the wilds of the Upper Hutt. A slow daybreak colored the edges of the clouds. My mind was filled with expectant visions of the real Minas Tirith set. Yesterday, I had already seen the most magnificent scale model over at WETA, and I wondered how the details of that glorious piece would translate to the full-size City.

When we got to the edge of the Dry Creek Quarry, we headed for the large "armor tents" which were filled with plate and chain armor, helmets, makeup chairs, and of course the necessary craft services! Inside, everyone was divided up into three categories ... one group for Hero Armor, and two others for "further back" soldiers who would be a certain distance from the camera. The furthest of the "further backs" actually wore cloth shirts with metallic fibers sewn in the arms instead of actual chain mail.

I got in line and after a while realized I would end up in the back of today's scene.

The WETA armor wranglers were in force this morning, busy as ants on a hill. Their task was to keep the group organized and get them fully armored up in a very short time. There was Sukhita, my singing partner, distributing helmets and breastplates. She greeted me warmly and I watched with amazement as the assembly line rolled on.

My outfit consisted of warm black leggings, a long-sleeve dark overshirt, shiny gauntlets for legs and forearms over that, topped off with the aforementioned breastplate mail. It felt so strange. The Gondorian armor outwardly seemed very bulky and heavy, but it was just plastic! It sure looked like real metal. The color was like the dark lead of a pencil, the shape of the plate clean and austere.

The helmet had extensions of black curly hair attached to the underside, giving the impression that every single soldier in Gondor had black hair. This of course was a stylistic choice by Peter Jackson and WETA to help create a different "cultural look" for Gondor. All the Rohan extras would have blond hair, light eyes — while Gondor boys would have black hair, dark eyes. Other standards were set for other races, inspired by Tolkien's descriptions, and the casting people followed these criteria in all their casting efforts.

Funny thing is — my eyes are blue.

After all was tightened and snug around my torso (with the help of at least two people), I hit the makeup chair. The makeup technicians worked on Minas Tirith civilians and soldiers in quick succession. They quickly sponged dark powder on all our faces, making us look rugged and unshaven. Soon my transformation was complete. There I stood, gazing at dozens of soldiers milling about, and I felt new courage flowing through my soul. If you've never worn the armor of Gondor, I highly recommend it.

* * *

A chilly sunrise peeked over the edge of the mountains as we up into the Quarry proper. There it was, Minas Tirith, standing stark and mighty against the mountainside. The walls were alabaster white. Towers and parapets circled around the structure, and I saw great colored banners unfurling above. Several unique walls and tower pieces zoomed up above our heads. How awesome! It actually was a giant, life-size version of the scale model!

We marched in file towards a huge holding area outside the first circle of the City. Weapons were distributed, according to each soldier's placement in the scene. Some received tall pikes, some had rubber swords (of course they looked like hard steel) and each had a glorious shield strapped to his back. This shield displayed a large White Tree with a stylized root system. I absolutely LOVED this design, as it was clearly the symbol of Elendil, only without the stars above it.

In the new sun, a strong breeze blowing down the ridge, the City called to us. And on we marched.

Entering through a small archway, we suddenly were inside the first circle. What an amazing construct! The boulevards were all made of flat cut stone that matched the masonry of the walls. Fountains and sitting gardens were tucked along the sides, adjacent to lovely arched doorways. People were busy setting props around these, dressing them up as markets and shops. Statues — hanging plants — smooth stone benches — buttressed windows — there was so much! Camera equipment was strewn everywhere, and by all appearances the technicians were gearing up for a busy day.

I thought: This is all kind of Ancient Romanesque. But it was not really. Some of the archways and statuary had the flavor of Rome, but many other architectural elements were clearly English. An interesting mix.

I wanted to run off and explore ... but we had to go straight up to the wall to man our posts. We were to look out over the wall, watching events unfold on the Pelennor Fields below. Dangling from a huge crane truck was the biggest piece of blue fabric anyone could imagine. I would spend the rest of the day staring at it.

The Second Unit assistants got everything organized. Sukhita and several others from WETA came along and brushed up the armor with this funny metallic powder. The tip of every spear was inspected and recolored. She could spot a rough edge a mile off ... and quick as lightning she was there with her brushes and colors. I met another friendly brunette named Laurelle who said, "Aren't you the one who sang at karaoke?"

Remind me never to go out drinking with Kiwis again.

* * *

The rest of the morning went something like this:
1) Stand at attention.
2) Hold your pike close to your side.
3) Look fearful and concerned!

The camera was mounted on another crane and passed slowly in front of us, getting a smooth pan across our faces. We were given direction by the Second Unit director David Norris. We had to imagine we were watching battle and carnage right below the outer walls, right under our noses. This was Gondor's darkest hour, and it was the "anxiety in our eyes" that he wanted to capture.

Around noon the heat became quite noticeable. ZOOM! the assistants were milling about with umbrellas and little cups of Gatorade for all of us. Everyone was to hide from the sun, as much as possible, in between takes. Funny seeing all these serious Gondorian soldiers propping themselves up against the wall with big red umbrellas waving over their heads. Dozens of takes were completed throughout the morning, and as soon as the megaphone yelled "CUT!" the drinks and umbrellas came flying right back for our relief. Quite different from the way extras are treated on a big Hollywood set, where they are regarded as so much cattle. They even brought us wee cups of sunscreen to dabble on our exposed necks and faces. I felt almost pampered.

* * *

During lunch break I was determined to go off and explore! How could I honestly say I had been to Minas Tirith if, at the end of the day, I had only stood on a parapet with my back to it?! Absurd.

Walking back out through the armor depository, Sukhita helped remove the shield and sword straps, and she suggested I go look around the left side. There I would find something very special.

I took off my helmet (delighted again at the beautiful wings traced along the sides) and I took her advice. I took that short walk around the outside wall. It was the most soul-moving, epiphanic walk I would ever take.

There stood the Main Gate of Minas Tirith.

I was a tiny figure standing mute before its glorious might. It was the most resplendent, awesomely crafted thing I had ever seen. Nay, I could never have dreamed up this. Standing almost 20 meters high (four stories), it was built into a solid wall of bleached white stone. The front of the Gate held carvings and bas-relief sculptures of beautifully dressed, terribly handsome Kings of the past. These were surely figures of Númenor. Two of the figures were proportionally large, other smaller ones were inset on the sides. Different hues of grey and white helped contrast the Kingly figures against the heavily drawn designs on the gate itself.

It made me feel, in an instant, that I had transported completely into a powerful, real history that dwarfed my comprehension.

My senses locked out all sound, as if the volume dial in my mind had been suddenly shut off. This was a moment that pulled me outside of myself. I felt incredibly moved at the glory and ancientry this Gate represented. I knew the history behind this Gate, the many thousands of years of turmoil and strife that was behind this noble structure. I knew what was behind it, and I knew the horror that would soon bring it down. I could feel the weight of it. I was overwhelmed.

What happened to my heart? Why am I crying?

Then out of the corner of my eye I noticed a transparent, vague figure, standing close. He was a slight, older gentleman, dressed in simple, academic attire and a tweed coat. He seemed very kind as he smiled at me. He chewed a small pipe in his mouth. I recognized this spirit immediately. In his arms he held a little orange cat, who purred softly. A feeling of comfort flowed over me.

He looked at me and then looked back up at the Gate, and smiled broadly, seeming to say, "They really got it right, didn't they?"

I said nothing. I could only stare up at it, the tears for some reason would not stop coming.

* * *

Going back up to the wall, I was determined to shake hands with *the* David Norris. He was very engaging and friendly, like everyone here in New Zealand. I told him I had come all the way from California to visit the set, on behalf of the fans. He said, "Well, let's get you into some *Hero Armor* and place you in front of the camera."

What a delightful and altogether fateful surprise.

In a flash I was hustled down to the changing area, and a very young lad named Micah gave up his Hero Armor in exchange for mine ... he didn't care. Seriously, he had been doing this for weeks, and with a surprising absence of ego he decided he would like to take a break. And he was exactly my size, too.

Now of course there's NO WAY this would ever happen in L.A.

The sublime moment had come. I was wearing real metal chain, a real metal Hero Sword, and stood with the camera two feet from my face. In fact, we shot additional scenes where we watched Faramir departing from the City to defend Osgiliath. The director barked many times at us through the megaphone: "You are horrified, you are sad! The Prince of the City who is dearest to you is leaving! You are worried he will never come back! What is that fearful Shadow rising up to meet him? That's it! Look frightened for him!" And so on.

The last scenes of the day were the most fun. We ran around trying to get away from the little orange ball. Really this was an orange ball stuck on top of the camera (to orient our "sight lines" to the correct spot). We were supposed to visualize the Witch-king, who was swooping down on his winged steed to terrify us all. When the camera rolled, we got into formation — then turned and looked up — then scattered in fright. From one end of the plaza to the other, we did it again, and again, and again.

All told, this had been (here comes the big cliché, everyone) the thrill of a lifetime. The little 12-year-old in me who had always loved *The Lord of the Rings* — loved it, felt it, memorized it, emulated it — had finally stepped inside it. I was a part of the legend.

If the scene doesn't end up on the cutting room floor, I will be doubly lucky. If so, come 2003 when you go to see *The Return of the King*, you will see me on the battlements right next to Beregond.

I will be the only Gondorian soldier with bright blue eyes.

Part V
* * *

I would spend the next day nursing the slow burn that moved across my aching body. I could write a whole chapter about my sore back. Frankly, I cherished the pain — this armor fatigue — this remarkable sensation. It reminded me of my other life as a soldier in the service of the White Tree.

Taking a whole day off from Middle-earth was like suffering withdrawal. I was supposed to be thinking about all the museums and shops I went to, the restaurants and historic sites. But a day of touring beautiful Wellington was not enough. My mind kept wandering back to Miramar and the studios. It was like a dream from which I kept waking, then feeling the great need to fall back asleep.

* * *

On December 7, 2000, I was called back to that fantasy world now manifest. I took a pleasant stroll straight to the set, leaving David's home on Lyall Bay. There, an inviting stretch of beach curved away, the cobalt water disappearing beyond the horizon. I simply walked along the beach and then turned inland, going north to Studios K and L. The same sets where Treebeard had marched on Isengard three days earlier were now occupied with other hobbits.

Sean Astin was busy shooting a unique effects shot. He was surrounded by bluescreen, of course, and was reaching up towards a camera high above him. He looked sweaty, dirty, and intense, and they had the wind machine going again. Though stationary, he moved as if climbing up and up, reaching towards the camera desperately. Was he falling? Or climbing? I had no idea what visuals they would place behind him ...

Now Samwise is my absolute favorite character (he is the true center of the story, you know) and it was very gratifying to meet Sean. He was very straightforward, very cool, very much himself. Those ninnyhammers back in Hollywood don't have a lick of sense compared to him — pardon me for speaking outright, sir.

Unfortunately, we chatted only briefly before he was called back to work. He's an excellent director in his own right, and it would have been great to get his angle on this whole big project. He did mention that Elijah Wood was nearby, just finishing some additional scenes for Frodo.

I looked everywhere for him. The Ring-bearer. The young hobbit lad who brought down the darkest Shadow. But alas, he was gone. My timing is usually good, but evidently not great.

But I was in for another treat: Philippa Boyens was running about, carefully working over her script and adding direction to Sean's work. One of PJ's closest collaborators, Philippa is a charming, delightful lady with real zest. Is it not great that she's a rabid Tolkien fan who also happens to be one of the screenwriters?

Watching the frenetic Second Unit crew, the makeup team, the laptops, and what with all the cell phones going off, one got the sense of real momentum. In just three weeks, the biggest motion picture project in history would call it a wrap.

* * *

I went next door to meet Shadowfax.

Now this was a horse. He stood by a group of gentle brown mares, all gathered around the large trucks that had brought them. A powerful, gorgeous white stallion, he sniffed and snorted as I stroked his mane. I get a little nervous around horses, but he was so utterly beautiful I had to say hello. One look in his eye and I could tell he was enjoying the attention.

Inside, the dark Fangorn set I had previously wandered through was now brightly lit and filled with mist. Many of the Fellowship were gathering in the green room. A rather dull room with a table of food and comfortable seats, it would soon be a hive of activity. The actors would kill time here waiting for the lights, boom microphones, horses, and everything else to be ready.

Dominic Monoghan and Billy Boyd arrived. I said hello, only the briefest of introductions, and then watched as the fruit started to fly. In perfect Merry-fashion, Dominic found a bunch of grapes and threw them across, one by one, to Billy, who tried in vain to catch them in his mouth. I had to duck several times to avoid the purple missiles. In truth, Pippin managed to catch some. These two fellows were simply perfect hobbits ... everything about their energy was hobbit-like.

John Rhys-Davies stormed into the room. There's hardly a better word for how John Rhys-Davies would walk into *any* room. He was a tower of energy with a basso profundo voice, buried under heavy Gimli armor. One of the greatest achievements of this movie will be how they effectively bring him down to dwarf size. John has a voice that could shake a mountain, too. What fun watching him flirt with and pester the makeup people! What a hoot.

Viggo Mortensen sat outside the door, very quiet, very to himself. At our first greeting he was kind and soft-spoken ... but I got the sense no chit-chat would be tolerated. As Aragorn, he will certainly elevate the role with his hardened good looks and his sharp-as-steel green eyes. I liked his intensity. It will resonate in his performance.

Orlando Bloom was there, being carefully fitted with a delicious Elven bow. The makeup folks were also trying to get his blond hairpiece under control. We then wandered outside and sat in the sunshine, talking about the phenomenon of online fandom and how the movie business was changing. Tolkien fans worldwide had turned the internet into a hotbed of rumor, literary debate, and busy chat rooms. I made predictions of what was next for Hollywood, as it bent to the forces of shared media. "Big changes," I said, "sure to get bigger than the studios can guess." Viggo came out and joined our conversation, and Bernard Hill, too, listened with great interest.

Legolas, Aragorn, and Théoden ... I had never had an audience quite like this.

Sir Ian drove up, fresh from central wig headquarters, and went straight over to greet his beloved Shadowfax. We went back into the green room and found a leather couch on which to lounge. We ducked a few grapes and a large peach during our conversation but managed to stay on track.

And then Karl Urban appeared — princely, tall, and virile. Let me say it plainly: a better-looking man than Karl does not live and breathe in New Zealand. His Éomer will be the breakout heartthrob of these movies. His future career has the trajectory that only Brad Pitt could have. Guys will want to be just like him, girls will daydream about him. Watch, you'll see.

It got kind of sticky when talk turned to politics. Someone spoke of the current American presidential election. Rather, the *non-election*, since nothing was decided at that point. Votes from Florida were still in dispute, VP Al Gore was behind by a miniscule number of ballots, and there was worsening controversy over recounts and litigation. It was confusing, and certainly no one felt good about the way it was being handled. Then John and Ian got into a spirited disagreement about the American political process.

I was pinned to my seat. Both of these actors, tremendously smart and articulate, were going headfirst into debate. A juicy one at that. What made it funnier was that both were in costume, getting ready to go out on the set. Imagine the sonorous stage voices of both Gimli and Gandalf, with some heat, going around the subject of presidents, Congress, and political mischief. Production assistants tried to gently separate them, but no luck. In a slow march towards Fangorn Forest, wizard and dwarf continued to bandy right up to their marks. How surreal.

* * *

The scenes from "Flotsam and Jetsam" were filmed that day, with the two hobbits meeting the entire group just coming back from Helm's Deep. The Fangorn set was now also used as the newly grown forest around Isengard — after the Ents had taken over.

I watched them ride in from the rear of the set: Théoden, Éomer, Aragorn, all atop their beautiful horses, followed by Gimli with Legolas, with Gandalf leading in front. Shadowfax seemed proud and spirited as he carried his rider. They were a regal troupe, come right out of my imagination and into the tangible world.

Merry stood up from the great crumbling wall on which he sat, smoking his pipe. "Welcome to Isengard!" This was the outer Ring of Isengard, broken and quite ruined, with scraggly overgrowth across the stones. Seems the Ents had done a fine job.

The perspective shots here were unique for Gimli. A remarkably tall body double in exacting Legolas costume stood on a box next to John. The camera moved in close, and with only the Elf's arm in the frame, Gimli could stand next to him, helmeted head coming even with the elbow. It really worked. Gimli was now dwarf-height, just by fooling the eye's reference point with Legolas's arm.

The shoot continued throughout the day — redoing all the entrances and exits of the horses — and more than a few reshoots of dialogue. You know the drill. Filmmaking demands more of its participants than you think.

However, the difference here was *love*. The great dynamism among all the people on *The Lord of the Rings* came from their love of the work. They were truly in love with the experience and it carried them through. How rare to see such unity of purpose.

I felt it too. I admit being on a "Middle-earth high." I was in love with these people, their surfeit of warmth, the way they held close together. I was drawn into their world now and it was hard, profoundly hard, for me to turn and leave.

But leave I did.

Something must be said here about Peter Jackson. He has shown the stuff of genius here. Against the worst odds he brought all these teams together, put his heart on the pages of a script, convinced the Money to put their hat in, and behold! Everyone lined up to champion his vision. They believe in him. They believe he is a sublime creative force.

And after a week of observing (and even participating), I was convinced. These films are fueled with passion and executed with great care. The incredible efforts of everyone involved are a blessing to us — the audience — the fans.

This is my acknowledgment to them.

* * *

That night, seeking the comfort of the moon, we took a walk along the inviting beach mentioned earlier. It was chilly enough to wear a coat, and the night wind flowed across the dark water of Lyall Bay. It was my last night in New Zealand and I wanted to smell the clean air once more before I left.

Down at the water's edge, I looked up at the sky and stared. Like a glittering blanket across the great indigo vault, stars shone brightly everywhere. Awe came over me. There were stars I had never seen before. Formations of stars I did not recognize. There was Orion, the mighty Hunter, but I was dumfounded when I saw him.... he had been turned *upside down*. I could not grasp it. What mind could take this all in? Was this really the far side of the world?

There was another shape in the heavens. This one had to be pointed out to me, for I could not have known it. I beheld the Southern Cross, floating in the dark like a gilded kite, a signpost on the way to Antarctica.

I felt very small then. Very small against the vast universe.

* * *

The morning of December 8, 2000, I was ready to fly out but not at all willing. While putting my luggage in the car I met a new friend. I think maybe it was a sign. He was a sturdy black tomcat, very affectionate, and he seemed to be talking to me.

What he wanted to say was important, evidently. I went over to where he sat, comfortable on his garden wall as if it were his own private parapet. He could safely watch the whole neighborhood from here. He purred and I petted. There was a communication going on, but you couldn't hear it with your ears.

He was going to take care of Icarus. He would be a new companion to him, sharing a world of new adventures. I am in danger of sounding maudlin, but I don't care. I understood what was going on.

The little spirit that had followed me all these days was staying. He would not come home with me. This was our final good-bye.

As I went back to the car, I knew he was gone. There was peace now. All had indeed turned out well.

Much too hasty,
Quickbeam

48. *The Fellowship of the Ring* Film Review

Ostadan

I suppose that everyone who has read *The Lord of the Rings* has daydreamed about a movie. As early as 1958, Tolkien was approached with a story treatment for a proposed animated movie (whose young author primarily impressed him with his "silliness" and "incompetence").

The first issue of the Mythopoeic Society's journal "Mythlore" in 1969 contained an article considering the possibilities of a live action movie. Fans have always been ambivalent about the possibility. Would it be something resembling Disney's rather free fairy-tale adaptations, with Galadriel singing "bibbity-bobbity-boo?" Could it be done live-action without looking silly? How many hours of film would it take to adapt the story? What would have to be trimmed? What would have to be changed? While everyone imagined what it would be like to see their favorite scene played out on the big screen, they feared that any screen adaptation might be more of an insulting caricature instead.

It is over thirty years since I first read *The Lord of the Rings*, and I have long been in the pessimist camp. Ralph Bakshi's attempt in 1978 was not as horrible as it was expected to be, and even had some very satisfying moments ... but its sense of being rushed (both in terms of slipshod production and in the sense of truncation) seemed to confirm that LotR was unfilmable. "Even George Lucas," I thought, "couldn't do it 'right.'"

Now, a quarter-century after Bakshi's film and *Star Wars*, Peter Jackson has attempted this impossible feat. Going into the screening room with the other TORn staffers, having seen so many stills and trailers (but having avoided the TV specials and soundtrack — there must be *some* surprises, I thought), I was cautiously optimistic. I figured that it would be like a competently made adaptation, and that there would be several moments where I would say, "Why ever did he make *that* change?" accompanied by occasional wailing and gnashing of teeth, balanced by at least as many moments where I would say, "Damn! It's *Lord of the Rings*!!!"

In a sense, I was right, although there were no moments of actual teeth-gnashing. As an adaptation, taken scene by scene and line by line, there are some questionable things and many wonderful moments. But what I hadn't counted on was that Jackson had gone far beyond merely presenting a series of scenes from the book — heck, Chris Columbus could have done that. Instead, he created Middle-earth anew on the screen, and it is captivating.

By the time the film was halfway finished, I wasn't really paying attention to what was changed, or what clever device was being used to make us think that Elijah Wood was under four feet tall, or whether Moria was a set, or a model, or a CGI screen. I was caught up in the story. I thrilled at Gandalf's escape from Orthanc. I had a sinking feeling when the Nazgûl were alerted to the Hobbits' presence at Weathertop. And I was near tears as the Eight Walkers fled the Bridge of Khazad-dûm.

I was perfectly aware of the differences from the book (and duly appreciated when something was preserved verbatim), and once everyone has seen the film, we'll talk about all those details endlessly (OK, until *The Two Towers* comes out), but somehow, in some magical way, all of that just doesn't *matter*. The movie is unmistakably *Lord of the Rings* — perhaps not *exactly* J.R.R. Tolkien's *Lord of the Rings*, but *Lord of the Rings* just the same. Throughout the film, it passed my ultimate test for any Tolkien-derived art: it felt like Reading It for the First Time. Not bad after 30-plus years.

If the other two films are of this quality, Peter Jackson will have produced the gold standard by which fantasy films will be measured for decades to come.

49. *The Fellowship of the Ring* & *The Two Towers* Film Reviews

Anwyn

When I watch Peter Jackson's *The Lord of the Rings*, either *The Fellowship of the Ring* or *The Two Towers*, there is no doubt about what I am seeing. I am *in* Middle-earth. The beautiful New Zealand scenery, the incredible artistry of the sets, the attention to detail in every character, and the luminous acting all combine to create a stunning visual illusion, a reality very easy to immerse oneself in. But against this background, characters I know better than any others in fiction speak trumped-up one-liners, twentieth-century jargon, and the simplest of explanatory lines. It's enough to make any Tolkien reader tear out her hair in frustration at the contradiction.

Tolkien's real story is text-based. It is not an action story. It is a word story with some really cool action scenes. Thus the biggest phenomenon in my mind after watching *Fellowship* — the "and yet" syndrome.

Legolas and Gimli. No character development whatsoever. Who are they? Where did they come from? "Hi, we just rode in with your friend Strider …"

… and yet, *damn*, could that Elf ever handle that bow. Fun action scenes there.

Boromir. Who is he again? Strider. Who is he again? He's a king? I didn't get that part …

… and yet, Boromir's attempt to take the Ring was all there, very true in spirit. Not only that, but his death scene was also masterful. And Strider leaping in to tackle the last Uruk-hai. Fun action scene there.

"What was the deal with Galadriel's freak-out? Why didn't the Ring affect Frodo that way?" Good question.

… and yet, what the Ring *did* do to Frodo was stunning. We were left in no doubt that the Ring was transferring him to the same world occupied by the Ringwraiths. Fun action scenes there.

The dichotomy here between "Hi, I'm Peter Jackson and I like to make action movies with cool effects" and "How do I make an action movie with cool effects based on this word-heavy book?" is staggering. To my way of thinking, he spent so much time showing off his effects that he wasted a lot of time he could have used to give us more story. The essence of Tolkien is language, language, *language*. When I contrast the brilliant dialogue of characters in the books, whether it be the light familiar discourse among the hobbits or a thunderous passage between Gandalf and Denethor, with the banal toss-off lines given us by Phillipa Boyens, Fran Walsh, and Peter Jackson, it makes me almost want to cry.

As for storytelling, when you know every in and out of a story before you see a movie and therefore know what was left in and what was left out, it's very difficult to tell how the movies did on a pure storytelling basis. But it's easy to tell which omissions, amalgamations, and additions hindered and which didn't hurt. *Fellowship* had its share.

For the record, I would like to state that I have absolutely no problem with Glorfindel being omitted and Arwen subbed in. It's a standard adaptation technique, amalgamating characters to reduce confusing extraneous people. What I *do* have a problem with is Arwen swooping in almost right after the attack on Weathertop, putting her sword to Aragorn's throat (a bit of playfulness that's just left hanging there), and riding off with Frodo, with all the Nine at her heels. When they finally make it to Rivendell (thanks to *her* trick with the river, faugh), Gandalf tells Frodo that Frodo has some strength in him. HOW HAD HE SHOWED IT? He started to be *really* messed up almost the second the knife pierced him. Arwen showed up and saved the day. We never saw what Frodo was capable of in the way of resisting the Riders and the Ring and the wound, all at once, and that cheapens Frodo's character considerably.

For the record, I would like to state that I have absolutely no problem with Tom Bombadil and the Old Forest being dropped. Again, adaptation requires that anything that is self-contained and can be jettisoned without affecting anything material in the plot *should* be ditched. What I *do* have a problem with is how curtailed the hobbits' meeting with Strider was. "Hi, I'm here, you'd better be scared, come with me." Um. Don't these hobbits have any brains at all? "The lesson in caution has been well learned." Not by Jackson's hobbits. It's like when Frank Darabont removed from *The Green Mile* the part where the Tom Hanks character proved by logical evidence that John Coffey *couldn't* have committed the crime because he couldn't tie a bow. You ditch the brain part, and the hobbits just went with Strider on faith because there was nothing else to do? Come on.

For the record, I would like to state that I have absolutely no problem with Lothlórien being curtailed. We got the idea that Galadriel is intimidating, that her woods are magical, and that we don't want her in charge of the Ring. What I *do* have a problem with is the Council of Elrond. As an acquaintance said after the movie, "There was a Council of Elrond?" Exactly. All I saw was a bunch of people sitting around in a petty quarrel. Not a lot in the way of thoughtful discourse.

Ultimately, I stand by my opinion that telling the story properly on screen in three hours cannot be done, and if it could be, it would not be the kind of film that most people would want to watch. Thus Jackson and his action scenes. But with the film so action-heavy, the casual moviegoer is denied much of the richness of the story. Moreover, film by necessity puts a stamp of contrivance on the story that does not exist in the book. Tolkien's story flows more naturally than any other book I have ever read. There is no need for long explanations of how magic works or where Angband is, because it's all in the nuances of the story — the *characters* know all the stories so well that they give them to us almost by osmosis. The need in modern movie making for snappy patter, clear cause and effect, and explosions gave us the confrontation between Saruman and Gandalf as well as the creation of the Uruk-hai, but it also gave us Sam whanging an Orc on the head with a frying pan and shouting, "I think I'm getting the hang of this!" Groan!

Thus *Fellowship*. My feelings upon seeing *Towers* were slightly different, and for an obvious reason. A friend remarked in the theater after the film that it was quite possible that we were "inoculated" to Jackson's particular style of changing things, and I think he's quite right. The "dumbing down" of dialogue, the deletion of much story and detail, and, of course, the mighty emphasis on action and slaughter — I expected that going in, so it was easier to focus on other things.

Moreover, I found more things to praise in *Towers* than in *Fellowship*, and thus some of the painful lapses of purism were easier to swallow.

In *Towers*, Jackson seems to display a particular talent for pushing things just one or two levels of intensity higher than Tolkien took them, in order to create drama. Examples: 1) Théoden was under the control of Saruman via Wormtongue; Jackson took it to the next level and had Saruman actually psychically possessing Théoden's soul. 2) Elrond was sorrowful about Arwen's choice; Jackson took it to the next level and had him actively condemning it. 3) Treebeard was doubtful about involving the Ents in the strife; Jackson took it to the next level and had Treebeard actually say "No." 4) Last but not least, the Number One Lapse of the Year, Faramir was stern with Frodo and Sam and a bit doubtful as to what to do; Jackson took it to the next level and had him actually hold Frodo with the intent of sending the Ring to Minas Tirith.

The shocking thing, for me personally, is not that he did these things, but that, with the exception of Faramir, I can accept them. Possibly through "inoculation," I softened my outlook a bit after *Fellowship* and realized that the average moviegoer "off the street" needs tension and drama, and all of the above-listed things injected that. Add to them things like Aragorn actually telling Arwen that she should desert him for the Havens and Legolas questioning Aragorn's wisdom in remaining at Helm's Deep, and you've got some drama in what otherwise would be a straight-up "We're good, they're bad, let's fight them" situation. Don't get me wrong, I've always loved this about Tolkien — that the good guys trusted each other and worked with one another and didn't bicker or doubt.

When I started reading Robert Jordan's *Wheel of Time* series, that was one of the things I Really Hated—the so-called good guys were *constantly* snapping and fighting and backstabbing and insulting and oh, it got on my nerves. But I think Jackson managed to inject some intrigue without ruining any of the above-mentioned plot lines—with the exception, again, of Faramir.

My overall feel for the film, and a nutshell comparison to *Fellowship*, could be summed up thusly: in *Fellowship*, with the exception of Tom Bombadil, etc., they went everywhere they were supposed to go and did everything they were supposed to do, but so much of it felt hollow and lacking to me. Bree was a dark, nasty, beer-smelling, lice-scratching nightmare with no logic (Gandalf's letter about Aragorn) or light-heartedness (the Inn song) to make up for it. Lothlórien was a shell of itself that not even the extended edition could entirely make up for — Sam's line "Are you out of those nice shiny daggers?" in the EE made my stomach heave in protest. True, there were a few great scenes — Frodo and Gandalf in Moria, Gandalf and the Balrog in Moria, Boromir's death, Weathertop — to try to offset them, but still, I felt rather let down at the end of every *Fellowship* viewing.

Whereas in *Towers*, they actually showed things that Tolkien didn't describe to us but which he does say happened—notably Théodred's death, the attacks on Rohan, and the evacuation of the people — and showed them with sensitivity and real feeling. Not to speak of the one name on everybody's lips since the opening — Gollum!

Gollum has always made me cry in the books, and I cried at the CGI version as well. The split-personality debates, the despair when he thinks "Master" has betrayed him, the growing hopelessness regarding his redemption, all wind their way straight from the books to the film reels. Much has been said about Gollum and everybody knows how good he is, so I shall limit my remarks to this: he evoked a wonderful emotional response, just as he should. That, and the pathos and humor of the "taters" scene with Sam. Priceless.

All of this acceptance and new sensitivity to the needs of the films as opposed to books has not blinded me, however, to the faults that I find most difficult to stomach. Namely:

For the record, I would like to state that I have absolutely no problem with Éomer saving the day rather than Erkenbrand at Helm's Deep. Amalgamating characters, when done with believability and sensitivity, is a great way to save time and make sure we know our main characters better. What I do have a problem with is the continued total lack of character development for Gimli and his restriction to comic relief only. Even Legolas was a bit more complex this time, but not good ol' Gimli, falling off his horse and just being a general blunderbuss. Sad, that.

For the record, I would like to state that I have absolutely no problem with Haldir bringing Elves to Helm's Deep rather than Halbarad bringing Rangers. A bit ouchy on first blush, perhaps, but again, introducing myriads of extraneous unknown characters when you already have one on hand who would do the trick nicely is danger zone for filmmakers. What I do have a problem with is Jackson's continued fetish for attempting to make us believe people are dead. He did it about three times with Frodo in *Fellowship*, and it was annoying every time. Here Aragorn is his target. That whole bit with him floating down the river is just … dumb. We who know the story are not in any danger of thinking Jackson is going to kill him off, and those who don't know the story ought to be savvy enough about movie making that they wouldn't think it either. Yes, I get it that he wanted to show Arwen and the conflict there, but why not have him think about her while sitting around at Helm's Deep? Thinking about the Elf while the human woman is actually in his sight would have been just as dramatic. Although it would have meant cutting Legolas's brilliant bit of dialogue "You're late. You look terrible." In Elvish, no less. Come on.

For the record, I would like to state that I have absolutely no problem with Treebeard at first refusing to take the Ents to war. As I said, it added drama. What I do have a problem with is the way he got turned around. Pippin: "Uh, wait, take us to Isengard." Treebeard (turning around): "Sure, okay, whatever." ?!?! Please. Just dumb. Even if he wanted to do it pretty much that same way, the dialogue could have been worlds better. Pippin could have outright *told* Treebeard what he would find and showed him where to find it and encouraged his rage. And if they'd done it earlier instead of showing so many shots of Pippin and Merry on his shoulders, he could have sent the Huorns to Helm's Deep with Gandalf and Éomer. It would even have been another chance for those geniuses who work for Richard Taylor to show their powers.

And now the mother of all story lapses: Faramir. He's been a favorite character of mine for time out of mind, and Jackson's Faramir is not at all the same man I knew in Tolkien. Yes, it was another example of what I said about Jackson taking things "to the next level," but in this case he went one level too far. Faramir was supposed to be the light side of Boromir's temptation, not the same or even worse.

While it's true that in the book he wavers, the crucial difference between him and Boromir is that *he does not fall*. Not even for a moment does he give way to the madness and lust of the Ring. Boromir wavered, gave way to temptation, and fell, for however short a time. Faramir did not. Perhaps the screenwriters are unwilling to believe that anybody could resist so strong a temptation; perhaps they think *we* would not believe it. We would. Especially if we saw the struggle and the resistance. We would. What a shame that one of the most important psychological elements of the story (and Tolkien is all too often criticized for his handling of human psyches!) is thus maligned in an otherwise better film than the first.

Two very similar films, two rather different reactions on my part. It is my hope that *The Return of the King* will be able to wind it all up for me and make me feel that Tolkien's story has been brought to life as best it could be in our current phase of movie history. Despite my negativity, I have a deep respect for Jackson's courage in taking on this project and for his creation of a world that draws us in, just as Tolkien's does. Bravo for a mighty effort, sir.

50. *The Fellowship of the Ring* Film Review

Quickbeam

My rating: 9 1/2 out of 10.

I am so grateful Peter Jackson made this movie.

It could have been a horrible mess. It could have been a cheap tinfoil mini-series made for television — you know the kind — with lame CGI effects and stock costumes out of the warehouse. Even worse, it could have been Disney, filled with dancing candlesticks and Gollum singing a tearful ballad by Elton John and Tim Rice. Happily, the end result is none of those things.

The Fellowship of the Ring stands on its own as a strong, visionary, and surprising film. Painted with sweeping strokes and equal measures of intimacy, the movie leaves you eager to see more. If the next two films match this one, then I can predict what movie fans will say years from now when they speak of PJ's work — "*The Lord of the Rings* is the *Citizen Kane* of adventure films."

But I tell you up front to bring Kleenex. Emotions run high in the latter part of the film, which is cut from the same epic fabric that Kurosawa used for *Seven Samurai*. Who knew that a fantasy movie could be so powerful and moving? Here you will find exceptional storytelling that elevates it above the label of "genre film."

But this movie is not the same *Fellowship* you have on your bookshelf. It is clearly NOT a replacement or a perfect mirror of Tolkien's work. It's not supposed to be. Indeed, many pieces and plots and people did not survive the translation from page to screen, but I don't fault the screenwriters for that. Look, I miss Tom Bombadil and the Barrow-wights as much as anyone, but I doubt they would find a place here to fit in.

Look at what happened with *Harry Potter and the Sorcerer's Stone* — where the best Chris Columbus could do was clone the book for another medium. That movie felt like a flat copy of J.K. Rowling's original story, sadly lacking any real zest, challenges, or satirical wit. But *Fellowship* screenwriters Philippa Boyens, Fran Walsh, and Peter Jackson avoid that mistake by serving up a unique distillation of Tolkien without aping him. Yes, they have made some eye-popping departures that fans are likely to fight over, but amazingly they never lose the soul of the story, and I believe the skill of their adaptation is more valuable than quibbles over differences.

The story begins with a sweeping prologue filled with spectacle. I would have been a satisfied customer with just this opening eight minutes ... Lo and behold there was an entire movie yet to unfold! You will recognize Cate Blanchette as the narrator, her voice brimming with authority and power. The essential background of the Ruling Ring is explained in a lucid way, and one of the film's themes is quietly introduced (the contempt that Elves hold against mortal Men, an erosion of race relations).

Much praise to the design work by Richard Taylor and the folks at WETA. Even if *Fellowship* clocks in at two hours and 45 minutes, it's still not enough time to soak in all the remarkable things WETA has created. All these details help immerse the audience in a Middle-earth that is organic, ancient, and sometimes harsh. *Fellowship* is a triumph of production design and special effects. PJ and Company can go ahead and dust off some space on the shelf for all the awards coming their way. Seriously. Don't wait, just give them the Oscars now (NOTE: My predictions proved true as the film racked up a staggering 13 Oscar nominations and during the 2002 Academy Awards ceremony took home four awards, including Best Makeup, Visual Effects, and Cinematography). They have created Middle-earth with such clarity. There's just so much beauty here.

The Shire is fresh and alive with hobbity goodness. I swear you've never seen a green like the green of those hills. There is a very effective shot where the early mist of morning rests around the Shire ... a gorgeous backdrop of hobbit-holes and gardens. It is pastoral to the tenth power. Then a terrifying Black Rider slowly enters the frame, very slowly, surveying the land with an ominous change in the music. The hobbits' peace is about to be shattered by an encroaching world they can no longer ignore. Now this is what I call damn fine directing.

The magical environments of the Elves really stand out. Rivendell is like a dream that not even the Elves could dream of. The open terraces are laced with fine carvings and soft leaves of autumn fall about the characters as they speak.

The embarrassment of riches continues in the Mines of Moria. How PJ managed to do it is beyond me. He combines breathless action, Dwarvish history, and devastating emotion into a virtuosic sequence that will go down in film history. A visceral experience by any measure. When the Fellowship finally comes out on the other side of the mountains ...

Howard Shore's music is perfect in every way. There is a sublime moment of longing as Enya softly sings *Aniron*, the theme for Aragorn and Arwen. The score is stunning all on its own, with themes of such beauty and sadness that you are moved to another place. But when the music is matched with equally vibrant images, you have achieved a special bliss. Waiter, could you wrap up that little gold statue, please, Mr. Shore will be taking it home tonight (NOTE: Howard Shore did indeed win the Oscar for Best Original Score).

What holds this magic tapestry together is the cast. Everyone can agree that the casting of these films is divine. I have a hard time pointing out my favorites because everyone is so superb.

Okay, I admit, Ian McKellen brings a heartfelt Gandalf to life as perfect as perfect can be. There is so much trust in his eyes and mysterious power in his voice that you can't help but believe Gandalf is real. His performance is almost transparent, if you know what I mean. He has a lock on the Oscar nomination, easily (NOTE: Yup, I got that one right too, but it was heartbreaking when Ian did not wi)]. Sean Astin had me in tears. Since Samwise has the most extreme range of moments in the whole trilogy — going from comedic to raging to otherworldly courage — it really is wonderful to see Astin up to the challenge. I loved Sean Bean as well. He stands out as an exceptional actor. His Boromir is deeply connected to the bigger canvas around him. Oh, the sadness and nobility he holds within him ... I told you to bring tissues.

And now I admit my shame for not trusting in Liv Tyler. She's actually quite splendid as Arwen ... we don't see enough of her, really. I had been downright awful in my early dismissals of Liv, but she really is a find. Her beautiful Elvish flows like wine and her tenderness with Aragorn is wonderful. And Viggo! When he looks into her eyes and his stern gaze turns to soft love ... it just gets you right there.

And there are such great performances from the others, especially Elijah Wood, who clearly shows the torment and uncertainty in his heart with his crystalline eyes. Orlando Bloom and John Rhys-Davies are impressive as Legolas and Gimli, but sadly their screen time seems abbreviated. I would have enjoyed seeing more of their bristling and banter.

This is one of my few complaints: the editing of the film moves things along at such a pace! Sometimes not enough time is spent on the characters settling in with one another before BAM you're on your way to another gorgeous vista or frightening encounter with danger. I appreciate the need for economy, story-wise, but for my taste I prefer *more* personal connections between lead characters instead of *less*. But PJ is a director with a very clear purpose, and in *Fellowship* he trusts his audience to keep up. He telegraphs things visually and quickly moves on, not going back for needless exposition.

Maybe when the DVD comes out next year, he might be able to return some of the excised material to the film. I hope to revisit some of those character set pieces that I know are there, waiting to be added in for the deluxe super-long edition (NOTE: The very fine *FotR Extended Edition* certainly made me and millions of other fans happy).

There's plenty to admire in the script, granted. And since I'm not such a prickly purist I was satisfied with the dialogue for the entire film up until one moment — just one small spot at the end that seemed like "Hollywood" dialogue creeping in. At one point Aragorn, Legolas and Gimli have just sent Boromir's body over the Falls, and everyone in the audience is deeply moved ... most are in tears. Then when Aragorn decides not to follow Frodo and Sam, he says some beautiful things about saving Merry and Pippin from the tortures of Isengard, followed by this statement: "Let's hunt some Orc." This was the only dialogue that squeaked a little, sounding too colloquial for a character like Aragorn. That's my only real gripe, small as it is.

Immediately after, we have Frodo and Sam gazing out across the Emyn Muil, with a staggering view of Mordor far, far in the distance. The two hobbits exchange hope, fear, and love in a few short sentences straight out of the book. As the music brightens, just a bit, a feeling of trepidation and wanderlust flows across the audience. Everyone simultaneously feels it: the sense of "what will befall our heroes next?" It is a beautiful emotional grace note to close the film.

All in all, *Fellowship* is brilliant and exciting ... and like I said before, carping over a few defects is silly when you look at the film's achievement as a whole. I must close by giving my congratulations to everyone involved. This is a new high-water mark for modern cinema.

Much too hasty,
Quickbeam

51. *The Two Towers* Film Review

Ostadan

This is a difficult review to write, because I *do* like the film so very much. And there, I think, is one of the problems — with me, not with the film — the first film, combined with the *Two Towers* marketing, has made me just a bit blasé. If I had seen this film two years ago, I might have criticized some of the story changes, but would have roared an approving "Wow!" And so, perhaps, I should do now. Instead, I feel a sense of mild disappointment.

Alas, it is too easy to say things like, "It goes without saying that Gollum is phenomenal; the hordes of Saruman's orcs are staggering; that Treebeard is a wonder ..." Except that it *shouldn't* go without saying. Likewise, the amount of Tolkien that *is* in the film is far beyond what anyone would normally expect in a movie adaptation, whether it is in Éowyn's fear of a cage, or "What's taters, eh?" or Théoden reciting the elegy for Eorl, or the vision of Elessar's death from the Tale of Aragorn and Arwen.

Finally, Jackson quite artistically uses the various characters to run a single thematic thread through this entire movie — the rejection of despair in the face of apparent certain failure and the importance of Hope (even in Arwen's flashback scene with Aragorn, the Sindarin spoken for the word "trust" is "estel," which Tolkien translates as both "hope" and "faith"). This is very much in keeping with Tolkien's themes — is not the whole theme of accepting mortality as the Gift of Men just this? Yet, thanks to the first film, and endless viewings of trailers for this film, I find that I take all these things just a bit for granted and focus more on the film's defects. The cost, I suppose, of success.

What are those defects? Not necessarily changes in the storyline. Indeed, at least one such change, the moving of Théodred's death onstage (with some of Gandalf's accusatory dialogue with Gríma given to Éomer), was an excellent way of establishing these characters and situations for the audience. Instead, the problems were general storytelling ones.

I think that some of the emotional power of the first film — the deaths of Gandalf and Boromir, Sam walking into the Anduin after Frodo — is lacking in the present film. Gandalf's reappearance should have been a lump-in-the-throat moment, but (probably because we'd already seen the moment in the trailer, due to a stupid New Line marketing decision), it was rather flat. The matter of Aragorn's Indiana Jones-style apparent death was particularly false — even someone unfamiliar with the books knows that this guy isn't getting killed off in this film — and so the other characters' reactions to it also rang false. And without an emotional payoff from Aragorn's disappearance, the whole Warg attack, while moderately exciting, really serves no purpose in moving the plot along (it kills off Háma, with whose young son Aragorn discusses swords, but this is probably lost on the audience anyway, and I might well be mistaken). The whole episode would have been better omitted. There were good moments, especially the afore-mentioned scene of Elessar's death, and Gandalf's dawnlight charge with the Rohirrim, but to me, these lack the impact of the Big Scenes in *Fellowship*.

I do not wish to go into a catalog of story changes and quibbles, but do want to say a word about the much-discussed Faramir. The first time I saw the film, when Faramir told Frodo that the Ring would go to Gondor, my reaction was a silent "Say what?" when Sam said that they shouldn't even be there (in Osgiliath), I thought, "Ya got *that* right." This took me "out of the movie experience," which isn't good. The second time, when it was not such a surprise, it bothered me less. It does, after all, allow Faramir to grow and understand the peril of the Ring and its bearer more directly than in the book. In *The Return of the King*, it may be that Faramir will seem all the more heroic for having given up the Ring in this way, so I will withhold judgment for now. I think the problem that a lot of us have with Faramir is that, unlike other characters in the book, he has a "signature line," spoken twice in the book, not just once, saying he would not take the Ring even if it lay on the roadside. I cannot help wishing that, once Faramir changed his mind in the film, he could have spoken this dialogue at the last. If he had, I think we would all somehow have been happier with the whole Faramir episode.

In my review of Jackson's *The Fellowship of the Ring,* I wrote that "it passed my ultimate test for any Tolkien-derived art: it felt like Reading It for the First Time. Not bad after 30-plus years."

In *The Two Towers,* the movie magic did not take hold for me so readily, and so I am not quite so enthusiastic this time around, but I think that on the whole, *The Two Towers* still passes my test. As I said last year, "If the other two films are of this quality, Peter Jackson will have produced the gold standard by which fantasy films will be measured for decades to come."

Still gold, Mr. Jackson, still gold.

52. *The Two Towers* Film Review

Quickbeam

My rating: 9 out of 10.

Last year at about this time, fans on the net were a nervous lot. All of us were wondering the same thing: could Peter Jackson really pull it off? Would his opening film, *The Fellowship of the Ring*, be glorious cinema or a misfire? Well, now, the proof is in the pudding. His work has been remarkably successful both artistically and commercially; indeed PJ was lauded to the top of the highest mountain and the fans are now all lined up, eager for more. The only way to go is forward. If you enjoyed *Fellowship* as I did and have now come to believe in the power of PJ's transcendent film direction, you are in for a grand time with *The Two Towers*. It is a triumph indeed.

However, you must be warned this movie is different ... it feels different ... the skies have darkened and doom hangs in the air.

The despair of the human soul does not make for popular entertainment. We would rather run away from the darkness of our own hearts, the feelings of hopelessness and isolation. Most forms of pop culture distract us from our troubles. Especially the output of Hollywood, the glamour of Tinseltown, where movies take us away from our lives — if only for a little while.

But in this amazing second installment of the *LotR* trilogy, PJ asks the audience to sit down and deal with despair. Middle-earth is darker and more disturbed this time around. There is no Shire where one can sit comfortably and have tea and cakes. There is no restful peace in a lovely Elven house. Every scene puts the characters further into emotional turmoil. The danger and threat is trebled as the story intersects a broken Fellowship scattered across a landscape of woe. It is not the first time I have seen an epic adventure story colored with so much hopelessness. Again I recognize the hand of Akira Kurosawa as a director's inspiration. It seems that PJ is determined to give us splendid sights of war and trials of bravery for our heroes, yet always he brings us back to the cost. The cost in lives, yes, but moreso the cost in broken spirit.

The Two Towers is a huge, spectacular movie that differs in tone from its predecessor. There are fewer moments of relaxing wonderment. Instead, PJ brings the story up high to thrill you, then brings his focus back to grief and heartache. It is an unusual thing for such a big time blockbuster movie. I sense the risk he is taking here. The audience that comes in for just a pleasant diversion is in for quite a different ride.

And that's really what makes it so fascinating. Beyond the huge battles and sublime special effects, there is a humanity to the proceedings, touching and rather sad. But that same quality always existed in Tolkien's writing, and it always attracted me to the story. For the antithesis of despair is hope, and how the beleaguered characters renew their hope is the very core of the film.

Let's get down to brass tacks. The very best things in *Towers* are so grand, so breathtaking, that I have to share them with you. Here is my short list of what I enjoyed most of all. And also a mention of the small problems I had with changes from the book.

Nothing can prepare you for the fall of Gandalf. It is the glorious battle of two great Maiar spirits, Wizard and Balrog, both falling into the bottomless pit underneath the mountains. I've never imagined such a violent clash of power. It is astonishing to behold. To say more would cause diminishment.

I do think this is worth repeating: the effort that went into this project was back-breaking ... and it shows. What you see onscreen is glorious, from beginning to end. Here we have a continuing vision of Middle-earth that is vast and wild. The pageantry of the landscape alone will make your jaw drop. The fantastic new images (Fangorn Forest!) and locations (the city of Edoras!) are delicious. Grant Major's production design, the vibrant cinematography by Andrew Lesnie, and certainly every beautiful sword, spear, and helmet from Richard Taylor's crew makes it all so perfect. More Oscars are going to be dished out, believe me.

And oh, my Lord, there has to be a special award for Gollum. How have they created such a creature? I don't think words can describe how compelling and fully realized this character is. He is just perfect. The entire look of him is wretched, sad, grotesque. Andy Serkis does more here, with the far-reaching assistance of WETA's digital animators, than just give Gollum a voice. He performed full on in every scene, alongside Sean Astin and Elijah Wood, and you have to marvel at the many months he was stuck in that motion-capture suit. The end result comes down to our emotional involvement with Sméagol. It is not how real he LOOKS as much as how real he FEELS. We respond when Frodo opens his heart to this twisted soul, showing him mercy and gratitude. While watching I always believed, without fail, that Gollum was sitting right there having a conversation with Frodo. The world of CGI has now seen its greatest accomplishment with Gollum. The sadness in his eyes was almost unbearable, especially in those scenes where he begins to talk to himself in two distinct voices, Sméagol and Gollum. Without ever falling into melodrama, his two sides have a compelling argument about loyalty and trust. Andy Serkis has finally brought Tolkien's most complicated character to life. Bravo!

Newcomers Bernard Hill, Miranda Otto, and Brad Dourif are superb here. The overwhelming threat of events brings out the best in their characters. Poor Théoden, who has suffered from the evil spell of Gríma and Saruman, finds it very difficult to get back his confidence. He has lost his son and seemingly lost his nerve as King. Watching his range of emotions is wonderful, as a fiery Éowyn tries to inspire her uncle to come back to his true form. I knew that Miranda Otto was perfect for the part the day I met her on the set. Seeing her come to life onscreen should make every Tolkien fan happy, for she is sincerely, truly the Éowyn that we have read in the books.

The finest single shot in the film is one of the smallest. The camera shows a burial mound, with a small stone door centered in the frame. A hand brings up a beautiful white flower, cold and pale in the foreground. The symmetry of the composition is precise, clean, and simple. Théoden kneels and grieves for his son, holding up a fragile *simbelmynë* as he weeps. The mounds outside of Edoras are sprinkled with these flowers. In a film overflowing with furious events, it is a rare moment of quiet reflection.

Another scene, perhaps even more touching, takes us back to Rivendell. We see the softer side of Aragorn when he is asked by a curious Éowyn to explain "the woman who gave you that jewel." She is of course talking about the Evenstar pendant. His flashback to Arwen is colored with dominant shades of deep blue and grey. He remembers the stern look on Elrond's face as the Lord of Imladris insists that he let her go. And later things turn even more somber. We see a private conversation between father and daughter and Elrond reminds her of her fate. Arwen sees clearly her future self, suffering the loss of her mortal husband after many years, standing by his sarcophagus. But all the Elven ships that would carry her have gone. This scene is handled with absolute, crushing sadness. Perfect.

Of course, the intimate scale of this film is nothing compared to the huge action set pieces. In the words of another great showman, it is a "Spectacular spectacular!"

What other word besides *awesome* can be used to describe the battle at Helm's Deep? You will be awash in thousands of Uruk-hai, storming across the Deeping Wall. You will revel in the outrageous MASSIVE software that makes the armies so lifelike and laugh aloud when the two friends Legolas and Gimli start their count of Orc heads. The sheer scope of the whole affair is striking. The movie slowly builds on the characters' feelings of uncertainty and fear.... so that the final cathartic hour is fraught with tension and high heroics.

The appearance of Treebeard is another jewel in WETA's crown. A giant, magnificent arboreal creation, Treebeard is unique. Later during the Entmoot, Merry and Pippin sit and watch as the Ents' slow, rolling back and forth becomes a conversation they cannot possibly understand. Treebeard actually seems more dangerous here than they way I remember him in the book, but perhaps that is a good thing. He is dangerous to Saruman, surely. Wait till you see the angered Ents march on Isengard, ripping everything to shreds in their wrath. Wow! Unfortunately my alter ego, Quickbeam, does not appear. Sorry, folks.

All these technical and visual marvels carry the film high above what I am used to seeing in the movies. Howard Shore takes his amazing, complex score and brings it to another level. There is softness, hurt, longing, majesty, and above all grandeur in his music. The WETA team has put every organic detail in just the right spot. The actors are especially fine (we don't get to see enough of Sir Ian McKellen, brilliant as ever). There is a synergy here among PJ's technical teams, his actors, and the score. It really is a remarkable, and fantastic, and satisfying film to behold.

So why am I not giving it a perfect 10 out of 10?

Well, I must be wholly honest here and say there is something slightly amiss in *Towers*. After I left the press screening, I went back and read my original reactions to *Fellowship*, and I realized a similar problem exists in both films. In this case, the culprit is the *editing*.

While watching, I got the strong sense that material was missing; trimmed and cut to bring the film down to a manageable length. You can easily imagine that PJ preferred to make *Towers* longer, but was obliged by the money-counters at New Line to cut, cut, cut. It is an unfortunate thing. There are scenes between characters that felt truncated — and scenes that did not have full emotional closure (for example, after the victory at Helm's Deep, we never go back to see the women and children come out of the Glittering Caves, happy to be alive in the morning light, and we never follow up with Legolas and Gimli to learn who won the final head count). I actually felt vacant spaces, like something should have been there. Sometimes PJ seemed to be cramming the narrative to its fullest, at the expense of solid storytelling rhythm. The very close of the film seemed like a sudden rush to wrap up the story.

This is not a critical fault. But it makes a difference when you know there is more to it, that some of the hard edges of the narrative are a little too hard. The edges needed smoothing. The "narrative beats," as we say in theater, were interrupted.

And then there is Faramir. He seems very much a different character than the one Tolkien wrote. Now, I'm not one to wail loudly about things being adapted and changed. I don't mind lots of Elven archers showing up at Helm's Deep. I don't mind that the healing of Théoden feels like a frightening "exorcism." All that is actually pretty cool to me. I don't fret much with all those changes from the book.

But David Wenham's Faramir is rather harsh. He is not always likable. When I read the original text of *The Two Towers*, I see proof that Faramir is stern but also wise, and a good listener — he is ultimately very kind and generous to the hobbits, after his tricky interrogation of Frodo. But the movie version of Faramir is not so open-handed. He keeps the hobbits as prisoners, making sure they know they are prisoners, and seems as prideful and rash as his older brother. It is important that Faramir be likable, for he is a foil to the arrogance of Boromir. In *Towers*, it is only after an extremely dangerous encounter with the Enemy, where Sam challenges Faramir with a passionate plea, that we see him begin to soften.

My good friend Matthew went to the NYC premiere and had a personal chat with screenwriter Philippa Boyens afterward. He had the chance to talk with her about the intense changes to Faramir. According to his report, Philippa "had some interesting things to say on the above — basically saying that Faramir's character is completely static in the books and thus wouldn't translate well filmically. She wanted to extend his character to give him more of a journey and also seemed to imply that it would seem incongruous were Faramir immediately sea-green incorruptible, whereas all other Men in the film (even Aragorn) definitely have to wrestle with their conscience to a greater or lesser extent."

Now this makes some sense to me. Perhaps this harsher Faramir will have the opportunity to grow and change during the third film. Perhaps he will show some of the charity and wisdom that makes Éowyn fall in love with him. So again I am reminded that this is a very different medium. It is not a novel, so it cannot succeed where a novel would have. It is ill advised to judge a movie adaptation such as this as one would judge a book. They are just horses of different colors.

And speaking of horses, just wait until you see Shadowfax's magnificent entrance!

Ah, there I go again. Praising it and going on and on about how much I truly enjoyed this movie. So that should tell you something.

Much too hasty,
Quickbeam

53. Those Pesky Questions

Anwyn

"I suppose there are two views about everything," said Mark.
"Eh? Two views? There are a dozen views about everything until you know the answer. Then there's never more than one."
— C.S. Lewis, *That Hideous Strength*

It's all a matter of perspective, or so I'm told. It's very easy, as a private reader, to slip into the trap of supposing one's own interpretation of an author's words is the only one available, that one's own point of view is decidedly correct. Then I went to work for TheOneRing.net. Forging the Green Books section of the site, which deals with matters of Tolkien's writing through essays, Q&A, and fan writing, opened my eyes. It wasn't until I was faced with answering mountains of detailed and pointed questions, many of which I never would have thought to ask, that I perceived that while there may be only one view about everything Tolkien, in many cases that one correct view has, alas, passed away with the Professor. I always said, as a little girl, that the first thing I would do when I got to heaven would be to get Tolkien to teach me Elvish. What working on the Green Books Q&A has taught me is that some folks just can't wait that long!

When the Green Books were founded, the members sat down and brainstormed about what kinds of sections to include. It was basically a forgone conclusion that we would have a Q&A section, primarily because the purpose of the Green Books was specifically to dole out information about the books, as opposed to the front page's mission of keeping fans up to date about the movie production.

What we could not have predicted is the overwhelming popularity of the Q&A portion of the site. The Q&A staffers get, on average, five to ten e-mails *per day* (and some days, many more!) asking everything from "Why didn't the Eagles fly Frodo and Sam to Mount Doom?" to "Who would win a fight, Gandalf or Elrond?" The unfortunate fact is that we get more questions than we could ever answer, but we always attempt one of three responses — either to direct the questioner to the URL wherein we have already answered his or her query, to give a short response directly via e-mail, or if we think the issue merits deeper consideration and wider perusal, to post an answer for all to see at Green Books.

Beyond the sheer volume of e-mails, of more pressing difficulty are the types of the questions themselves. They are generally divided into a few categories, namely questions of fact, questions of theory (aka wild speculation), and questions that reference a system outside Tolkien. These topics can be divided further.

A basic question of fact could go a couple of different ways. It could simply ask about an event outlined in Tolkien that can be answered by a quick look at the appropriate text, like "What are the Grey Havens and why does everybody go there at the end of the book?" Or it could be a complicated technical query about the mechanics of Elvish linguistics. Other questions, while they too are questions of fact, rely substantially on facts that only Tolkien knows, like "What happened to the Blue Wizards?" (Those are the other two out of a total of five, if you're wondering.) Unfortunately, while Tolkien vaguely hints at their fate, we just aren't given the specifics. However, there are lots of fascinating questions of fact that can be answered by piecing together text from *The Silmarillion*, from any of the *History of Middle-earth* volumes, and from various other Tolkien sources. The Green Books staff deals with many of these every month and tries to find all of the pertinent information from the right books.

Questions that reference a system outside Tolkien are quite beyond our capacity. We get lots of questions that clearly are predicated on the supposition that Tolkien characters work like Dungeons and Dragons characters — "What power level was Gandalf?" "Who was more powerful, Gandalf or the Witch-king?" Not only are the D&Ders very active in their questioning, but also cropping up are proponents of the well-intentioned old game sets that gave names to the Nazgûl that had nothing to do with Tolkien. More recently, we are also dealing (of course!) with questions that directly reference Peter Jackson's films. While we would love to be inside the minds of the screenwriters and Mr. Jackson, we just can't answer why they did something a certain way in the movie that was different from the book.

Questions of theory (aka wild speculation) can also take different forms. Some of the most interesting problems deal with matters of interpretation, like "If the Three were never handled by Sauron, how could the One have any influence over them?" In cases such as that, we staffers carefully give our most educated opinions and then let the chips fall! Others are strictly flights of fancy, like "What would have happened if Faramir instead of Boromir were part of the Fellowship?" While interesting to contemplate, those questions are capable only of completely subjective supposition.

In the pages that follow, we are pleased to offer a selection of the most fascinating and intelligent questions we've answered over the years since the inception of Q&A. We don't claim to be perfect and have been corrected many times by our alert readers.

Ultimately, we are honored that so many readers come to us with their Tolkien wonderments, and there's nothing more broadening to one's own perspective to read, on a daily basis, the thoughts and ideas and questions of others. Enjoy!

54. Questions & Answers

Where page numbers are given, they refer to the Houghton Mifflin three-volume hardcover edition of *The Lord of the Rings* and to Houghton Mifflin's *The Silmarillion*.

Q1: Why did Sauron never come forth himself to do war? Couldn't he have flattened all of Minas Tirith with one outstretched hand?

A: Perhaps. But perhaps not. Remember that without the Ring, Sauron was not at his full power. Tolkien tells us that when Sauron created the Ring, he allowed a significant amount of his own native power to pass into the Ring so that he could control the others. This allotment of power to the Ring seems to have been permanent. This is evidenced by the fact that if he *could* have won the war without the Ring, he would have done so. *With* the Ring, he would have been terrifyingly unstoppable. Without it, he had perhaps half, perhaps as much as two-thirds, of the power he possessed at the end of the Second Age, when it took all of the combined power of Elves and Men to defeat him — the Last Alliance of Gil-Galad and Elendil, when both races brought out and sacrificed their best to achieve victory.

When at last he was defeated and the Ring stripped from him, he was crippled by the loss of the power contained in the Ring. Tolkien seems to imply that he was able to nurse himself back to health somewhat when he states that always, after being defeated, the Shadow takes shape and grows again. But it is clear that he could never return to full power without the Ring.

So the conclusion is that if Sauron could be attacked and defeated by Gil-Galad, Elendil, Elendil's sons, and the hosts of Elves and Men while he held the Ring, then it is well within the realm of possibility that he could be vanquished through the combined might of Gandalf, Aragorn and the Rangers, the sons of Elrond, Théoden, Éomer and

Éowyn, Denethor's and Théoden's armies, and Faramir when he no longer possessed it.

Also remember that his immediate objective was not to crush Gondor and the Free Peoples (not yet), but to regain the Ring. A character inside the story asks the very same question — basically wondering if Sauron wouldn't just crush them all with his pinky finger as he would swat a stinging fly. The answer comes back that no, he would try to trap the fly and take the sting (meaning, of course, the Ring), because he lived in constant fear of his enemies using it against him. I think it's safe to say that if he could have captured Frodo and regained the Ring, we probably would have seen him make some frontal attacks in a more personal way, in his ultimate campaign to conquer the world. Denethor sums it up in Minas Tirith (in "The Seige of Gondor") when he explains to Pippin bitterly that Sauron gets his minions to fight his battles — as does Denethor himself, sending out his own sons into deadly risk. Until Sauron's triumph is complete, Denethor doesn't expect him to appear in person. (*Return of the King*, p. 92)

— Anwyn

Q2: What tangible powers does the One Ring *really* have? We've seen its powers of invisibility, but what is it about the Ring that would allow Sauron to conquer Middle-earth if he had it?

A: We know that the Ring causes invisibility in mortals. We also know that it looks out for itself; it can remove itself from fingers unexpectedly, which it has done on several occasions, causing Isildur's death, Gollum's loss of the Ring, and Bilbo being seen by goblins at the back gate. Not only that, it can slip *on* to fingers unexpectedly, as it did when Frodo disappeared in the Prancing Pony. You might remember that Frodo had the feeling that the Ring did that to reveal itself in obedience to a wish or command that was emanating from the environment; presumably from Bill Ferny and the squint-eyed Southerner or else from the Black Riders lurking around the village.

The Ring draws servants of the Dark Lord because so much of his power is vested in it. Aragorn told Frodo as much. We know that the power in the Ring and the power in Sauron were akin and thus were drawn to each other, as well. We know that the One Ring has power over the Nine, the Seven, and in a more limited fashion, the Three.

Anybody holding one of the Nine or the Seven would be subject to Sauron's will, as we see with the Nazgûl.

All right, but how will all that help Sauron control the world? It's simpler than you might think. How does anybody control the world? They conquer by force, as several of our own worldly dictators have tried to do. With what force? Armies. What holds armies in thrall? One of several things. Either loyalty, personal or patriotic; money; ideology; hope for personal gain; or the fear that something bad will happen to people who refuse to serve. The Ring provided Sauron with a form of mental and/or spiritual control over his armies, and I have no doubt that he made sure bad things happened to any with enough willpower to resist or refuse.

Do you remember what happened at the battle before the Black Gate after the Ring had been destroyed? The Captains looked up after the pause occasioned by the destruction of the Ring to find their enemies flying from them or surrendering where they stood. Tolkien goes so far as to liken it to a hive of bees or ants when the queen dies — there is no longer a sense of control over the hive. It is quite clear that the Ring provided this hive control even though Sauron was not in possession of it. It was Sauron's power that was in it, and he was clearly able to draw upon it in a limited fashion even while the Ring was out of his immediate physical control. Though Sauron did not possess direct mind control, the Ring gave him a measure of sway over the wills of others already inclined to evil.

Tolkien goes on to state that this control was exercised primarily over the beasts and the Orcs. The beasts and Orcs were held in thrall to the power of Sauron, even without the Ring in his hand. But what about the human beings who were fighting for him? Tolkien tells us that some fled, some sued for mercy, and some, the most steeped in "evil servitude," fought on.

Evil servitude. Why were they serving evil? Most likely they were not completely in Sauron's thrall as long as he did not hold the Ring. But many of the above reasons would serve nicely. They hated the West; that's ideology, and in fact, it is the same ideology that the Soviet Union tried to hold over its people for so many years. They saw a chance for personal gain if the West fell: power and rule over rich lands.

So to conclude, the power of the Ring lies in the fact that Sauron is able to use its power to bend susceptible mortals and beasts (Orcs, etc.) to his will and to use other mortals (humans) whose goals are already roughly aligned with his, such as power-hungry Easterlings, Southrons, and the kings who were the Nazgûl.

Continuing in this line of thought, Gandalf informs Frodo that Sauron, with the Ring, is quite capable of enslaving the entire Shire and indeed the entire world. This says to me that with the Ring in hand, Sauron would be able to bend the wills of whomever he chose. Without it, he was able to control beasts and Orcs and ally to himself Men who had similar lusts for power. With it, his hold over the peoples of Middle-earth would have been terrifying.

— Anwyn

Q3: Why does this Ring that is so spiritually powerful also make people invisible? Was Sauron invisible when the Ring was cut from his hand? How could he have allowed that?

A: Now, why would a Ring, endowed with the greater power of Sauron, capable of corrupting a strong mind to evil, make the wearer invisible? The answer lies in the concept of fading: that in the end the keeper of the One Ring who wears it too much will become permanently invisible. What is the nature of this invisibility? Nothing more or less than being drawn completely into the spiritual world — the same effect that happened to the Ringwraiths.

Because the Ring is trying to draw the wearer into the world of spiritual evil that Sauron and the Nazgûl inhabit, making the wearer invisible to the natural physical world must be the first step. When you are cut off from your natural environment, it can do strange things to your mind. Can you imagine what it must be like to be in solitary confinement in prison? Take Gollum. Invisible, he could slink around and hear the secrets other people didn't want known. Secrets are a form of power over other people, and power over other people for the sake of manipulating them is evil. Thus the first tiny step on the road to corruption.

Taking the wearer from his natural state and closer to an unnatural state of spiritual corruption is a large step on the road to soul devouring, which, as with Satan in the Christian structure, is one of Sauron's goals.

Was Sauron invisible when Isildur cut the Ring from his hand? Perhaps, but perhaps not. Remember that Frodo was invisible when Gollum bit the ring from his hand, finger and all. If you are desperate enough, you can fight without seeing. But I'm not so sure that Sauron was invisible. Remember that Tom Bombadil did not vanish when he put on the Ring. I subscribe to the view that Tom is a form of Maia, so I put it to you that any corporeal form he might take on is a projection of his own power. Since the Ring's power does not affect Tom's personal power (although with Sauron wielding it, it might be a different matter, as Elrond pointed out), it does not affect his corporeal form.

I have no doubt that Sauron could have been invisible had he wished, but certainly that the Ring by itself would not make him so. As for why he did not cause himself to be invisible to facilitate escape, I submit that the forces of the West had overcome so much of his army by this time and battled him for so long that he was weak. They had overcome or killed many of his minions; these forces were held in thrall by his power, so presumably having them killed was weakening to him. Even though he was a spirit with great power, he had let a large part of his power pass into a physical object, so there was less power available for him to draw on for survival and evasion.

— Anwyn

Q4: Gandalf tells Frodo in the chapter "The Shadow of the Past" that Sauron had believed the Ring destroyed. But we know that if the Ring is destroyed, Sauron would be too, so shouldn't the fact that Sauron still exists tell him that the Ring does too?

A: In *The Fellowship of the Ring* (p. 61), Gandalf explains to Frodo that until Sauron knew the One Ring was found, he had believed that the Elves had done what they ought, long ago, and destroyed it. He goes on to recount how the Ring was cut from Sauron's hand, his spirit was "vanquished," and that he fled until taking shape again in Dol Guldur. So far so good; Sauron did indeed think that the Ring was destroyed. It thus follows that if he thought it was destroyed, he could not possibly have realized that the Ring's destruction would also mean his own.

The Council of Elrond discusses what would happen to the other Rings if the One were destroyed, and they talk about Sauron losing his grip over his slaves and lands, but they never really theorize on what would happen to Sauron himself if the One were sent to the fire. Looking at the problem logically, if Sauron knew the personal consequences of the Ring's destruction, then he never would have supposed that it had been destroyed. As Sherlock Holmes used to say, "When you have eliminated the impossible, whatever remains, however improbable, must be the truth."

Sauron thought the Ring had perished; therefore he was not under the belief that his own existence was connected with the continued existence of the Ring. I like to think that it came as a shockingly nasty surprise for old Sauron that once the Ring was melted, he was toast! This, of course, merely begs the question of whether Sauron or any other spiritual being with a soul, however twisted, could actually be destroyed or whether he was merely rendered innocuous or imprisoned in a particular form of hell or chained in the Void with his mentor. In my understanding of Tolkien so far, he really does not say.

— Anwyn

Q5: Why is the famous inscription on the One Ring written in the Elven script of Eregion, when Legolas states that Sauron does not use the Elf letters?

A: Legolas remarks, when one of Saruman's Orcs is found with the S-Rune on his shield, that "Sauron doesn't use Elf-runes." (p. 406, *LotR* one-volume, 1999). The script in the One Ring is in the Tengwar, which Tolkien always translates as "letters;" runes are an entirely different writing system. So Legolas may be, at least, technically correct — Sauron — may not use runes at all, only the Tengwar.

— Ostadan

Q6: Why do the Black Riders, though painted as so utterly terrifying, seem to have so little power for actual harm?

A: My answer to this is in two parts: the answer that is indicated by the content, i.e. what it is about the characters that makes them this way, and secondly the fact that it constitutes a literary device that Tolkien used.

Part One: Yes, the Black Riders are terrifying. But what is the main strength of their image? Just that: an image. The tall black shadow, towering over smaller creatures, intimidating them. Tolkien tells us their weaknesses flat out. They do not see well, hardly at all, in daylight. Thus they are at the mercy of the black horses for direction and guidance much of the time. They can smell. Well and good, but it takes time to sniff out prey, and as we've seen, rescue or help can come in the time it takes to track somebody by smell. The five Black Riders, advancing over the lip of the dell … horrifying image.

But what was their physical weapon besides the sheer terror they generated? The knife. They had to rely on steel weapons just like the good guys, and it's no small irony that it was a steel blade, albeit poisoned and spiritually charged, that would drain Frodo's spirit to the point where he would become a wraith and hand over the Ring willingly. Again, in *Return of the King*, we see the Witch-king relying on a weapon, his mace, to kill Éowyn.

So when it comes to actual physical combat, they are hampered by their limited daylight vision and just as reliant upon weapons as any mortal. We're not talking about Dungeons and Dragons dark mages or dark clerics here, who can cast spells with a single word. No. These are formerly mortal beings who have crossed into the spiritual realm but are still able to wield a presence in the physical world. Personally I think they're fortunate to be able to generate the influence that they do!

Now, if Frodo were to put on the Ring, it would be another matter. They got him with the knife when he put it on at Weathertop, and they would have done more had not the others with their flaming brands driven them away. At that point they let him alone not because they couldn't do more, but because they believed there was no need; they assumed the wound would overcome Frodo and that all they had to do was follow and wait for him to fall into their hands. So spiritually, they are a horror to any rational being, but physically, they are hampered and can be foiled by fire, rushing water, and even broad daylight.

Part Two: I believe Tolkien deliberately used them this way to create a literary device by which Frodo would have no choice but to continue the journey. Everybody has to have some strong motive for leaving their home and pursuing a quest. Desire to serve the good is one motive, but fear is usually stronger. With these creatures driving behind, Frodo and the gang had no choice but to continue to Rivendell or risk capture and turning into wraiths at the hands of the Black Riders and the Dark Lord.

— Anwyn

Q7: What are the names of the Nazgûl? I know of Khamul, but I have not found the names of the other Nazgûl. Who were they prior to their transformation?

A: Khamul seems to be the only named Ringwraith. What we know of him is given in the section "The Hunt for the Ring" in *Unfinished Tales*. He was second to the Chief, and his name is given as Khamul the Shadow of the East. Some more about the Nazgûl, or the Úlairi, can be found in some of the volumes of the *History of Middle-earth*, particularly in the section "The Story of Frodo and Sam in Mordor" in *Sauron Defeated*, and in the work on the Appendices to *The Lord of the Rings* as printed in *The Peoples of Middle-earth*. But unfortunately, the histories of the men who became the Nazgûl seem nowhere to be specifically illuminated.

There is an additional possibility that Gothmog, who is described as the "Lieutenant of Morgul," is a Nazgûl, but this is by no means certain. (He may instead be an Orc, or even a Man.) In any case, a Captain can have more than one Lieutenant, so if Gothmog is a Nazgûl, and Khamul is the second to the Chief, Gothmog could have been the name of another Nazgûl.

Last, I note that in one of the Middle-earth games, there are names given to all the Nazgûl, but since those names were made up by the people who created the game, and not by Tolkien, we don't view them as authoritative. They're simply not in Tolkien anywhere.

— Turgon

Q8: Is water an effective weapon against the Nazgûl, as they are so afraid of it? Further, what specifics are written by Tolkien about the Witch-king of Angmar? What kind of weapons were Merry and Éowyn using that were effective enough to harm the Witch-king, when he was impervious to all other blades?

A: It is sometimes hard to find detailed information on the Nazgûl, or going by their Elvish name, the Úlairi. Although I know most people skip over them, I always recommend looking at the Appendices. Specifically, look closely at Appendix A, and deep within the *Annals of the Kings and Rulers*, you will find an account of "The North-kingdom and the Dúnedain," which reveals fascinating details of the Men who were Aragorn's ancestors and their strife with the Witch-king of Angmar. There are details of the climactic battle that joined Elves from the Grey

Havens, a fleet of Men from Gondor, and skilled Hobbit archers from the Shire, all united in a last front against Angmar. Concise maps of the battle, which are very helpful, can be found in Karen Wynn Fonstad's *The Atlas of Middle-earth,* my favorite reference book.

As for the Nazgûl being harmed by water, I'm not certain that's the case. They did not like crossing any body of water, true, and as Frodo tried to escape them, only three of the Nine stepped forward into the river. More accurately, the Witch-king himself and two other Ringwraiths were compelled by the Ring itself right in front of them. But the others were driven into the Ford of Bruinen at a crucial moment by Glorfindel and Aragorn. Of course burning fire in the hands of an Elf-lord was a greater threat to the Ringwraiths, as Gandalf explained later on. But remember Elrond commanded that river and it was certainly not ordinary; thus the brute force of his magic flood was strong enough to sweep away the horses of Mordor (and of course Riders too).

Unfinished Tales has a section called "The Hunt for the Ring" that contains plenty of interesting material on the Nazgûl. The most fascinating bits include an account of the Ringwraiths' arrival in Hobbiton the very day Frodo was setting out. We learn from Christopher Tolkien that JRRT had drafted material about the Nazgûls' fear of water but then finally made the concept less specific because it was problematic, saying: "My father did indeed note that the idea was difficult to sustain."

So it seems Tolkien was thinking about this for some time and ultimately would make the distinction less pronounced. I should also say that it is a common motif of European folklore that ghosts or spirits are unable to cross bodies of water.

Now about this business of weapons against the Witch-king. Only magical blades laden with spells could harm a Nazgûl. Consider the episode where Merry and Éowyn face the Lord of the Nazgûl and defeat him. One Hobbit using a Númenorean blade; one human woman using steel of the Mark. I must be very specific here: the most lethal implements against a Ringwraith were those imbued with some greater skill or magic beyond common steel. Be it the magic of Elves or the high spirit of Númenor — it would be some component that upheld the legacy of Valinor and scorn for the works of Shadow. Also remember that in Tolkien's stories, an artifact is usually powerful because of the wielder's force of will. Merry had the proper instrument and delivered a blow breaking the spell of the Witch-king's invulnerability. And

Éowyn may have been wielding only a "regular sword," but the rules of the game had changed at that point. Éowyn's role was to fulfill the prophecy, and being not a "mortal man," she brought fate full circle to the dreaded Morgul-lord.

— Quickbeam

Q9: When the hobbits and Aragorn were attacked at Weathertop, Frodo attacks the Nazgûl with his sword, but he also screams an Elvish phrase. Aragorn later says that what Frodo yelled was more powerful than his sword. How does this make sense given the later demise of the Witch-king?

A: At the time of the incident on Weathertop, Frodo's sword did not actually strike the Nazgûl, but only his cloak. Aragorn finds the cut in the fabric later, and comments that the cloak was the only thing Frodo's sword harmed; the Ringwraith took more harm from the name of Elbereth, shouted by Frodo as he attacked. The first thing to realize is that the Ringwraiths were spiritual beings, and as such, they could be harmed by invocations of other spiritual beings. Words and ideas have great power over the spiritual realm in many of our world's stories and myths. Do you recall the legend that evil spirits cannot dwell in your house or possess your body unless you invite them in? The Bible describes the disciples of Jesus driving out demons by invoking the name of Christ. Calling on spiritual powers of good can be a grievous blow to enemies who are spiritual powers of evil.

In this specific case, Elbereth Gilthoniel is the Sindarin name for Varda, queen of the stars and wife of Manwë, lord of the heavens. So to draw a rough parallel to the Catholic spiritual structure, since Mary is called "the queen of heaven," Frodo using the name of Varda to ward off the evil power of the Nazgûl was the same as if a Catholic, beset by demons, used the name of Mary, mother of Christ. Who is to say what invoking her name did to Frodo's enemies, effects perhaps unseen by the company? I will say, however, that it was beyond Varda's power to *destroy* the Ringwraith, just as it is (presumably) beyond the power of the spirit of Mary to destroy demons. You notice those Biblical demons weren't destroyed but only driven away. This brings us to the next question: whether the name of Elbereth was more deadly than a sword.

Merry's sword was not just any run-of-the-mill blade, and Éowyn was not an ordinary warrior. It was the destiny of the Witch-king to be destroyed by these two, and Tolkien states clearly that no other sword but Merry's, bound as it was with ancient spells, could have dealt that blow in that time and place. So we see that while Aragorn means that the name of Elbereth was more deadly than Frodo's sword, that doesn't necessarily mean more deadly than all other forms of attack.

Merry's sword did, in fact, melt into mist and vanish after he struck the Nazgûl, but it accomplished its purpose first — dealing a wound both physical and spiritual to his spiritually evil foe. In the end the doom that was foretold to the Witch-king came upon him at the hands of a woman and a hobbit, both bearing brave, self-sacrificing hearts — and darn good swords.

— Anwyn

Q10: Could Gandalf have slain the Witch-king? Also, how did Éowyn's sword work against the Witch-king? Tolkien seems to state that only powerful blades forged by Elves or by the Men of Westernesse would have been any use.

A: Gandalf himself did not know whether or not he could have slain the Witch-king in a one-on-one. He states that the ultimate fate of the Witch-king is "hidden from the Wise," and that includes "hidden from Gandalf." He did not know if he was overmatched, because it was not his time to face the Witch-king. That comes later, in the gate of Minas Tirith, and although they do not fight, Gandalf is able to drive him away because the wraith cannot claim victory yet; Rohan shows up to contest the field. As we see later, of course, "not by the hand of man" simply means "by the hand of woman and hobbit." For myself, I believe that a one-on-one contest between Gandalf and the Witch-king would have been almost as iffy as the battle between Gandalf and the Balrog. Gandalf and the Balrog are both Maiar, and though the Witch-king began as a normal human, the ring he wore, one of the Nine, gave him power approaching the spiritual realm. So there is really no telling.

I believe Gandalf was aware that the fate of the Witch-king did not rest with him, and that's why he responded to Denethor as he did. But also he didn't know with whom the fate actually *did* rest. As we see later, the Witch-king was so off his guard that there was no actual fight. He believed he was invincible to anything currently on the field and probably did not realize there were those on the other side who were not men, but hobbits and women. Tolkien states that when the Witch-king realized he was facing a woman, he was filled with sudden doubt, and we all know what happened next. After Éowyn managed to dispatch the flying beast, Merry got in one for the Shire at the wraith's knee, and the very unexpectedness of the stroke, along with the magic wound around Merry's blade, broke the wraith's concentration to the point where his will no longer held as steady, and Éowyn was able to drive her sword into what was left of his power, shattering it.

To sum up, I believe that A) Gandalf did not know at whose door the death of the Witch-king would be laid, and he didn't know if he would be the winner in a fight with him. B) Éowyn's sword, so far as we know, was indeed a plain old Rohan sword, but Merry's blade was forged long ago by the men of Númenor. It is clear to me that Merry's stroke shattered the spells that allowed the Black Rider his cohesiveness of form and his concentration of will, and this allowed Éowyn's sword to demolish the center of his power, the spiritual head. Moreover, it seems apparent that it took both of them to get the job done.

— Anwyn

Q11: Yes, Merry was aided by a blade of Westernesse when he attacked the Witch-king (and also the fact the he was a Hobbit, not a Man). Can we theorize that the three Hobbits at Weathertop, with Númenorean blades, could have successfully defeated the lesser Nazgûl on their own?

A: Remember that Gandalf tells Frodo in Rivendell that the Ringwraiths would be difficult to destroy. Tolkien tells us this to augment how fearful and dangerous they are and to foreshadow their return later in the story.

Looking back on Anwyn's previous discussion of this, I am inclined to say no to your hypothesis. Merely holding a blade of Westernesse would not be enough to slay such a creature. But you can easily correlate the wielder's force of will to the effectiveness of his blade, as in Merry's case of despairing rage on the Pelennor (and also in Sam's moment of fury against Shelob). The directed force of will, or you could call it the focused spiritual essence (or moment of blind epiphany) is a major component relating to artifacts and weapons. It's how Tolkien makes these things work: the Palantír, the Phial, the Ring. Yes, Merry helped facilitate the Witch-king's demise, but the death-stroke belonged to Éowyn. She was the key element to his destruction, in keeping with the demands of the prophecy and the extension of her fierce resolve.

— Quickbeam

Q12: Since Sauron could easily conquer the whole of Middle-earth with the power of the Ring, and if all the power of the Ring was natively his to begin with, then why did he put so much power into a small object that could be lost or stolen?

A: Without the existence of the Ring, Sauron would not have had a reliable method of controlling the other rings and, through them, their wearers and their actions. Despite his great powers as a Maia spirit, Sauron is not capable of direct mind control — if he were, then he would not have spent years insinuating himself by trickery into the counsels of the Kings of Númenor or of the Elves of Eregion.

When the Elves made the Three, Sauron saw his chance — the rings had a spiritual connection with their wearers, and if he could gain influence over the rings, he could gain influence over the bearers and their works. Tolkien never spells out what the Three were capable of, but he gives the impression that many of the special qualities of Rivendell and Lothlórien were created and maintained by the power of the Elven rings.

Sauron never touched those, but he learned all about their forging and actually helped in the forging of the Seven and the Nine, so that he learned enough about the power that was imbued in all the rings to make a Ring that would control all the others, their wearers, and their creations. However, the power in this Ring, the power to control the others, had to come from somewhere. So Sauron put a great deal of his own will and power into the forging, transforming his power into a specific channel: that of controlling the other rings. He assumed he could always keep this Ring with him, thereby having access to all of his power *and* controlling the other rings at the same time. Clearly he didn't reckon on the Last Alliance.

— Anwyn

Q13: Since Sauron never touched the three Elven rings and had no control over them, why would their power be unraveled when the One was destroyed?

A: Ah, but look carefully. Tolkien very clearly states that the One

Ring *did* have a measure of control over the Three. The Three were not given to the Elves; the Elves made them, and Sauron was deep in their counsels when they were made. Once he saw how they were being made, he aided and advised in the making of the Seven and the Nine, and then, as we know, he forged the One all on his own, allowing a large part of his own power to pass into it with the specific purpose of controlling all the others. Sauron used his own life force and channeled it into the Ring so that its force would be made similar to the forces of the Three, Seven and Nine in order to control them and their users.

The Elves did the best they could; they hid the Three from him, and I believe this lessened his power over them, but what the rest of the story says to me is that even though the Three were made separate from the One, the One had a part in the doings of *all* the Rings, that it lent a part of its power, perhaps the part that was forged with the knowledge and skill Sauron gleaned from the Elves, to the creating and guarding of the Elves' works, and thus, when the power of the One passed away, the things created with the Three would fade, because they didn't have that "extra power" to draw on.

I am indeed aware, however, that the One was evil and nothing good could be done with it. I'm simply theorizing that perhaps the life force of Sauron was a sustaining factor behind the power of *all* the Rings, and that because the wielders of the Three were purely good, they were able to use their power for good, but that when the One was gone, the Three would fade.

— Anwyn

Q14. How could Gandalf conceal his Elven Ring when he was imprisoned in Dol Guldur — before the events recounted in *The Hobbit*? Would not the Necromancer know that Narya was there in his stronghold, right under his nose?

A: First let me clarify one important thing: Gandalf was never held prisoner in Dol Guldur: rather he paid visits in secret there, more than once, throughout the Third Age. If Sauron had ever captured our dear Gandalf, that would have been the end of him and the certain end of the War of the Ring (before it even started)! It was actually Thráin II who was imprisoned by the Necromancer, later discovered by Gandalf during one of his covert visits.

As for Sauron not perceiving Narya, the Ring of Fire: it seems most unlikely he would have such prescience without himself bearing the One Ring. Even though his influence upon the lesser rings was potent, he still did not possess the One while Gandalf wielded Narya. Also remember Sauron's ability was greatly diminished wherever the Three Rings were concerned, as he had never touched them and had no direct part in their making. I assume the whereabouts of the Three was forever kept secret from him. He knew nothing of Galadriel having Nenya or Elrond holding Vilya, and for good reason.

— Quickbeam

Q15: Gandalf reported that Saruman wore a ring. Did Saruman forge it in the fires of Orthanc or was it another ring provided by the Dark Lord? Second, why would Gandalf not take this ring from Saruman but break his staff? And why would Saruman not initially do the same, breaking Gandalf's staff when Gandalf refused to join him?

A: I have only speculation to offer on this one. True, Saruman's ring is mentioned in Gandalf's anecdote at the Council of Elrond, but not anywhere else in the books. The Seven had all been destroyed or reclaimed by Sauron. I would guess as you have done, that this ring was an example of Saruman's tinkering with Ring lore. I'm sure he had spent countless years searching through the secrets of Ringmaking, and the results of his efforts may have been one or two trifles with some unique powers. However, not being a master as the original Elves of Hollin were, this ring Saruman bore was not considerable in quality or power. If it were, we would have heard more about it during the Scouring of the Shire.

Saruman's staff was definitely an implement of power and a symbol of his high station in the White Council. The ring Gandalf had noticed on Saruman's hand was not taken later because A) it wasn't as important as the staff, and B) he really didn't get close enough to Saruman, as the treacherous old goat refused to come down from Orthanc. Breaking Saruman's staff was symbolic of him being cast out of the Council forever. His power removed, his effectiveness thus forfeit.

Honestly, I don't think Saruman ever wanted to cast Gandalf out of the Order of Istari. He was still hoping, somewhere down the road, to convince Gandalf to join him. Or, in another light, Saruman never really had the true means to kick Gandalf out. He had betrayed his Order, and after that decision he would not redeem himself (see also chapter 11 of this book, "Justice, Mercy, and Redemption," an excellent article by Anwyn where she explores this subject). It was then Gandalf who became "the White" and had authority over all of the other Istari, so to speak.

— Quickbeam

Q16: We are shown that the three Elven rings give powers of wordless communication. Why then can't Elrond and Galadriel communicate about the Company? Why is there the fuss about Gimli? Wouldn't the Elves have known who and what was coming?

A: Galadriel and Celeborn already knew who and what each member of the company was; they were in no way surprised when the Company arrived at Caras Galadhon. But clearly the border guards were not informed in a timely manner. Though they knew of Elrond's messengers passing up to the Dimrill Stair, the ones he sent out to try to scout the whereabouts of the Black Riders, they would have spoken to the rulers, not to the guards. When the guards saw a Dwarf, they followed the law of the land, which stated that he wouldn't be allowed to enter Lothlórien. It was only on the say-so of Aragorn and Legolas that they let him in at all, because they were simply following the rules and didn't know how a Dwarf would be received in the City of the Galadhrim.

Their information was incomplete, but later we see that Galadriel had full information. Elves come out the forest and bring messages to Haldir from Celeborn and Galadriel, saying that the Fellowship are to be allowed free passage, even Gimli. "It seems that the Lady knows who and what is each member of your Company. New messages have come from Rivendell perhaps." *Perhaps.* Haldir didn't really know how the Lady got her information; he just knew enough to know that she knew there was a Dwarf in her land and she was commanding that he be allowed to walk free. For all we know, these messages may have come through the power of the rings. But here's another question to throw on the fire.

Is it really the rings that convey the power of communicating with thought? Does Tolkien actually state that? The quote about their "council" in "Many Partings," at the end of *Return of the King* (p. 263) describes Gandalf and the Elves sitting silent and motionless as statues, looking into each other's minds, with only their shining eyes stirring and kindling with the thoughts that passed between them.

Keep in mind that we are not speaking only of Gandalf, Elrond, and Galadriel, but also of Celeborn, who did not hold a ring. So was this a power of the rings that came to Celeborn by extension through Galadriel, or was it a power of the Eldar and of Gandalf as a Maia? Tolkien doesn't really say.

So while I'm sure they used messengers when it suited them, I'm also willing to bet that Galadriel and Elrond and Celeborn, between them, had other ways of communicating, and since Tolkien didn't specify how she got her information, we don't really know how Galadriel knew what was going on. Also, don't forget that Lothlórien was built and defended largely with the power of Galadriel's ring, and I suspect that the ring gave her power to see what was passing on the borders of her land, possibly in the Mirror. So she had many ways of gathering news, and we're left not knowing whether the telepathy was a function of the rings or a function of the minds of Eldar and Maia.

— Anwyn

Q17: How was Gandalf's staff recovered after the confrontation on the Bridge of Khazad-dûm? Further, in the violent battle between Gandalf and the Balrog atop the peak of Silvertine, how does the wizard recover Glamdring after his death?

A: The moment Gandalf fell with the Balrog from the bridge, his staff was shattered, but he still possessed his sword. But yes, it is difficult to explain how Glamdring escaped destruction in the depths of Khazad-dûm.

In Gandalf's account in *The Two Towers* it is clear that he somehow managed to hold onto Glamdring as he fell. Specifically he says that "ever I hewed him" during the lengthy chase below the mountain. Thus he had the sword with him at that point. After that, it is not mentioned when he speaks of the Endless Stair and the ensuing Battle of the Peak. I assume he still wielded it and that it was instrumental in the final doom of Durin's Bane. There's no specific wording of how it survived Gandalf's physical destruction and re-embodiment. Indeed, he says "naked I was sent back," and by this I assume Valinor. I would take a leap of faith and assume that Glamdring survived the ruin atop the Silvertine and was perhaps later recovered by Gwaihir.

I would even go so far as to say our Olórin was sent back as "a brand new Gandalf" with a new staff. If the Valar returned him to Middle-earth as a new being (The White Rider) to replace the treacherous Saruman, then maybe he was given a new token of office, a new device of power, before returning. Or maybe the Elves of Lothlórien crafted a new one for him (out of Mallorn wood, perhaps?).

— Quickbeam

Q18: What is the source of Gandalf's power? Is it his birthright as a wizard and Maiar, or is it because he wears Narya, the Ring of Fire, or is it linked to his knowledge of Elvish incantations, as for instance when he raises fire on Caradhras by saying, "Naur en adraith ammen?" (p. 283, *LotR* one-volume, 1999).

A: In *The Silmarillion,* there is the incident of Felagund's battle with Sauron in "songs of power." Gandalf's fire spell echoes this as well as his words of command for shutting the door against the Balrog in Moria (and his unsuccessful opening spell at the West-gate). Gandalf could doubtless choose to speak words of command in whatever language he chose; the power is not in the words per se but in the one who is speaking them.

Gandalf has assumed bodily form, and for him, the use of language is habitual. In an essay entitled *Ósanwe-kenta* (Enquiry into the Communication of Thought), Tolkien explains that such habitual use of language, being more precise and clear for Incarnates than direct thought transference, the practice and use of such direct thought transference is dimmed, even (to some degree) among the Valar, if they are habitually clothed in incarnate form.

It seems likely that the magical calling forth of power to shape the world operates much the same and that Gandalf focuses his power better through the use of spoken spells. Sindarin simply may be the language that Gandalf has used the most in his dealings with the Elves, and so is his language of choice and habit. A couple of thousand years is, after all, quite a lot of time to get into a habit.

The Three Rings made by the Elves were not forged as weapons, but as tools of healing and preservation. Remember Círdan's words to Gandalf, "Herewith, maybe, thou shalt rekindle hearts to the valour of old in a world that grows chill" (p. 304, *The Silmarillion*). Gandalf's healing of Théoden likely has more to do with the Red Ring of Fire than the fire-spell has.

— Ostadan

Q19: At the Black Gate, Gandalf and the Mouth of Sauron confront each other, with the latter revealing Frodo's mithril coat and Sam's blade. But why does Gandalf not accept the offer if it would save "the prisoner?" He did not know Frodo was still alive (but the reader does), so would he have let him die at the hands of Sauron?

A: This is my take on the dramatic game of words played out before the Morannon. Gandalf and the Mouth of Sauron were playing a game of "stare-me-down." Whoever blinks first is the loser, or rather will give away their strategic weakness to the other. The dark Lieutenant brings out the hobbits' gear in an attempt to get Gandalf to blink.

In other words, Sauron had precious little information about the spy (he believed one was operating alone) who had broken through his fences. What was this halfling doing in Cirith Ungol? What were the Lords of the West really up to? This display of the cloak, sword, and mail were a ploy to get some more information about the hobbit's mission and also to cruelly destroy the morale of the Lords of the West.

Gandalf would not truly have let Frodo die, for it was obvious to him in that instant the trickery being attempted. He knew that Sauron did not yet have possession of the One Ring, for in such case all trickery would be moot. Gandalf was playing along (rather convincingly I'll say) at this crucial point to buy time for the Ring-bearer and to assert his presence to Sauron's emissary.

— Quickbeam

Q20: When Gandalf returns as Gandalf the White, he tells Aragorn, Legolas, and Gimli that none of them has any weapon that could hurt him. Does he mean that the weapons will actually physically not work or that he simply cannot be killed?

A: There is another passage further on (*The Two Towers*, p. 107) where Gimli jokes that now Gandalf's head is untouchable, he'd better find a more appropriate target for his axe. But though he was being humorous, I think there was a grain of truth in his words — Gandalf had clearly become imbued with an even greater spiritual power than he had previously possessed. Whether Gandalf simply meant he could stop their weapons without thinking twice or whether their weapons wouldn't bite, I can't say. I would tend to think the former, although the mental image of a battle axe whistling harmlessly through Gandalf's midsection is moderately amusing. However, I think the key to the puzzle lies in Gimli's words, not Gandalf's: sacred.

I believe that in the sacrifice Gandalf made in the battle with the Balrog, his old worldly form was taken from him. How could it have survived? The fall into the Abyss, the fall through deep water, the burning of the Balrog's fire ... I believe his old form was shattered/burned/drowned, what have you, but that the Maia spirit within him lived and defeated the Balrog, as a sacrifice for his friends.

The Eagle, when he picks him up off of Zirak-zigil, tells him he is light as a feather and that he can see through him. Gandalf's reply is telling: he fears to fall. (*The Two Towers*, p. 106). He gasps this as he feels life returning to him. This tells me that his spirit has been given a new form, that of Gandalf the White, and moreover, it is temporary. He states that he was sent back, naked, *for a brief time*, until his task is done.

Naked — without form. His spirit lay on the mountain top and gathered a form about it for its brief stay in Middle-earth, until his task, to be the Enemy of Sauron, was done. Bottom line is that this form cannot be hurt by physical weapons, although I do think he still could have lost his soul. I believe that the forthcoming battles with Nazgûl and the chat with the Mouth of Sauron at the Gate, etc., were all instances of spiritual warfare upon Gandalf's part, and his standing firm helped lead to the victory.

He would not have been the first Maia to succumb to Sauron and Morgoth, but he does not do so, and his spirit continues on until he returns to the Blessed Realm.

— Anwyn

Q21: In the appendix story (in RotK) of Arwen and Aragorn, when Aragorn is about to pass away, he asks if Arwen would repent of her choice to remain mortal with him and sail away into the West. Arwen says that is no longer possible, that there is no ship left that would bear her. Why would there not be a ship, when we know that

Legolas built a ship later and even took Gimli with him to the Blessed Realm?

A: I think the answer to this question lies in Arwen's statement that "that choice is long over" and *not* in the statement that no ship would bear her. To my mind, that doesn't mean that there aren't still ships capable of sailing to the Blessed Realm, because we know that at least one more (carrying Legolas and Gimli) did sail after the passing of King Elessar.

I think it simply means that, once Arwen made her choice to live out a mortal life span and to die from the world, no ship carrying her would be allowed to make landfall on the shores of Valinor. She would have been trying to have her cake and eat it too — to live out her blissful wedded life with Aragorn and then, when he kicked the bucket, reclaim her immortality and sail. That seems not to be allowed.

Gimli did indeed go with Legolas, but I'm quite certain he did not become immortal. I believe he lived out the remainder of the life span allotted to him as a Dwarf and then passed away in Valinor. I believe the same thing about Frodo, Sam, and Bilbo. They were granted the grace to spend the ends of their lives on the blessed shores but not the immortality of the Elves.

Arwen had long ago made her choice to become mortal, and since the Elven immortality is not granted to mortals, she would not have been allowed to revoke her choice but would have to live out the remainder of her human years. Legolas, of course, retaining his Elven rights, was received on the shores and lived out his Elven immortality.

The sweet in the bitter, however, is what Aragorn says to Arwen about immortality: that beyond death is more than memory and that they will meet again. Even if she *had* been able to reclaim her Elven heritage and sail for the West, she would have been denouncing forever her chance to be with the one she loved for all time — he having died a mortal death and she continuing to live out her immortal life. Clearly if this had been what she wanted, she never would have chosen to become mortal in the first place. She looked forward to another time beyond death when once again she would be with Aragorn.

— Anwyn

Q22: Why were the Elves of the First Age so much more powerful than those in the Third? During the War of the Ring they seem inconsequential compared to the great Elven Lords of *The Silmarillion*. Further, why must the power of the Three Rings fade when the One is gone — and the Elves too? It is sad that the altogether good works of the other Rings must also diminish.

A: It's not a matter of the Elves having less power as time went on; rather they were playing a less and less active role. Many Elves in LotR (Galadriel, Círdan) certainly did compare to the "Elves of yore" because they were the exact same people appearing in the First Age — or before! They strove against the Enemy in mighty battles, as you say, but that was no longer the case during the Third Age. Most of the more powerful Eldar had returned to Valinor by this time. Though fewer in number, the remaining Elves were still puissant; only their participation in world events waned. These smaller populations that stayed behind receded from Middle-earth, preferring to stay in enclaves such as Rivendell and Lórien. This period of history was deliberate in Tolkien's greater design, of course.

This brings me to the bigger point. The Delaying of the Elves is a larger, more profound, theme found in LotR. Consider it is Galadriel's Ring that is at work in Lothlórien, slowing down the flow of time and preserving the unearthly beauty of the land. In *The Letters of J.R.R. Tolkien*, # 131, Tolkien described the Elves' use of the Three Rings to keep alive their memory of past beauty, "maintaining enchanted enclaves of peace where Time seems to stand still and decay is restrained," and making a place in Middle-earth that echoes the "bliss of the True West." The Elves are destined to leave behind their small pockets of preservation, to depart Middle-earth and thus return to the Undying Lands.

The various reasons and circumstances of their lingering are endlessly fascinating (especially when you are rereading *The Silmarillion*). In *Letters* you can learn much about the Elves' pursuit of "timelessness" and why Tolkien considered it a dynamic failing in their character. The Eldar burdened themselves with the memory of the West as if it were a yoke, yet still longed to stay in Middle-earth where they would enjoy their prestigious standing. Much more comfy for them to remain the greatest race of the mortal lands than to return West and be the bottom rung on the ladder. It is quite revealing stuff to learn that the High Elves' most compassionate efforts to preserve beauty in Middle-earth was indeed an attempt to recreate their own private Valinor!

But the primary theme in all of Tolkien is that all things must fade. This is a cornerstone in the Professor's mythology. After the fall of the Shadow, the remaining inhabitants of this mythical world are faced with inevitable transformation.

Consider that Elrond expressed woe that the Elven Rings were ever made in the first place. Remember that the Three were forged in alignment with Sauron's designs, even though he never touched them himself. Still, Celebrimbor developed the art of Ringmaking alongside Sauron. This means that the Three were not, as you say, "altogether good" though they were often used with typical Elvish ambitions.

Here's the rub. The great sin that befell Elves and Men was their rejection of time and change. Sauron played right into the Elves' worst character trait with this grand scheme. The power of the Rings, by Sauron's design, would allow the Elves to continue their primary folly — the pursuit and preservation of their own little timeless dream worlds. The Elves in Rivendell and Lórien who lingered, never leaving for Valinor, were especially guilty of this. For Tolkien, it was noble of the Elves to heal beauty and nature while the rest of Middle-earth suffered from war and strife, but terribly misguided as well! This was not the way Ilúvatar planned things to work out.

For Men, the Dark Lord offered a way to avoid the Doom of Men, which was an ultimate death and removal from the Circles of the World. Their Nine Rings would slow time, stretching their existence and allowing them to cheat a death that was truly theirs to embrace.

All of the material output of the Rings, and the greater plan that had first brought them into existence, was based on *Sauron's thought*. No more One Ring means no more Sauron — and thus no more nice little side-benefits like eternally golden mallorn trees. Saddening and bitter-sweet, that was what Tolkien wanted us to walk away with: all things must fade.

— Quickbeam

Q23: Why would the Elves be motivated to aid the Ring-bearer and fight against Sauron? At the unmaking of the One Ring their way of life would fail, as the Three Rings would become powerless. The Elves could simply sail to Valinor, so does it not seem they always had an "out?"

A: You have touched upon what is, to my mind, a great irony within Tolkien's story. Of course they were concerned about the Three Rings fading — and the cessation of all their protective and healing works — and it put them in a difficult place. However, their main duty was to counter the threat of the Shadow (either in the form of Morgoth or Sauron). There was no question they would assist the other Free Peoples in some fashion during the War of the Ring, though achieving victory would ultimately be an end to their time of habitation in Middle-earth.

But they did not always have an "out" as you have suggested. If the Elves were to completely abandon Middle-earth and Sauron then won the War (and his erstwhile Ring), what would be the next likely progression of events? Firstly, the dominion of Sauron would rise to such insurmountable strength that all of Arda would be enslaved or destroyed. Second, with no hindrance to his advance, Sauron would find a way to assault Valinor and ultimately fulfill the original designs of his Master. Just because Valinor was removed from the world does not mean that it was beyond Sauron's arts to descend upon it. So it was equally important for the Elves to participate in the War as it was for any other race.

— Quickbeam

Q24: Why would the Elves leave Middle-earth just when Sauron had been vanquished?

A: Now, as for the Elves bolting the farm as soon as it was saved from the creditors, so to speak, I believe that without the power of the Three, the power of the Elves in Middle-earth was greatly lessened — power to make their realms special places where evil did not enter. The deciding factor on this, though, is that Tolkien clearly states that there would be a time of the Firstborn (Elves) and a time of the Followers (Men).

That is, when the power of the Three passed away, that signaled an end to the dominion of Elves in Middle-earth, and with the reclaiming of the throne by Aragorn, the dominion of Men was at hand. In passing over-Sea, the Elves were simply "going with the flow," as Elves generally do.

— Anwyn

Q25: Are Elwing and Lúthien able to shape-change because of some power they inherit from Melian, who was a Maiar? Is Tolkien saying these powers are hereditary only to Maiar, or can other Elves do it?

A: Sometimes we need to remind ourselves that Tolkien's view of magic was not the sort of mechanical, rule-based affair of more modern fantasy stories (post-Dungeons and Dragons). It was mysterious in its operation and not necessarily understood by those thought to be telling the tales. When Pippin asks if the elven cloaks they receive are magical, the leader of the Elves says that he does not know what Pippin means by that; to him, what mortals call magic is simply how the world works.

So it is difficult to answer these two questions, which both are different aspects of "How does 'magic' work?" To the first question, we know that all Elves have an affinity for (what mortals call) magic. Recall, for example, that "Felagund strove with Sauron in songs of power, and the power of the King was very great." (p. 171, *The Silmarillion.*) Perhaps some Elves have greater and lesser talents (as we all have), and Lúthien (and Elwing afterwards) had a greater talent for changing her appearance or form (and, at least, the length of her hair). Not much more can be said of this.

— Ostadan

Q26: Does Elvish ancestry lengthen human life spans, and conversely does human ancestry shorten the lifespan of an Elf? Why is Elrond "Half-Elven" so long-lived if he's half-human?

A: Although Elvish ancestry is said to "ennoble" the bloodlines of humans, and seems to have resulted in long lifespans for Elros and his heirs, the classification of a being as a Man or an Elf is an either/or choice.

With the exception of the heirs of Beren and Luthien, all the descendants of Men retain the Gift of Men and die and leave the world, even when Elvish blood is evidently present, as, for example, in the royal house of Dol Amroth. Anyone who is of the kindred of the Elves (even if they are given the grace to claim this kinship freely, as in the case of Elrond and his children) is immortal and bound forever to Arda.

— Ostadan

Q27: Legolas (and Gandalf) rode his horse in "elf-fashion" (i.e., without saddle or bridle), yet when Glorfindel lets Frodo ride his horse at the Ford, he "shortens the stirrups up to the saddle skirts." Why wasn't Glorfindel riding elf-fashion?

A: In *The Fellowship of the Ring*, at the first appearance of Glorfindel on the road, he is described riding a white horse whose bit and bridle had glittering gems worked into them that sparkled as they approached out of the shadows (p. 221 of the first edition, 1954). Later, Glorfindel gets Frodo up on his horse, offering to shorten the stirrups for him (p. 223).

In 1958, a reader of *The Lord of the Rings* asked Tolkien the following question: "Why is Glorfindel's horse described as having a 'bridle and bit' when Elves ride without bit, bridle or saddle?"

Tolkien's answer was as follows: "Actually *bridle* was casually and carelessly used for what I suppose should have been called a *headstall*. ... Glorfindel's horse would have an ornamental *headstall*, carrying a plume, and with the straps studded with jewels and small bells; but Glor. would certainly not use a bit." (*The Letters of J. R. R. Tolkien*, # 211, p. 279)

In the second edition of *The Fellowship of the Ring*, the reading of "bridle and bit" was changed to "headstall" on p. 221, but the reading on p. 223 remains the same as in the original edition. So, for whatever reason, Glorfindel must have been riding with a saddle, even though that is not normally elf-fashion. Perhaps in riding out to aid Frodo, Glorfindel anticipated the need for a swift horse that could be ridden by someone other than an elf.

— Turgon

Q28: *The Silmarillion* tells of the curse that Mandos put upon the Noldor when they left for Middle-earth. The curse forbade them to return to Valinor, and yet at the end of the Third Age, Galadriel was permitted to return. Why was this curse lifted in Galadriel's case?

A: Tolkien spoke of this in his translation of "Namarië" in the *Road Goes Ever On* songbook:

> She was the last survivor of the princes and queens who had led the revolting Noldor to exile in Middle-earth. After the overthrow of Morgoth at the end of the First Age a ban was set upon her return, and

she had replied proudly that she had no wish to do so ... But it was impossible for one of the High-Elves to overcome the yearning for the Sea, and the longing to pass over it again to the land of their former bliss.

Tolkien explains that Galadriel was granted permission to end her exile because of her part in opposing Sauron during the War of the Ring, but more importantly, as a reward for her rejection of the Ring when Frodo offered it to her.

But the story is not so simple; in later essays (seen in *Unfinished Tales*), JRRT modified the story. In a very late writing, Galadriel was wholly opposed to Fëanor in every way and fought against him with Celeborn at Alqualondë. She wished to go to Middle-earth not in rebellion against the Valar, but for the exercise of her talents; for "being brilliant in mind and swift in action she had early absorbed all of what she was capable of the teaching which the Valar thought fit to give the Eldar." (p. 228, *Unfinished Tales.*) In this account, she was not forbidden from returning to Valinor at the end of the First Age, but refused to do so out of pride.

— Ostadan

Q29: Since the One Ring exerts so much mental influence upon the bearer, why then did it not prevent Gollum from running around and falling into the Crack of Doom? Further, we realize that Frodo has failed as Ring-bearer, as he could not ultimately complete his task. Did Frodo use Gollum as a proxy?

A: The first question is about the Ring's ability to overpower an individual. You could say it was a function of the Ring to bring anyone who held it (or would wield it) closer to the will of Sauron, .sort of "attuning" them to Sauron's ultimate will and of course using them as pawns to find any possible way to get back to its Master. The Ring could not solely control the physical behavior of a person; that's something else entirely. It could not force its will on Gollum to stop him from jumping wildly in ecstasy any more than it could force Frodo to turn around and walk down Sauron's Road to go knocking on the front door of the Dark Tower.

Now when you speak about Frodo's failure as Ring-bearer, you get into the same area Tolkien himself considered and wrote about in 1956, in a letter to Mr. Michael Straight (see *Letters of J.R.R. Tolkien*, # 181). If you do not have a copy of this book you absolutely must get one. Here Tolkien explains that Frodo did NOT use Gollum as a proxy nor did he write a scenario of randomness that falls under "deus ex machina." Tolkien summarized that the final critical moments where the Ring was unmade were carefully considered and reasonable for all the characters involved.

He goes on to say the entire final "catastrophe" marked a point where Frodo was rewarded for his continual forgiveness and pity of Gollum. Frodo had the chance but did not kill Gollum; even after being betrayed to Shelob and attacked again on Mt. Doom, he pitied him and let him go free. This was the most important aspect of Frodo's failure as Ring-bearer. Even if you assume Frodo, all by himself, had failed in his task, Tolkien also says:

> ... the 'salvation' of the world and Frodo's own 'salvation' is achieved by his previous *pity* and forgiveness of injury.... [Gollum's] last betrayal was at a precise juncture when the final evil deed was the most beneficial thing anyone could have done for Frodo! By a situation created by his 'forgiveness,' he was saved himself, and relieved of his burden.

In a fuller context, the Professor wanted this scene to be a dynamic way of exemplifying the most famous line from the Lord's Prayer: "Forgive us our trespasses as we forgive those that trespass against us. Lead us not into temptation, but deliver us from evil." You can see how profoundly Tolkien's beliefs are present in the story, and with what skill the author shows us the deeper points of meaning. Please refer to Letter # 181 for a complete discussion.

— Quickbeam

Q30: Doesn't the Ring attract the attention of Sauron and the Nazgûl whenever somebody puts it on? Neither of them were very far away when Sam put the Ring on at Cirith Ungol. How come they didn't locate him then?

A: Frodo had grown, and his wearing the Ring was a "Significant Event" in Sauron's eye. By contrast, Sam, who had never been tempted by the Ring, was humble and seemingly nearly immune to the Ring's corruption. He is almost like Bombadil, in the sense that both are uninterested in Power — Sam dismisses his brief daydream of Samwise the Strong with little effort and yields the Ring relatively easily to Frodo, hesitating only because he is unwilling to burden Frodo with it again. So Sam probably was no more visible to Sauron than if a rabbit had accidentally eaten the Ring.

It must also be remembered that Sauron's attention at the time was elsewhere. A week earlier, the Heir of Elendil revealed himself to Sauron in the captured Palantir of Orthanc; and the fleet at Pelargir was overcome when Frodo lay in the Tower. Sauron probably thought he had a pretty good idea of where the Ring was — which was indeed Aragorn's purpose. Personally, I think people overestimate the "ring is a beacon" business; even on Amon Hen, which is a somewhat magical place, Sauron doesn't locate the Ring, though he is "aware" of it.

— Ostadan

Q31: We are shown a scene of Gandalf encouraging Frodo to try to destroy the Ring in Bag End. Frodo is unable to summon enough willpower to cast the Ring into his little hearth fire. Given this, how did anybody expect him to possibly be able to hurl it to certain destruction in the Cracks of Doom?

A: The Ring's ability to drain willpower had already been witnessed in Frodo himself, and yet he was still appointed to be the Ring-bearer. Why?

One reason is to be found in the nature of hobbits. Gandalf says that both Gollum and modern hobbits are much tougher than the Wise might suppose. He says that hobbits in particular can resist the evil powers of the Ring far longer than other beings — witness how reluctant Gandalf is to take charge of it himself, even for a short while, and how quickly Galadriel refuses. Each of them knows that they would take the Ring and immediately be tempted to use it, while a hobbit, more patient and more humble, does not try to use it, but only keeps it.

So forget giving it up; anybody else would have taken it and used it long before reaching Mount Doom. So it was kind of a choice between two evils — nobody's going to have the willpower to throw it into the fire, but anybody else but a Hobbit would rise up and use it. So give it to the hobbit, and hope for the best.

How could they hope Frodo would pull it off? Well. We know the ending, that Frodo was not actually able to do it, but they didn't know. They had to hope for the best and trust that an entire journey with Frodo's mind bent on destroying the Ring might somehow be able to overcome the terrible hold the Ring would try to take. They were hoping for the best, but not quite blindly — Gandalf said that his heart foretold that Gollum would have his part to play, and how correct he was!

In essence, I believe it was a leap of faith. Maybe the leap was unjustified from a certain point of view, but Frodo did have enough will to carry him mile after terrible mile to Mount Doom with the Ring weighing him down, which is likely much more than any other being would have had, and a merciful Eru had no intention of allowing all that good effort and good intention to go to waste.

— Anwyn

Q32: Why are Merry and Pippin, two "green around the gills" hobbits with no significant or worldly experience, accepted so quickly by two great rulers, Théoden and Denethor? Other soldiers spend years in training for important positions, yet the hobbits seem to be accepted on a whim.

A: I believe that Gandalf had a far-reaching foresight in these matters, and we see this foresight come to play in Rivendell as the wizard soothes Elrond's doubts and advises that the two young hobbits be granted a place in the Fellowship. Gandalf knew something was up. Perhaps he even knew of the future connections the hobbits would have to the great rulers of Rohan and Gondor.

I don't find it unusual that Merry and Théoden bonded with such immediate warmth. Théoden had just been healed and was riding on the afterglow of his triumph at Helm's Deep, and I see the Lord of the Mark as opening up his eyes to life as he never had before. It is a unique transformation for him through a close series of events. And suddenly there is a "legend out of the past" that comes strolling into the King's life, a *Holbytla*, eager to help and begging for a way to be of use to the Kingdom. I too would be completely charmed by Meriadoc's tenacity. Young Merry feels a sudden devotion to the old man and follows his natural instincts to serve, rather than feel isolated and miserable after Pippin's departure. Makes perfect sense to me, and I find it quite moving.

Pippin, however, doesn't bond nearly so naturally with the grouchy old Denethor. Nor does he really need any training for his "honorary position" in the Citadel. Initially, the Steward of the City is suspicious and badgering, playing a mental chess game with Pippin (a metaphor that Tolkien effectively uses twice in the same chapter). At a pivotal point in this tête-à-tête, Pippin rises to the challenge and offers his sword to the service of Gondor, effectively doing the only thing that will earn Denethor's trust and repay his life-debt to Boromir. This is a brilliant counter-check that Denethor immediately recognizes as admirable, indeed grace under pressure. Thus Pippin is granted a token position in the Guard, given in a rather conciliatory manner. Not bad for a fool of a Took!

— Quickbeam

Q33: Why does Sam act as a servant throughout the story of *Lord of the Rings*? Is he of lower social status than the other three hobbits?

A: In a word, yes. Baggins, Brandybuck, and Took are three of the most highly regarded names in the Shire. The office of Thane has been in the Took family for time out of mind, and they have their own little patch within the Shire, the Great Smials. Brandybucks the same; they founded Buckland and keep a seat at their Brandy Hall. Baggins is described in the very beginning of *The Hobbit* as being a greatly respected (not to mention rich) name.

Now apply that to our world, to Tolkien's own time and country. Being a servant in somebody's house or garden was a widely held occupation in England around the turn of the last century. In that time and place, rich people's money came not from working hard and saving and investing, usually, but from estates that generated revenue which was then capitally invested, yielding enough interest for most everyday expenses. These people had land, houses, horses, carriages, gardens, and servants to look after it all — people who did not come from money and who had to work for a living. Money confers power through employment of those who don't have as much. Servants addressed their employers and their employers' peers as "sir" or "madam."

Now, take all this back to Middle-earth. It's as if Bilbo was a Carnegie, the Brandybucks were Vanderbilts, and the Tooks were the Rockefellers (to Americanize the British concept). Sam's father, Hamfast Gamgee, was directly employed by Bilbo as Bag End's gardener and was

361

training his son to take over in the same job, so when Gandalf basically orders Sam to go with Frodo, it's as if the son of the castle gardener has been directed to be the personal plant keeper of the crown prince. There were social strata in England; so too in the Shire, where the image of "country squire," with his little empire and his wife, his children and his servants, was alive and well.

This is why we later see Sam addressing Pippin and Merry as "sir" and Pippin rather cavalierly ordering him around near the beginning of the journey in the matters of bath water and breakfast preparation. He was of the "servant class," where as Pippin, Merry, and Frodo were of the "gentry."

The fact that in the Shire people in general were treated better than in our modern world and that these people were friends across the social lines just speaks to Tolkien's love of "the way things ought to be." And conversely, Sam took very seriously his assigned duty to "watch out for Mr. Frodo," again an example of "the way things ought to be." He took his tasks seriously, with a zeal born of true affection for his employer, which we later see turned to love between friends on equal footing.

— Anwyn

Q34: Why are the Hobbits not disposed to use the immense power of the Ring? It seems to have only been a simple tool for invisibility (but of course it lengthened the hobbit life span). Hobbits seem to be the strongest-willed of all the Free Peoples, so why is there no sense of threat that one of them would use the Ring to become the next Sauron?

A: The short answer is in the actual *ambition* of the bearer. Don't confuse a person's capacity (willpower) with his lust for greatness. Frodo and the other hobbits have tremendous innate will but initially they are not disposed to the typical wielding of the Ring as Sauron would have used it: control, coercion, and manipulation. That's just not the Hobbit way. Frodo would not initially be interested in dominating others or pushing his will towards that goal. Yet Galadriel tells him that the Rings give power according to the measure of each possessor.

And very interestingly we see a little later in the story the first seeds of Frodo's ability to truly wield the Ring: where he effectively uses it to tame Sméagol.

— Quickbeam

Q35: Tolkien claims that *The Lord of the Rings* is based on records available to him such as the fictional *Red Book of Westmarch*. Did he go to a lot of effort to link his mythology to recorded history? How did he explain the difference between our present geography and that shown on his maps?

A: The conceit that the tales of Middle-earth refer to our own world at some mythical earlier point in time has been part of Tolkien's world since its earliest beginnings (see, for example, the history of Eriol in *The Book of Lost Tales*). Whole stories, such as "The Lost Road" (found in the volume of that title) or *The Notion Club Papers* (in *Sauron Defeated*) are based on the idea that Middle-earth could be rediscovered by someone in a later period of history. There is no question that Middle-earth is conceived to be our world at another time.

In the *Akallabêth* (and also, less explicitly, in the discussion of the fall of Númenor in Appendix A of ROTK), it is explained that the Valar called upon Eru to intervene when Ar-Pharazôn invaded Aman and that the world was then transformed from its previous "Flat Earth" form to its current shape" — all the seas were bent" — so that only special ships could sail the "straight path" to Aman thereafter.

But as Christopher Tolkien shows in the section entitled "Myths Transformed" in *Morgoth's Ring*, sometime after *The Lord of the Rings* was published, Tolkien had second thoughts about the "Flat Earth" cosmology of his mythology and had decided — at least tentatively — that such tales as the kindling of the stars by Varda or the tale of the Sun and the Moon were unacceptable to modern educated audiences, and must be erroneous myths received via human (e.g., Númenorean) sources. On the other hand, in 1968 he wrote a letter (#297) that indicated that Eärendil and the Silmaril represented the morning star (Venus), so he may have decided that such a complete restructuring of his cosmology was unnecessary after all.

So, like so many other matters concerning Tolkien's creation, "how Tolkien pictured Middle-earth" is not easily described; it was constantly in flux.

— Ostadan

Q36: I am fond of astronomy and the legends and myths of our own constellations. In rereading *The Lord of the Rings*, I noticed that some references to stars in Middle-earth mirror those in our own lofty skies.

For example in *The Fellowship of the Ring*, when the hobbits meet Gildor, they speak of "Remmirath, the Netted Stars," and Borgil the red star, and "the Swordsman of the sky, Menelvagor with his shining belt." (LotR one-volume, p. 80.)

These descriptions seems to correspond with the Pleiades star cluster, red Aldebaran and Orion the Hunter, which seems to show that Professor Tolkien knew his stars extremely well. Are the names Remmirath, Borgil and Menelvagor relevant? Has Tolkien composed some sort of mythology surrounding the heavens of Middle-earth as we have done looking at our own stars? And this brings another question: is it possible for Elves to have myths? Or is everything "history" to them? By the same token has anything ever been said or written about Tolkien the "astronomer?"

A: To take your questions in almost reverse order, I don't know of any pieces written on Tolkien as astronomer, but it would be a very interesting topic.

As to the Elves and their "myths" or "histories," that seems to be a matter of perspective. Isn't *The Silmarillion*, in one sense, just that — a collection of myths about the origins of the world? At least, according to Men, it would probably be considered myths, though the Elves might instead call it history. A lot of myths emerge out of a misty interpretation of history, so it's hard to say where "history" itself ends and myths begin. In any case, I don't see why Elves themselves wouldn't have myths about some things and recognize them as such.

As to Tolkien composing some sort of mythology surrounding the heavens of Middle-earth, yes indeed: there is a fascinating cosmological essay with diagrams called "Ambarkanta: The Shape of the World," which is published in *The Shaping of Middle-earth*. But I don't think this is quite what you want — which is, I gather, something more like Middle-earth legends about the constellations. I don't recall Tolkien writing much about this, other than the fascinating passage you cite in the chapter "Three Is Company" and the passage in chapter three of *The Silmarillion* where Varda kindles the stars (p. 48). Several stars themselves are named, including Carnil, Luinil, Nénar, Lumbar, Alcarinquë, Elemmírë, Wilwarin, Telumendil, Soronúmë, Anarríma, Menelmacar (with his shining belt) and Valacirca.

Menelmacar (Menelvagor in *The Lord of the Rings*) is clearly the constellation Orion. Valacirca is the Great Bear (or Big Dipper). Of Wilwarin, Christopher Tolkien notes that the word meant "butterfly" in Quenya, and the constellation was perhaps Cassiopeia. Carnil is apparently the name of a red star — perhaps this later became Borgil? Luinil is a star shining with blue light. Borgil could perhaps be Aldebaran or perhaps Betelgeuse. Remmirath does seem to be the Pleiades.

Another highly interesting source to look at regarding Tolkien's knowledge of astronomy is his unfinished "Notion Club Papers," published in *Sauron Defeated*.

— Turgon

Q37: The battle between good and evil depicted in *The Lord of the Rings* is full of religious and spiritual implications, but are there examples of specific theological understanding or organized worship of a recognized deity?

A: It all depends on your definitions of "specific theological understanding" and "worship. " First of all, *The Silmarillion* makes clear the hierarchy of supernatural beings: There was Eru, the One, Ilúvatar, creator of all. Beneath him were his created servants, the Ainur, some of whom became the Valar, the Powers of the World.

The Valar went down into Middle-earth to help in its creation, each doing the part that he or she was best at, and they stayed to guard it, to fight off Melkor (Morgoth), and to defend and guide the Children of Ilúvatar, Elves and Men. There is a sentence in *The Silmarillion* that states that men afterwards considered them gods, which indicates that the men of Middle-earth were at least aware of the existence of the Valar and the Blessed Realm, but it is equally clear that despite this perception of them as gods, the true power rested with Ilúvatar.

Now, as far as worship or prayer, what there was of it seems to me to be manifested in the songs of the Elves. Their songs refer to Varda, queen of the stars, companion of Manwë, who was chief among the Valar. So it seems to me that if you're talking about an orthodox church structure, obviously there was none. But the Elves, at least, were very conscious of the Powers, the Valar, and through them the Creator, and they made this clear in their songs.

In general, from the songs of the Elves and their overall behavior, especially in the latter Ages when they had "grown up," it seems that perhaps the Elves had less need of structured worship since they tended towards the good already.

Worship or prayer among Men, well, they seem to have far less overt knowledge of the Valar and Eru than the Elves. It is said that the Sleepless Dead of Erech were men who worshiped Sauron in the Dark Years, but he deliberately made himself manifest to them and craved their worship. Beyond that, I think Tolkien was projecting the fact that most men knew the difference between good and evil and made different choices in various situations.

It is recorded that in Númenor there was an established form of worship consisting of the kings making pilgrimages to the top of Meneltarma, their highest mountain, which was sacred to Eru. However, this was in ancient times, well before the events recorded in *The Lord of the Rings*.

The only hint of respect for the Powers on the part of Men and Hobbits in the Third Age is the passage in which Faramir and his men, and Frodo and Sam, look to the West before sitting down to eat — an archaic, more distant form of our "saying grace" today. Beyond that and the songs of praise of the Elves, there is no form of church or regular worship described in *The Lord of the Rings*.

— Anwyn

Q38: In *The Fellowship of the Ring*, at the Council of Elrond, Elrond says that he was there when Isildur cut the Ring from the hand of Sauron. He tells the Council that both he and Círdan told Isildur to cast the Ring immediately into the fires of Orodruin but that Isildur would not listen to their counsel.

The question is, then, why didn't Elrond and Círdan force Isildur to throw the Ring in? Failing that, why didn't they pick him up and throw him in, Ring and all?

A: I believe it's safe to say that Elrond and Círdan did not approve of such "direct measures." Elrond says right out that Isildur took the Ring without reference to what the Elves wanted, "whether we would or no." He implies that the choice was Isildur's and there was nothing he and Círdan could have done to stop him. Elves have been known to fight for what's theirs, certainly, but manhandling another into doing their will for the higher good is not their thing. Remember, not even the Valar forced people to do things; they even left it to Fëanor to choose whether he would continue his madness for the Silmarils. Elrond makes it clear even in the "present time" that he would not force anybody to take the Ring to the fire, that nobody could lay that burden on another.

Elves learned early and well the great truth: you can't control other people's behavior. Besides that — if they had tried to take the Ring from Isildur by force, would they have succeeded? Near the beginning of the story, Frodo asks why Gandalf can't just make him destroy the Ring. Gandalf rejects the idea that it is up to him to make or let Frodo do anything against his will (*The Fellowship of the Ring*, pp. 69-70) and adds that attempting to do so would break Frodo's mind. Elrond and Círdan may have reasoned that it was not for them to break Isildur's mind deliberately — that the course of events must run. He most likely could have lashed out, with the Ring, at them, and thus they would have accomplished nothing but their own deaths. We just can't know what would have happened, but it seems obvious that they didn't want to find out.

— Anwyn

Q39: In *The Illustrated Encyclopedia of Middle-earth* there is a time chart of Middle-earth and the Undying Lands. In the chart concerning Middle-earth it says "Sauron's spirit vanishes," but in the chart of the Undying Lands it says "Valar reject Sauron's spirit." Do you know anything about that? Where is the source? It would be an interesting point that the Valar are not once again fooled by Sauron and do not give him a second chance like they did before with him and Morgoth.

A: It is possible that the statement that the "Valar reject Sauron's spirit" is an interpretation of the events at the Field of Cormallen, where Gandalf announces that the realm of Sauron has ended, and a shadow rears up like an enormous hand and a great wind blows and disperses it.

This description is similar to that of the death of Saruman, as described in "The Scouring of the Shire," when a grey mist gathers above Saruman's body, but a cold wind comes blowing out of the West and the mist dissolves into nothingness.

The spirit of Saruman seems very clearly to have been rejected by the Valar, with the cold wind from the West. And though the passage about Sauron is not as explicit, it seems likely that his spirit too was rejected in a similar manner.

— Turgon

Q40: When Boromir tried to take the Ring from Frodo, was there another influence at work besides the Ring? Was there perhaps some evil associated with the place and specifically with the falls of Rauros?

A: To the contrary: Aragorn decides that they will give him a river burial on the Anduin and let the falls of Rauros take him, for in that way his remains will be safe from the defilement of evil creatures." (*TTT*, chapter one) Generally, water is considered a "good" element in Arda, associated with the beneficent Ulmo. The idea, never fully realized, of the Nazgûl having difficulty crossing water (seen in *Unfinished Tales*), also supports the idea of water as a "pure" or "good" element.

Tolkien is more explicit about this in his "Notes on motives in *The Silmarillion*" found in *Morgoth's Ring*. There he explains that in Middle-earth, all gold tended towards evil — but silver did not. And Water is an element that was almost entirely untouched by Morgoth's influence, though individual bodies of water could, like anything else, be "defiled."

— Ostadan

Q41: What exactly are these Barrow-wight creatures?

A: First let us examine the etymology of the actual word, Barrow-wight. My fellow Green Books staff person Turgon (who is held high among the Wise) shared the following with me:

A barrow is an earthmound marking a grave (from Middle English "berw," Anglo-Saxon "beorg"). But "wight" is also an archaic word, meaning 1) a human being, or 2) a preternatural or supernatural being. It derives from Middle English "wight" and Anglo-Saxon "wiht," meaning "creature, animal, person, thing." So of course the terms have a perfect resonance for Tolkien's use of them ...

Put the two together and you have "supernatural creature of the grave." This is a shining example of Professor Tolkien's erudition with these languages. Let us look closely at the history of the lands surrounding the Barrow-downs, as it is most germane to your question.

Early in the Third Age, the race of Men (the Dúnedain) held power in two main Kingdoms, Arnor and Gondor. In the north, Arnor was split into three principalities: 1) Arthedain, 2) Rhudaur, and 3) Cardolan. This triad of the Dúnedain had a capital city at Annúminas (and later Fornost). There was constant strife between them and the Witch-king of Angmar, who reigned from his cold seat in Carn Dûm.

The power of the Witch-King was undoubtedly great — he was chief of the Nazgûl, after all. He took into his service Hillmen of the North, Orcs, and other foul creatures including the demonic spirits that would eventually become the Barrow-wights, but I'll get to that in a minute.

Many battles were fought over the centuries between the Dúnedain and the Witch-King, and Elrond makes specific mention of them during the high Council, saying that of all the vast kingdom of the North, little was left but burial mounds after the lordship of the land ceased. Those "green mounds" he speaks of are the same ones the four hobbits passed through only a few chapters earlier. The men of Cardolan used the fields of Tyrn Gorthad (the Barrow-downs) as a refuge and also as a burial field for their fallen kings and warriors. The white monoliths marked the gravesites of many of the fallen.

When the Witch-king was ultimately defeated, he fled into the shadows of dusk and vanished from the North. Many tortured servants and spirits also fled from Angmar after his power was broken, no longer having their Lord to rule them (or enslave them, if you prefer). There were also demons, now disembodied and wandering aimlessly, looking for other bodies in which their evil spirits could dwell. And so that's how I speculate the Wights came into being, as they traveled southward from Angmar to the Barrow-downs and inhabited the bones and jeweled armor of the ancient dead.

The wights could crush the will of an unwary traveler. Apparently they wielded spells that rendered the victim mindless, thus they could lure him into the treasure tombs below ground. After the hobbits are rescued by Tom Bombadil, there is a moment where Merry returns to consciousness. The golden circlet around his head falls over his face, and it somehow brings out the voice of the dead man who was originally buried with it. The young hobbit speaks of the Men of Carn Dûm and then snaps back to himself as the dream of dead spirits leaves him. Very spooky.

Having a good understanding of Arnor and the history of the Dúnedain makes many of these small details more vibrant as you read.

— Quickbeam

Q42: Was Sauron actually controlling the Balrog of Moria or was the Balrog just a separate, powerful entity outside the Dark Lord's influence? Certainly the Balrog felt the presence of Sauron, so would the demon not have headed to Mordor to ally itself?

A: Well, I'm curious about this too. There may have been more than just the one Balrog that the Fellowship encountered (a faint possibility), but none were ever mentioned. We assume that the demonic thing fled for its life when the Host of the West cast down Thangorodrim way back during the War of Wrath in the First Age ... thinking of nothing but finding a safe, dark place underground. So off it went until it found a pleasant little pit to curl up in.

We also know from reading Appendix A of RotK that the unfortunate Dwarves would be in that exact same spot (Moria) many centuries later and they delved much too deep looking for mithril, waking the thing from a very long sleep. Then there's a footnote suggesting that the Dwarves' excavations had perhaps given it a way out of its prison, and it was also possible that Sauron's evil will may have roused it already.

So there you have it. The Balrog fled to the East and lay completely dormant, like an egg not yet hatched, until the Dwarves stumbled upon it. Maybe it had recently awakened, maybe not. Tolkien seems to enjoy the suggestion. Perhaps Sauron knew it was there and was content to let it reside in Moria, destroying the Dwarves for him, without him having to lift a finger.

I honestly don't think Sauron could control the Balrog, not as he specifically would control armies or slaves. They were both servants of Morgoth, "peers" in their original relationship to him, though Sauron was certainly a greater power than a Balrog in several respects. It is fun to speculate what would have happened if the Balrog responded to Sauron as it had to its original master so many centuries earlier.

— Quickbeam

Q43: So who is Tom Bombadil anyway? Is he a Valar, Maia, or something else entirely? And who was the eldest — Fangorn or Tom Bombadil? Fangorn is said to be "eldest" in one spot, and elsewhere Bombadil is referred to as "oldest" and "fatherless."

A: Tom Bombadil is another really tough person to place and define in the whole scheme of Tolkien's legendarium. This topic also has been debated for many years. About the best answer one can give, and it is still only speculation, is that Tom Bombadil was some lesser form of Maia. After all, Tom refers to having been around Arda from very early on, for he "knew the dark under the stars when it was fearless — before the Dark Lord came from Outside." (*The Fellowship of the Ring*, p. 142.) And the reference to the Dark Lord must refer to Morgoth, rather than Sauron. Treebeard's title as "Eldest" must be some sort of honorary title, for he and the Ents as a race seem likely to be slightly younger than Tom Bombadil.

— Turgon

Q44: Gandalf and the other wizards were obviously powerful Maiar sent to protect Middle-earth. If Tom Bombadil is a lesser Maiar, then why was Tom completely unaffected by the Ring when he placed it on his finger? Tom didn't even disappear.

A: It seems plausible that Tom Bombadil was uninterested in the kind of power that the Ring conveyed. Tom also clearly had his own boundaries, at least geographically, for when he takes leave of the hobbits he declines to step over the borders of what he considers his own country. (*The Fellowship of the Ring*, p. 159.) If Tom could have been persuaded to take the Ring, it would, over time and in the end, have worked its power upon him and corrupted him. But for the short time of its passage through his own country, it seems not to have affected him, and within the boundaries of his own realm, Tom seems certainly to have been Master.

Some people have suggested that Tom was unaffected by the Ring because he was actually Eru, the One God. However, there are a few passages in *Letters* where Tolkien refutes this idea, and in the drafts of a letter to Michael Straight Tolkien states explicitly that, in Middle-earth, "there is no embodiment of the One, of God, who indeed remains remote, outside of the World, and only directly accessible to the Valar or Rulers." (*The Letters of J. R. R. Tolkien*, # 181, p. 235.)

— Turgon

Q45: In *The Silmarillion* I have found mention of so-called Guardians of the forest. These creatures were, apparently, created by Yavanna to protect the forests. Are these the Ents?

A: The passage concerning Yavanna and her role in creating the Ents, or the Shepherds of the Trees, can be found in *The Silmarillion*

("Of Aulë and Yavanna"). Ents were not originally part of Tolkien's *Silmarillion*, and they emerged during the writing of *The Lord of the Rings*. Tolkien had to add them into *The Silmarillion* afterwards. In a rough note on a letter from 1963, Tolkien wrote that no one knew whence the Ents came, but some believed that Yavanna "besought Eru (through Manwë) asking him to give life to things made of living things not stone, and that the Ents were either souls sent to inhabit trees, or else that slowly took the likeness of trees owing to their inborn love of trees" (*The War of the Jewels*, p. 341).

— Turgon

Q46: Does Tolkien name any of the Seven Fathers of the Dwarves besides Durin?

A: Yes. The only other information about the seven houses of the Dwarves is in a late untitled essay (late 1960s) concerning Dwarves and Men. Here, the other six houses of the dwarves, beside the Longbeards, were named, apparently for the first and only time. These were the Firebeards and the Broadbeams, and (arising further east) the Ironfists, Stiffbeards, Blacklocks, and Stonefoots. (I cannot help wondering if the Stonefoot dwarves insisted on being called StoneFEET!) The Firebeards and Broadbeams were, apparently, the kindreds of Nogrod and Belegost. This essay appears in "The Peoples of Middle-earth," the last of *The History of Middle-earth* volumes.

— Ostadan

Q47: How is it that the sword of Túrin, Gurtholfin, was able to speak?

A: Túrin's sword was named Gurtholfin, "Wand of Death," in *The Book of Lost Tales*. In later writings, particularly in the published *Silmarillion* and in the "Narn i Hîn Húrin" in *Unfinished Tales*, it was called Gurthang, or "Iron of Death." It was named thus after it was reforged in Nargothrond from Anglachel, the sword of Beleg. *The Silmarillion* describes it as being "though ever black its edges shone with pale fire." And Túrin's use of it on the Guarded Plain made him known as Mormegil, the Black Sword.

To turn back to *The Book of Lost Tales*, it is described therein as follows: "It was made by magic to be utterly black save at its edges, and those were shining bright and sharp as but Gnome-steel may be. Heavy it was, and was sheathed in black, and it hung from a sable belt, and Túrin named it Gurtholfin the Wand of Death; and often that blade leapt in his hand of its own lust, and it is said that at times it spake dark words to him." (*The Book of Lost Tales*.)

The important passage where the sword itself speaks is found first in *The Book of Lost Tales* and later in revised forms in the "Narn i Hîn Húrin" and in *The Silmarillion*. In the latter, when Túrin draws forth his sword, he asks the sword if it will slay him swiftly, and a cold voice answers from the sword: "Yea, I will drink thy blood gladly, that so I may forget the blood of Beleg my master, and the blood of Brandir slain unjustly. I will slay thee swiftly." (*The Silmarillion*, p. 225.)

Within the world of Middle-earth it is indeed odd for a sword to speak. There are some instances of animals speaking (I am thinking here of Huan in *The Silmarillion*, of the eagles and spiders and ravens in *The Hobbit*, and then there is that curious fox in *The Lord of the Rings* who passes the hobbits sleeping out in the Shire, in Book 1, Chapter 3, and "thinks" for a few sentences...), but the speaking inanimate object seems very unusual.

Yet it is highly interesting to note the history of Gurthang from the time before it was reforged. It was originally called Anglachel and was made by Eol the dark elf out of iron that fell from heaven as a blazing star. Melian the Maia, wife of Thingol, said of Anglachel: "There is malice in this sword. The dark heart of the smith still dwells in it." (*The Silmarillion*, p. 202.) That some of the spirit of Eol remained in the sword after reforging might help to explain why the sword was able to speak.

There is another answer to this question that comes from a study of Tolkien's own sources. While a student at Oxford, Tolkien had become enamored with the Finnish epic *Kalevala*, in the W. F. Kirby translation. The *Kalevala* includes the story of the hapless Kullervo, whose basic story resembles Turin's very closely. (In fact, Tolkien himself wrote a verse-version of "The Story of Kullervo" in 1914, but this has never been published.) In both stories, Kullervo and Túrin, after similar upbringings, fall in love unknowingly with their own sisters, and when the sisters learn of their incest, they drown themselves. Kullervo, like Túrin, seeks release from his life by his sword, asking it if it will drink his blood. Kullervo's sword answers very similarly and takes its master's life in an identical manner. The following quotation comes from the W. F. Kirby translation of the *Kalevala*:

Kullervo, Kalervo's offspring
Grasped the sharpened sword he carried,
Looked upon the sword and turned it,
And he questioned it and asked it,
And he asked the sword's opinion,
If it was disposed to slay him,
To devour his guilty body,
And his evil blood to swallow.
Understood the sword his meaning,
Understood the hero's question,
And it answered him as follows:
"Wherefore at thy heart's desire
Should I not thy flesh devour,
And drink up thy blood so evil?
I who guiltless flesh have eaten,
Drank the blood of those who sinned not?"
Kullervo, Kalervo's offspring,
With the very bluest stockings,
On the ground the haft set firmly,
On the heath the hilt pressed tightly,
Turned the point against his bosom,
And upon the point he threw him,
Thus he found the death he sought for,
Cast himself into destruction.

— Turgon

Q48: How did King Elessar manage to reestablish and revitalize the entire Northern Kingdom in the Fourth Age? The area was underpopulated and Gondor was so far away, unable to offer resources and manpower. How was the realm of Arnor effectively restored and Annúminas rebuilt?

A: Good question, but one has to remember the factor of time when considering these events. The Ring was destroyed 25 March, Shire Reckoning 1419. Seventeen years later in S.R. 1436, we learn that King Elessar went north to visit Lake Evendim (see Appendix B of *RotK*,

"The Tale of Years"). We assume he was there to survey the ruins of Annúminas and assess the land, making plans for it to be restored. I can only guess that the process of breaking new ground and ordering the new City's plans started at that time.

In S.R. 1541 Elessar died. That's one hundred and five long years between his first visit to restore the North Kingdom and his final hour as King ... and a lot can happen in a century! Just compare with a century of American history, let's say from 1800 to 1900:

- 1803: Jefferson makes the "Louisiana Purchase"
- 1804-05: Lewis and Clark's expedition to the Pacific
- 1819: Florida acquired from Spain
- 1836: Texas wins independence from Mexico
- 1861-65: American Civil War is fought
- 1862: Emancipation Proclamation
- 1867: Purchase of Alaska
- 1898: Spanish-American War
- 1898: Hawaii annexed

Thinking along those lines, within a hundred years power can shift, cities can be destroyed and rebuilt, great territories can be expanded, and freed slaves can become part of the populace. Even in Middle-earth.

Elessar gave the lands of Nurn to the freed slaves of Mordor, and peace was made with the Easterlings and Haradrim. It's doubtful that these thousands of people stayed locked away within their native lands, even though they were once enemies. Movement, migration, and new settlements would certainly come to pass throughout Gondor and Ithilien. In peacetime there would likely be a terrific baby boom in all of Middle-earth! With no wars to fight and young soldiers staying at home, what else are they going to do but thrive, make babies, and rebuild their civilization? People were no longer afraid to travel in the open country, so agricultural and mining trade probably flourished in Eriador. With trade routes reinvigorated and safe to traverse, Arnor would have been readily connected to her neighbor the Shire and with her sister in the south.

I think the restoration of the Reunited Kingdom continued actively for many centuries into the Fourth Age, long after Elessar's death.

Given enough time, there would be plenty of resources and migration of people to accomplish this.

— Quickbeam

Q49: Are the Undying Lands so named because they bestow immortality upon any who set foot therein or because of the nature of the folk who dwell there (Valar, Eldar, etc.)? This may seem simple, but it is stated in *The Silmarillion* that when Ar-Pharazôn and his men landed in Aman they were buried in the Earth and are now imprisoned in the Caves of the Forgotten, until the Last Battle and the Day of Doom.

A: The Undying Lands is the name given to the lands inhabited by the immortal Valar, including Valinor, Eldamar, and the island Tol Eressëa. It was Eru, or Ilúvatar, who designed death as the Gift of Men (or as a release from being bound to the Circles of the World) while the fate of the Elves was bound within the Circles of the World, where they would remain through their very long lives (not quite "immortality"). (Elves could be slain, but their spirits went to Valinor and remained within the Circles of the World.)

The Valar had rewarded the Númenoreans with long life, but could not alter the nature of man so as to bestow upon them immortality. Thus the Undying Lands do not appear to be inherently immortal. See in *The Silmarillion*, the statement of Manwë's messengers to the Númenoreans: "It is not the land of Manwë that makes its people deathless, but the Deathless that dwell therein have hallowed the land." (*The Silmarillion*, p. 264.) It was apparently one of the lies of Sauron to suggest otherwise.

The statement about Ar-Pharazôn and his men reads as follows: "But Ar-Pharazôn the King and the mortal warriors that had set foot upon the land of Aman were buried under falling hills; there it is said that they lie imprisoned in the Caves of the Forgotten, until the Last Battle and the Day of Doom" (p. 279). I think the key here lies in the phrase "it is said," for it must be a legend of Men that the writer of the "Akallabêth" is here referring to, not an explicit statement of fact.

— Turgon

Q50: Who was Queen Berúthiel and what's the story about her cats?

A: The story of Queen Berúthiel exists in an outline, and this outline appears in *Unfinished Tales*. Berúthiel was the solitary, loveless wife of Tarannon, the twelfth King of Gondor. Tarannon was the first of the Ship-kings and took the name Falastur, Lord of the Coasts. Berúthiel had ten cats, nine black and one white, that she used as spies, so that all of the people of Gondor were afraid of both her and the cats. She was eventually cast adrift in a ship on the sea, with only her cats, and her name was erased from the Book of Kings. For a fuller recounting of her history, see *Unfinished Tales*, pp. 401-402.

— Turgon

TheOneRing.net®

FORGED BY AND FOR FANS OF JRR TOLKIEN

Servng Middle-earth Since the First Age

Since its publication, J.R.R. Tolkien's *The Lord of the Rings* has become one of the best-selling books of all time. In 1999 Peter Jackson and New Line Cinema began the momentous task of bringing Tolkien's epic to the big screen.

TheOneRing.net (TORn) was forged by the combined vision of the four founding members to meet the groundswell of interest in the film adaptation of the book. Since May of 1999, TORn has become something scarcely imagined at its inception. With 45 staff members living in 15 countries and readers from over 150 countries, TORn must be thought of as a culmination of worldwide Tolkien fandom.

About TheOneRing.net:

• #1 internet source of up-to-date *Lord of the Rings* news and information.

• Front Page News updated at least three times daily.

• One of the original and most trusted Tolkien movie websites.

• Features more than 10 different sections with over 800 pages.

• Contains extensive information about Tolkien's books and film adaptations.

• Offers up-to-date news and information about the cast and creators of *The Lord of the Rings*.

Cold Spring Press

An Imprint of Open Road Publishing
P.O. Box 284
Cold Spring Harbor, NY 11724
Jopenroad@aol.com

Our quality fantasy books include:
Myth & Middle-earth, by Leslie Ellen Jones, $14.95
The People's Guide to J.R.R. Tolkien, by TheOneRing.net, $16.95
Tolkien in the Land of Heroes, by Anne C. Petty, $16.95
The Tolkien Fan's Medieval Reader, by Turgon, $14.95 (available Spring 2004)
Dragons of Fantasy, by Anne C. Petty, $14.95 (available Spring 2004)

For US orders, include $5.00 for postage and handling for the first book ordered; for each additional book, add $1.00. Orders outside US, inquire first about shipping charges (money order payable in US dollars on US banks only for overseas shipments). We also offer bulk discounts. *Note:* Checks or money orders must be made out to **Open Road Publishing**.